OF LIGHT
AND
DARK

TDS
5

Of Light and Dark

Copyright © 2021 by Danah Logan

All rights reserved.

Fourth Edition

Editor: Jenn Lockwood | Jenn Lockwood Editing

Proofreader: Mary | On Pointe Digital Services

Cover Design: Danah Logan

Interior Formatting: Danah Logan

ISBN: 978-1-7360990-2-5 (ebook)

ISBN: 978-1-7360990-5-6 (paperback)

ISBN: 979-8-9851796-9-9 (paperback - discreet cover)

ISBN: 978-1-7360990-9-4 (hardback - discreet cover)

A NOTE FROM THE AUTHOR

Trust Lilly and Rhys.

Of Light and Dark (OLAD) is the <u>final</u> book and **CONCLUSION** of Lilly and Rhys's trilogy within The Dark Series.

Everything will be explained throughout the series. The books are labeled dark due to the themes that may be considered **TRIGGERS** for some. **Reader discretion is advised.** *(For a more detailed list of potential triggers, visit www.authordanahlogan.com.)*

While the entire series is intended for **MATURE** (18+) readers, please be aware the trilogy is a **SLOW BURN**.

Each book in The Dark Series is unique to its main characters. They write the story; I'm just along for the ride. As they get older, their characters grow throughout the series, make mistakes that can have you either relate to, like, or dislike (possibly even hate) them. They are raw and flawed, but we love them anyway.

For my husband. You are my best friend, my partner in crime, the most amazing father to our girls, and a real-life hero. Thank you for supporting me from the day I announced I'm writing a book to when I finally emerged, three and a half years later, with a trilogy.

PROLOGUE

HER

SIX DAYS AGO

I'M the last to climb the steps and enter the private jet.

MY LITTLE LAP dog followed through. By mid-Sunday, the news of Lilly McGuire being victim number one had broken everywhere. They even gave Nate a cute serial offender name: The Babysitter. How very fitting.

I can imagine how he reacted when he got the alert. I hope he lost his temper in front of his dimwitted fiancée; he has never been able to handle it when someone bad-mouths his family.

AS SOON AS I tasked my informant, I set everything else in motion. It was not easy to organize transportation for my pawn and the medical staff I require to keep him in check, let alone a place for all of us to stay. It needs to be secure and large enough so I don't have to listen to him yell at the nurse every time she administers the paralytic drugs. I thought, after years of not using his legs, he would be too weak. Obviously, I was wrong. Last week's escape attempt was proof of that. A mistake I will not make twice.

GRAY ASSURED *me the house he procured is far away from any other residence in the area, close enough to drive to Westbridge on short notice, and still meets my aesthetic requirements. This is going to be interesting, knowing Gray's taste in interior design.*

EVERYONE IS ON BOARD, *and he is secured in the back of the plane. As far as the pilots and flight attendant are concerned, the unconscious man is my terribly ill husband that will be receiving medical treatment in the United States.*

Standing in the door, I take in the interior of the jet. This will do for the next ten hours.

CHAPTER ONE

RHYS

MOTHERFUCKER, THAT HURTS!

I shake my hand, looking down at Jager's busted face. My *friend's* eyes are wide, and blood is gushing out of his nose like a freaking waterfall.

"What the fuck, McGuire?" He tries to push himself off the ground, but I plant my boot in the middle of his chest, holding him down.

Thanks to the farce of a press conference, followed by Lilly's revelation about trench-coat creep, and an endlessly long call with Nate and George, I was two hours late for school. I arrived just as the bell announced the end of second period. With one objective in mind, I made my way through the crowded corridors, ignoring the conversations that halted mid-sentence and the fact that everyone, except the freshmen who are too chickenshit, openly gawked at me. Entering the senior hallway, I spotted Jager coming out of his classroom.

Perfect timing.

As I let my tunnel vision take over, I picked up my pace and reached his side precisely as we were in front of the guys' bathroom. My hand shot out, gripped his neck—probably tighter than necessary—and steered him through the door.

"LEAVE!" I barked at the two juniors taking a leak. Both whirled toward my voice and immediately scrambled to get out —one of them still having his dick in his hand as he headed for the exit.

I pushed Jager against the closest stall and let my fist fly—a well-aimed cross punch straight at the nose. Dude went down like a ragdoll.

Pussy.

WITH MY FOOT now on his chest, I contemplate what to aim for next. As much as I want to let all my pent-up frustration out on the fucker, Spence's number one rule won't allow for it. Unless it's a life-or-death situation—*for you*—you never use your feet on someone that's already down.

That would make hands acceptable, right?

I shift so my knee replaces the shoe on Jager's sternum and am about to strike again as something wraps around my wrist.

"What the fuck are you doing?" my best friend's voice penetrates the pounding in my ears.

Still in a full-on rage, I whirl on Wes, and he takes a step back, holding his hands up. "Dude, you gotta snap out of it. They called Harvey."

I want to laugh. Wes is fully aware that my baby sister would have a better chance holding me back than Harvey. He's the school's forty-some-year-old security guard. Five-foot-six and two hundred-plus pounds—he's a joke. He's also a huge wrestling and football fan and kisses my ass whenever he sees me.

"Let him come," I scoff, turning back to Jager who is halfway to his feet. "Did I tell you to get up?"

Hand in front of his face, which is completely stained crimson, my teammate lets himself drop back to the tiled floor.

The door flies open, and Harvey walks in, in all his nonthreatening glory. "What's going on here?" he booms then does a double-take between the guy on the floor and me. "Rhys, my man. You're back!" His face lights up like a Christmas tree.

"Sure am, Harvey, my friend." I slap his palm as if my classmate is not lying at my feet behind me.

Wes rolls his eyes behind the security guard's back.

"Uh, is everything okay in here?" Harvey glances around me.

"Ab-so-lute-ly." I plaster a fake grin on my face and point my thumb behind me. "Jager here slipped and hit his pretty nose on the edge of the sink. Isn't that right, Kellan?"

I don't bother turning around to make sure he'll confirm my explanation. My superfan bobs his head slowly. I didn't take him for being that dense, but whatever.

"Well"—Harvey clears his throat—"if that's all, I'm not needed here."

"Yup, it's all good," Wes chimes in, plants his hands on Harvey's shoulders, and steers him out the door. He then moves in front of it so no one can come back in.

I lock eyes with my best friend and rub my hands together, slowly turning. "Let's continue our chat."

Jager's eyes widen. I'm channeling my inner George and must have succeeded, because the boy on the floor looks like he's about to shit himself.

"Rhys, bro, we're c-cool. N-no hard feelings," he stammers.

"No hard feelings? I thought you were hard for *my* girlfriend. Didn't you want to tap that?" I force my tone to remain eerily calm. If I learned one thing from George, it was the calmer you act, the scarier you are.

"Fuck!" Jager hisses. "Man, that was just a joke. You know I would never..." I cock my head to the side, and he trails off.

"I know, huh? Wes, did you know when you came back to school last week, and Lilly was still kidnapped? From what you overheard, the entire team—*my team*—ran their mouths." I don't take my gaze off of the shaking boy in front of me.

"Nope, he seemed pretty set on making a move." It's audible in his reply that Wes has his trademark smirk on full display.

"That's what I thought." I slowly sink to a crouch until I'm at eye-level with Jager. He shrinks even lower, and I get in his face. "So, what are we going to do about that?"

"I...I swear, I was joking. I would've never touched Lilly. She's always been off-limits—for all of us. We were just talking shit. Kat started it!" His voice pitches at the end of his speech, and I bite at the inside of my cheek to not burst out laughing. What a fucking loser.

"Oh, now you're blaming it on my ex. That's rich."

Behind me, Wes can't keep his composure and snorts loudly.

I pat Kellan's cheek. "I would advise you to watch your trap going forward. I may not always be around, but I *will* know."

"Uh, dude?" Wes's tone makes me shift my focus.

No fucking way.

"Did you seriously just piss yourself?" My eyebrows shoot up as I take in Kellan's ashen skin.

He closes his eyes briefly but remains mute.

My best friend cackles behind me. "I don't think we have to worry about him." A flash lights up the bathroom, and I can't contain myself anymore. Laughing, I stand up and walk out. Wes took a picture of a bloody and pee-stained Jager.

A slight sense of satisfaction settles in my chest. I'm done with him. On to the next one.

As I walk through the door this afternoon, I am proud to say I didn't get suspended. It was a close call when I finally caught up with Owen in the locker room after last period, but Coach let me off with a warning.

Note to self: Be more careful next time.

Oddly enough, I didn't run into Kat the entire day. We have three classes together, and I saw her car when I pulled into the lot. The only explanation was that she heard I'm back and made a run for it.

I stop abruptly in the empty kitchen. Camden and Lanning are nowhere in sight, making the room look weird after their asses have been basically superglued to the chairs for weeks. Natty enters the room as I'm heading for the stairs.

"Where are the suits?"

My little sister shrugs then looks me up and down. "Were you in a fight?"

I squint at her. "Are you psychic now?"

The tiny human in front of me rolls her eyes. "Your knuckles are all busted up."

Instinctively, I shove my hands into the pockets of my jeans. "Just had a minor disagreement with someone."

"Uh-huh." With a scowl that tells me she doesn't buy my lame excuse one bit, she moves past me.

Shaking my head with a grin, I make my way upstairs two steps at a time.

I knock once and push the door open. Lilly sits at her desk and closes the laptop quickly as she turns. My chest tightens, and my grin falls.

What now?

I cross the room, pull her up, and wrap my arms around her slender waist. She's getting too thin. Burying my nose in her hair, I whisper, "I missed you." Her signature scent of coconut and vanilla instantly calms my nerves.

Her arms wind around my midsection, and she squeezes tightly. "How bad was it?"

"Not bad at all." I'm not lying, but I'm also not telling the truth.

By the time lunch had rolled around, word had gotten out about what happened to Jager and Maxwell. Tyler Maxwell didn't participate in the online smear campaign, but I overheard him telling someone that I wouldn't have been able to jump him like that. He'd still plan on going after Lilly; if she were so eager to fuck her brother, she'd be more than satisfied with what he had in mind. I contemplated letting Lilly's real brother handle it but decided against it. The damage Nate could inflict on Maxwell would most likely result in consequences for years to come, but planting my foot in the back of his knee and sending him to the floor was much more satisfying.

He was upright, so I didn't break any rules.

After that, the stares and whispers stopped. When I entered the cafeteria, the conversations halted, but no one looked my way. Suddenly, the floor seemed to be tremendously interesting for the entire student population. My teammates, sitting at the table I used to occupy, scrambled, assuming I would want my old seat back. Wrong. Yet, the gratification of their reaction made me grin inwardly. With Wes on my heels, I carried my tray to Lilly's table. Den was already there, nibbling on some carrot sticks and ignoring her surroundings. Sloane and Emma, next to her, looked around frantically as I approached.

"Ladies. And Den." I greeted, winking at her as I dropped into Lilly's usual chair.

Denielle flipped me off but smirked. The shift in the social hierarchy over the last few weeks had our classmates unsettled. It was never a secret that *The Bulldog* and I didn't see eye to eye. Den was Lilly's guard dog, shielding her from me, and now we acted like best friends. Correction, we don't have to act. I consider her one of my closest friends.

After I made my stance clear throughout the day, no one would dare come after me, but I had my doubts about Lilly— especially once Kat emerges from wherever she had hid today.

"I know what you did to Kellan and Tyler," Lilly announces against my sweater.

I assumed she'd find out, but that was quick. "How?"

She pulls back and looks me straight in the eyes. "Someone filmed you; it's all over social media. You could've seriously injured him with that push kick to the knee."

Shit, I didn't notice someone taking a video.

"He deserved it," I defend myself.

Lilly sighs. "So, it's bad."

With a bitter taste on my tongue, I admit, "Yes."

She turns and walks to her bed. Sitting down on the edge, elbows on her knees, she covers her face with her hands. "I should've stayed in California."

CHAPTER TWO

LILLY

"What the fuck are you talking about?" Rhys is at my side in an instant. Squatting down, he pulls my hands away. I was mostly talking to myself, but he's searching my eyes for any hint of seriousness.

"I'm sorry. I didn't mean that," I mumble, swallowing over the sudden lump in my throat.

Did I, though?

I stare at our interlaced fingers.

Rhys rolls back on his heels, not letting go of me. "Babe, talk to me." His tone is wary.

I'm a coward. I didn't think twice about chasing my past, despite being fully aware of my kidnapper being out there. But the mere thought of walking back into Westbridge High makes me want to run. Add Francis Turner into the mix, and I'm more scared than when I woke up at the vineyard.

I force myself to make eye contact. "Nate doesn't think it's safe here."

"What do you mean?" Rhys cocks his head, watching me closely.

I feel sick just thinking about what my brother found out today. "Francis Garrison Turner died thirteen years ago."

His face drains of color, and I continue, "Turner was a former Army Ranger. He was dishonorably discharged for attacking a superior officer under the influence of narcotics. He died not long after. His car went over a cliff on the Pacific Coast Highway."

"California?" Several emotions flash across Rhys's face at once.

I nod. *This is not a coincidence.*

"Are we sure it's the same guy?"

Standing up, I pull Rhys with me into the bathroom. I motion for him to take a seat on the closed toilet while I dig through my feminine products. With the burner phone in hand, I move in front of him and hold it out. "Check the texts."

Rhys does as he's told. I don't have to ask if he found the evidence my brother sent over; his grip on the phone intensifies to the point of his knuckles turning white.

Nate discovered the proof that we're dealing with the same guy after doing some *digging*. Don't ask me how he did it, but he got a hold of Francis Garrison Turner's old driver's license picture, as well as the police accident report and death certificate.

Rhys looks up. "The report says the body was unidentifiable."

"Keep reading."

I memorized it hours ago. The accident happened in the middle of the night; the crash site wasn't discovered until mid-morning. Turner's SUV went through a barrier and crashed onto the rocks. The car caught fire on impact, just to later be submerged by the tide. The first responders were able to secure the vehicle enough to pull the body out. The DNA evidence indicated that the remains were Turner's, who owned the SUV.

"What are we gonna do now?" Rhys's question snaps me out of recapping the gory details in my head.

He is so *not going to like the answer to that.*

I pry the phone out of his hands out of fear he'll send it flying. "Nate wants me to come to LA, and George wants me to stay put and act as bait to figure out what Turner wants."

Crash.

And there goes my toothbrush holder. Damn it!

"ARE THEY FUCKING INSANE?" he yells.

"Lower your voice! Tristen is home," I whisper-shout.

Rhys stands, jamming his hands in his hair and tugging on the strands. With his back to me, he exhales, "I can't take this shit anymore!"

Those are his parting words before I'm alone in my bathroom.

Unsure what to do, I stare at my bed through the now open bathroom door. I'm about to return the burner to its hiding spot to follow Rhys when it starts vibrating in my hand. Quickly, I close the door again and answer the call.

"He didn't take it well, did he?" my brother's voice greets me.

"What did you expect?"

"Not that he would storm out of the house like a little toddler throwing a tantrum," Nate sneers.

"He did what?" I jump up from my crouch in front of the vanity. Even before racing into the hallway, I know I'll find Rhys's room empty.

Not paying attention, I slam straight into a body coming down from the third floor: Tristen. Stumbling back, we stare at each other. His eyes dart to the device plastered against my ear before he scans my face.

"Lilly? You there?" Nate's voice filters through the speaker.

Tristen's gaze snaps back toward my lifted hand. "Whose phone is that?"

Heather hasn't gotten around to getting me a new one since the accident, and I haven't pushed the issue. I'm with the people I'd contact anyway. One of them always has a phone I could use —not that I need to.

My mouth opens and closes several times. I glance toward the stairs. If Rhys left the house, he's already gone. My mind begins to race. If I stay here, there is a likely chance of my adopted father cross-examining me. I do the only thing I can think of. I dart around Tristen and break into a sprint, taking two steps at a time to the first floor.

"Lilly."

I pretend not to hear him calling after me. Standing in the doorway to the garage, I realize my mistake. I don't have a car.

Shit, shit, shit!

Footsteps on the stairs make me react on instinct. I grab the keys to Tristen's Raptor from the hook and make a run for it, slapping the garage door opener on the wall in passing. Thankfully, no one in this family ever locks their cars inside the garage, and I climb in.

Starting the truck, "Hail to the King" by Avenged Sevenfold blares out of the speakers, and I jump. Jeez. Twisting the volume button down all the way, I hear my brother's voice.

"Lilly Ann, if you don't tell me, right this fucking second, what the fuck is going on, I'm going to send George to pick you up. I don't give a fuck what he wants to do; I'm the one writing his fucking paychecks!"

Lifting the phone back to my ear, I scoff, "You realize that you just used the word fuck four times."

"I don't give a flying fuck!" Nate barks.

A knock on the driver's side window makes my head snap around. Heart beating in my throat, I lock eyes with Tristen. I hold his stare for several breaths before putting the Raptor in reverse and pulling out of the garage. My adopted father stands, hands on his hips, in the spot his car occupied a few seconds ago. His face is expressionless—as usual—and I push the garage door button on the visor. I'll deal with the consequences later.

Lancaster's car is still parked on the street. Thankfully, the windows to Tristen's black monstrosity are so tinted that the guy doesn't recognize me, and I hit the gas as soon as I have the massive truck in the middle of the road.

I PUT the phone on speaker and place it on the center console. "Sorry, I'm back. Tristen caught me with the burner, and I kind of just stole his truck." Heat creeps up my neck.

That makes my brother burst out laughing. "Now I want to hack into the feed to see his face."

"How did you know that Rhys left if you weren't already watching?" I assumed he was when he called.

"His tracker started moving again. Fast. I know he just came home, so I figured you told him, and it didn't go well."

Of course they're following everyone's movements like a hawk after what we found this morning.

Nate stays on the phone but doesn't say anything else. I drive by Wes's but don't see the Defender anywhere. "Where is he?"

I should've asked that first.

"Almost at Woodland Park." I hear the clicking of keys in the background, and I wonder what Nate's doing.

Focusing back on the road, I turn right at the next intersection. Wes's house is not far from the park, but I was heading in the wrong direction, and the following streets are all one-ways or cul-de-sacs. I come to a halt at the light in front of Café Chai. It's similar to Magnolia's, but the cheerleaders had declared it their spot years ago, so I never ventured into the enemy's territory. The light turns green, and I take my foot off the brake when someone darts across. Pushing the pedal back down, I roll my eyes at the idiot. Why can't people wait the extra minute until it's their turn again? Suddenly, *the idiot* pivots back. That's when it registers who is standing in front of me: Katherine Rosenfield.

This is the first time I've seen her since I had let my rage take over and planted my fist in her face. A red haze forms in front of my vision, remembering the confrontation. How was that less than three weeks ago?

Neither of us breaks eye contact, and my surroundings fade into the background as I tighten my hands on the steering wheel. It's just her and me. Everything I've read over the last few days about myself floods my brain at once. *She* started it all.

Head tilted, Katherine pulls something out of her purse. Her arm lifts, and with a mixture of a sneer and a smug smile, she takes a picture of me.

I press the gas pedal down, not paying attention that my signal has switched to red again. I go around her but cut off another car that was in the process of turning. The driver beeps at me, and I swerve just in time. Looking in the side mirror, I have a clear view of Rhys's ex. She moved all the way into the street—filming me.

"FUCK!" I hit the steering wheel. The burst of adrenaline is now accompanied by pounding in my ears.

"Did you just say the *F-word*, little sister?" my brother chuckles.

I totally forgot that he's on the line.

Forcing myself to calm my voice, I joke, "Can George make someone disappear for me?" Okay, maybe I'm a little serious.

"Why?" The humor is gone from his tone.

"I ran a red light, trying to get away from Katherine, and the bitch just took a video of me."

"You really know how to keep a low profile." Nate attempts to lighten the mood but achieves the opposite.

"Shut up." My eyes start to sting, and I blink.

"Want me to send her a virus?"

That makes me laugh, and my chest feels a little lighter. As much as I want to say yes, I reply, "She'll find a way to blame that on me as well."

"It's your call. Though, you could probably do it yourself with as good as you already are." Nate's praise distracts me from the Wicked Bitch, and the corners of my mouth turn up.

"I miss you, big brother." The words are out before I can think about it.

"I miss you, too, little sister." I can hear him smile as he returns the sentiment.

"I'm almost at the park. I'll call you later, 'kay?"

"Be careful. George is working on tracking down Turner. We need to figure out what he wants."

"I will."

Nate disconnects as I pull into the lot by the picnic area. I park next to the Defender and let the car idle as I watch Rhys sitting on one of the tables. He's facing away with his feet planted on the bench below and his elbows resting on his thighs.

Getting out, I shove the phone into the back pocket of my black jeans. With everything going on today, I'm still wearing the clothes I had picked out for the press conference. A shiver runs through my body. It's definitely too cold for what I'm wearing: a denim jacket over a thin tee.

Wrapping my arms around myself, I try to keep warm.

Rhys's back is to me as I approach, and his voice startles me. "How did you find me?"

Climbing the picnic table, I take a seat next to him. "Nate."

I want to scoot close enough for our thighs to touch, but an invisible force won't let me. It's as if we're two like poles of a set of magnets, repelling each other.

He huffs. "Of course." A little quieter, he adds, "And here I thought we still had the bond that always led us to one another."

What?

"What do you mean?" I ask, puzzled.

Rhys turns toward me. I can't read his expression, and my chest tightens.

"When we were little, I used to take off a lot. You would always find me. It became like a challenge. In the beginning, I would leave small clues for you to follow. Eventually, I stopped. No matter how far I ran or where I hid, you would come for me. It was like we were connected somehow."

I draw in a deep breath, but my chest only constricts further. "I don't remember that." A lone tear runs down my cheek, and I close my eyes.

The sensation of his thumb swiping away the wetness on my skin makes me face him. His eyes are filled with sorrow.

"I know." His sadness opens up the floodgate, and my tears are flowing. I'm not sure if I'm crying for him or me. How can I mourn something that is no longer there, something I have no recollection of? But Rhys...he remembers it all. I may have lost parts of my memory, but he lost us. What we had from the day I was born.

He bridges the distance between us, wraps his arm around my shoulder, and pulls me into his side. I latch onto his jacket, burying my nose in the crook of his neck.

Home.

We sit like this until the urge to scream overtakes every cell in my body. I'm sick of being in the dark, then finding answers—finding the light—just to be thrown back into the black void. I know life consists of light and dark; one cannot exist without the other. Yet, mine seems to be lacking the gray that should connect the two. I'm tired of being someone's chess piece—a game that has been going on for years and has used me as its pawn.

My breath quickens, and I jump off the bench, taking several steps until I'm in the middle of the clearing. My fingers curl into fists, nails digging into my palms as I give in. I'm sure I resemble a crazed banshee, but I don't care. Let them hear me.

Arms encircle me from behind, and Rhys draws me against his chest. "It's okay. Let it all out."

And I do.

When my throat feels like sandpaper, I turn in his embrace and hold on for dear life. "Please tell me you forgive me." His clothes muffle my words.

"There is nothing to forgive, Cal. None of this is your fault. I'm sorry I flipped my lid earlier."

At his warm breath against my ear, butterflies erupt in my stomach. It's always him reassuring me. I pull back, and Rhys studies my face. I place my hands on either side of his neck, right underneath his ears, the spot that drives him crazy when I kiss it. He lowers his forehead to mine, and I inhale his exhale, tasting the mint from his gum on my tongue.

"There are no words that can express how sorry I am for what you had to go through because of me, because of what happened and is still happening. You've been by my side, even when I thought you weren't. You watched over me time and time again." A brief chuckle escapes me. "You let George, every grown man's nightmare, drive you to God knows where for a chance to talk to me."

Rhys smirks. "He's not so scary once you get to know him."

A smile tugs at the corner of my mouth, but I continue. I'm not done. "I need you to know that no matter what happens, no matter where we are or how long we're apart, I'm yours. I'll always find my way back to you. You are my home. I love you."

Rhys's gaze jumps back and forth between my eyes before he lowers his mouth to mine. The kiss starts as a featherlight caress, but it's not enough. The fluttering sensation in my belly spreads to my chest. I want more. Need more. I raise to my toes, and his arms around me tighten. Arching my back to get even closer, my lips part, and I nip on his bottom lip. Rhys groans and immediately follows suit. His tongue invades my mouth with tender strokes, and the initial peck turns into a frenzy of mind-numbing kisses. Heat builds in my core, and I don't want this to end. By the time we break apart, my body is on fire, and I no longer feel the chill from the cool March temperatures. Rhys watches me closely through hooded lids before he pulls me into a tight embrace, resting his chin on the crown of my head.

We remain like this until, suddenly, another hand lands on my shoulder, and I squeal in surprise.

"Miss Lilly." George's soft tone breaks the little composure I had gathered just moments ago by distracting myself with Rhys's expert tongue.

I let go of Rhys and fling myself at my bodyguard, head of security, friend—whoever this man has become to me. George goes rigid at my assault but then relaxes and hugs me back. I wonder when he was hugged last.

"Did you find anything?" Rhys asks him.

"I have. But it's not safe to talk here."

George disentangles himself from me and gently pushes me toward Rhys, who interlaces his fingers with mine. I sweep the park. We are the only ones here, but I understand what he is saying. After this morning, we have no clue who is watching. And here we assumed Nate is the one who has eyes on everyone —aside from Tristen, that is.

I guess there is a third party that no one knew about until today.

CHAPTER THREE

HER

"YOU TOLD THEM YOUR NAME! YOUR REAL NAME, YOU IDIOT!" It takes every ounce of self-control not to wrap my hands around Gray's throat as he drives us back to the property. I told him to reveal himself to her, not to lay himself—and, by extension, me—out on a silver platter.

I know what Nate is capable of. He'll find out everything there is to know about Francis Garrison Turner by the end of the day. More accurately, that there has been no Francis Turner in thirteen years. Not since I helped him disappear. It was the one time I ever did the dirty work myself. To this day, I can smell the decaying body as we maneuvered it into the SUV. The only reprieve was that the rigor mortis had already lessened. But it was necessary for Gray to become invisible. To put the plan in motion. Getting my revenge was the added bonus. Back then, I didn't intend to keep him around for over a decade, but he has served his purpose over the years.

As soon as Gray parks the car in the garage, I make my way into our new—and definitely temporary—home. The place is filthy, and even after two days of Elise cleaning it from top to bottom, I can barely stand setting foot in it.

Just a few more days.

There is one thing I know will lift my spirits. Since my personal physician is adamant that I cannot increase my dosage, I need to find other ways to numb the violent urge to punish someone for Gray's irresponsible actions. Opening the door to his new bedroom, I take in the dark space. It's a joke compared to our previous houses—not that I care where he is stored. I'm only keeping him around until I have what I want and he's no longer needed as potential leverage.

His eyes find mine. He's awake. Perfect.

"How do you like your new accommodations?" I haven't spoken to him since we left South America.

"Are you fucking serious?" he snarls at me. "I wake up in this shithole, and Elise refuses to talk to me. Where the fuck are we?"

He is almost cute when he tries to appear threatening. If it weren't for the restraints on his hands and feet, I might even buy it. Why couldn't he have shown this type of backbone when we met?

I move until I am right beside his bed and pull out my phone. While hiding in the shadows, I made sure to take a picture of his precious Lilly. I hold the screen in front of his face.

"We are home, my dear."

CHAPTER FOUR

LILLY

"Dad gave you the Raptor?" Rhys peers at me suspiciously.

We're approaching the cars. Another black SUV is on the other side of the Defender—George's mode of transportation. I avoid direct eye contact when I mumble, "Not necessarily."

I feel myself blush and speed up my pace as George rats me out. "Your father caught her with the burner. She *took* the truck as she made a run for it."

Maybe I should just broadcast my every action since I have zero privacy as it is.

Spinning on my heels, I'm about to snap a retort when Rhys snorts. "You're giving me a run for my money in pissing Dad off."

He's referring to the fact that the Raptor has replaced the Defender on the *do-not-touch* list. No one but Tristen drives it. He loves his black monstrosity, but the real reason is that he has an AR stashed in a locked box under the backseat, and when Heather found out, she laid down the law. Her kids would not drive an assault rifle through town—loaded or not.

I don't have any desire to continue this conversation, plus I want to know what George found out. "Where are we going?"

"You are both going home. I will be in touch later. We can't risk being seen together, and as soon as your mother is home, Tristen will be on his way here," George explains and then levels Rhys with a glare. "You didn't leave your phone."

"Fuck! I forgot."

He couldn't get away from me fast enough.

Rhys reaches inside his jacket and pulls out his cell. Three sets of eyes take in the device. The movement makes the screen light up with several social media notifications, and when I lean closer, I read the one name I didn't expect to see: Kat Rosenfield.

Narrowing my eyes at him, he lifts both hands in a surrendering gesture, his phone between his thumb, index, and middle fingers. "I'm getting push notifications whenever she posts. I want to know what she's up to and who I have to deck next."

I rub my hands over my face. I have a good idea what she's posting about this time. I let my arms drop to my sides and gaze past the two men into the distance.

"Calla?" Rhys says my name carefully.

"I ran into Katherine on my way here," I admit.

Rhys swipes over the notification and starts reading with George hovering behind him, focused on the screen as well. Rhys's nostrils flare, and a knot starts forming in my stomach.

"What?"

When neither of them responds, and George's mouth turns his usually stoic features into a slash of disapproval, I tear the phone out of Rhys's hand and scan the newest rumor.

KAT ROSENFIELD:

If banging her brother isn't enough, now she's trying to run me over. Check out that bitch's deranged face when I tried to cross the street to Café Chai earlier. Psycho much?

. . .

COMMENTS:

Meghan LG: OMG, she's insane!

Nora Ross: R u ok? What's wrong with her? First she steals ur bf, then she tries to kill u? Someone do something!!!!!!!!!

Owen J: Don't u think ur exaggerating a bit? What's with all the !!!, Nora?

Kellan J: I'm with O

Lisa Bennett: U guys r just pissing ur pants that Rhys finds out.

Kat Rosenfield: If you don't believe me, here is the proof. She almost crashed into poor Mrs. Heatherway.

IN THE COMMENTS, Katherine posted the video of me cutting off the other car in the intersection, followed by speeding down the road. Sure enough, it's Mrs. Heatherway's ancient Honda I almost slammed into. I didn't recognize her in my haste to get away. She's the sixty-plus-year-old woman who owns the tailor shop next to Café Chai and does all the alterations for the school's cheer uniforms. She took in my homecoming dress last year and is the sweetest lady. Kat using her to make me look certifiable ignites a rage I haven't felt in a while. I skim over more comments.

NORA ROSS: They better not let that crazy slut come back to school. None of us are going to be safe. We all know what T. McGuire drives around in that truck.

Kellan J: Oh, come on, N.

Kat Rosenfield: Nora is right. What if the #boyfriendstealingbrotherfuckingwhore walks into school with a gun?

Meghan LG: What if the whole kidnapping is just made up and her parents actually sent her away for seducing their son?

Kat Rosenfield: Megan:: OMG, you're right. She probably was in some military mental place.

Meghan LG: Psych ward for incestuous sluts.

Kellan J: M is using big words. Did you Google that one?

Meghan LG: Fuck you, KELLAN. Start using our full names, or do you need help with spelling like a big boy?

Lisa Bennett: That would definitely make sense. I mean, who would want to kidnap her? She has nothing anyone could ever want. #skinnybitch

Kellan J: Meghan, I'd fuck you any day. Name the time and place.

Meghan LG: OMFG, someone block this asshole!

Emma: I told Sloane we should no longer sit at that table, even with her not being there, but she's too scared of D.

Nora Ross: Fuck Denielle, she's probably cheating on Charlie with Wes. We all saw how those two all of a sudden stick together. #theyaresodoingit

I STOP READING. Emma, *my friend*, sided with Katherine. Denielle has a target on her back because of me. My throat starts aching, and I close my eyes for a second to collect myself. None of them would've dared to badmouth my best friend before...*I need to get out of here.* I thrust the phone at Rhys, who barely catches it, and turn on my heels.

"Calla!"

I don't make eye contact as I climb into the Raptor, put the truck into reverse, and leave him and George standing in Woodland Park.

PULLING INTO THE GARAGE, I expect Tristen to be hovering in the door to the kitchen. I stole his truck, after all.

I gently close the driver's side door, minimizing any sound—not that the roar of the engine isn't enough to announce my arrival—

and hesitantly approach the entrance leading into the house. Voices are audible inside, but I can't make out what's being said. Heather is talking, Tristen is responding, and Natty is laughing. Suddenly, the door swings open, and Tristen halts abruptly. Our eyes meet, and we're locked in a stand-off. When black spots start appearing in my vision, I suck in the breath I was unconsciously holding.

My adopted father lifts something, and I lower my gaze. Oh, he was taking out the trash. Sidestepping, I let him through, and he dumps the white plastic bag into the bin by the roll gate.

On his way back, he pauses and leans in. "Mom doesn't know. I told her you needed to get out for a bit, and I let you take the truck. Don't do it again."

My eyes widen, and I jerk my head up and down.

"Oh, and sweetheart?"

"Yes?" I squeak.

"We are going to talk about that phone."

My pulse is thrashing in my ears, and I murmur, "Okay."

I follow him into the kitchen, and Heather's face lights up. "You're back! How was the drive?"

My cheeks are aflame, and I'm about to reply when Rhys enters through the front door. He must have left the Defender in the driveway. Another quick escape?

I'm not bitter at all. Lie.

All eyes swivel to him, and Heather's expression falls. "I got a call from your coach earlier." She doesn't elaborate, but we all understand the meaning.

Rhys smoothes his features, not letting what went down at the park show. "They deserved it." No excuses.

"I agree with you, son. But next time, don't do it on school property." I whirl around to confirm I'm not hallucinating. Tristen stands slightly behind me, arms on his hips, and levels his son with a gaze I can't decipher. It's something between pride, disapproval, and a smug grin.

"Tristen!" Heather admonishes.

I turn back toward the rest of the family. Heather's lips are pursed, Rhys's eyes nearly bulge out of their sockets, and Natty tries to cover her snicker behind cupped hands.

Tristen steps forward and shrugs. "You know what these little shits said about our daughter. They deserve much more than what Rhys did to them."

Heather throws her hands up and turns toward the stove. Rhys seems to be in the same state of shock as me because we just stare at his father, slack-jawed. Tristen walks over to his son, places a hand on his shoulder, and squeezes before leaving the room.

I haven't seen that type of affection from him in years.

LATER, after Heather and Tristen retire to the third floor and Natty is sound asleep, Rhys and I sit in my bathroom in front of the open vanity cabinet, each having one headphone in our ear.

I haven't been able to concentrate on anything all evening. My nerves have been in a state of permanent buzzing since Tristen's proclamation that we will *talk* about the phone.

"George. Let's recap what you could find out from your guy." My brother's voice brings me back to the present.

"Unfortunately, not much." George's frustration is clear. When no one speaks, he continues, "I reached out to some old contacts. Francis Turner was a loner. He didn't socialize."

"Sounds familiar," Rhys mumbles, and I elbow him in the side.

George chooses to ignore the comment. "Turner had a drug problem that, in the end, got him dishonorably discharged. He was not married, but there was a rumor of him having a child. Supposedly, he got some eighteen-year-old girl pregnant and moved her close by, but no one ever saw her. He kept an apartment on base as well. The speculation was he only used that to meet with his girlfriends. He was never caught with the actual drugs."

"Girlfriends? Plural?" I ask incredulously. I stop listening after that. The guy is so...eww. I shudder and Rhys side-eyes me.

"That's what was said," George confirms, oblivious to my thoughts.

"Do we know when that was? The year or base?" Nate is typing in the background.

"Georgia. He wasn't clear about the timeframe. I will get back to you on that."

"Sounds good," my brother replies absently. We can still hear the faint clicking of keys.

"Do you think his girlfriend or kid are involved in this?" Rhys's question makes the hair on the back of my neck stand up.

Who are these people?

"I'm still saying Lilly should come to LA. At least we know she's safe here." Nate has stopped typing.

At that, Rhys barks out a non-comical laugh. "And do what? Hide in one of your mansions and hope it all disappears?"

"Nate, I strongly advise against pulling Lilly out of her current environment. It would raise too many questions and would make any future reintegration extremely difficult. You don't want her to be on the run her entire life, do you?" George attempts to reason with my brother.

"What life is that? Did you see what her so-called friends have been plastering all over the Internet? I want to send all of them a nice virus or, even better, put some unpaid parking tickets into the database, or give them a fun STD on their school medical records and leak them all over the Internet."

Oh boy, one really doesn't want to get on his bad side. He's hella inventive—and vindictive—which, embarrassingly, I quite enjoy at the moment.

Nate needs to show me how to do all these things—only theoretically, of course. Maybe. One practical execution test on the Wicked Bitch won't hurt, right?

In the end, we settle on me staying in Westbridge, but George will be keeping me under 24/7 surveillance. Nate doesn't want to miss anything on the Turner front. George has not been able to locate him since the press conference, which I sense neither of the men in my immediate life like very much. They're not used to being in the dark.

Who is Turner, and what does he want with me?

"Have you made any progress on Brooks's transactions?" I'm desperate to change the topic.

Hearing Nate type again, I assume he's pulling something up on his computer. "Some. I was able to trace it through four shell corporations down to South America, but I'm hitting a roadblock. The last one was owned by someone who died around the same time the transfers started in the U.S. Whoever set this up knew what they were doing, how to create false trails, use deceased individuals as a decoy, etcetera. Since there is no information exchange between these countries and the U.S., no one questioned it."

The frustration in his voice is palpable. Nate is one of the best, and yet he's unable to find who's behind this or who Brooks transferred money to all these years.

"Do we really care who he paid off? Maybe he had a gambling problem? Plus, it's not like he didn't have the money for it." Rhys remains unconvinced.

"It's all connected. I know it," I say to no one in particular. My gut feeling has not been wrong over the last five months.

RHYS SKIPPED HIS MORNING PRACTICE. He said if he sees Kellan or any of the guys, he'd probably end up pounding their faces for no reason other than breathing.

Entering the kitchen, I stop in my tracks. Camden, Lanning, and both of my adopted parents sit at the table, talking in hushed tones. Rhys is still upstairs, getting dressed, and I intended to make my tea while waiting for him. Taking in the scene in front of me, I get the feeling I should've stayed in my room and let him bring me my tea. Lanning clears his throat, and four sets of eyes instantly are trained on me.

Well, if that isn't uncomfortable.

"Lilly, you may want to sit down." Heather's voice forces my focus on her. I don't like where this is going.

Slowly, I approach the empty chair at the end of the table and lower myself down. Heart pounding in my chest, I scan the faces of all four adults. Agent Camden returns my gaze with a wary expression. Lanning radiates pity, and where Heather has concern written on her forehead, Tristen is once again indecipherable.

I swallow hard. "What's going on?"

Camden exchanges a look with Heather, both women seemingly debating how to breach the news to me, when Lanning slides his tablet over to me.

"Connor!" Camden barks at her partner.

"What? She has to deal with it one way or another. There is no way to sugarcoat this," he defends himself as I draw the device closer.

I lower my eyes to the screen. A news article with today's date shines back at me from the display. It's not one of the big, reputable papers, but it's still a well-known source for entertainment news. The headline alone makes me want to throw up.

KIDNAPPING VICTIM #1, Lilly McGuire, in a Secret Relationship with Her Adopted Brother

UNDERNEATH IS the famous picture of me wrapped around Rhys, tongue down his throat, and his hands on my ass in front of Denielle's house. I force myself to read one line after another until I can't stomach it anymore.

. . .

The above photograph has been circulating on dozens of social media accounts linked to Westbridge High, the school Lilly and Rhys McGuire are currently attending. A reliable source revealed to us in an exclusive interview that the illicit affair between the adopted siblings seemingly has been ongoing while Mr. McGuire was still in a relationship with his longtime girlfriend and head cheerleader, Katherine Rosenfield.

Shortly after the relationship news broke, Miss Rosenfield attempted to confront Miss McGuire to clear up the rumor, which resulted in Miss McGuire attacking her peer violently in front of the entire junior and senior class, followed by her fleeing the scene of the physical altercation.

That was the last time she was seen until her reappearance, six days ago, at Hill Crest Medical Center in Nebraska. An independent media source was able to get a visual of Miss McGuire after her admittance and told us that she appeared to be heavily medicated but was unable to determine if said medication was self-administered or by the hospital. The question that arises now is, was she really a victim of The Babysitter? Could this all be an elaborate scheme to redirect from the lack of adult supervision in the McGuire household? Or is this something Miss McGuire did to herself because of the guilt of seducing her adopted brother?

MY PULSE INCREASES with every word until my hands are trembling so badly that I let the device drop back onto the table. I'm going to be sick. Pushing the chair back with too much force, it topples over. I'm unable to look at the four people in the room. The chance of them, the public, not believing my memory loss was a possibility, but this?

Mortified, I spin and slam straight into Rhys's chest. His hands shoot out to steady me, and our eyes lock. His jaw tenses, but he doesn't ask what's wrong. He wraps his arm around me and leads me upstairs to his room.

CHAPTER FIVE

RHYS

LILLY HAS COMPLETELY WITHDRAWN.

I brought her to my room, despite it facing the front of the house and our reporter stalker, Lancaster, being camped out underneath my window. The dude has not left his post in days. At this point, I'm convinced he has a *Luggable Loo* in the back of his tinted SUV. He is careful not to set foot on our property, but his fucking camera is permanently angled toward my window. It's beyond me what he expects to record.

She curled up on her side on top of my comforter before I fully closed the blinds, saluting Bomber Jacket in the process. I lower myself to the edge of the bed and carefully place my hand on her hip. "Babe?"

Staring blankly ahead, she doesn't respond. A dull pain forms in my chest. This is worse than when she found out whatever my father did to her—*let happen* to her.

She almost appears catatonic, and I have no clue what to do. I rub my free hand against my jeans. "Babe, what happened? Please talk to me."

Still, no answer. I'm this close to getting on my hands and knees and start begging.

Fuck.

Do I call Nate? He'll immediately dispatch George to *extract* his sister. His stance on all of this is clear. George wants Lilly to stay, but in the end, he works for Nate. He'll do whatever his orders are.

What the hell could've happened in the eight minutes it took me to get dressed? The tablet! Lilly read something on the federal douche's iPad. With one more glance at her, I place a gentle kiss on her temple and whisper, "Be right back."

Nothing.

Unsure what I'm going to find but determined to get answers, I take the stairs three steps at a time. I'm in the kitchen and grab the device that's still where Lilly left it. My parents and the federal wastes of oxygen are where they were a few minutes ago, talking in hushed voices. As I reach for the iPad, Mom's gaze jerks to me. "Rhys!"

I have no idea if she's admonishing me for taking the guy's property without saying *pretty please* or if she doesn't want me to see what's on there. It's a news article. I'm able to read the head-line before it disappears from my grasp. I level my father, who is now holding the device in his hand.

"What the fuck is this?" I attempt to take it back, but Dad just throws it at its owner, who catches it with an oof sound. "Dad?" I growl. My fists curl into themselves, and my nails dig into my palms. I've shown less and less respect toward my father, and I wouldn't be surprised if he snapped soon.

"Let him read it, Tristen," Agent Camden speaks up, and I peer at her.

"Vivian!" My mother tries to insert herself.

"She's right. This impacts all of us, Rhys just as much as Lilly, even though they try to put the spotlight on my daughter." I don't miss how Dad claims Lilly as his, and a rush of adrenaline bursts through my body.

Is it possible our family is not as broken as I thought it was?

"Sit," my father orders, and I reluctantly comply. I need to know what is on that screen. His head swivels to Agent Mouthbreather. "Give it to him."

Lanning stares incredulously, like he wants to say, "You just threw the damn thing at me," but he doesn't have the balls to use his actual voice to follow through.

Dad cocks an eyebrow at the clearly inferior man, and the iPad is back in my hand before I can suppress the snort building in my throat. Could this guy be a bigger joke?

I scan the article in front of me, but it's like my brain has shut down. I don't comprehend the words and have to read it twice before it sinks in. There is only one person who could be the *reliable source*. Right about now, she can thank the Lord that she has a fucking pussy, or she would be in the hospital, eating through a straw, by the end of the day. My grip is so tense that the plastic case around the device crackles.

Dad pries Lanning's tablet from my fingers, and my hands instantly curl back into tight fists. My entire body is shaking, and I can't make out my mother's words through the pounding in my ears. Jumping up from my chair, I kick the one beside mine across the kitchen, where it crashes into the island.

"RHYS!" My father's commanding tone finally penetrates the red haze. I clasp my hands on the top of my head and turn away from the audience. I need to get a grip. The urge to punch the drywall across from me is taking over my senses. I'm ready to take the three steps it would require to turn the kitchen and living room divider into my next victim when a band of steel wraps itself around my upper body. Dad immobilizes me with his arms.

The man is strong for his age.

"You need to calm down, son!"

I struggle against his hold until my father says the three words that can deflate my rage. "Lilly needs you!"

Stopping my fight, I sag against his chest, giving him all the power. He instantly releases me, and I crouch down, trying to get my labored breathing under control.

A hand lands on my shoulder. "Go upstairs and take care of her. We'll talk later." These last few days, my father has shown more emotion than in the previous years—hell, the last decade. I follow his order without a second glance back.

Was his behavior also connected to all of this?

I DIDN'T GO to school. Instead, I lay in bed, wrapped around Lilly—not in a sexual way. She didn't speak one word. Mid-day, she got up to use the bathroom, but as soon as she was done, she aimed for the bed, curled into a tight ball again, and that was it. I returned to my big spoon position, one arm under my head and the other tightly around her belly. The first sign of life was when Lilly took my hand, which was splayed on her flat stomach, between hers and placed a kiss on the inside of my palm. In response, I pressed my body even closer. The weight in my chest had gotten heavier as I watched the minutes tick by on the alarm clock. The feeling of losing her had been growing all day.

I've ignored the buzzing coming from my desk. I have a decent idea who is blowing up my phone and what it's about, but I refuse to let go of Lilly. Something deep down tells me that I may not have many more chances.

It's dark when someone knocks. After the last bathroom break, I moved us out of the dual fetal position—my back couldn't take it anymore. I'm sitting against the headboard, and Lilly is tucked under my arm, with her head on my chest. Our fingers are intertwined on my lower abdomen, and I'm playing with the strands of her hair with my free hand.

"Come in."

The door slowly swings inward, and Mom's face appears in the gap. She zeros in on her daughter immediately but doesn't enter. "Sweetheart?"

When Lilly doesn't react, her eyes shift to me, asking a

million questions without uttering a single word. Drawing in a deep breath, I flex my fingers around Lilly's. "Babe?"

"Hmm?" Her eyes still don't focus, but this is the first sound all day.

I tilt my head down. "Cal? Mom is here." I squeeze her hand again and rub my other up and down her back, mentally preparing myself to have to shake her out of this lifeless state.

Lilly's head slowly turns toward the other side of the room.

Thank fuck, she's back. I think.

"Hi, sweetheart." Mom's tone is wary.

"Hi," Lilly croaks. Why am I surprised at the rasp in her voice? She hasn't had a drop of water all day.

My mother's eyes flick to mine before she addresses the girl in my arms again. "Dad and I were wondering if we could talk to you."

My mouth is already open to protest when she amends, "Both of you."

I shift away from Lilly to see her entire face and for her to see me as well. When I'm sure I have her attention, I speak. "It's up to you, babe. Your decision."

Out of the corner of my eye, it's apparent that Mom is about to argue, but I throw her a glare. She pinches her lips together.

Lilly searches my face, and I smooth my features in an attempt to appear confident and strong—two of the last emotions I feel at the moment.

"Okay." It's just a whisper, but Mom hears it and expels a long breath.

"We'll wait for you in Dad's office. Whenever you're ready."

I give my mother a curt nod in acknowledgment without averting my eyes from Lilly.

TEN MINUTES LATER, we find Dad behind his desk and Mom in the single chair in his office, leaving the sofa for us. I expect to see my father's usual stone-cold demeanor. What I find, instead, makes a pit the size of the Grand Canyon form in my stomach. His hands are clasped tightly on top of the desk—to the point of the skin being stretched over his knuckles. His shoulders are stiff, and under the desk, I can see his leg bouncing. A small but —for my father, the man without emotion—clear sign that something is very wrong.

Leading Lilly to the two-seater, I pull her down next to me. I'm in the same position as the day we met with Madeline, my ankle crossed over my knee and my arm stretched over the back-rest. Yet, I don't feel the confidence I'm attempting to portray. My insides churn in anticipation of whatever my parents are about to drop on us. It can't be good if they asked both of us down here.

Dad clears his throat and makes quick eye contact with Mom. I follow his gaze and see her nodding at him. Lilly misses the exchange, being focused on her hands in her lap. I pull her into the crook of my arm, needing the contact more than her at the moment. Once she is settled, I hold my other hand out, palm up, and she automatically interlaces her opposite hand with mine. Both my parents follow our movement but remain mute.

The silence stretches, and I stroke my thumb over our inter-twined fingers. It's as much to calm my thrashing pulse as it is to reassure her.

"You have both seen the article that was published this morning," Dad begins.

A low growl builds in my throat.

"Other news outlets have already followed suit. We have received multiple requests to comment throughout the day." Lilly's eyes fly to my Dad's as he speaks, but he continues, "After long deliberation with Agents Lanning and Camden, we have issued a statement this afternoon."

"Why would you give them the fucking satisfaction to react? This has Kat written all over it," I burst out, barely able to contain the pent-up rage that has surged back to the surface.

Lilly's head jerks to face me. "How do you know? Why would she do that?"

Instead of making me answer, Mom leans forward and places a hand on Lilly's knee. "It was easy to force the paper to give up her name. All I had to do was threaten them with defamation and other legal actions. You are the victim of a crime, and this has nothing to do with it." Lilly's eyes flicker to me as Mom mentions her being a victim.

"But with that being said," Dad amends, "we had to react to the accusation of turning a blind eye to your relationship. The last thing we need is the state trying to take Lilly away and bringing charges against all of us—including you, Rhys."

My eyes bulge, and Lilly's hands fly to her mouth.

What the fuck?

"Can they do that?" A hollow vacuum builds in my chest.

"I haven't looked into all the legalities yet, but Lilly is under-age, even if just for another week. And no matter how you turn it, once the suit is out, it will follow us forever. Not only would you"—she levels me with her courtroom face—"be *labeled*, but Dad and I would be charged with neglect. I'm confident we could fight it, but it will ruin everyone's reputation, even if we'd win."

"So, what did you do?" Lilly's whispered question drags me out of the rabbit hole I was already halfway down. They could charge me with rape because of my ex talking to the media.

How did this happen?

"Agent Camden released a statement that Mom and I were fully aware of your relationship. Lilly has known of her adoption for some time, but we decided, as a family, to keep it on the down low until she was ready to talk about it. Your emotional relation-ship evolved over the years. We didn't encourage it but also didn't permit it, knowing this would only push you more toward each other. We kept open communication with both of you, and once it became clear that you two had developed feelings for each other, we set clear rules for both of you. We have raised all our children to be responsible and honest. You are mature for your age, and along with the rules, we trusted you to make the right decisions." Dad concludes his recap by pushing himself off of the desk chair.

"So, you lied your ass off," I deadpan.

"We did." There is no remorse in my father's tone.

I begin to question my judgment on his motives all those years. Maybe he is not the emotionally compromised robot I made him out to be? Along with a sense of gratitude, the gut feeling that his actions are linked to everything that has happened to this family is growing.

"What happens next?" Hearing Lilly speak after a day of silence still startles me.

"We expect there to be more reports about the kidnapping. So far, the clusterfuck your ex has caused has distracted everyone from that," Mom sneers, and I stare at her with wide eyes.

"Mom! Did you just drop the F-bomb?"

My mother smirks at me sheepishly. "I do curse when it's warranted, honey." Then she turns to Lilly. "As for what happens next, this is what we wanted to discuss with you."

I'm so not gonna like this.

Dad rounds his desk and leans against the front of it with his arms crossed over his chest. A silent communication passes between him and Mom, and the vacuum in my chest expands.

He nods at her, and she inhales deeply before speaking. "We would like for Lilly to return to school tomorrow."

A whimper escapes the girl in my arm, and I tighten my hold on her.

"Are you crazy? Have you not seen what everyone's been saying about her?" There is zero point in trying to rein in my temper.

Both of my parents remain calm. "Hear us out, son," Dad begs. He actually pleads with me. This man never so much as asks; he demands. And people follow. That's who Colonel Tristen McGuire is.

I press my lips together, waiting for the second *Danner*—not any regular shoe—to drop.

"The longer Lilly stays in hiding, the worse the rumors get. Camden got a hold of another article that is set to print tomorrow, questioning Lilly's memory loss."

Dad cocks his head, scanning both of us intently. I'm ninety percent sure he questions it himself.

If the FBI chick found that article, why hasn't Nate?

The prolonged silence is beginning to choke me. I don't want Lilly to face WH. I can only do so much in school—meaning I can only rearrange the faces of the male student population. Kat has the female one cowering at her feet, and I don't think even Den has the power to prevent the things that will happen. My ex is their *Queen Bitch*.

"Okay."

All eyes in the room swivel to Lilly. I lean forward to get a better look at her face, and what I see there is such a surprise it makes my brows furrow. Her eyes are hard and determined, but her flipping of her thumb against the rest of her fingers tells me the opposite.

Reaching up, I turn her face toward me. "Are you sure?"

Lilly bobs her head, and I peer at my mother. Her narrowed eyes show that she's not buying it either.

Lilly excludes herself from the remaining conversation where we discuss that she will drive with me, but we will keep our distance. We are making a statement by going together, but we don't need to fuel the fire.

Back upstairs, while Lilly is taking a shower, I check my phone for the first time since this morning. I missed several texts from Wes and Den. Both have read the article, and with me not being in school, they want to know what's going on. I'm surprised they haven't shown up at the house.

A message from Jager says: **It wasn't me. I SWEAR !!!!!!!!!!**

I really did a number on that asshole. Good!

Several more texts from my former friends, similar to Jager's.

Pussies.

And one from UNKNOWN: **Answer the fucking phone, or I will come to pick her up personally.**

I probably should call him back before he jumps on his fancy jet and reveals himself.

WE HAD SPENT ALMOST an hour on the phone with Nate last night, who, needless to say, was pissed with a capital P—scratch that, make all the letters caps. When we didn't respond to his twenty-three missed calls and forty-four messages, he hacked into the security feed to check on his sister. After that, he sent the text to my personal cell and waited for us to reach out. Asking why he didn't check the cameras right away was on the tip of my tongue, but I swallowed the question not to push him further.

By the time we finally called him back, George was camped out one street over, waiting for his boss's orders. George agreed with my parents' plan of offense, versus Nate, who still insisted she should not be here. He's grown extremely protective of his little sister.

The first genuine reaction Lilly showed all day was when her brother admitted that he sent a couple of viruses to Kat. She activated one of them on her phone, and every single photo she had was copied to Nate's cloud, followed by the device being wiped. Nate then went through the pictures and videos and extracted the ones that would serve as future blackmail material. According to him, there is a lot to choose from. Lilly barked out a laugh, and the sound made the hollow vacuum finally shrink to a manageable size.

. . .

Now, on the drive to school, Lilly is sitting next to me in the passenger seat of the Defender, flicking her thumb against her remaining four fingers. I fight the urge to grab her hand; the movement is starting to make me twitchy.

When we pull into the parking lot, I drive past my usual spot and pull in next to Denielle's Q3. She's already leaning against the driver's side next to Wes's 4Runner, but my best friend is nowhere in sight. That's odd.

At the sight of my car, students stop walking mid-step. I notice Lilly stiffen out of the corner of my eye, and my breathing speeds up. I have no fucking clue how this day is going to go.

I reach over and touch Lilly's leg lightly. Her nervous tick stops immediately, and her head jerks toward me before facing forward again. She scans the front of the school with wide eyes.

I don't give a fuck if anyone sees me touching her, but I retract my hand nonetheless. "Cal?"

She slowly turns back, but her eyes don't follow until she has to focus them on me.

I hold out my hand, palm up, and she glances down.

"What is this?"

"The spare key for the Defender. If you want to leave, leave." I need to know she can get away if she has to.

Lilly slowly reaches out and takes the key from me, tucking it into the front pocket of her faded blue jeans. I take in her outfit, and besides her skinny jeans, she is wearing my old hoodie—definitely a statement—black John Fluevog boots, and her black leather jacket. Her hair is up in a messy bun, and she neglected her usual minimal makeup. I don't think she's ever gone to school like this. The boots were from last Halloween when she dressed up as Abigail Whistler, and she refused to buy any boot but the exact same. I just hope she never added the blade modification as she originally intended. That could end disastrously today.

"Ready?" I ask her after she makes no move to leave the car. Den has already planted herself in front of the Defender's hood, arms crossed and ready to bite anyone's face off who comes too close.

Without another word, Lilly opens the door and joins her best friend outside. In an attempt to calm my nerves, I expel one last breath and follow suit.

May we all survive this day without suspension—or a murder charge.

Denielle and I flank Lilly on either side, and together, we walk toward the main entrance. It's fair to say every single head is tracking us. Conversations halt, cameras point, and the hushed whispers cannot hide the exclamations of *slut, she fucked her brother, it's all a lie, psych ward,* and *does Kat know* assaulting us from all sides.

Lilly holds her head high, and her gaze is straight ahead. We don't touch, and neither do Denielle and her, who used to link arms all the time.

As we near Lilly's locker, my best friend comes into view. I narrow my eyes, and my heart rate doubles. Wes is scrubbing ferociously on the door. As we get closer, I can make out the words written neatly across Lilly's and the *surrounding* lockers in various types of paint and markers, all probably requiring a different method of removal.

"LILLY MCGUIRE IS an incestuous slut who fucks her brother and lies about losing her memory. We don't want you here!"

WE'RE NOT GOING to make it through this day. If Lilly doesn't lose it, I will. Or Nate will send George to torture half the student population if he finds out.

Either way, we're fucked.

CHAPTER SIX

LILLY

I SPENT YESTERDAY GOING DOWN ONE RABBIT HOLE AFTER another, trying to figure out how to feel or react. The shock of the article and my impending return to school had eventually worn off, but I was still no further than before. My fight-or-flight instincts were in a battle of tug of war. One moment, I was ready to take the entire Westbridge High population with its *Queen Bitch* at the top head on—who are they to pass judgment over me? A minute and four seconds later, I was close to dialing George's number to pick me up—because why would I do that to myself? Or my family and friends, for that matter? I expected a lot, but statutory rape? This was spiraling out of control at an inconceivable rate, and I felt more helpless than when I was trapped in my crashed Jeep.

Nate's small act of revenge gave me some satisfaction, though Katherine deserved a lot worse after this article.

Rhys fell asleep around one in the morning, but no matter what I tried to relax, it didn't work. Finally, I gave up and snuck out of bed.

Sitting in front of the vanity, I typed in Nate's number: **Hi.**

The bubble immediately popped up: **What's wrong? It's one in the morning in VA.**

I can read the clock. Thank you very much, dear brother.

In response to my sassy reply, he sent me the emoji with the straight mouth and raised eyebrow. Who knew that bantering with my big brother would give me the type of normalcy—the distraction—I needed?

I can't sleep, I admitted.

Talk?

I thought that over. **Can't. I don't want to wake Rhys up.**

We ended up texting for over an hour, and I confessed how my conflicting emotions confused the hell out of me. Shouldn't I be one or the other? Nervous/worried *or* don't care.

We talked through my different trains of thought, and in the end, Nate helped me realize that both extremes are a reasonable reaction to my current situation.

My (at times) unstable brother made a pretty decent therapist.

NOW, standing in the school's hallway, a semi-circle of probably more than fifty juniors and seniors forms around me. I stare at the words on my locker. And stare some more.

Wes has taken a step back, sponge in one hand and what looks like a Clorox wipe in the other. He won't look at me. "Dude, I tried. I have no fucking clue what they used to write this shit." Contempt drips from every word.

Rhys and Denielle have gone rigid on either side of me. Where Rhys is shaking with rage, Den is eerily still, eyes narrowed on the words.

Out of the corners of my eyes, I notice the number of students surrounding us increases. Everyone wants to have a front-row seat to the show.

Nate's last message before saying goodnight reverberates

through my head: **Remember what's important. You've done nothing wrong. Your boyfriend and adopted family love you and would do anything to protect you. And so do I. Nothing they do will change that. You're in charge. Don't let your emotions overpower your intelligence. That's what they want. George will be outside the school if you need him.**

I'm in charge.

I pull my shoulders back, take two steps away from Denielle and Rhys, and unlock the door to the little space of privacy I have at Westbridge High. My books are where I had left them over three weeks ago. Grabbing what I need for my morning classes, I turn, look at Denielle, and plaster a smile on my face that makes my cheeks hurt. "Ready?" I chirp, ignoring my audience and envisioning blinders around my face like at a horse race. I will not give them the satisfaction of acknowledging them —or worse, cowering.

Den narrows her eyes at me, peers at Rhys sideways, but plays along. "Sure thing, babe."

We fall into step beside each other, and the mass of students shrinks away as we make our way down the hall. Rhys and Wes follow close behind. There is no way he'd let me walk alone, so I don't even attempt to leave without them.

After we say our goodbyes, and I promise to stay put until one of them is back to walk me to my next class, I swivel on my heels. Having to spend my first three classes without my best friend, my senses go on alert as soon as I enter the classroom. All conversations stop, and the air is instantly charged like lightning is about to strike. Just as I sink into my chair, Bria and Hailee, two girls who were always friendly with me and occupied the desks surrounding mine, get up and move to the back of the room. My body tenses, and I concentrate on keeping my breath steady. I zero in on a spot in the front and put on my best George expression—none.

Don't let your emotions overpower your intelligence.

The only person not abandoning his seat is Lucas, a boy from the chess club. He meets my eyes when he approaches his desk in front of mine but turns his focus quickly to his shoes. Miss Foy, our American History teacher, furrows her brows at the new seating arrangement until her gaze lands on me. Her eyes widen for a microsecond before she composes herself. This is only her second year of teaching, and she probably has no idea how to handle the situation. Hence, she ignores it.

Class itself passes quietly, and when the bell rings, I take my time gathering my things. I can't leave anyway until one of my bodyguards arrives. I'm bent sideways, dropping my notepad into my messenger bag, when my textbook shoots off the table and lands under the chair next to me. I inhale to the count of four before slowly turning in the direction my book got launched from.

"Oops." Bria shrugs, a sweet smile turning her mouth into the perfect target for my fist. Instead, I do nothing. When she doesn't get a reaction from me, she walks away with a huff.

I exhale slowly through my nose and lean down to reach for my book when something slams into my head, and I can barely catch myself before face-planting onto the linoleum floor.

"Slut," the owner of the bag—the weapon of choice—whisper-coughs.

Blood starts pounding in my ears. Balling my fists, I take a deep breath, uncurl my fingers, and grab my book.

Do. Not. Engage.

THE NEXT TWO periods go similar, and it's getting increasingly more difficult to keep my cool.

Instead of my classmates moving away, my lab partner in AP Chemistry, Arianna (Ari), *stumbles* and spills the nitric acid we're using for our experiment. It ends up all over my chem book and splashes on my lab coat. After ripping the white fabric off and making sure it didn't hit anywhere else, I stare at her incredulously.

"Oops." She smirks and begins cleaning up, acting as if nothing happened.

Is that all these girls can say?

Of course, she timed it perfectly with our teacher rummaging around in the back of the room. By the time he pulls his head out of the supply cabinet, everything appears as before —minus my lab coat.

I've never talked to this girl outside of class, and I didn't think she was associated with Katherine. I'm starting to wonder if the Wicked Bitch has put a hit out on me.

In third period, Algebra II, I find a big fat "WHORE" carved into my desk. My pulse quickens, but I keep repeating my new mantra in my head. My pointer finger traces the indentation. It's a good quarter of an inch deep. How the hell did they manage that without Mr. Mann noticing?

Cocking my eyebrow theatrically, I place my textbook over the word. I count back from thirteen, unclenching my jaw before I do permanent damage to my teeth. It won't do any good using them as my personal punching bags. Though, I'd probably feel a lot better.

Fourth period, I get my first reprieve. Denielle and I share P.E., and as soon as she is at my side, no one glances at me twice. Lunch passes similarly. People stare at the four of us sharing the table, but no one dares to speak up or fake cough an insult in my direction. I don't keep what happened in periods one through three from my friends; there is no point. One of them would find out eventually. I've been *the talk* all morning. So far, I was kidnapped, followed by my kidnapper kicking me out when I sucked in bed. (The thought of Nate and any intimacy triggers my gag reflex.) The next rumor was that I was pregnant and faked my kidnapping while I was getting an abortion. Some guy even suggested I delivered the baby and gave it up, to which I made the first eye contact. The speaker was some dude from the soccer team. He's probably middle class in the school's social hierarchy and therefore seemed to have missed what happened to Rhys's *friends* who ran their mouths. I bit my tongue. Asking him if he had paid attention in sex ed would've been a waste of oxygen—I had a flat stomach three weeks ago.

My last class of the day is French, a subject I always looked forward to. However, after the previous six periods, pretending not to hear any of the whispers—some not so quiet—I'm mentally drained. Rhys will pick me up from here, as he's right above me on the senior floor, and then we can finally go home. Thinking about getting out of here, I miss the noise level in the class rising. When the mumbles and gasps register in my brain, it's too late. Something wet hits me from behind, and I instinctively duck. Not fast enough, though.

What the fuck?

My shoulders scrunched up to my ears, hair dripping into my face, I take inventory. I'm not hurting, so it's not chemicals this time—or at least nothing that could burn my flesh off. Then, I take a whiff and gag. The stench of algae and...fish penetrates my nostrils. I don't want to touch whatever is at the back of my head, but I have no choice. With a trembling hand, I slowly reach back and disentangle the object from my bun. Holding it between thumb and forefinger, I force myself to look at it—*it* being a half-dissected fish from, I'm guessing, the biology lab. The liquid still dripping down my face is probably water from the numerous tanks the school has for said fish. I swallow the pool of saliva in my mouth but end up choking in the process. The stench and visual make my stomach revolt. I let the dead animal fall to the floor, and after briefly closing my eyes to collect myself, I turn in my seat. The row behind me is occupied by several cheerleaders, including Emma and Sloane. I scan both of them with narrowed eyes, and where Sloane looks shocked, Emma is radiating glee.

Did she throw this thing at me?

Madame Morel chooses that moment to enter the room and

stops in her tracks. "Mon dieu, ce qui s'est passé ici?" *What happened here?* Whenever she gets upset or flustered, she falls back into French, even though she's lived in the U.S. since she was a child. I face my teacher, and when no one answers her question, I speak up for the first time all day.

"It seems this fish ended up in the wrong classroom. May I please go clean up?"

There are a few snickers around me, and I hear a huffing sound from the cheerleader's row, probably pissed that I don't burst into tears or lose my shit. But I swore to myself that I wouldn't do that, no matter what happens today. They will not see me bow down. Between Turner and all the other secrets Nate and I still need to get to the bottom of, I refuse to let a bunch of girls in too-short skirts and over-curled hair break me.

"Absolument. Vite. Go get cleaned up."

As I exit the room—with my bag, since I have no intention to return—I hear my teacher demanding who's responsible for the mess. Of course, she doesn't get a response.

After a quick detour to the bathroom, where I hold my entire head under the faucet followed by wringing my hair out and putting it back into a bun on top of my head, I strip out of my hoodie. It caught the brunt of the attack, and for that alone, I want to sic my big brother on them. This is my favorite piece of clothing these days. I stop at my locker, grab my jacket I had stashed there earlier, and head to the Defender.

Sitting in the security of Rhys's car, I pull out the new phone Heather handed me before school this morning and send him a message: **Waiting in the car for you.**

I follow that with a text to Den and Wes, in case they had planned to come to pick me up as well: **Left early. Waiting in the Defender for Rhys.**

When none of them respond, I double-check that the bubbles have the small "delivered" underneath.

Did I put their numbers in wrong?

I haven't finished that thought when the front door of the

south wing bursts open, and I see Rhys and Wes rush toward the parking lot. A few seconds later, the side door of the west wing opens and reveals my best friend, turning in the same direction.

Uh oh.

All three stop in front of the Defender, and we stare at each other through the windshield. Rhys takes three more steps and tears the passenger door open.

"What happened?" Then, he inhales and holds his hand over his nose. "Jesus Christ, Cal, what the fuck is that smell?"

"Dead fish." The adrenaline spike from the incident has worn off, and I'm too exhausted to even be upset at this point. All I want is to go home and take a shower.

Denielle comes to the side of the car and scowls. "Why is your hair drenched?" Then she takes a whiff and mimics Rhys's reaction. "Oh, my God."

I really don't want to rehash this now, but I am fully aware that neither Den nor Rhys will let it go until they know what happened. I recap the fish incident, and Denielle immediately does a one-eighty on her heels to head back into the building. Wes grabs her around the waist and holds her in place.

"LET ME GO! I will show that little skank what it means to smell like fish. Wait until I get my hands on that bitch!" My best friend is kicking, and with every word, her voice gets louder, but Wes keeps a firm grip on her. He murmurs something in her ear, and she goes limp.

Since when does he have that power over her?

I watch the scene with my head cocked to the side. Den and I need to have some girl time. I seem to have missed a lot over the last few weeks.

Rhys rounds the Defender and plants himself behind the wheel. "Let's get out of here."

I sigh. "Best words I've heard all day."

CHAPTER SEVEN

LILLY

Neither Heather nor Tristen are home when we pull into the garage. Spotting Lancaster aim his damn camera at the Defender as soon as we come into view, I sink lower in my seat, shielding my face. Who knows what headline my wet-dog appearance will cause?

With the garage door securely lowered, I straighten up and reach for the door handle.

"I want to kill these motherfuckers." Rhys's tone is low and menacing. Those are his first words since reversing out of the parking spot at school. As much as I relished the silent drive after this day of insults, my sweaty palms were a clear indicator that I was just waiting for Rhys to lose it. Not that it was my fault, or he'd blame me, but he's already been through enough in the last few weeks. I don't want to see him make the entire school his enemy.

I turn my head and see emotions ranging from rage to utter helplessness play across his face. It kills him that he can't be with me during class.

"Did anyone say anything to you?" We only talked about what happened to me, not if he experienced similar treatment.

Rhys's nostrils flare, and his hands grip the steering wheel tighter. "Yes and no."

I narrow my eyes, waiting.

"The guys learned their lesson. Jager won't make eye contact, and Owen even ran the other way and ditched class, but Kat...she's challenging me." Rhys is referring to their position at the top of the school's food chain. "She knows I can't do anything to her...physically."

He's holding back.

"What did she do?" After what I experienced first-hand in the past few hours, it can't be good.

"She's been telling everyone and their mother how you threw yourself at me when she and I were together. That she's suspected for *years* that something was wrong with you. The first kidnapping fucked you up to the point of your parents not being able to handle it anymore, and the second was all just a ploy to divert from our relationship."

I let it all sink in, and besides my parents not wanting me, it's similar to what I've already heard. *My parents didn't want me because I was too fucked up.* My heart rate seems to slow. Is that the real reason, after all? Is that what Heather and Tristen are keeping from me?

Without another word, I exit the Defender and head upstairs. As soon as I'm over the threshold of my room, I begin to strip, leaving pieces of clothing on the floor on my way to the shower.

By the time Rhys enters the bathroom, it's full of steam from my scorching shower. I haven't gone through my purging ritual in a while. Today, though, I need it. I didn't give them the satisfaction of breaking me, but I can't deny that it's been challenging. I trace the small crescent-shaped indentations on the heels of my hands with the tips of my fingers. The dozens of times I balled them into fists throughout the day have left permanent marks.

The glass door opens, and Rhys steps in. It took every ounce of energy to keep my façade in place throughout the day, but I can finally let it slip off. Standing directly under the spray, the water pelts on my skin, and my hair is plastered against the sides of my head. I stare up at him through my wet lashes, and he reaches for me, pulling my body against his. My arms circle his waist, and I press my cheek against his chest.

Rhys tightens his hold. "You did good today."

His praise is my undoing. All the comments and humiliations —some whispered, some not—come back and assault me from all angles: Slut. She's crazy. Whore. Brother-fucker. Lying skank. Bitch. The first tear starts flowing, followed by a second and a third until my body is shaking with gut-wrenching sobs, the running water muffling my cries.

What have I ever done to any of them?

Rhys hugs me tighter and places a kiss on the top of my head, but he doesn't speak. There are no words that can make it better. We remain like this until I run out of tears and the shower starts to cool. He hasn't moved the entire time, and as my body calms, I listen to the low thud of his heartbeat against my ear. The sound stirs a new emotion inside of me, and I loosen my grip. I turn my face to place a chaste kiss on his chest, right above his left pec. It was meant as gratitude for him being there for me once again, but when my lips connect with his skin, he jolts ever so slightly. He didn't expect me to do that. His embrace loosens, and his hands slowly glide down my back until they rest on my hips. My eyes flutter closed as the tips of his fingers press into my flesh, and his thumbs start circling my hip bones. Heat surges to my core, and I feel myself become wet. *More,* a voice inside my head all but shouts at me.

Where his hands traveled down, I let mine move up his torso, trailing each muscle of his ripped abdomen, over his pecs, until my arms intertwine behind his neck. My hands bury in the wet strands of his hair, and I tug ever so slightly. A low rumble of approval erupts in his throat, and my need to touch him—*let him touch me*—overwhelms all rational thought.

His breath quickens, and I know if I were to press my ear against his chest right now, his heart would beat anything but steady. I tilt my head up, blinking my eyes open. Rhys's chin is dipped down, and his lids are hooded. He's hardening against my belly, and I lick my lips. I'd be lying if I say his arousal doesn't please me.

When he stepped into the shower with me, neither of us intended for this to become anything other than the means of me working through my emotions. Rhys knows of my little ritual. But as we stand in front of each other, the air around us shifts to something else entirely. I raise myself on my tiptoes and press my lips lightly against his jawline, teasing him with the tip of my tongue. He hasn't shaved, and the scruff on his chin gives him an edge that makes me clench my legs together. Looking at him like this, water dripping down his taut body, chest heaving with desire...*I want him.*

Noticing my—no doubt, heated—gaze, Rhys inhales sharply, and the gleam in his eyes reminds me of the night of our first kiss right before he flipped me over on the couch and took charge. As if on cue, he shifts and grabs me at the back of my thighs. His hold pinches my skin, and a soft moan escapes me. Instead of it registering in my brain as painful, I react instinctively and wrap my legs around his back, right above his ass. He stares down at me, scanning every inch of my face, while my painfully hard nipples are pressed against him. What the hell is he waiting for? I rock myself against him, and he arches an eyebrow at my impatience, the corner of his very kissable mouth quirking in a cocky smirk. But despite his attempt at acting nonchalant, the rapid rise and fall of his chest is a dead giveaway to how much he wants this as well. Everything else, the reason we ended up in here, becomes unimportant.

I need this. No, I crave this. Him.

I stretch up, but before my lips reach his, Rhys's mouth is on mine, tongue inside. Finally. With a whimper, I clasp the back of his neck, pressing myself further into him. He groans into my mouth as he grinds himself against me, creating friction against my most sensitive spot that makes me roll my eyes back inside of my head. I stop holding back. My hips begin to move up and down, coating his length with my wetness. Rhys's hold on my thighs tightens to the point of me being convinced that he's leaving marks. I can't bring myself to care, though. My body vibrates with need, and I try to shift in his grasp so he's aligned with my entrance.

He suddenly pulls back, and I whine in protest. No, no, no!

What is he doing?

"Cal, wait." Rhys gently pushes me back as I try again. He holds my confused gaze. "Condom," he clarifies almost scoldingly.

Oh.

"Oh!" My face flushes. I briefly debate pushing the topic. I've been on the pill since I was fifteen—irregular cycles and all—and he knows it, but he wants to be responsible.

"Whoops." I shrug sheepishly and untangle my legs, albeit a little reluctantly. Rhys places me on the tiled floor of the shower. I don't want this to be over.

He shoves the door open. "Stay here," he orders, but before I can say anything, he disappears, dripping wet, into my bedroom, leaving footprints on the carpet.

I guess we're done?

The water has turned almost cold, and I quickly turn the spray off. Stepping out, I reach for the towel on the rack to dry off when a low growl makes me halt. "What do you think you're doing?"

I turn and watch this sexy-as-hell guy stalk toward me. My eyes widen at the determination written across his features. Aiming straight for me, he finishes rolling on a condom, and I take him in in all his glory. Dear Lord. Another wave of heat hits me straight to the core.

A wicked grin spreads across his face, and as soon as he reaches me, I'm back in his arms. I yelp at the sudden loss of contact with the floor and cling to his broad shoulders.

Nose to nose, Rhys's tongue darts out, tracing the corner of my mouth. "Where were we?"

I moan at the sensation, all coherent thought escaping me. "I'm, um...not sure." My response is no more than a breathy whisper. Closing my eyes, I nip at his bottom lip, which makes him hum in approval.

Without another word, he attacks my mouth with his, moving hard against mine, forcing his way in. Despite the initial force, his tongue does the opposite. He caresses me with soft strokes until I lose all self-restraint. The pulse between my legs throbs, and I want him inside of me. Now.

I'm on fire, my heart beating so fast I can barely catch my breath. Still moving my lips in sync with his, I flex my arms and pull up enough to align myself with him. Before he can stop me this time, I let myself sink down on his dick, and a guttural groan comes from Rhys. "Shiiit. Cal..."

I have no idea what he was attempting to say, but I don't really care, either. I deepen the kiss as I move up and down his length, letting him stretch me from a whole different angle than the first time.

Rhys adjusts his grip, and his hands move to my ass. He pushes farther into me, and I cry into his mouth. "Oh, God. Yesss."

He is so deep, the ecstasy steadily building as he keeps driving into me. I let my lips trail down his neck, kissing and nipping along the way. As one thrust hits my cervix, I instinctively moan and bite down on his shoulder.

With a growl, Rhys flips us around so my back is against the cold, glass wall of the shower, and I cross my ankles behind his back, not wanting to fall.

"I got you, babe." His fingers knead my butt, and the friction against my clit makes every nerve ending inside of me come to life.

My breasts bounce with every thrust, and when Rhys tilts his head and captures my nipple with his mouth, I'm done for.

"Rhys...shit..." My orgasm is beginning to crest, and he pumps into me harder.

"Let go, babe. Come for me." His voice is muffled as he moves to my other breast.

I don't want it to end, but as Rhys gently tugs with his teeth on my pebbled nipple, I go over the edge. My vision clouds, and I clench around him. After only two more thrusts, I feel him shudder against me. "Fuuuck."

His mouth is back against my neck, and his incoherent mumbling makes me smile as I come down from a high I've never experienced before.

We stay like this until our breathing has returned to a normal pace. He blinks down at me with a lazy grin on his lips. "You are so fucking beautiful when you come."

I swat his arm, blushing, and slowly unwind my legs from behind his back. Rhys pulls out and lowers me down until my feet touch the ground. I'm glad I'm still leaning against the glass, because my legs barely support my weight. He cups the sides of my face, bending down. His warm breath is like a caress to my skin. "I love you, Cal."

I gaze up at his green eyes. "I love you, too."

He places a gentle kiss on my mouth. "We can do this. Together."

I don't respond.

LATER, in my room, Rhys sits against the headboard of my bed, playing with the strands of my hair while I'm nestled into the crook of his arm. My arm and leg are draped over his body, and I relish the goosebumps his twirling of my hair causes. My new phone begins to vibrate on the nightstand, and a shot of adrenaline puts me on instant alert. I disentangle myself from him to check the caller ID, and when Den's picture on the screen registers, my rapid pulse begins to calm.

I swipe to answer the call. "Hey, babe."

"Hi," she says hesitantly. "I just wanted to check in on you." Her tone is less than cheerful.

"I'm...okay." It's not a complete lie. I do feel better. Letting everything out in the shower has helped. Then, a mental image forms of what happened after, and my face heats. My thigh automatically pushes against Rhys's leg, and he chuckles, knowing exactly what just went on inside of my head. Yup, that definitely distracted me from the shit show at school today.

When my best friend remains silent, my momentary happiness disintegrates like a dried flower petal. I prepare myself for the worst. Finally, she expels a long breath. "I got a call from Rhys's BFF."

Rhys is close enough to hear Denielle's statement, and his eyebrows knit together. "Why wouldn't Wes just—oh..." He leaps off the bed and charges into my bathroom. It takes me longer to comprehend the meaning of Den's words. When I hear Rhys rummaging through the vanity, it clicks.

His BFF. George.

I follow with my cell phone still pressed to my ear and find Rhys sitting on the floor, scrolling through something on the phone.

"That little cunt. If I get my hands on her tomorrow." His body is shaking with rage.

"Call me back later?" Denielle's voice filters through to my brain as I'm staring at Rhys white-knuckling the device in his hands.

"Hm-hmm." I lower my phone without hanging up. Crouching in front of him, I try to get his attention, but he is focused on whatever he's looking at.

"What is it?" I whisper.

His eyes snap up as if he just now realizes I'm in the room. He draws in a slow breath and expels it at the same pace, which makes his nostrils flare. "Nate messaged."

"Okay?"

What has him bent so out of shape?

"He stopped the article that was supposed to print today. I forgot about it with the shit show in school."

Tristen mentioned another press release yesterday, but like Rhys, I didn't remember it until now. His face, however, tells me that this is not all. I wait.

"Your brother figured out who tagged your locker. Seems like he's been *following* you all day. And he wants to know why you left French class early with wet hair."

There are no cameras in the classrooms, just the hallways, cafeteria, auditorium, and gym, etc.—all the places big groups of students congregate. It makes sense that he didn't see the actual incident but was able to find out who wrote *the lovely message* on my locker.

"What did he do?"

Please tell me you didn't do anything stupid, Nate.

He made it clear that he will do anything to protect me.

Rhys hands me the phone, and I start scrolling. The first message contains a video and several stills from the security footage. Even from the frozen picture, I instantly recognize who vandalized my locker: Emma.

Something breaks inside of me. Emma. Why? We've been friends for years. Maybe not *best* friends, but friends, nonetheless. I ungracefully fall out of my crouch onto my butt. My gaze meets Rhys's, and the betrayal he feels for me is written all over his face. I take in the pictures that follow the video and see Kat huddled with Emma in a corner. According to the timestamp, their meeting was shortly before Emma tagged the school property.

My brother's next message is about the article.

Below is the article that was supposed to print today.

I was able to "remove" it from the paper's server and sent the fucker who wrote it a little present, but that won't stop it from being published. We just delayed it. He's already in the process of rewriting it.

It still baffles me how Nate does all this without being traced. I move on to the message that contains the actual article.

LILLY McGUIRE—Is Her Memory Loss Real or Is It All Just a Ploy?

MY BREATH HITCHES at the picture underneath the headline. I'm staring at myself sitting on my hospital bed at Hill Crest Medical Center. My eyes are bloodshot and wide with shock from the reporter invading my hospital room. I'm in the clothes George dropped me off in—the clothes I wore the day I crashed the Jeep. This was all part of the plan, but seeing myself like this makes my throat close up. My hair is wild, unkempt. I look crazed.

Parts of the timeline fall back into place. I didn't remember much from when the guy snuck into my room to when the nurse helped me change out of my filthy clothes, but things are starting to come back. My breath is getting labored, and I faintly register Rhys's hand on my leg. He's saying something, but the memories flash in front of my eyes. The nurse and doctors had just placed the IVs to counteract whatever was still in my bloodstream. It was like I'd had one too many drinks. Everything was fuzzy, and concentrating was impossible. I was waiting for the nurse to come back with a change of clothes—the only reason they discovered the intruder so quickly.

WE GOT a first-hand glimpse at Miss McGuire right after her discovery at Hill Crest Medical Center. Miss McGuire is the alleged first victim of The Babysitter, who was taken a second time by the perpetrator on

March 2nd and reappeared on March 21st. When we spoke to Miss McGuire, she kept asking where "he" was. A fair question of a real victim if she hadn't followed with the statement of "I can't go home. We need to figure out what happened."

OH, no. What did I do? I don't remember this at all.

THE MEDICAL STAFF of Hill Crest Medical Center refused to let us continue the interview, and we, therefore, have to speculate what Miss McGuire meant with her words. Who was she referring to? Is she somehow involved with The Babysitter? And what does she need to figure out? Is her memory loss real, or is she playing all of us? Is she lying to the families of the other victims to protect herself or, worse, the perpetrator himself? We tried to get a statement from the McGuire family, who refused to comment at this point on anything other than their children's relationship.

THERE IS MORE, but I stop reading. This is so much worse than anyone could've anticipated.

I skip to the following message.

Call me as soon as you get this. We need to talk about what happens next.

WITH TREMBLING FINGERS, I switch to the Phone screen. It takes me three tries to type in Nate's number, and when Rhys attempts to help me, I snap at him in return.

"I can do it!" Closing my eyes briefly, I follow my outburst with, "I'm so sorry."

Rhys nods, but his features turn to stone. I know he's not angry with me, but I can't help the need to keep apologizing.

It only rings twice before Nate answers. "Hold on a sec."

The line goes quiet as if he muted me. I stare at the little clock over my sink, and it takes three minutes until my brother's voice comes through the earpiece again. During the entire time, Rhys's hand rests on my leg, but neither of us speaks. I can't look at him. This is all my fault. Maybe I shouldn't have come back.

"Sorry, I was just leaving the office. Hank was with me."

Nate answering my call while he is in public—with his business partner, nonetheless—tells me how serious the situation is.

"Is it safe?" Still paralyzed from what I just read, I'm not sure what else to say.

"Yes, I'm in the car, heading home."

The typical tick-tocking of a turn signal is in the background, along with the sound of what I assume is LA traffic. Exhaling, I voice the question I'm afraid to hear the answer to. "What are we doing now?"

I listen to more traffic noise until Nate replies, "You know my stance on it, but removing you from the situation will make everything worse. I spoke to George earlier, and he will be shadowing you more than he already is. You'll stick to the story of memory loss; you don't remember ever saying what the reporter claims. I was unable to locate the original footage on his computer before sending the second virus. My guess is he's storing it somewhere else. I'm still looking for it."

"Second virus?" Rhys interrupts my brother. I didn't put Nate on speaker, but since we neglected to turn on the water, he can easily follow the conversation in the small space.

"The first one was to access his laptop. The dumbfuck fell for the *get-one-month-free-porn* trap. Why is humanity so predictable?" Sarcasm drips from his words. "The second one wiped his hard drive, but I made sure a watcher remains in place for the future—even when he reinstalls the OS." This time, you can hear the grin in his voice.

"But that is only one out of who knows how many trailing Lilly. I mean, look at the piece of shit that is camped out under my window."

"Leave Lancaster up to me."

Of course he knows who we're talking about. I meet Rhys's gaze, neither of us asking for the meaning behind my brother's words. Better not to know.

I decide to change gears. "What did you do about what happened in school?"

"Which incident are you referring to?"

Shit, crap, shit!

I play dumb. "How many are there?"

"Do you take me for an idiot, little sister?" Nate sneers.

"No?" I answer meekly, but it sounds more like a question than a convincing response.

Rhys stifles a laugh, and I narrow my eyes at him. I'm glad he thinks this is funny.

"Well, then let me enlighten you." My brother deadpans. "I took the liberty to send the footage of the locker incident to another news outlet with the comment that Westbridge High seems to ignore vandalism of school property, as well as students getting ostracized by their peers for being a victim of a traumatic experience. Said news outlet might have received a small contribution to publish an article with the footage by morning."

Where I suck in a breath in shock, Rhys cackles, "Dude, that's fucking awesome! I'm starting to like you more and more."

"What is wrong with you guys?" I burst out. "You just made it ten times worse for me tomorrow. Now I really have a target on my back."

Nate's voice comes through the phone. "Lilly, you already had a target on your back. The size of that hasn't changed. And I'll be damned if I stand by and let them terrorize you."

His protectiveness makes the empty cold in my stomach shrink the tiniest bit, but I can't help the fear of what they will come up with tomorrow. More graffiti, more physical assaults with random objects... The possibilities are endless.

I press my lips together. It doesn't matter. They can't break me.

CHAPTER EIGHT

LILLY

LAST NIGHT'S DINNER WAS THE FIRST TIME WE HAD EATEN AS A family since before I...*left*. Our federal guests are no longer camped out in the kitchen 24/7. Camden and Lanning only swing by to bring Heather and Tristen up to speed or to form a new plan of attack.

Tristen brought pizza home. While we were eating, Heather attempted to get information about school, but I made Rhys swear that we wouldn't involve them in my war at WH. It's bad enough that Nate inserted himself into the mess. Thinking of Heather taking legal actions or Tristen pulling *strings* to deal with the issue...no, thank you. I gave them the toned-down version of being called names, and tomorrow, by this time, they'll have heard about the locker incident, but until then, I don't need anyone else tangled up in that mess.

WALKING down the hall toward my locker on day two of being back, I hold my breath—prepared for anything. I'm flanked again by Rhys and Denielle, with Wes in the rear. Instead of being stared at, though, most are averting their eyes as soon as they spot the four of us—everyone except the cheerleaders, who continue to openly glare.

When we arrive at my locker, I'm surprised to see that *the message* is almost gone. You can still see the faint outline that something was there, but not what it said.

I place a change of clothes—just in case—in my locker, and my friends walk me to American History. I keep my head down, Miss Foy still ignores the new seating arrangement, and besides some whisper-coughed *slut* and *whore* insults, class runs smoothly. I don't get attacked by objects, and none of my books end up on the floor—or worse.

Entering the AP Chemistry lab, I find a new partner standing at my table. Approaching the station, I make eye contact with the boy I have certainly seen around but never exchanged a word with. Theo transferred in earlier this semester from somewhere in the south. But that's where my knowledge of him ends. He keeps to himself—not sure why, though. He has the whole bad-boy vibe going. He wears faded, distressed jeans with Frye boots—the purposefully aged kind—and a matching leather jacket. His tight, black, long-sleeve shirt clings to his bulging biceps and broad shoulders, showing off his athletic body. I briefly wonder what he does to be this...ripped. His ebony hair is tousled with a little gel in the perfect messy style, and his blue eyes and sharp features give him an edge that screams danger. Add to the whole package that he seems uber smart whenever he does speak up in class. You'd think the female student body would form a line for him. They don't, though. Everyone gives him a wide berth. My curiosity is piqued as to why *he* is here at my table, and I quickly scan the room, finding Ari at Theo's old table.

Deep breath. Here we go.

"Hi," I greet him as I place my bag under the table. I try not to stare, but he is freaking gorgeous, after all.

If I had any interest in anyone other than Rhys, of course.

We'll see what his strategy is: ignoring, attacking, or indifference.

He glances over while arranging some of the materials for today's class. "Hey."

He speaks; that's something.

We listen to our teacher explain the assignment, and once everyone is busy, I address the elephant in the room. "Why are you here? At this station, I mean."

There is a beat of silence while he keeps messing with the beaker, and I assume he has switched to ignoring, but then Theo replies in a low tone, "Arianna requested a transfer. Better not ask what her reasoning was."

I snort. "Oh, I can guess. So, you got the short straw?"

This time, my new partner faces me head-on, and the corner of his mouth quirks up. "Nah, I volunteered."

His smirk would melt the panties off any other girl, but I'm instantly suspicious. I scrunch my eyebrows. "Why?"

He shrugs a shoulder and turns back toward the experiment. "I have no issue with you. From what I heard, you've done nothing wrong." With a sidelong grin, he adds, "Maybe a bit kinky, with the adopted brother and all, but I'm not judging."

"Um..." My mouth hangs open. What do I reply to that?

"Don't read anything into it. Take it as one hour of not being harassed. I'm in your French class, remember?"

He has a point. I don't realize how tense my body had gone until it all melts away. We settle into a comfortable silence and finish the assignment just as the bell rings.

WES IS on babysitting duty and walks me to Algebra II. We haven't talked much since I've been back. He is either with Den, or the four of us are all together.

I bump his elbow with mine. "So...how are you doing?"

Rhys's best friend glances at me out of the corner of his eye. "Fine."

Neither Rhys nor Wes have been back to practice, and I heard from Rhys that Coach is starting to get frustrated with them. So far, he's given them slack—probably because he also wants to avoid further injuries not caused by practice—but that won't last forever. Especially because Wes got scouted for a scholarship to his dream school, and it'll look bad not finishing his athletic activities, even though we're past football season.

We're approaching my classroom, and I mumble, "I never meant for you and Den to get pulled in like this." The guilt has been steadily building, but so far, I've been too scared to voice my thoughts, not wanting to hear what my friends would potentially have to say.

Wes pulls me into a side hug. "You and Rhys have been my best friends forever. Did you honestly think I wouldn't stay by your side, Lil?"

This is one of the most serious conversations I've had with him in the ten years we've known each other, and I give him a tight smile.

"Plus, I'm finally on the bulldog's good side. I never would've anticipated that happening in this lifetime." He grins down at me.

I huff out a laugh. "Don't let D hear that."

Wes gives me one more squeeze before we say our goodbyes, and I enter the room. Bria and two cheerleaders are in this class with me, and I get greeted with, "Oh look, she not only fucks her brother but also the best friend. QB. Tight end. Who's next? Wide receiver? Safety?"

My adrenaline level instantly spikes as she addresses not just me but everyone else who's already here. Kellan and Owen are in said positions. The thought of them coming anywhere near me...no thank you. I've never had an issue with either; they've been Rhys's teammates and friends for years. They used to greet me in the halls, but since I read what they had to say about me on social media, just looking at the guys makes my skin crawl. I hear some guy bark out a laugh and mutter something inaudible, but I force myself not to look around.

I want to tell Bria where she can shove her petty remarks, but instead of sinking to her level, I hold her gaze until I reach my table. I keep my expression blank, which causes the reaction I was looking for. Bria scowls and then looks at her friend for support. I sit down at my desk, placing my bag over the carving with a loud thud, and allow the satisfying smirk to appear on my face.

They won't break me.

EMMA'S SUSPENSION is all over school. The rumor that she might get expelled was *the topic* over lunch. As promised by my brother, the article hit the paper this morning, and several screenshots appeared all over social media by the end of first period.

With this being the second time Westbridge High has been mixed up in a bullying scandal, the school's board is already involved, and I am supposed to meet with the school's guidance counselor tomorrow afternoon. Today, it seems, they're trying to do damage control.

When I muse why Kat's name is not mentioned anywhere, despite the footage Nate pulled from the school's server, Rhys smirks. "Probably because he has a special plan for her."

"Where is the Wicked Bitch, anyway?" Denielle looks around the cafeteria.

Rhys's smile falls, and the guys glance at each other.

"Rhys?" I slant my head at him.

His lips are in a thin line, and he holds my gaze.

"Kat has been extra lovely this morning. Your man got into it with his psycho ex," Wes clarifies.

My eyes widen, but before I can recover, Denielle asks, "Is there anything worse she can say or do at this point?"

My best friend is referring to the possible statutory rape charge that's still hanging over our heads.

Wes picks up on the meaning. "Well, maybe not jail-time bad, but definitely ruin-your-school's-rep bad."

Rhys takes a sip from his water bottle, not making eye contact and speaking toward the table. "She cornered me in class and demanded to know how we got the footage of Emma. With her minion gone, Kat lost one of her best cheerleaders. It was also clear that she was fishing to find out if we saw their conversation. She didn't make a secret out of her involvement. She's getting bold."

My chest tightens. "Why does she think it was us?" I mean, it was us—Nate, technically—but how could she know?

Rhys finally looks up, pinning me down as he explains, "I guess she's starting to put two and two together. That there is a third player. Otherwise, how would she have gotten the picture of you and me that started it all."

Denielle huffs. "Fuck, when did she grow brain cells."

"You need to be careful," Rhys says in a low tone, which makes the hair on my nape stand up.

"Why do you say that?"

"She insinuated that no one takes what's *hers*. And now you've taken her boyfriend and cheerleader." He pauses for a breath. "She's planning something, and it won't be pretty."

I pull my sleeves over my hands and hide my trembling hands by sitting on them. We all know Katherine; she is ruthless when her position is threatened, which makes her feared by almost all the girls in school.

So much for 'the size of the target hasn't changed.'

After Rhys's revelation during lunch, I contemplate skipping French. But with Emma not there, the remaining members of the bitch squad suddenly are rendered mute. Surprise, surprise. Sloane shrinks so far down in her chair that her butt hovers in the air in front of the seat, and I'd be lying if I don't admit to the gratification I feel seeing my former friend like this. Theo notices as well and winks before focusing on something on his notepad.

. . .

ARRIVING HOME, we're greeted by Heather and Tristen, waiting for us sitting in the kitchen. Startled, I come to an abrupt halt, and Rhys bumps into me. Stumbling forward, I catch myself before tripping over my own feet.

Why are they home?

Taking in his parents' grim expressions, Rhys narrows his eyes. "What's going on?"

Tristen leans back in his seat and crosses his arms over his chest. "It's time we talk."

Heather glances sideways at her husband before straightening her back and interlacing her fingers on top of the table. Her attorney pose.

I slowly approach the closest chair and pull it out, my heart hammering in my chest as I lower myself down. I peer at Heather but am forced to focus on my adopted father when he begins to speak. "We would like to know how the article Agent Camden informed us of *disappeared*, and instead, Mom and I get phone calls to comment about our daughter getting bullied in school."

Rhys mimics his father's posture. "What makes you think we have the answers to that?"

"Do. Not. Treat me like an idiot, son," Tristen barks, and I jump in my seat. He levels me with a glare that could make grown men pee their pants. "Whose phone was that the other day? And who did you talk to?"

Crap, crap, crap.

"What phone?" Heather interjects, confused.

Speaking to his wife but not taking his eyes off me, Tristen explains, "The day Lilly *took* the truck, I caught her with a phone that we didn't give her."

My adopted mother opens her mouth, but Rhys beats her to it. "I gave her the phone. I wanted to be able to reach her. It was just a prepaid one."

Following the exchange, I try to appear unaffected, but let's be honest, I might as well have a billboard with "She's hiding something" hovering over my head. Between my rapid pulse and sweat pouring out of every pore, I look either guilty as hell or like I just sprinted a mile at full speed.

Where Heather purses her lips, Tristen's cocked eyebrow screams *bullshit*.

"Who was on the phone then? I know it wasn't you." He levels his son.

Because your tracker would've recorded a call coming from Rhys's phone.

"Wes!" I blurt out without thinking.

Two sets of eyes focus on me, and the needle in their built-in lie detectors goes haywire. Both remain mute, and I'm ready to confess when Rhys deadpans, "After all the secrets you've been keeping from her—from us. What makes you think we'd tell you anything?"

Tristen slams both fists on the table, and I yelp in shock. "Because this is not a fucking game, Rhys! This is all for Lilly's safety. And yours."

Wha—?

Rhys narrows his eyes at his father. "What is that supposed to mean?"

Heather places a hand on Tristen's forearm. "We wish you would tell us what's going on so Dad can protect you."

Rhys barks out a laugh. "Could you be more cryptic? Protect us from who?"

When neither of them speaks, Rhys pulls me up by the hand. "And *that's* why we don't tell you jack shit!"

I let him lead me from the kitchen. Not good.

We spend the remainder of the day upstairs in my room, without dinner.

· · ·

REPLAYING Heather's and Tristen's words in my head over and over, I barely slept that night. In the morning, I waited until I heard the Raptor pulling out of the garage and Natty was downstairs eating breakfast before leaving the safety of my room. Using my little sister as a buffer to not deal with Heather is cowardly, but it's all I can think of not to get confronted again.

I'm starting to believe that there is something other than just the threat of my kidnapper—which is not a threat at all, but they don't know that.

As I USE one of the bathrooms between second and third period the next day, I discover some new *love notes* inside the bathroom stalls.

LILLY MCGUIRE IS A BROTHER-FUCKING SLUT.

CLASSY.

IF YOU WANT A CHEAP LAY, call the QB's little sister. She spreads her legs for everyone!

NOT SURE WHY this is in the girls' bathroom, but okay. The tags go on, and eventually, I stop reading.

I manage to get through my first three classes with minimal insults and am glad the next few periods are with Denielle. I stayed true to my mantra and didn't let my emotions overpower my intelligence, but I'm drained. The lack of sleep and the energy of keeping my guard up at all times are taking their toll. I'm going to need this weekend to recharge and prepare for the last five days before spring break.

. . .

FRIDAY IS track day in P.E.—unless it's pouring rain or a blizzard outside—something I used to enjoy but now have to mentally prepare myself for. The idea of showering with the enemy has my mind coming up with all kinds of mean-girl scenarios. I've seen too many movies where clothes get stolen and whatnot.

I've successfully avoided it for the last two days since we played badminton and I was able to keep the sweating to a minimum, but I know I won't be that lucky today.

I take solace that my best friend will be with me and nothing would happen with her around.

CHAPTER NINE

RHYS

I'M SITTING IN U.S. GOVERNMENT, BORED OUT OF MY SKULL, when I hear the sirens. Everyone's heads start turning questioningly, and the ones with a window seat peer outside. I glance over at Wes, who is shrugging a shoulder dismissively. It's not the first time someone has hurt themself in Chem. Usually, once a year, some dumbass whose IQ never developed past the single digits has to *test* if acids really hurt when you pour them on your hand or other body parts.

Then, my gaze lands on my ex-girlfriend. She's already zeroed in on me, waiting for me to look at her.

I study her expectant expression. Something isn't right. At that moment, my phone starts vibrating in the back pocket of my jeans, and I know. I'm out of my seat and in the hallway before I have the device pressed to my ear.

My teacher yells after me, but I don't stop.

"WHERE IS SHE?" I bark into the phone.

"Locker room. Hurry!" Denielle's hysterical sobs assault my ear, and my legs threaten to buckle as several scenarios flash through my mind. Denielle is never hysterical.

With Wes on my heels—apparently, he came to the same conclusion—I take three steps at a time down to the first floor and push through the double doors with so much force they slam into the brick wall, bounce back, and almost hit my best friend in the face. Thank fuck the guy has good reflexes. Without checking that he's okay, I break into a run and aim for the gym.

As I'm turning the corner from the east wing, an ambulance pulls into the small parking lot next to the fieldhouse. The paramedics jump out and rush inside with multiple bags strapped to their bodies. The sight makes me pick up my pace to almost tripping over my feet—my athleticism has officially exited.

Wide-eyed juniors file out of the doors of the gym as I approach and force myself to slow my pace. The whispers and murmurs stop instantly, and one guy flattens himself against the wall. I faintly register a random voice saying, "He's going to lose it."

The closer I get to the girls' locker room, the slower my legs move. My feet feel like I'm dragging them through knee-deep mud. Commotion from inside filters into the hallway, and— Lilly yells out. Not in an *I'm-having-an-argument-with-someone* way, a full-on scream of pain. My throat closes up, and my hands shake violently as I push through the last barrier separating me from her. I have no idea what to expect.

The girls' locker room is a mirror image of the guys'. The paramedics crouch on the floor near the entrance to the showers. One is rummaging through his bag while the other is examining someone—*please no*. Not someone. Lilly.

I can't move.

Her P.E. teacher and my coach stand off to the side, hands deep inside their pants pockets, and watch with a mix of worried and horrified expressions.

Another scream fills the room, and between the legs of the paramedic who's prodding on Lilly's back, I see her hand curl into a fist.

"Rhys." My head swivels to the side, and I take in Denielle's tear-streaked face. She's clutching her cell phone to her chest. Her eyes are wide, and she is anything but *The Bulldog* right now. She reminds me of a helpless child.

Lilly's whimpers get louder, and my head whips toward the sound so fast my neck cracks. Fuck, that hurt. My gaze turns to tunnel vision. I dart toward the group on the ground, getting my first direct glimpse of her, the sour taste of bile immediately coating my tongue.

What the fuck!

Lilly is on her stomach, one arm goal-posted, the other alongside her body. A bunch of school-issued towels are padding the tiled floor underneath her with more draped over her lower half, covering her legs and butt. Her back is fire-red with blisters ranging from marble size to golf-ball size across her shoulder blades to her lower back. I lift the back of my hand to my mouth.

Don't throw up.

"Rhys, you can't be—" my coach starts but clamps his lips shut as I glower at him, daring him to continue.

I circle Lilly's body to not interfere with whatever the EMT is doing to her back. My mind has gone blank, but somehow, I can think logically enough to understand that pushing the medic away from her would be counterproductive.

Dropping to my knees next to her, my shaking hands hover in the air, not knowing where to place them.

"Cal?" I rasp over the razor blades in my throat.

"Rhys?" Lilly attempts to lift her head and groans. I bend my upper body down farther to meet her eyes without her having to move. Her eyes are red and puffy, and despite lying on the cold floor—pretty much naked—she's covered in sweat. Her fingers inch toward me, and after a moment of hesitation, I gently place mine over hers. I'm scared to touch her. Her arms are as red as her back but show no blisters—at least from what is visible.

"I'm here, baby." I'm not sure who needs to hear the words more, Lilly or me. A sob escapes her, and my lungs close up.

I'm going to kill whomever is responsible for this.

"What happened?" My best friend's question registers in my brain, but I can't focus on the reply. All I see is my injured girlfriend. I don't avert my eyes from hers and carefully interlace our fingers.

The paramedics treat Lilly's back, and words like "hot water," "burns," and "hospital" filter through the pounding in my ears. Whenever they come near one of the blisters, Lilly's hand in mine turns into a vise, and I clench my teeth to not make a sound. My emotions are all over the place. I border between numb—most likely shock—and losing my shit, wanting to trash the room and clock the damn guy causing Lilly pain—more pain, that is.

I have no clue how long they work on her until she is ready to be moved onto the stretcher that seems to have appeared out of thin air. After her lower half is covered with an emergency blanket, they place a light cloth on her upper body. Her long, wet hair is falling off to the side, and I briefly wonder if it should get tied up to not tangle in the stretcher's legs.

What the hell am I thinking? Lilly just got her back almost scorched off. Her hair is the least of our problems. I mentally slap myself out of my stupor.

Get your fucking brain to work, dickhead.

The wait, while two guys secure the straps around her without touching the burned areas, makes me want to pull my hair out. It can't be more than a few minutes, but it sure as fuck seems like hours.

I stand with the stretcher, not letting go of her hand. Exiting the locker room, we pass Wes and Denielle. With Wes's arm draped around her shoulder, Den is still strangling her cell phone, fresh tears creating black trails down her cheeks.

They fall into step behind us with the teachers pulling up the rear.

I ignore the murmurs that get louder the closer we get to the doors leading to the parking lot. We're instantly surrounded by half of WH's student population. Since it's still the middle of fourth period, some fucktard must've wanted his or her five seconds of fame and sent a blast out. I better not find any pictures of Lilly's injured body on social media.

Gasps run through the crowd as we emerge, the murmurs and questions getting louder, but my focus is on Lilly's closed eyes as she's wheeled along the side of the building.

The paramedics are about to lift the stretcher into the ambulance's back, and I reluctantly let go of her. Peering to the side, my gaze lands on my ex-girlfriend. Her arms are crossed over her chest, and instead of shock or compassion, she radiates pure gloating. My heartbeat stutters.

She did this!

Wes and Den follow my line of sight. The EMTs are busy getting Lilly settled, and a red haze settles over my vision. At their own volition, my feet start moving slowly toward the person responsible. Wes grabs Denielle around the waist as she must've come to the same verdict. No one stops me, though. The sea of students parts as I zero in on my target. A growl builds in my throat, and my hands curl into fists. All bets are off.

I'm going to jail for this.

I'm just a couple of feet away from Kat when two arms wrap themselves around my upper body.

I fight against the hold of whomever is stupid enough to interfere. "LET ME GO! I'm going to kill this fucking bitch! It was her. SHE DID THIS!" I'm going ballistic in front of everyone.

Kat's expression turns from smug to wary to panic, and her eyes flick left to right.

Oh yeah, you better run, you cunt.

"Not here, Rhys!" The low tone of the last person I ever expected snaps me out of the rage, and I go limp.

"George?" My voice is shaking.

"Let's go. Miss Lilly needs you." He lifts me and turns me the other way like I'm my ten-year-old sister, not six-one and two hundred pounds. His grip loosens slightly, but he doesn't let go until he deposits me into the back of the ambulance.

Once I sit next to the paramedic, George takes charge. "He is her boyfriend; he's going with you." The man's eyes turn to saucers as he takes in my BFF and jerks his head up and down.

"Rhys?"

"Yes?" I force myself to look away from Lilly's body in front of me.

"You will not let her out of your sight until I get to the hospital."

I nod, too stunned to comprehend what just happened.

George turns and looks at Wes and Den, who are off to the side of the ambulance. "You two are coming with me." Both are visibly pale but trail after the man without a word.

THE DRIVE to the hospital is a blur. The raging river of adrenaline that kept me going since Denielle's call has turned into a dried-up stream. The EMT removes the cloth they placed over Lilly during the transfer from the locker room to the ambulance. He asks her questions about her pain level while making sure nothing touches the burns, to which she replies with a grimace.

Kat's satisfied bitch face flashes in front of my eyes, and my fists keep clenching of their own volition. She is responsible for this. If George hadn't shown up, I'm not sure what I would've done. I remain mute despite the million questions I have. I need to get my temper under control before we reach the hospital.

The paramedic glances over several times, opening and closing his mouth. I cock an eyebrow at him.

Spit it out.

"Who was the guy with the scar?"

The corner of my mouth pulls up to a one-sided, most likely lunatic smirk. "Someone you never want to see again."

That was the only time he talked to me.

We arrive at the emergency room entrance, and I follow the two EMTs, never letting go of Lilly—my hand placed either on her leg or foot. Her eyes are closed, but she's awake. The thin line of her lips is as much a giveaway as her thumb flipping against the remaining four fingers of her hand.

After she's transferred off the stretcher onto a bed, the two guys leave us just as a nurse enters the small room and stops in her tracks when she spots me. "You need to wait outside."

"He is not leaving." George's voice comes from behind the woman, and she jumps in surprise. However, that is nothing compared to the reaction when she *sees* him. She yelps and bumps into the small table next to Lilly's bed, various items clattering to the ground.

"O—oh goodness, I—I'm s—sorry," the poor nurse stammers.

"George?" Lilly's rasped voice makes all eyes snap to her. It's the first time she's said anything since the locker room.

I'm fucking sick of seeing her in a hospital bed.

One side of her face is pressed into the mattress. The EMTs removed the pillow to accommodate her prone position, and she lifts her head slightly.

"Yes, Miss Lilly?"

"Don't scare the nurse." Even in her battered state, she ridicules this bad-ass former Marine, and a snort escapes me.

I love this girl.

George moves closer to make eye contact. "My apologies, Miss Lilly. I am simply ensuring you are not alone until Heather and Tristen arrive."

My parents! "Did someone call Mom and Dad?" I ask no one in particular.

George turns to me while his hand rests next to Lilly's head on the bed. "Yes. Weston called your father, who informed your mother. Your mother was in the city and should be here within the hour. Your father is"—he pulls out his phone and glances at the screen—"about eight minutes out."

The flustered nurse's jaw hits the floor.

George addresses the woman. "I didn't mean to startle you. I'm Miss McGuire's..."

There is a beat of awkward silence.

"Uncle," Lilly supplies.

"Uncle," George and I parrot simultaneously, though our response sounds more like a question.

The woman peers at the dangerous-looking man out of the corner of her eye but knows better than to question Lilly. I clamp my mouth shut. I'm not getting into this.

She turns to her patient. "Miss McGuire, how is your pain level? The doctor will be with you shortly; he's finishing up with another patient. Once he assesses the wounds, I will clean them up."

"Whatever the guy in the ambulance gave me is working," Lilly declares groggily. At least she is not in pain anymore—or at the level she was at when I first saw her on the floor.

"I'm glad to hear that. I will be back shortly. If you need something in the meantime, please press this button over here." She places a small remote on the mattress next to Lilly's hand. "Or one of your, uh...family members can come to get me from the nurses' station."

"Thank you," Lilly whispers, and it's apparent how exhausted she is.

As soon as the nurse leaves the room, I square my shoulders and round on George, who is staring at his phone.

"Dude, where the fuck were you when this went down? I thought you're supposed to 'shadow'"—I make air quotes— "Lilly?" Logically, I know he didn't have eyes in the locker room, but my irrational side needs to blame someone.

"Your father just pulled up. I will be waiting outside. Weston knows where to find me." And with that, he's gone. The only thing missing is George dropping a black curtain like a magician and purple smoke remaining in his place.

Motherf—

I slowly walk to the other side of the bed and lower myself onto the rolling chair probably meant for the medical staff. I wrap my fingers around Lilly's, and she blinks at me.

"What happened?" My voice breaks, and I avert my gaze from her exposed back.

She draws in a shuddering breath. "We were running track today. We were on our way to the showers when a sophomore showed up with a slip for Den to come to the office. She said she'd go after she showered, but Mr. Landon told her to go immediately. The other girls were already done and almost out the door, so I figured it wasn't a big deal. Den would be back in a few." Lilly pauses, and I swipe away the lone tear running down her face with my thumb. I wait for her to collect herself.

"I even brought my clothes with me out of fear they would take them." Lilly breathes out a non-comical laugh. "I was rinsing the shampoo out when the water turned scorching hot." She squeezes her eyes together but keeps talking. "I tried to turn it off but couldn't get to the lever fast enough. The water burned me. When I tried to get out of the stall, someone pushed me back in." Lilly's breathing picks up. "I...I couldn't see. My wet hair was in my face, and I tried to get my head away from the water. Someone held my hands and shoulders, and the water hit my back." Another tear escapes. "Rhys, it hurt so bad."

I gently place my palm on her cheek. "I'm so sorry, babe."

I feel sick and have to fight the urge to haul the tray with medical supplies across the room.

"I heard Den scream. That was when they finally let go." Lilly's lids spring open. "They're going to pay!"

A cold shiver runs down my spine. In all these years, I have never seen the girl in front of me anything but kind and compassionate—even with what I put her through for two years. She is one of the most empathetic human beings I know. But at this moment, her eyes are wild, almost...deranged. Everyone has their limits, and Lilly has reached hers.

I make sure our eyes are locked when I speak. "They will,

babe. I promise you." She will get revenge. The question is only when, how, and who gets to execute it. The list of people who would do anything for my girl is long. Anything from torture to erasing the target from existence—in a cyber sense—is possible between George and Nate alone.

Just as I'm about to place a kiss on her forehead, Dad storms through the door. He stops abruptly and zeros in on Lilly's exposed back. His eyes turn wide, and he presses the back of his hand against his mouth, mimicking my own reaction earlier.

His gaze jumps to me. "Who did this?"

"Still working on it, Dad." He will find out soon enough.

My father jerks his head in a nod. He has seen some of the worst shit a human can be forced to endure during his time in the Marine Corps. He hasn't talked openly to us kids about it, but I've heard bits and pieces over the years. He has never so much as shown concern or remorse about it, but the emotions playing on his face now tell me that this will end badly for everyone involved. Maybe not in a physical way—unless one of my *former* friends had anything to do with it—but between Nate and my parents...they messed with the wrong family.

MOM ARRIVES as the nurse has finished cleaning Lilly's skin with saline and is putting aloe on her back. Nurse Julie, as I find out when I finally take the time to read her name tag, explains the process as she goes along, and Dad and I are standing in the corner, letting her do her job. Every time Lilly winces, I'm about to punch Julie's lights out. Not that it's her fault, but I can't take much more of seeing her in pain. Dad eventually has his hand firmly planted onto my shoulder, aware that I'm holding on by a thread and may lose it at any point.

Mom's eyes water immediately at the sight of Lilly, and her eyes fly to Dad. He holds out his other hand, and she launches herself at him, unable to hug the person she wants to embrace.

The doctor, who assessed Lilly's burns earlier and declared

them to be second degree, enters the room again, and it's getting crowded. He seems to come to the same conclusion. "We only allow two visitors at a time. May I ask one of you to wait in the waiting room while we finish up with Miss McGuire?"

"Rhys." Dad looks at me, and I want to protest.

The thought of letting Lilly out of my sight causes my chest to constrict. I try to inhale, supply my lungs with the oxygen they demand, but it's like I'm breathing through a pillow.

However, seeing my mother about to fall apart, I can't do that to her.

"Okay," I concede. Before leaving, though, I take the two steps to Lilly's bed and squat down so she doesn't have to raise her head.

"I'll be outside with Den and Wes." *And probably George,* which I don't say aloud.

She smiles at me tightly. "Okay."

"I love you." I place a kiss on her nose, not giving a fuck about who's watching.

"Love you, too," she whispers.

As I straighten, the doctor says, "We will discharge Miss McGuire shortly. I don't see a reason to keep her overnight. You want to watch the burns, keep them clean, and when the blisters burst, do not pick at them. They will heal in seven to fourteen days. No lotions or creams and loose clothing. She can take Motrin for the pain and sleep on her stomach..." He keeps going on, but I exit the room in search of Lilly's head of *failed* security.

CHAPTER TEN

RHYS

I FIND WES AND DENIELLE HUDDLED IN THE FAR CORNER OF the ER's waiting area. The large, rectangular room is packed to max capacity between people who need to be here and students who want to get their hands on the newest WH gossip. Lilly's *former* friend Sloane sits next to Jager, her hand between both of his. That's a surprising development, but I can't bring myself to care at the moment. My coach and two of Lilly's teachers are in another section. I ignore them, not willing to answer potential questions. Jager notices me first, and his lips part. Sloane follows his gaze, and her eyes turn wary. I probably look unhinged. If I find out any of them had something to do with what happened to Lilly, pissing his pants will be the highlight of Jager's week. I pass them, not taking my eyes off him, and he gets the meaning. He inclines his head, and with an unspoken message, I know he wasn't part of this. My former friend is a cocky fucktard who thinks with his dick most of the time, but he would never physically harm someone on purpose, let alone a female.

Wes stands as I approach, and Denielle follows suit, her hand gripping his bicep. Without a word, he makes his way toward one of the many doors leading from the room. I trail after them, my fists deep in my jeans pockets so I don't accidentally clock someone who looks at me the wrong way. A new wave of anger hits me when I see all the assholes camped out in the waiting area. I'd bet George's fancy AR on the fact that half of them don't even know Lilly personally.

We're in a hallway we have no business being in as my best friend stops in his tracks, pulls out his phone, and types something. A few seconds later, he starts moving again, and after two more turns, we're in a staircase that's definitely not open to the public. Heading down two flights, we find George standing on the landing between the floors.

He has his phone pressed to his ear, listening intently before he replies. "I have to advise against that." Pause. "No, you cannot force her." Deep breath. "You and Miss Lilly are my first priority." Pause. The person on the other end is getting louder, yet I cannot make out the words. "I am fully aware that this was possibly our only shot, Nate, but—" George clamps his mouth shut, and it's clear that he is struggling to keep his cool. "I understand. Keep me posted on what else you find."

He extends the hand with his phone toward me, and I lift the device to my ear.

"Yes?"

I expect Nate to go apeshit on me, but instead, a shuddered breath comes through the earpiece. "How is she?"

My inner asshole wants to blame him. If he hadn't come back, stalked and kidnapped Lilly, none of this would've happened, but even I know that that's not true. He had nothing to do with my psycho ex's plan of revenge.

"She's in pain, but whatever the doc gave her is helping. They're releasing her later."

"Thank you, Rhys. I..." He hesitates for a moment. "George will fill you in on everything else."

The line goes dead, and I pull the device away from my ear, frowning at it. Fill us in on what? I don't like the sound of that.

George plucks his phone out of my hand and pockets it. "We need to talk."

I'm used to zero-expression George. I've even seen amused George—not much, but I was privy to get a glimpse of him. Yet, what currently shows on his face makes the blood in my veins turn to ice. Denielle seems to come to the same conclusion, because she shuffles closer to Wes.

Nate and Lilly's head of security leans against the wall across from the stairs and motions for us with a jerked chin-dip to sit. The last thing I want is to plant my ass on these damn stairs, but I follow his silent order, knowing he probably will make me sit if he wants to.

"The reason I wasn't there to 'shadow' Miss Lilly"—he makes air quotes around shadow, referring to my earlier yelled accusation—"was that I was following a...lead."

"What lead?" Denielle frowns at George. She's no longer scared of him.

"I was parked in my usual spot off of Baxter Drive when I noticed an SUV idling not far from the main entrance." Baxter and 11th make up the T-intersection the school is located at. I want to question why that would be suspicious; students often have to park off-campus when they're late and the parking lot is full. Or someone gets picked up outside the gate. But George keeps going. "Something was off. I had Nate run the plate, and it came back registered to a recently deceased veterinarian."

"Fuck." Wes curses under his breath.

I have an idea where this is going. "Turner?"

George levels me with a look that I've only ever seen from one other person: my father. "I couldn't confirm one hundred percent that it was Turner, but from the brief glimpse I got of the driver, it was likely. I informed Nate and decided to follow the car."

"Did you lose him?" Denielle inserts herself into the report. I throw her a glare that hopefully tells her to shut up and let the man talk.

"No. I followed him to a warehouse outside of Alexandria. Nate tracked my location from his end." George halts, and I scan his face. What is he not saying? This man never needs time to collect his thoughts, and the waiting makes the hair stand up on the back of my neck. He stares at me. "I need you to stay calm."

What the—?

I narrow my eyes, and he expels a long breath. "Once he arrived at his destination, I confirmed that the driver was, indeed, Francis Turner. He walked into the warehouse and returned later with a large duffel bag."

My heart rate increases. Before I can ask what that means, though, Wes inserts himself into George's report.

"Okay, the guy went shopping. What's the big deal?" He tries to play it off—for whose benefit, I don't know. He's not *that* brainless.

"The big deal is that this particular row of warehouses belongs to someone under investigation for running a sophisticated network of illegal substances. Specifically, medical-grade sedatives and paralytic drugs you cannot get from your local drug dealer at the street corner."

George waits for us to put two and two together.

When it clicks, I jump up and punch the nearest concrete wall. "FUCK!" *Punch.* "FUCK!" *Punch.* "FUUUCK!" *Punch, punch.* I shake my hand, followed by flexing and unflexing my fingers to see what damage I did. While doing so, I let out another string of very explicit and beyond X-rated phrases. My pulse is pounding in my ears. Can this day get any worse?

Denielle flinches at my outburst, and I round on the former Marine. "He's coming after Lilly."

Stoic George is back. "That's a likely conclusion."

"How do you know about the drugs?" Denielle voices the question I ignored.

I'm still in the process of assessing if I broke anything but turn my attention back to the conversation.

"Nate traced the owner through a couple of shell corporations after I gave him the address. Once he had the name, it didn't take long to find what we know now. I was following Turner back toward Westbridge when I got your call." George looks at Denielle. "I was another twenty-five minutes out."

This time, it's my eyes that nearly bulge out of their sockets. I stare at her. "*You* called him?"

Denielle looks something between guilty and proud. "I had to. I mean, Lilly was injured."

My gaze swivels between the three people in front of me, and I stop at Wes. "You also have his number?"

Wes's tone is almost apologetic. "I do."

I scowl at George who remains mute.

What the fuck? He might as well give it to my parents.

AFTER GEORGE all but took a blood oath that he would not abandon his post again, we made our way back upstairs, waiting for Lilly to get discharged.

Neither of us move to enter the ER's waiting area, and my father finds us in the hallway outside of Lilly's room.

"We're ready to leave. Mom is with Lilly, but I want you in there while I'm pulling the car around." Dad doesn't allow for any questions or negotiation. The man who could give George a run for his money when it comes to emotional paralysis looks like he had about one too many coffees. I don't think I have ever seen my father this jumpy. Tristen McGuire is a professional. The man in front of me...is not.

I give him a curt nod and walk toward Lilly's door. I'm about to enter when I hear my father address our friends. "I spoke to your parents. You two take Heather's car back to our house." I glance over my shoulder and meet Wes's confused gaze.

Does Dad know that they don't have any mode of transportation here?

As he steers my two friends toward the exit, probably telling them where Mom parked, I enter Lilly's room. She sits at the edge of the bed, a hospital gown covering her front and the back loosely tied, most likely so that the one size fits all—or not—won't randomly open and fall off of her tiny frame.

Our eyes immediately lock, and relief is written all over Lilly's face. "Hey," she breathes.

"Hey, babe." I force my voice to remain steady and calm, even though my pulse has been somewhere above the 150 range since George confirmed my conclusion that Turner is after her. It'll be a miracle if Lilly is allowed to pee in peace going forward. Nate is probably going to implant a tracker in her arm or neck.

Lilly frowns. Of course she reads me like an open book—I can't keep anything from her. I imperceptibly shake my head. *Not here.* Instead of nodding, she slowly blinks in affirmation. I want to pat my back. We totally have this silent communication thing down.

I continue my way to her and interlace our fingers, placing a kiss on her forehead. "How are you feeling?"

She smiles weakly. "I just want to go home." My breath hitches, and I study her face.

Which home is she referring to?

Mom remains mute. I glance over and see her watching us intently. Her face is closed off, and it's almost as if my parents have changed roles. She takes a step forward and addresses her daughter. "Let's get you ready. Dad is going to pull the car around any minute."

Lilly eases herself off the bed, and I grasp her elbow as her feet hit the floor, and her legs wobble. "Easy, Cal."

Leaving the room, Mom walks ahead of us alongside Julie, who leads us through back corridors to a set of elevators not accessible for someone who is not staff. Lilly's nurse takes us down to an underground bay meant for the ambulances to deliver their patients. Dad's Raptor is idling as close as possible to the elevators without blocking any emergency vehicles.

I climb in the backseat ahead of her, and once she is inside,

Lilly lies down in my lap, making sure her back doesn't touch anything.

Mom and Dad take the front without a word, and we're off. As we come out of the delivery bay and around the side, I understand why we chose this route. Once again, the hospital entrance is lined with news vans.

Fuck.

AT HOME, only our friend Lancaster awaits us. The rest of the vultures are likely camped out in front of the hospital. I already see tomorrow's headlines:

First victim of The Babysitter attacked in school's locker room shower stall. Did she try to boil herself to distract from the incest with her stepbrother or her suspected illicit relationship with her kidnapper?

AT THIS POINT, nothing will be a surprise.

DAD PULLS STRAIGHT into the garage, where we find Mom's GLS 580 in its spot. Den and Wes are already waiting in the kitchen, and Lilly's best friend is by her side as soon as she follows me through the garage door.

Reluctantly, I let go of Lilly's hand as Denielle leads her upstairs without a word, which leaves me with Wes and my parents in uncomfortable silence.

"Where is Nat?" Now that we're home and the tension leaves me like air out of an untied balloon, I realize that my little sister is nowhere in sight. I grimace. I was so preoccupied with Lilly that Natty's absence completely escaped me. I'm a shit brother.

"She went home with Olivia after school," Mom explains. "I'm going to pick her up in a few minutes. We didn't want her to have to sit in the hospital."

I nod at no one in particular and silently promise to make

more of an effort with my little sister. I need to be there for her as well.

Dad walks over to the fridge and pulls out a bottle of water. "Camden arranged for Lilly to give her statement tomorrow morning." He takes a sip. "A police officer will be here at eight o'clock. I want all of you to be there."

"All?" Wes's croaked question makes it clear that he did not anticipate that.

"Yes. You are all witnesses," my mother clarifies in her attorney voice then amends more emotionally, "Whoever did this to my daughter will be charged with the max penalty we can demand." Her stern gaze lands on me, and I have a hunch she suspects my ex to be involved somehow.

"I'll make sure she's ready," is all I say before walking past them and up the stairs. I hear Dad tell Wes that their parents are aware of him and Denielle spending the night. Mom says something I don't understand, and Wes mumbles a response. By the time I step on the landing on the second floor, he's beside me.

"Dude, I thought your dad was scary, but your mom almost made me piss myself just now. She makes the chick from *The Ring* look like your girl next door. Kat will regret fucking with your family."

I snort a laugh. "Tell me about it."

Entering Lilly's bedroom with Wes on my heels, we find Lilly sitting on the edge of her bed with Denielle squatting in front of her, holding each other's hands. Both girls have tears running down their cheeks, and an instant knot forms in my stomach.

Den turns and launches herself at me. "I'm so sorry!"

I'm shocked by her sudden attack, we stumble backward, and Wes puts his hand in the middle of my back to stop us from falling over. My eyebrows knit together as I try to comprehend what she's apologizing for. Lilly meets my gaze, but I'm no closer to understanding.

"D, let the man go to his woman." Wes carefully pries her away from me and envelops her in a tight hug, where she completely breaks down, holding onto him like a lifeline. Denielle sobs into his shoulder. I've never seen her this way.

I slowly make my way over to the bed and sit down, taking Lilly's hand in mine. I was about to drape my arm over her shoulder as usual but caught myself at the last moment.

We watch our friends, and Lilly whispers, "She blames herself for leaving me."

My head jerks to her. "That's ridiculous. If someone is to blame, it's Kat and whomever she got to do it." My tone is way harsher than I intended. I glance at Denielle to make sure she knows my rage is not directed at her.

She has calmed down some and turned in Wes's embrace to face us. "I'm sorry, Rhys. I shouldn't have left."

I grind my teeth, hating that she thinks she is to blame in any way. I stretch my hand out, and Wes nudges her toward me. When she's within reach, I grasp her hand. "D, no one blames you for any of this. And if anyone *ever* so much as suggests that, you tell me, and I'll sic good ol' George on them for some fun torture time. He'll have a blast." I wink at her, and a half laugh, half sob bubbles up in her throat.

Wes steps beside her. "Did you see who did..."—he hesitates mid-sentence—"it?"

Denielle levels each of us before speaking. "There were four. I recognized three. The fourth bolted as soon as I came in. Only one was a cheerleader. Two juniors. The third was a sophomore. I've seen all of them suck up to the Wicked Bitch before."

Where Wes exclaims a string of curse words, Lilly and I remain quiet. I don't have it in me to get the names of everyone involved right now, and it seems neither does Lilly.

She sighs. "I'm exhausted."

I take that as her cue that she wants to get some rest, and I scoot back until my head hits the pillows on her bed. Lilly follows me and drapes herself over my chest, tucking her fingers between me and the mattress. Having her this close, an instant sense of peace settles in my chest. Her head is nestled under my chin, and I try to figure out where to place my hands when the hospital gown she's still wearing falls open. Wes flinches, and Den's eyes widen, but neither of them say anything.

After a beat of silence, it's clear that Lilly is done for the day. Our friends slowly turn and head to my room, leaving both doors ajar.

CHAPTER ELEVEN

LILLY

I TURN TO MY SIDE AND STIFLE A GROAN. WAKING UP ON TOP of Rhys's chest, my neck is stiff, and all I want is to turn on my back. The urge to change position and alleviate the stabbing sensation overcomes me. However, it takes about .3 seconds after starting to roll over for yesterday's events to come back alongside the feeling of someone peeling the worst sunburn off my back—with a blunt knife. During the blissfully numb hours of sleep—courtesy of pills the nurse made me take before we left —I suppressed what had happened.

Where are the pain meds they handed me last night?

Rhys begins to shift underneath me at my sudden movement.

"Babe? Everything okay?" His voice is raspy from sleep, and it stirs something inside of me that makes me momentarily forget everything else. Instead of responding, I press myself closer to him, nuzzle my nose in the crook between his ear and collar bone as he lifts a hand, gently pushing the strands of hair from my face.

"Cal, talk to me."

I angle my head upward to meet his gaze. "I'm fine," I lie. Of course I'm not fine, and he knows it. His narrowed eyes say as much.

"Try again, babe." A smug smile tugs on the side of his lips. He can read me as well as I can read him. Why I try to pretend is beyond me.

"I'm angry." I pause. "No, scratch that. I'm fucking pissed!" My tone is hard, and Rhys cocks an eyebrow.

"You have every right to be upset—" he begins, but I interrupt him by jerking into a sitting position.

"I'm not *up-set*," I enunciate the two syllables. Upset doesn't come close to covering the turmoil inside of me. "I'm pissed. Furious. Livid. All of it. Those bitches attacked me like cowards in the shower. Naked. Four against one. Who does that?" By the time I finish, I'm breathing heavy, and I'm fisting the duvet, one of the pin-tucks having ripped.

Just awesome.

Gaping with an open mouth, Rhys clearly didn't expect this outburst from me upon waking up.

I inhale and exhale slowly. "I'm sorry. It's just... I'm sick of being a target."

He dips his head in a small nod before asking warily. "What do you want to do?"

I sigh. "I have no idea. Yesterday changed things."

Once again, my emotions are all over the place, and I need time to sort through them. The anger clouding my vision when I think of what happened in the locker room makes the fear of the unknown—my past and future—shrink to a barely noticeable tickle in the back of my mind. But it's there. The question of what Turner wants with me hangs over my head. Between the kidnapping and incest scandal, the media follows my every step. The desperate need to hide is at war with my instinct to fight back. To get revenge. I'm not a naturally violent person, but I refuse to cower to Katherine Rosenfield with her psychotic delusions.

"I'm gonna take a shower," I announce. That wasn't the

response Rhys was looking for, but that's all I can give him at the moment.

"Do you think that's, uh...okay? With your injuries, I mean?" His forehead wrinkles. He doesn't press me for more answers, and the ache in my heart lessens, knowing Rhys is on my side.

Sliding off the bed, I turn. "They said as long as the water doesn't hit the burns, I can shower. It just has to be quick."

How fast is up for debate. I'm in desperate need of my purging ritual.

IN THE END, reason wins out. I keep the shower short, not to worsen my condition. The skin on my back feels like it's stretched to the max, and every movement hurts. After letting the hospital gown drop to the floor, I chance a glance in the mirror. I wish I hadn't. I heard the nurse and doctor talk about the blisters, but seeing them is a whole different thing. I'm not super squeamish, though taking in the extent of the burns makes my stomach churn.

Sitting in front of the vanity, I have a towel wrapped around my lower half and one on my front side, tucked under my armpits. The cool air feels good on my back, and I need to ask someone to help put more aloe on.

Slowly, I lean forward and pull the cabinet door under the sink open. I study the pink box with its writing for a moment before digging out the burner and headphones I left there.

Without thinking, I initiate a video call. The phone rings five times before his face appears on the screen.

"Lilly." My brother is breathless. In the background, a door closes behind him before he lowers himself into a desk chair similar to the one he has at the vineyard. His face is red, his blond hair plastered to the sides of his forehead, and sweat drips from his chin.

"Are you okay?" I tilt my head to the side.

"Shouldn't I be asking you that?"

If the dark circles under his eyes weren't a dead giveaway, him rubbing his hand over his face for the third time since picking up the phone would be. His demeanor mirrors his behavior from when the first article about my kidnapping was released.

"Talk to me, big brother," I prod gently.

He stares at something past the camera. When his focus is back on me, he confesses, "I was on my way to the jet yesterday when I got the call about...what happened. I lost my shit. Ran out of a business meeting. George was still on his way back from Alexandria, your friends didn't pick up their phones, and there are no cameras in the locker rooms. I couldn't check on you."

George was in Alexandria?

I drop the question of why George abandoned his post—for now. It must have been something important. Or why neither of my friends mentioned that they had a missed call from my brother. They either didn't notice or didn't want to put anything else on me.

"Please don't expose yourself," I whisper. *Not yet.*

Nate's eyes gentle. "You come first, little sister."

A sad smile makes the corners of my mouth turn up. "I know. But I need you...*out*. There are too many unanswered questions." The selfish side of me is not ready for him to go away.

He nods his head in understanding.

"What were you just doing?" I force a change in topic.

"Running. I needed to move after..." Nate trails off. I pinch my brows, and he elaborates, "I've been...busy. It was that or coming to Westbridge. George threatened to call my pilot if I so much as breathed in the direction of the airfield again." He rolls his eyes.

"He wants you safe as well," I say softly.

Nate inhales slowly. "I needed to distract myself, and I'm still at a dead-end with the money our father transferred. Whoever owned the account withdrew all the money. I need to try a different approach on that front." He pauses, and I wait.

I can read between the lines, though, and my pulse speeds up.

"I found Hector Lakatos."

"Who?"

"Your memory doctor."

I blink. My memory... My hand tightens around the phone, and a wave of dizziness hits me. "How?" The question is barely audible.

My brother explains, in the detached business-like tone I had become used to at the vineyard (whenever his genius mind switches to task orientation only), how he informed George about Tristen's revelation. And how our head of security put two and two together. Through George's connections, they were able to track Hector Lakatos to the continental U.S., and Nate took it from there. My brother had to keep himself distracted after the attack, and this was his contribution—he found the person who messed with my mind. According to Nate, Lakatos seems to have mostly retired from his *profession* and only in rare cases still makes an appearance in public. However, my brother found him—in rural Oregon, of all places.

"He set up a specific protocol of how to contact him. Even I couldn't narrow down his location further than a post office box in the middle of nowhere. He has nothing in his name," Nate concludes.

"Sounds like his choices caught up with him. Why else would he try to disappear this way?" I scoff. I mean, seriously, this guy fucked with brains for a living; I'd be surprised if more people don't want to get their hands on him.

That makes him chuckle. "When did you become so ruthlessly sarcastic? But yes, I agree with you. He probably made quite a few enemies with his *services*."

"What's next?" I hold my breath as I wait for his answer. What are we going to do about the man who rearranged my memories?

"George will set up a meet. It'll take some time since he won't leave your side for the foreseeable future."

"Why don't you contact him?" I don't want to wait.

"George is the better choice. His name is well known in his, uh, line of work," Nate explains then switches gears. "How do you feel?"

Is he asking physically or mentally? "It hurts." Describing the actual sensation of razorblades shaving the skin off my back whenever I move won't do any good, so I add, "I want revenge. They went too far."

A joker-like grin spreads over Nate's face, but before he can respond, the door creaks open, and Rhys's head appears in the gap.

"Hey." His tone is hesitant.

"Hi." I turn away from the small screen.

His sleepy appearance makes me smile.

"The cop taking our statements will be here in a few minutes. I just wanted to see if you need anything." His gaze flicks to my exposed back.

"Um..." I glance at the phone and back at Rhys. "Yeah, can you help me with the aloe? And I'll need one of your shirts. The doctor said to wear only loose clothes for now."

Nate's voice filters through the headphones. "I'll let you go. We'll finish our conversation later."

I'd rather talk revenge plans with him than deal with another cop, but I don't have a choice.

We say our goodbyes while Rhys goes to get something for me to wear, and I get ready to give my statement.

TO MY SURPRISE, the police officer had the names of all five girls when she walked in. Five, not four, which made everyone's jaws drop. The female cop, who introduced herself as Officer Martinez, was accompanied by Agent Camden. She informed us that the school handed over the security footage. The attackers were traced back by who entered and didn't leave the locker room after P.E. The girls—one senior, two juniors, and a sophomore—gave their statements last night and ratted out the fifth member of my attack squad—another junior. Number five was the one who manipulated the shower by shutting off the cold water in the maintenance room. How the girl knew where to go and what to do remains under investigation, but in the end, they got released into their parents' custody. All of them have been suspended, effective immediately, and Camden commented that they most likely will be expelled.

No one asks me if I want to press charges, which I do, but apparently, it was already done. The girls admitted to the attack. Their reason: I seduced the school's QB, aka my adopted brother, and ruined his *and* the school's reputation.

What the fuck?

As soon as Officer Martinez concludes her report, shouts erupt around me.

"Are you fucking kidding me?"

"That's complete BS!"

"That fucking cunt!" Which comes from Rhys and earns him a good tongue lashing from Heather. She does not want to hear the C-word in this house. Tristen remains quiet, as usual.

I watch the scene like a passive observer. Everyone is basically foaming at the mouth, but the small crescent-shaped indentations on the insides of my palms are the only visible sign of how I feel about this.

"Are you saying someone else is behind the attack?" Camden inserts herself.

Rhys balls his fists on top of the kitchen table and growls between clenched teeth, "This was all Kat. She's a fucking psycho. Her mindless bitch followers did what she would never attempt herself."

"That's why there were four in the locker room! Everyone knows Lilly can put any guy at WH on their ass in less than a minute," Wes adds. The last part is spoken with a proud under-tone, and I can't suppress a tiny smile.

I'm lucky to have friends like them in my life.

"Do you have proof for your accusation?" Officer Martinez tilts her head.

"We don't need proof. The Wicked Bitch has had it out for Lilly since Rhys broke up with her," Denielle snarls.

Heather purses her lips but doesn't chastise Den for her choice of words—probably because she thinks the same.

Camden glances at Heather and Tristen before her gaze settles on my best friend. "Without evidence, Officer Martinez cannot bring Miss Rosenfield in."

She believes my friends, but she's right. They can't touch Katherine unless one of her minions comes clean. Rhys's ex may be an evil, manipulative—not using the C-word despite it being an accurate description—but unfortunately, she's also smart. That's how she got where she is in the WH hierarchy.

When I don't jump on the blame-the-ex train, all eyes land on me.

Chewing on the inside of my lip, I remain quiet. Heather scans me with concern. My friends look at me in disbelief, most likely wondering why I don't back them up.

Martinez reads my silence as me being upset. "Miss McGuire, I ensure the responsible parties will be held accountable."

Yes, they will.

Rhys and Den both snort sarcastically, and Wes mumbles something along the lines of, "Yeah, right!"

Only Tristen sees through me. I swear this man knows more than he lets on. Way more! And in this case, he is right. Katherine Rosenfield will pay, and I'll get my revenge. Though, I won't admit that here. She talked five students into attacking me. Of course, they could've said no, but their actions of taking the blame speak for the fear Katherine Rosenfield has instilled in the female population of Westbridge High. They ruined their futures for the approval of *one* girl.

We finish our statements, Denielle's taking the longest since she was the one that saw the most. The entire time, Tristen's gaze doesn't leave me.

When we're done, Officer Martinez takes more pictures, in addition to the ones the hospital took yesterday, followed by Camden walking her out. I guess since the female agent basically lived here for weeks on end, I shouldn't be surprised how casually she moves around the house.

Heather gives me a careful hug. Our relationship is still on thin ice, but I let her. She busies herself with an early lunch, roping Denielle into cutting the onion for her, and Rhys and Wes are deep in conversation with Tristen when I head upstairs.

I stop at my little sister's door. Natty has remained in her room, and besides a short glimpse on my way down, I haven't seen her since before school on Friday.

We sit on her bed while she scans me up and down. All my injuries are covered, but it's as if she can see right through Rhys's t-shirt.

"Are you okay?" my observant little sister inquires. I'm growing tired of the question, but she's not the one I'd let my frustration out on. They are all worried, but I'm over talking about it.

"I am. It's not that bad." I smile at her.

"You're not supposed to lie," Natty scolds.

What is it with the McGuires and their built-in lie detectors?

I try a different approach. "I know, baby girl. I just don't think I need to unload my, uh...*stuff* on you."

"You could, though. I'm your sister."

Needles prick at the back of my throat. Her words bring the first tears since the attack to my eyes. "Yes, you are."

I swipe with my index finger under my eye and motion for Natty to lie down on my lap. Her face lights up, and genuine happiness settles in my chest. We used to do this when she was a little girl. Natty would lie down in my lap, and I would comb her hair with my fingers. We haven't spent time together like this since it all started, and I swallow hard over the guilt.

"Tell me about your newest book," I say after she gets comfortable on my thighs. I don't have to ask if there is a new book. Natty always reads.

That's where Rhys finds me twenty minutes later. He leans against the doorframe, watching us with his arms crossed over his chest as Natty talks about a new series she discovered. The books play out in Virginia and follow two brothers solving mysteries.

Rhys locks eyes with me and mouths, "I'll wait in your room."

I nod my head in confirmation and focus back on the girl on my lap.

CHAPTER TWELVE

LILLY

THE REST OF THE WEEKEND FLIES BY.

Tristen takes Wes and Denielle home after lunch on Saturday, and both return Sunday afternoon. We hang out in Rhys's room. The boys sit at the foot of the mattress, playing video games, and Den and I are just...us. We lounge on the bed—me mostly on my stomach—when she announces that she is thinking about surprising Charlie during spring break. He's been distant, missing their usual video chats, and she hopes that some quality time together will help. Rhys and Wes exchange a glance I can't interpret, but neither comments on Den's plans. I'm not used to seeing my best friend anything but confident. She's the one with the I-don't-give-a-fuck attitude. Something is up with her, but I also don't want to put her on the spot in front of the guys.

I avoid every phone and computer in the house—except the burner—needing a break from the social media drama and news articles. Rhys confirms that there are a handful of news reports covering the attack at school. Surprisingly, though, most of them are factual. They describe how four female students attacked me, and a fifth was charged as an accomplice. Since no one (officially) knows about Katherine's involvement, the conclusion is that the girls wanted revenge for their own personal gain—the same B.S. they served the cops.

Rhys barely leaves my side. He makes sure I have everything I need, including letting me sleep on top of him, as that's the only bearable position. The dark circles under his eyes are proof of him forfeiting his rest for mine, and a pang of guilt hits me.

Monday morning, I wake up before the alarm goes off. Rhys is going back to school today; I'm excused until after spring break. Though, I've been playing with the idea of online classes and the possibility of graduating early. I have the credits due to the summer classes I took over the last few years, and after this coming Thursday—my eighteenth birthday—I'll have the financial means to support myself if Heather and Tristen had any issues with that plan.

The sensation of getting the skin shaved off my back at every move has also lessened. It still hurts—a lot—but it's manageable. I prop myself on my elbows, taking in the sleeping boy next to me. His long lashes fan over his cheekbones, and his hair has grown out over the last few weeks, the slight waves standing up all over his head. His eyes flicker under his closed lids, and his mouth presses into a thin line. He's dreaming, and from the looks of it, it's not a good one. The need to stop whatever is going on in his brain makes me lean in. With a flutter in my chest, a sensation I experience every time we touch *anywhere*, I gently press my mouth to his. *Home.* Rhys's tense features soften, and I sweep my tongue over his bottom lip ever so slightly.

A hum rumbles in his chest, and my butterflies morph into their hornet form. Eyes still closed, Rhys's hands slide up my arms, and he caresses my biceps with his thumbs as he returns the kiss. He doesn't wrap his arms around my back like he usually would, which tells me he is awake and aware of his actions. I part my lips, and his warm tongue instantly invades my mouth. I can't stop the moan escaping my throat, nor do I want to.

Thank goodness the door is closed.

I move until I'm completely on top of him, and he grinds his hips against me in response, never breaking the contact to my mouth. Feeling his hard length against my core makes heat shoot through my body, and I inwardly curse my injuries. I want him so bad, his hands all over me, him inside of me. But my limited movements make it impossible. Not impossible, but it definitely wouldn't be the most enjoyable *experience* for either of us. Despite not breaking the kiss, Rhys isn't oblivious to my inner battle of desire, anger, and frustration.

"Stop thinking, babe," he murmurs against my mouth.

I grin against his lips; he always knows. "I want you so bad." To drive my point home, I push my hips forward and create more torturous friction for both of us.

Moooore, my insides whine.

He pulls back, and our gazes meet. "Trust me?"

There is a gleam in his eyes that instantly put me on guard. What's he planning? He'd never do anything to cause me (more) pain, so my answer is the only obvious one. "I do."

Rhys shifts until we're both on our sides, facing each other. He scans me carefully, and I smile. "I'm okay."

Slowly, never looking away, he leans back in and starts a gentle assault of my mouth with his. I love the feel of his tongue against mine, and a tingling sensation spreads through my entire body. Why can't it always be like this?

Suddenly, the waistband of my sleep shorts is pulled away, and Rhys's hand dives under the fabric. I jerk at the unexpected contact and latch onto his arm with my hand to not fall backward. The heel of his palm presses against my sensitive spot, and he enters me with one finger.

Yesss.

My eyes flutter closed, and a whimper escapes me. I part my thighs, draping one leg over his, to give him better access. I deepen the kiss and press my throbbing clit against him.

"Already so wet, Cal?" He smirks against my mouth.

"More." The word comes out in a breathy moan, and Rhys chuckles. I'm so turned on that I can't bring myself to care if he laughs at or *with* me.

"You know I never say no to you." And with that, another finger joins the first.

Fuck me—literally.

I nip on his bottom lip and most definitely leave claw marks on his arms, but I can't stop myself. Rhys changes his angle, and now his two fingers pump in and out as his thumb circles my clit.

"Ahhh. Rhys, I..." I want to tell him that I'm about to come, but he speeds up his movement, and I lose all train of thought.

"Shhh...just let go."

And that's what I do. I completely fall apart. I clench around his fingers deep inside of me, Rhys not stopping until the last shiver has wracked through my body.

I slowly peel my eyelids back and gaze at him in my post-orgasm fog. He pulls his hand out of my shorts and does the last thing I'd ever expect. He licks his fingers with a devilish grin on his face. "Mhmmm."

My eyes nearly bulge out of their sockets, and I cover my face with my hand that had been holding onto him.

"You did not just do that," I exclaim, peering at him between my fingers.

"If that wasn't a wake-up call—" He winks.

At that precise moment, the alarm goes off, and both of us burst out laughing.

God, I love this boy so much.

EVERYONE IS at school or work. I try to pass the time, but I can't concentrate on anything for more than a few minutes, and by lunchtime, I am so bored that I cave. Typing my name into the search bar, I expect all kinds of results, but not this. With Rhys and me not giving them more ammunition in the kidnapping or incest category, the attack already being covered, and the

FBI not releasing any leads toward the capture of The Babysitter, the media begins to grasp at straws. And said straw is my little sister.

Is Natty McGuire a Victim of Parental Neglect?

READING THE HEADLINE, my pulse skyrockets, and my fingers clench around the edges of my laptop.

A SOURCE BROUGHT to our attention their suspicion of Natty McGuire, the younger adopted sister of The Babysitter's first victim, Lilly McGuire, being neglected by her parents.

Tristen and Heather McGuire have previously been under crossfire for condoning the relationship of their son, Rhys McGuire (18), and their underage, adopted daughter, Lilly McGuire (17). The secret affair was exposed by very incriminating photographs leaked by Westbridge High's students via various social media accounts.

Since then, Tristen and Heather McGuire have issued a statement regarding the accusation of turning a blind eye to the relationship, which resulted in the case being dropped.

How the McGuire family was able to evade legal actions, despite the evidence presented by an undisclosed source, is currently being questioned by several enraged Westbridge residents, as well as other members of the press.

This morning, our office received reliable evidence that during all this, the youngest member of the McGuire family, Natty McGuire, is being neglected by her family. Not only was she deposited at a family friend's house the entire time her older sister was held captive by The Babysitter, but she also has been banished to her room whenever she is home.

· · ·

WHAT THE FUCK?

I stop reading and take in the picture below. Natty sits in her window on the second floor, reading a book. She is content. I know my little sister; this is where she spends most of her time. Her room faces the backyard, which is enclosed by a tall privacy fence and several trees lining the edges of the adjoining properties.

Did someone sneak onto our property to take that photo?

I scramble to my bathroom, digging under the sink for the phone.

The line rings twice before George picks up. "Miss Lilly?"

Adrenaline level through the roof, I stammer, "I saw...Natty...backyard...photo..."

"Miss Lilly, please calm down." His voice is quiet. Professional.

I inhale slowly and exhale at the same count before asking, "Did you see the article about Natty?"

The sharp intake of breath tells me he hasn't. "No. I was busy with a different matter, and Nate is in meetings all morning. I assume he hasn't been able to read or act on it yet. I would be aware of it if he had."

Shit, shit, shit.

"I need to talk to him." I don't remember if there are cameras in the yard, and even if George knew, he can't pull up the footage.

"Let me see what I can do." George disconnects without a goodbye.

I remain sitting on the bathroom floor, chewing on my thumbnail. I don't have to wait more than five minutes before the burner begins to vibrate in my hand.

Knowing my brother will drop everything when necessary, I don't check the screen for his number before answering. "Someone was in the backyard!" My voice borders on hysterical. Thank goodness I'm alone in the house.

"What do you mean?" Nate's confused question is accompanied by footfalls.

"Th—there is an article about Natty. That Heather and Tristen are neglecting her. Someone took a picture of her sitting in her window." I rush everything out. Nate is familiar with the property's layout.

"Fuck!" He doesn't say anything for several moments until a car door slams in the background. "Okay...I'm going home. Tristen doesn't have cameras besides the entrances and inside the house, nothing pointing at the house or far enough away from it, but George put up surveillance all over the neighborhood. I'll go over those.

"Can I help somehow?" The thought of sitting here useless makes me want to scream. Even in my sitting position on the bathroom floor, my knees won't stop bouncing.

"I'm sorry, little sister. I wish I could give you access." *But it's not secure*, I complete my brother's sentence.

I stay on the line until Nate pulls into his garage, promising to call as soon as he finds something. He has a similar setup in his LA house as at the vineyard and can search several cameras simultaneously. He assures me that he should have something in a couple of hours.

It's 1:30 when we hang up. Another hour and a half until Rhys gets home. I have the urge to pick Natty up from school, but replacing my totaled Jeep was low on everyone's priority list. I'm stuck here. Restless, I walk down the hall to my sister's bedroom and step up to the window. After glancing down at the photo on the laptop in my hands, I scan the outside. It's not hard to narrow down the spot. Someone could've taken the picture across the fence from Mr. Hollencomp's backyard. Mr. Hollencomp is a consultant for some big firm and never home, so no one would've noticed a stranger marching across his lawn.

I've just placed the laptop back on my desk when I hear the humming sound of the garage's roll gate. My gaze flicks to the clock at the top of the screen. This is not good.

Running through all the options of who could be home this early, every possibility results in the same conclusion. Something happened. *Again.*

I take two steps at a time and round the entrance to the kitchen when my little sister bursts through the door from the garage. Tears are streaming down her face.

"Natty, what—" But she hurries past me and up the stairs before I can finish the question.

Heather appears in the kitchen with a somber expression, and our eyes lock.

"What happened?" I whisper, palms pressed against my chest.

She sighs, setting her purse on the kitchen island. "Some girls got a hold of the article that was published today." She scans my face to see if I know what she's talking about. I nod, and she continues, "They cornered her in the bathroom and must've said some awful things. I got a call from the counselor that Natty got into an *altercation* with a girl named Victoria Rosenfield. Natty refused to go into details."

No way!

"Rosenfield?" I choke out in disbelief.

Heather turns to face me head-on. "Did you know Katherine's little sister goes to school with Natty?"

My hand fists my shirt near the neckline. "No! I didn't even know Katherine had a sister."

When did the Wicked Bitch get a sister?

"Rhys has mentioned her once or twice. But last I heard, she was at a boarding school in Maine." She lets herself drop onto the barstool. "Lilly, this is getting out of hand. What is happening?" Heather's eyes gloss over, and I swallow over the lump in my throat. By forming a relationship with my biological brother, I've turned my entire family into targets.

This is all my fault.

. . .

I ATTEMPT to check on Natty, but she refuses to open the door. I could easily pick her lock, but the coward in me chickens out. Instead, I sit in the middle of my bed, clutching a throw pillow until screeching tires announce Rhys's arrival at home.

Natty is getting targeted because of me. Because I chose to protect the man who kidnapped not just me, but four other girls. Because I fell in love with her big brother. It's all on me.

Rhys storms into the house and up the stairs with Wes on his heels, heading straight for his little sister's room. I stand in my doorway, and as soon as Rhys hammers against her door, she opens up, flinging herself into his arms. I cover my mouth with my hands.

Wes's gaze swivels to me, and as Rhys disappears with Natty into her room, his best friend slowly moves toward me.

I stare up at the blond boy who's been part of my life for so long. He has always been the one with a joke on his lips, the one with the ability to dissolve any tension and make you feel better. But at this moment, none of that is present. Hurt, anger, and sorrow flicker in equally quick succession across his face. Wes and I are toe to toe, neither of us speaking, and my heart beats a million miles a minute.

Does he blame me as well?

I shuffle backward, ready to hide in my room, when his arms shoot out, and he pulls me into a tight hug, interlocking them behind my neck, careful not to touch the injured skin below. The motion is so sudden that my body stiffens. Wes places a kiss on my hair, and I melt into the embrace. I swallow hard.

"It'll be okay," my friend murmurs.

This brings back the memory he and I share from over two and a half years ago. Rhys had made his first public appearance with Katherine in school. I was hiding near the side entrance of the east wing, wiping away tears, when Wes found me. Back then, he did the exact same thing. He hugged me and told me it would be okay. In the end, it was, but what did we have to go through to get to that point?

. . .

WES and I sit in silence on my bed when the burner phone I kept in the pocket of my sweatpants starts to vibrate. I jump off the mattress as fast as my raw back allows and speed-walk into the bathroom. Wes follows at a slower pace, and I've already accepted the call by the time he closes the door behind us.

George's face fills the screen, and I suck in a sharp breath. George, the man who could be the poster guy for Botox—with the lack of facial expressions and all—looks back at me with a scrunched forehead and unsmiling mouth—not that he smiles a lot. His scar is stretched around his eye and chin, which makes him appear more menacing than usual.

"This is not good." Wes glances over my shoulder and comes to the same conclusion.

"Miss Lilly," George greets me. His gaze flicks behind me. "Weston."

"What did he find?" I peer over at Wes, whose narrowed brows express his confusion.

"I'm going to send you two photographs Nate was able to pull off our surveillance cameras. You will notice on the time-stamp that they are from Saturday morning—around the time you met with Officer Martinez."

Natty was alone upstairs.

"Nate will explain everything to you later. He had to go back to the office since he left a meeting with two board members this morning."

I'm about to question why George can't give us the details when he adds, "I need to make a phone call in twelve minutes and still have to set up a secure line."

He is more cryptic than usual, but I let it slide—for now.

"Is he getting in trouble?" It's the second time my brother ran out of work for me.

"The alarm at his home was triggered, and he went to check on it."

I have to smile. I'm sure Nate actually triggered the alarm somehow to back up his story. Nonetheless, we are getting careless.

It takes less than ten seconds after George disconnects before a text message alert pops up. I click on the first picture and stare.

"MOTHERFUCKER." Wes's shout echoes through the bathroom.

CHAPTER THIRTEEN

LILLY

"FRANCIS-FUCKING-TURNER. WHO IS THIS FUCKING COCKSUCKER?" I snatch the burner out of Rhys's grasp before he can launch it like my poor toothbrush holder—which I haven't replaced yet. Wes and I were still in my bathroom when he walked in. He had spent the past hour talking to Natty and, therefore, was already high strung.

The first picture Nate found was of Turner walking down Chester Drive—the cul de sac parallel to ours. Why George installed cameras there is beyond me, but right about now, I'm just grateful. The second one is of him driving down Grand Avenue, which is the one our street breaks off of. There is no question in my mind; Turner is behind the photo of Natty. But is he also the source of the article? What the hell is his endgame? It makes no freaking sense.

Rhys rubs his hands over his face. "Babe, Nat was a mess. No one has ever treated her like this. She didn't know how to respond to being bullied. You know her, she's the sweetest kid. Everyone likes her." His fists ball at his side, and he growls, "I want to fucking strangle Vic."

"Why did you never mention Katherine's sister before? Let alone that she goes to school with Natty?" My question comes out like an accusation, and I quickly take his hands. "I'm sorry, I didn't mean it the way it sounded." I sigh. "I hate hearing how upset she was. She wouldn't talk to me."

Rhys huffs. "Because Kat's sister has never been of any concern to me. She's two years older than Nat and attended some fancy boarding school up north for as long as I've known Kat. I've seen her once or twice during breaks. The Rosenfields always travel over the holidays, so our paths haven't crossed. I had no clue she was back. Nat's school is a K through eight, which is the only reason Vic has access to her. Otherwise, they would've never met."

"She sounds like a mini version of your psycho ex." Wes's tone is equally as harsh as mine was a minute ago. Not what I'm used to from him.

"Which is why she was sent away," Rhys deadpans.

Glancing sideways at Wes, he also waits for Rhys to elaborate, but he remains mute. I'm sick of Kat, and now her sister, messing with our lives. We have enough going on as it is.

All because of you, a voice echoes in my mind.

I shake my head, willing the thought to go away, which makes both boys scowl at me.

"Will this turn into another Kat *situation?*" Translation: Will Victoria Rosenfield physically attack our little sister?

Rhys glares at the wall behind me, not making eye contact and deliberating. "I don't think so. Kat probably sicced Vic on Natty, but people would put two and two together if anything happened to her—with your attack and all."

It's some consolation, but I'm still worried about what nonviolent bullying will do to Natty.

WES LEAVES AROUND FIVE. Natty refuses to come down for dinner and won't talk to me either. Guilt gnaws at my insides as I lie in bed that night. Rhys is the only one Natty lets into her room, and that's where he's been since dinner. All I can do is sit in my room and wait.

I spot him heading into his bedroom around 9:30, and a couple of minutes later, he walks across the hall in sweats and a clean t-shirt. He takes his place on my bed, and we stare at each other, tears pricking in my eyes.

Rhys leans forward, swiping under my eye. "Don't cry, babe. Nat's fine. We talked. I gave her some big brotherly advice on how to handle it when she gets cornered again. Everything will be okay." His tone is soothing, and my nerves calm a little.

"I hope you didn't tell her to sucker punch the mini witch." I smirk, blinking against the moisture in my eyes.

"I might have." He grins but then sobers. "No, I told her that the only reason these girls are doing this is to hurt her. They can't touch her, and spewing lies is their way of trying to get to Nat." His tone is gentle, and I'm grateful that he was able to talk her down. Nonetheless, I can't help the hollow sensation that has settled in my stomach and has been growing since this afternoon. The feeling of being responsible for all of it.

As we move into our new sleep position, "Lover. Fighter." by SVRCINA comes through the speaker next to my bed. How fitting. I forgot I added the song to my playlist a while ago. Rhys pushes a strand of hair from my face and places a soft kiss on my forehead. "Get some rest, babe."

THE LAST TIME I had glanced at the clock on my nightstand was around two a.m. My mind kept running through all the consequences my adopted family has had to deal with because of my selfish need to hold onto my brother a little longer—to find the answers to my past.

I wake up with the alarm and watch Rhys from the bed as he gets ready in my bathroom. While he brushes his teeth, I take the opportunity and walk down the hall to Natty's room. Her door is ajar, and I knock against the doorframe with a trembling hand. My pulse accelerates with every step that brings me closer to her. She sits in her window nook with a book—even this early in the day—and her head whips around.

"Hey, baby girl." I chew on my thumbnail, waiting for her response. I've never bitten my nails until the last few months. Now they're basically nonexistent.

"Hi." She smiles genuinely, and relief crashes through me.

I cross the room and lower myself down next to her. "I just wanted to see how you're doing and tell you how sorry I am."

"What for?" Natty's brows knit together.

"For what happened in school. If Kat didn't have it out for me, her sister wouldn't have come after you. I—" my voice cracks. I shouldn't have to have this conversation with my little sister.

"Are you kidding me?" Her incredulous expression makes me freeze. When I don't speak, she leans forward. "Vic thinks she is *someone* because of who her sister is. She can say whatever she wants about you, me, or our family. I know the truth. She is just a bully hiding behind a mask of insecurity."

Excuse me, what?

It takes me a good minute to form a coherent sentence in my head. "Uh, how old are you again?"

And why don't I have this confidence?

Natty giggles. "I heard Mom say that a while ago when she talked to Grandma about Kat and thought it sounded cool. And it fits in this situation, right? Vic *is* Kat's sister."

Unsure of what to reply, I agree with her. "Uh, yeah. Right." Still skeptical if she's truly okay, I force myself to dig deeper. "So, you're not upset? You were crying yesterday, and Rhys told me these girls said some awful things to you."

The ten-year-old—going on thirty—girl in front of me sighs. "Sure, I'm upset. They talk about you and Rhys, people look funny at Mom when she drops me off, and all my teachers watch me like a hawk, but none of this is your fault."

My eyes begin to gloss over. *But it is*, I want to yell. If I had handed Nate over, none of this would've happened. Probably. Maybe. Not to this extent, at least, I tell myself.

"Cal?" Rhys stands in the doorway, and we both turn at my name. "Hey, Nat. How're you doing?" he greets his little sister.

"I'm good," she chirps.

He arches an eyebrow, peering at me, and I shrug. It looks like his advice took root.

"Well, okay. I'm giving you a ride to school today."

"Sweet!" Natty jumps up, grabs her backpack, and waves before disappearing into the hallway. "Bye, Lilly. Don't worry so much."

Uh, that went...well?

THE DAY GOES BY QUICKLY. After my *talk* with Natty, I can relax enough to get lost in a romance novel by this fairly new indie author, S.J. Sylvis. I started the book weeks ago and never finished it with my life turning into a roller coaster of disastrous proportions. The main character, Ivy, falls in love with this boy, Dawson, in seventh grade, but of course, it's not that easy. *It never is.* I sure hope they end up together. I heard that the beginning of the book is based on how the author met her husband, which sucked me in instantly. Plus, her husband is a Marine like Tristen. That makes it a must-read, right? I just got to the part where the main characters meet again after years apart when Rhys walks in, and I place my e-reader down on the comforter.

He plops down next to me on the bed. "You're reading." His eyes light up.

I haven't touched a book in what feels like months. "I am." I smile back. "How bad was it today?"

"The usual." Rhys shrugs it off, and I take it as: *don't ask*. "D said she'd call you in a bit and that she'll swing by tomorrow after Oliver heads back to school."

"Sounds good." Lying on my stomach, I cross my arms underneath my head, resting my cheek on my forearms to face Rhys. Den texted yesterday that her brother, Oli, showed up unannounced this weekend, introducing his new girlfriend, Elena, to the family. Everyone was shocked. Oliver Keller has never had a serious relationship in his life. I think he's been the role model for many of Westbridge High's male student body over the years with his talent of picking up girls using ten words or less. And for Den to also instantly approve of Elena means this girl is something special. I can't wait to hear all about her.

"Have you talked to Mom?" Rhys's question catches me off guard.

"No. Why?" I lift my head to get a better view of him.

"I don't know. She's been acting weird since last week," he contemplates.

I mull that over for a moment. Rhys is right. Heather has been withdrawn. After the attack, I would've expected her to be a helicopter parent, no matter how we left it after their revelation about how I lost my memory. But she hasn't. "Do you think it has to do with what they won't tell us?"

"Who the fuck knows? There are too many damn secrets in this family," Rhys grumbles, and it feels like a punch to the gut.

I'm the one keeping the biggest secret from everyone and, in the process, forcing him to do the same.

I drop the topic, and we spend the rest of the afternoon in more or less comfortable silence—him on his phone and me reading. It almost feels...normal. Almost.

"DINNER!" Tristen's voice travels through the house, and I glance at Rhys.

Family dinner?

He shrugs, climbs off the bed, and reaches his hand out

toward me. When I don't immediately move, he sighs, pulls me up, and wraps his arm around my shoulder. I'd rather be hiding in my room without food, and he knows it.

As we enter the kitchen, we look more like Rhys having me in a chokehold than a loving embrace. I pretend it's because my back is off-limits to touch and not that he had to literally *force-lead* me downstairs. Facing the people in this house has become increasingly more difficult over the past week and a half.

Lord, was it just a little over ten days ago that I found out how my memory got erased, Francis Turner came into my life (officially), Rhys almost got charged with statutory rape, Heather and Tristen faced accusations of negligence, I got attacked in the school's showers, went to the hospital *again,* and Natty became a target to a bunch of hateful middle schoolers?

Silently listing off everything that has happened has me so distracted that I jump at Rhys's euphoric shout.

"OHHHH...spinach lasagna!" He lets go of me and shoots over to his mother, who is pulling two baking dishes out of the oven.

She smiles up at her son. "One spinach and one meat. You know your father."

"That's right. Real men eat meat." Tristen winks at Natty, who's already in her usual seat.

I'm rooted in the entryway. *Am I in the freaking Twilight Zone?*

This whole scene reminds me of a family dinner that would've happened three years ago, but not in the recent past. Rhys seems to read my mind and makes his way over, leaning down to whisper in my ear, "Don't question it. Let's just enjoy it for as long as it lasts."

It lasted all of twenty minutes. Twenty minutes of us being a *regular* family.

"Nat, how did it go today? Did the Rosenfield girl give you any more trouble?" Tristen asks flat out after swallowing a mouthful of his *manly* meat lasagna.

I hold my breath as we wait for her to answer.

Natty looks up from her plate. "It was fine."

Both her parents narrow their eyes at their youngest.

"Love?" Heather pushes. That's all she needs to say. It's her special mom-power. She can make her kids spill their guts by simply addressing us with her nickname for us. Rhys calls it her attorney hypnosis.

"Fiiine." She sighs dramatically. "In homeroom, some girls talked about how you and Dad are going to go to jail for letting Rhys and Lilly have sex."

Some of the water I was in the middle of drinking goes down the wrong pipe, and I begin to cough violently. Rhys makes a choking sound himself, but Heather and Tristen remain stoic.

I gape at her while Rhys is strangling his fork and knife. Yet, Natty continues as if nothing happened. "Some girls called me names, but I ignored that."

Something tells me this wasn't all, and Tristen seems to come to the same conclusion. "Is there more, Nat?"

She remains mute until her father puts his utensils down at either side of his plate, palms flat next to them, and levels her with a *start talking* glare.

Rhys lets go of his knife and places a hand on my bouncing thigh.

"Vic came up to me after lunch. I ate outside on the front lawn with Olivia, and she kept going on and on about how Lilly faked her kidnapping to distract from what's really been going on. I told her she should go tell her lies somewhere else. That's when she got into my face and pushed me against the shoulder."

Heather's eyes go wide as her daughter recalls the event.

"I dropped the rest of my lunch, but when a teacher came over, Vic took off."

Everyone at the table exhales a sigh of relief until she finishes her recollection.

"My apple rolled down the pathway toward the gate. This reporter guy picked it up for me and gave it back."

My heart stops a beat. Reporter? Since when does the media hang out at Natty's school?

"What reporter, love? You know you're not supposed to talk to the press without Dad or me present." Heather slants her head. Her tone is sincere, but the lawyer in her rises to the surface.

"That was the first time. Swear!" Natty rushes out. "I know I'm not supposed to talk to them." She rolls her eyes as if to say, *I'm not stupid.* "All I said to him was thank you."

"He? Have you seen the guy before?" Rhys inserts himself into the conversation with a hesitant tone, his fingers starting to clench down on my leg. I place my hand over his and pry it off, interlacing our fingers instead.

"Oh yeah, the guy was at the press conference last week. The one in the front with the trench coat. Frank or Francis or something. His name sounded like two first names."

I grip Rhys's hand until I sense one of his fingers crack. He doesn't show any sign of feeling it, though. His jaw is locked as he stares at his little sister.

"Francis Turner?" Tristen asks in confirmation.

No!

"Yes! That was it. Like I said, two first names." Natty grins proudly.

I drop Rhys's hand and clamp both of mine over my mouth. Pushing the chair back, I sprint up the stairs and make it to my bathroom just in time before my dinner comes back up.

The man who is after me was at my sister's school. He spoke to her. He took pictures of her. I'm putting her at risk—my entire family. Tears are streaming down my cheeks as I grasp the toilet bowl, retching.

LATER THAT NIGHT, after I assured my adopted parents that the pain meds must've messed with my stomach, I lie next to Rhys, listening to his even breathing. Instead of lying on his chest, as I have the past four nights, I'm on my stomach beside him. He is facing me on his side, holding my hand between both of his.

Once Heather and Tristen were satisfied that I didn't need medical attention, Rhys helped me change into a fresh t-shirt. I washed my face, and we ended up sitting in the bathroom in front of the vanity.

"Turner did this to scare you. From everything we know, he has no interest in Nat." I'm not sure if he was saying that for his or my benefit.

"I know." I did. But that didn't change the fact that this man had stalked her. And based on him taking the photo of her, it's likely he was the source for the article accusing Heather and Tristen of neglect. Is this all part of his plan? To achieve what? Isolate me from my family. Forcefully removing them from my life by having them accused of a crime they didn't commit.

I can't let this continue.

"Do you want to talk to George? As long as you're at home, he can follow Nat," Rhys suggested. He was right. That *would* be an option.

But that wouldn't keep them safe. "No." I didn't explain myself, and apart from scowling, Rhys didn't press the issue.

Eventually, we settled back in my bed, and long after Rhys fell asleep, I was still watching him.

TAKING in his stunningly gorgeous face in the dim light, my breath hitches. This boy is mine. Knowing what I have to do next makes me want to cling to him, but I'm too scared of waking him up.

As I recall what I said to him not two weeks ago, tears begin to pool. *No matter what happens, no matter where we are or how long we are apart at times, I'm yours. I will always find my way back to you. You are my home.*

When I uttered those words, I didn't expect them to become

a reality so soon. I knew we'd be apart eventually, but I thought it would be because of something *trivial* like college.

I hope he will forgive me—one day.

Gingerly, I push myself up on all fours and crawl off the bed, careful not to make any sudden movements.

With the burner in hand, I head across the hall to Rhys's bathroom. I can't risk him overhearing this conversation. Sitting on the closed toilet seat, silent tears run down my face. I type in my brother's number but then hesitate.

No, I don't have a choice.

Hitting the dial button, it only rings twice before Nate's anxious voice comes through the phone. "What's wrong?"

We haven't spoken since he called about the surveillance camera stills of Turner that George had texted me.

After dropping everything twice for me, George insisted that Nate focus on his life in LA before someone—namely, Hank or Margot—starts asking questions. George has kept me up to date with the progress on the Hector Lakatos front—the call he had to make yesterday—and the lack of progress on the Turner front. Little did we know, he was following Natty.

It's almost midnight in LA. Thanks to my brother's fiancée being a social media serial poster, I know he was at some charity event with her, Celeste, and Julian that ended at eleven.

"I need you to do me a favor." My heart is pounding in my ears, and it takes every ounce of strength to steady my voice. My body wants to break out in violent sobs, but I don't allow myself to lose it.

"Anything. You know that."

"I do."

I haven't told either of them about Turner showing up at Natty's school yet, and I'm going to wait until I see my brother.

"What do you need?" Nate presses carefully.

I take one more breath before speaking the words I have thought but have torn me apart inside since the first article was issued and dragged my family into my mess. "I need to leave."

Nate is quiet for so long that I'm not sure he's still there. "Nate?"

"George will be outside in twenty minutes. Pack only essentials and bring the burner. We'll set you up with everything once you get to your destination."

Relief floods through me, and I whisper, "Thank you."

After a moment, Nate asks, "Does he know?"

He. Rhys.

"No."

"I see." His disapproving tone surprises me.

"Can you do one more thing for me?"

He seems to understand the seriousness of the second request and simply replies with, "Yes."

"I need to be able to get a message to Rhys and my family."

"Okay." He doesn't ask why or what. He simply says, "Send me what you want to say from the burner."

Then the line goes dead.

I wrap my arms around my stomach and bend forward. Biting the inside of my cheek, I rock back and forth, letting the tears stream down my face but refusing to make a sound. A metallic taste fills my mouth, and I swallow several times, forcing the coppery taste down my throat. I count to 193 before my body stops shaking and I trust my legs to carry my weight.

Heading back to my room and into the walk-in closet, I move slowly, not to make any sound. I pull out the small duffel bag I stashed in the back of it on the second day after coming home. For some reason, I had a feeling this day would come.

Dropping the bag again, I cover my face with my hands and breathe in slowly. I can still back out. Tell George that I changed my mind.

No. Before I can talk myself out of it, I drop my hands from my face, pick up the bag, and walk back into my bedroom.

The duffel contains everything I need, which is not much. The only thing I add on top of the pile of clothes is the ten-year-old framed photo of Rhys and me from my desk. I can't bear to leave it behind.

I gingerly pull Rhys's old hoodie over my head, wincing as the movement makes the healing skin on my back stretch. I slip into my Adidas Superstars and tighten my hand around the handle of the bag. My vision turns blurry once again as I take one last look at the sleeping boy in my bed.

CHAPTER FOURTEEN

RHYS

BLINKING, I REALIZE IT'S STILL DARK OUT—TOO FUCKING early. My body and brain are beat from the last few days. I haven't had a decent night of sleep since Thursday. Though, knowing Lilly gets the rest she needs is all I care about.

God, I'm tired.

My eyelids sag again. Turning over, I expect to find Lilly's sleeping body, but instead, my hands touch only the cold, empty sheets. I shove my face into the pillow she slept on not too long ago and inhale deeply. Her scent of vanilla and coconut lingers in the fabric. A picture of her lying on her side, one hand tucked under her cheek, smiling back at me, forms in my mind. I can't wait until I can let my hands roam again, hug her sexy body to mine without the fear of causing her pain. Every time I see the healing burns on her back, the adrenaline coursing through me makes me all twitchy. I have to fight the urge to punch someone —or something, since the person responsible is unavailable.

I lift my head and glance over my shoulder. The bathroom door is open, and the light is off.

After shifting around to push myself up and lean against the headboard, I dig the heels of my hands into my eyes. Waaake uuup.

A buzzing sound comes from the nightstand, and I pull my hands away from my face. A text message lights up my phone. I glance at the alarm clock. It's not even six.

No one texts me that early unless— My heart stutters a beat, and I stare at the device.

When it lights up again with the repeat notification, it's like it's taunting me. I can't move. Lilly is not in bed with me. It's too early for anyone but two people to message. Lilly is not here.

Two minutes later, the third alert makes my phone move across the wooden surface once more. Why the hell did I set the damn thing to three alerts? Oh right, because pussy-whipped me doesn't want to miss a text from his girlfriend.

The illumination of the screen appears like stadium lighting to my heightened senses.

My heart rate has already doubled, but I can't stall any longer. Seeing my hand tremble in the dim light, I reach over, pick up my phone, and tap the screen with my thumb. UNKNOWN.

Fuck! Fuck! Fuck!

I want to chuck the device but, instead, clench my fingers around it.

I don't understand. He hasn't used this caller ID since...*before*. Whenever he had contacted me directly, he'd make sure to be extra obnoxious and use "PSYCHO."

I slide my legs off the side of the bed and sit with both hands now clutching the phone. My stomach churns as I tap the screen once more—yup, still there. UNKNOWN. I swallow over the lump in my throat and swipe the message open.

MY RHYS. My best friend. My love.

. . .

By the time you read this, I'll be on my way. There are no words to describe how sorry and heartbroken I am.

I thought I was doing the right thing by coming back. That I could find the answers to my questions while being in Westbridge—while being with you—and move on at the same time. And in the end, once everything is over, for him to be able to take responsibility. But all I have done is bring misery and pain to you, our family, and it is only a matter of time before Wes and Denielle will be part of the crossfire.

None of you should have to go through this because of my lie. I asked too much of you by keeping my secret and protecting him for me.

I promise you, I tried to stay. I really did. But between the media camping out in front of the house, the potential lawsuits against you and our parents, Katherine targeting me, Natty being bullied in school, and now Turner following her, I couldn't risk it any longer. There are too many odds against us, and I would never forgive myself if something happened to any of you.

None of this changes my feelings for you. You are and will always be the love of my life, and I hope with time, you will understand and forgive me. I want nothing more than to build a future with you, but for that, I have to say goodbye to the past and make sure the demons hiding in the dark are no longer following me to find my starlight.

I'm getting poetic, and you can probably guess what's been on repeat on my playlist as I'm writing this.

I'm sending messages to Heather and Tristen, as well as Den and Wes. Please don't worry about me. I'm going to make sure you have a way of getting in touch with me—if you want to. He promised he would set everything up, and I will contact you as soon as I can. I'm safe with both of them.

I love you more than life.
    Calla

. . .

READING the message two more times, it finally sinks in. She went back to Nate. George picked her up. He fucking picked her up in the dead of night. *Motherfucker!*

I glance around.

Lilly is gone. *Again.*

I'M NUMB.

At first, I was pissed. How could she fucking leave me? *Leave us!* Then I bawled like my mom when she watches those shitty, made-for-TV movies. Why is Lilly giving up on us? After that, I started planning my revenge on everyone who caused her to run —until logic set in. I couldn't do shit about the media or Turner. I was useless. Cue the self-pity. I grabbed one of the pillows off the bed, lifted it to my face, and bit down, letting out the scream that had been building up in my chest since the moment my phone lit up. I screamed until my throat felt like sandpaper, then I sent the pillow flying. It hit something across the room on Lilly's desk, and as I looked over, I noticed the empty spot next to her laptop. Her glass cup with pencils was toppled and broken, its content scattered all over the tabletop. But that was not what changed everything. I didn't give a flying fuck about the damage or glass shards everywhere. She took our picture. She's not coming back. Suddenly, there was nothing. No anger. No sense of loss. No more resentment. Just...numbness. She left me.

Still sitting in the same position as when I read the message, I stare where our picture used to be for years. Light has begun to come through the window when my phone vibrates, this time with an incoming call. It's too soon for it to be Lilly. Wherever Nate sends her, there is no way she's already at her destination. So, I let it go to voicemail. It only takes a couple of seconds before it starts right back up. Resigned, I lift the screen to meet my line of vision: Wes.

Guess he received his message.

I accept the call. "Yes?"

"YES? What the fuck is this, dude? Where is she?"

"I don't know." My voice sounds computer-generated. Emotionless.

"You don't know? He fucking doesn't know. HOW THE HELL CAN YOU NOT KNOW?"

"What do you mean he doesn't know?" Denielle's pissed-off bark is audible in the background.

My eyebrows draw together. "Why is D with you at"—I peer over to the nightstand—"6:52 in the morning?"

"I woke him up, asswipe!" Lilly's and, as it seems, now also Wes's best friend sneers. Looks like I'm on speaker.

"Who're you calling an asswipe, *Bulldog*?" My nails dig into the palm that's not holding the phone. Why am I lashing out at her? None of this is Den's fault. But I am no longer numb. I feel again. Rage. And I want to let it out. She simply gave me an opening.

"Man, I have no idea what's going on with you guys, but—" Wes tries to reason with me, but he gets interrupted by the door to Lilly's room crashing inward with so much force the door handle makes an indentation on the wall.

Fucking great. Couldn't she have spaced the messages out a bit?

I spin slowly so one leg is angled on the mattress while the other foot remains on the ground, and I lock eyes with my father —my extremely red-faced, nostril-flared father who, with his wide stance and balled-fists, takes over the entire doorway.

"Where. Is. She?"

I snort and shake my head at the mindfuck I woke up to. Did Lilly really think a simple message saying *I'm fine* would satisfy these people?

"I'm gonna have to call you back," I say into the phone. Not waiting for a response, I press the red button.

"Who was that?" My mother's question comes muffled from behind Dad.

"Wes," I reply in a flat tone. "If you want to be precise, Wes and Denielle, asking the same question."

Mom pushes past my father and slowly walks into the room, scanning it like Lilly is going to pop out from the closet or some shit.

"She's gone, Mom," I snap.

My mother's eyes fly to mine and instantly begin to water.

Aw, crap.

I stand up and walk over, wrapping my arms around her. "I'm sorry. I'm just..." I trail off. Maybe remaining numb would've been better after all.

I need to get out of this damn room. The urge to trash every piece of furniture in here is too overpowering. I shift so my arm is around my mom's shoulders and lead her past my father. Thankfully, he lets us by without the third degree.

WE'RE SITTING in the kitchen, Dad in his usual chair at the head of the table. Mom is next to him, both hands strangling the coffee mug in front of her, and Natty is next to our mother, glancing warily between the three of us.

After I led Mom downstairs, I busied myself making coffee. I had to do something to delay the inevitable conversation. Once I placed cups in front of my parents, I leaned against the wall next to the garage door. Arms crossed in front of my chest, I refused to make eye contact. I couldn't. I had no clue what their message from Lilly said, so I wasn't going to make the first move. Resentment was fully present since the numbness had left, but despite her running away, I wasn't going to throw her under the bus.

Just as my father opened his mouth to start what most likely would've been a military-style interrogation, Natty walked in. All eyes turned to her, and my little sister stopped in her tracks, staring like a deer caught in the headlights.

"Uh, what's going on?" Her tone was hesitant.

Without a word, I pushed away from the wall and made my

way over. Placing my hand between her shoulder blades, I gently guided her toward the chair next to Mom, followed by planting my ass in the seat at the other end of the table, the space between my family and me serving as a barrier.

Now, I glance at the clock on the microwave. We've been sitting here for seventeen minutes. Someone needs to speak up.

"Where is Lilly?"

Aw, fuck. Not her.

My father's eyes swing from Nat, to Mom, to me, and he raises his eyebrows expectantly. Slowly, Mom's gaze follows until three sets are trained on me.

I clear my throat. What the fuck am I supposed to say? Opening my mouth, nothing comes out, so I snap it back shut.

"Is she with him?" My father's question hits me like a push-kick to the balls.

"Uh, what?" is my very profound response.

"Him who?" My mother wrinkles her forehead, her gaze ping-ponging between both ends of the table.

Without taking his eyes off me, Dad answers, "Whoever was on the phone the day I caught her with a burner Rhys did not give her. Whoever was not Wes." His tone is eerily quiet.

Fuck me.

My lips part. "Uh..."

My father slams his flattened palms onto the tabletop, and everyone jumps. "DAMN IT, RHYS! Start fucking talking. I'm sick of your secrets."

My secrets? Is he for real? I bare my teeth at him. He wants to play this game? Bring it on! I mimic the position of his hands, but instead of remaining in my chair, I shove myself up and look down at Colonel Tristen McGuire. "My secrets?" I seethe. "*You're* one to talk."

My father scowls at me, and I cock my head in a challenge, daring him to push me. I'm ninety-nine percent certain Mom has no clue about the surveillance features in her home.

The wheels in his brain are turning. He can't figure out how much I know. Past caring, I raise one eyebrow and peer toward the corner where one of the cameras is located. Looking back, I smirk, and my father's face pales.

Who is keeping secrets now?

"Rhys?" My mother inserts herself into the standoff, and I glance to the side. "She says she has to leave for us to be safe. What does she mean by that? Where is my daughter?" The floodgates open, and tears are streaming down her face again. Natty wipes under her nose to stifle her sniffling, and Dad reaches over and takes one of Mom's hands.

He exhales a long breath, and calmer than before, he pleads with me, "Please tell us where she is. All we ever wanted was to keep her safe."

His change in demeanor momentarily throws me off. I can handle angry, pissed-off Tristen McGuire. Even scary, Marine Corps Tristen McGuire. But the desperate father...

My anger disintegrates. How much does she want me to reveal? I rub my palms over my face.

"Fuck," I mumble into my cupped hands. Pulling my hands away, I lock eyes with my father. "Lilly is with her family."

"Oh, my God!" Mom's eyes widen in shock.

"Excuse me?"

I think, for the first time in my life, I've truly stunned him.

"What family?" My mother's voice is shaking.

I have to give them something, but telling them who Nate is... I refuse to betray Lilly in that way, even though she *left* me. Instead, I stall. "What did her message say?"

My father's mouth flattens. He doesn't like to be the one who's not in charge. After a moment, he concedes, "She said she had to go away to keep us safe. That the reporter that showed up at Natty's school is not who he says he is and that she is afraid that if she stays, she puts us in danger." Natty stiffens next to our mother, and Mom wraps her arm around her. Dad continues mercilessly. "I'm asking you again, son. Who is Lilly with?"

Still standing, I finally lower myself back into the chair and cross my arms over my chest. "Her brother."

What I see next on my parents' faces confuses the shit out of me. Relief. Both school their features quickly, but I know what I saw.

What the hell?

"I don't understand. What brother?" Mom is the first to speak up.

Time to lie my ass off. Again. One would think this is second nature for me by now. "After she came back, her biological brother got in touch with her."

"How does she know this person is who he says he is?" My mother has gone into lawyer mode, and Dad lets her take the lead.

"Henry was not her father." I give them a pointed look. Lilly had blurted that out the day in my father's office, so from a time-line perspective, I'm telling the truth. Though, I am also convinced they knew that already. "They did a sibling DNA test," I continue, pulling shit out of my ass.

I want to smack my forehead and pat my back at the same time.

"Why does she believe she is safer with this...person? Who is he?"

I have to be careful about my next words. "I've never spoken with him in person." Not a lie. Face to face, yes. In person, no. "He has the means to keep her safe. She said she'd be in touch once she gets there. You can ask her yourself when she calls." The ice is getting thinner, and I'm sick of the lies. The part of me that resents Lilly for leaving me wants her to sweat as she comes up with an explanation for our parents.

Dad is about to speak when the front door opens, and Wes, followed by Denielle, stalks in. Seems like Wes still has the spare key I gave him years ago. My two friends take in the scene in the kitchen, and my father sighs. The conversation is over. He's not going to push the topic with them around, no matter how much they already know. He slowly raises himself out of the chair. "I'll be in my office." Before he rounds the corner to the hallway, his eyes meet mine. "We're not done."

Of course we're not. He'll probably boot up all the cameras in the house, hoping to catch something between Denielle, Wes, and me.

Mom shuffles Natty to the stove, ordering her gently to help with breakfast. It seems to have become Mom's go-to way of distraction. I doubt anyone wants food at this point, but I don't give a fuck.

With my friends on my heels, I make my way upstairs.

CHAPTER FIFTEEN

HER

"WHAT DO YOU MEAN SHE IS ON HER WAY TO CALIFORNIA?" I shriek into the phone. *Deep breaths. I need to control my temper.*

I don't like talking to this imbecile directly. Informant or not, I avoid speaking to him when possible. That's what the encrypted emails are for. But when I received his message five minutes ago, I immediately dialed his cell phone.

"I notified you as soon as possible," he defends himself. "He sent the jet to Westbridge in the middle of the night. I wasn't able to message until now. I didn't have my laptop, and you said not to call you directly."

Dear Lord, his high-pitched lamenting makes me want to stab the wine opener I'm still holding in my hand into his jugular and watch him bleed all over himself. I smile at the visual forming in my head. That would be the highlight of my week.

Glancing at my white knuckles wrapped around the Code38—a gift from my sweet girl—I force myself to unclench my hand and slowly place the tool on the table in front of me. Focus.

Why is Nate bringing Lilly to California? How could that happen? That doesn't make sense. Something must have triggered the move.

"Where is he?" I growl into the phone. What do I pay this idiot for? I'm losing patience with him.

"I haven't been able to reach him since he woke me up. My best guess? He is on the plane."

What? Why would he risk getting seen together with her?

The closing of a door alerts me that I'm no longer alone. I turn to see Gray making his way to the cream-and-white barrel accent chair I had him pick up the day we moved into this dump. He lets himself fall into the cushion, his unkempt exterior in contrast with my clean décor. Per usual, he displays no manners and just barged in without knocking.

I hold his gaze as I speak into the phone. How do you know that the jet is not picking up Weiler?"

Gray frowns when understanding sets in. His eyes bulge for a fraction of a second before he averts them, and he begins to fidget with his black KA-BAR. It's a habit I don't believe he's aware of. He never leaves the knife out of his sight. For as long as I've known this man, he's always had a blade with him. This particular knife is a remnant from his active military days. Maybe it makes him feel less of a failure than he is. And whenever he is nervous or on edge, he pulls it out.

I narrow my eyes at Gray. Without a word, I disconnect the call and slowly make my way across the room until I stand between his legs. When he just stares ahead, I place my pointer finger under his chin and forcefully tilt it up. He doesn't put up a fight, but the little nudge that is needed confirms my suspicion.

"Do you have anything to tell me?" I keep my tone calm, but my other hand automatically clenches at my side.

When the man I've known most of my life finally locks eyes with me, I know he is to blame for Lilly's sudden departure. I bend down and pry the knife out of his hand, slowly moving the sharp tip down his leg.

"Gray," I warn.

He draws in a breath. "I went to the little McGuire's school. She saw me." His admission is no more than a whisper.

Without hesitation, I raise the hand holding his prized possession and bring it down on his thigh. The blade slides in without resistance, and it reminds me of that day thirteen years ago. The day I got my revenge. He *also saw the knife coming, just like Gray today. But he never expected me to have the guts to pull through with my threat. My threat of cutting his eye out if he so much as looked at me again.*

Gray's spasming in front of me rips me out of the memory. He's gripping the armrests of the chair but not making a sound. He knows better.

I let go of the hilt and straighten. Looking down, I see a speck of blood on the linen covering my legs. Just wonderful. I just bought these. I open the drawstring that holds the pants up and let them fall. Stepping out, I leave them in front of the chair and head toward the door. "Get everything ready. We're going to California."

I pull the door shut behind me and leave him to clean up the mess in my office.

CHAPTER SIXTEEN

LILLY

IT'S PITCH BLACK. DARK CLOUDS COVER THE NIGHT SKY. IT'S as if the impending storm is a reflection of the havoc my life has become.

Through sheer luck, Lancaster was passed out—asleep, not literally—in his car. George was prepared to distract him somehow, but for once, something worked in our favor.

I stumbled twice due to my trembling legs as I crept along the fence to meet George two properties down the road. The second time, I remained on my hands and knees for several minutes, trying to get my breathing under control. I didn't bother wiping the tears away anymore. The moment I stepped out the back door, I let them fall freely.

We've been driving for forty-five minutes, and neither of us has said a word. Even when I opened the passenger door and climbed into the Navigator—which I finally identified today— George just gave me a solemn look. He disapproves of my decision. I almost wish he'd say something, yell at me, tell me I'm making a mistake. The silence is worse. It leaves me alone with my thoughts, regrets, doubt...guilt.

His phone has lit up a few times, but he would just check it and then place it back in the cup holder without responding.

I shift restlessly, trying to keep my healing back away from the seat. But no matter how I position myself, eventually the muscles in my back (upper and lower), my neck, even my butt start cramping. Driving anywhere for longer than five minutes in my current physical state is as pleasant as running a marathon wrapped in barbed wire.

Eventually, I can't take the quiet anymore and whisper, "Please say something."

George takes a deep breath, and I prepare myself for a scolding, but instead, he reaches over and gives my knee a gentle pat. I don't think George has ever initiated physical contact with anyone in the few weeks I've known him.

"I will do whatever it takes to keep you, your brother, and your family safe. Rhys will not take it well; you have to prepare yourself for the consequences. But I'm sure you've thought long and hard about it."

His insinuation is clear: I haven't thought this through.

That's where he's wrong. I've been thinking of nothing else since Turner revealed himself at the press conference. It's all connected; I can feel it. Despite it being the opposite of support for my decision, his words bring the reason "why" back to the forefront of my mind, pushing the guilt and doubt further back. The longer I stayed, the more I put my family in danger.

I'm doing the right thing.

WE'RE PARKED inside a hangar of a small private airfield in God knows where.

After our brief conversation, we drove for another twenty minutes. George pulled up to a gate, exchanged a few hushed words with the security guard stationed there, and then pulled in. Through all of it, I averted my face out of the window. Keeping a low profile has become my number one priority.

Whenever doubt and guilt tried to take hold again, I kept repeating '*You're doing the right thing*' silently in my head. I know this will be a continuous battle until I can speak to Rhys and explain myself. *Rhys.* My throat closes up, and I squeeze my eyes shut.

I'm doing the right thing. I'm protecting the people I love.

Once George stops the Navigator in the back of the structure, near a small office space, he gets out and walks around the SUV. He opens the passenger door, staring at me expectantly.

"It's warmer in the office, Miss Lilly. There is a heater in there. It'll be a while." His tone is low yet commanding.

I unbuckle myself, swing my legs out, and let my feet hit the ground. The slap of my soles echoes through the massive hangar as I trail behind my bodyguard. Inside the square room is a metal desk, a few metal chairs, and a military-style cot.

"What is this place?" I scowl.

"The best I could come up with on such short notice. We can't fly commercial now, can we?" George deadpans, walking past me and depositing my duffel bag on the table with a thud.

I slowly follow him. "So, how are we getting...wherever we're going."

He swivels around and leans against the desk, leveling me with a glare that gives me the chills. He is truly disappointed in me for *running*. "Nate is sending the jet. But since we have to stay under the radar—the Altman jet does not necessarily blend in—I had to find a private airport that will keep this under wraps."

Meaning, my brother had to drop a good chunk of change.

Guilt charges to the front like a 5.56 leaving the barrel of an M-4, and I swallow hard.

"We have approximately another three hours; you might as well get some rest." He nods toward the cot.

I blow out a non-comical breath. Is he joking? There's no way in hell I'll be able to sleep. Nonetheless, I sink onto the makeshift bed and pull out my phone, aka the burner. Plugging in headphones, I click on the notes app and start typing. "Good Goodbye" by Linkin' Park and "Under Your Scars" by Godsmack are blaring on constant repeat through the small speakers into my ears. As soon as I type the first word, my vision blurs, and by the third line, I can barely make out the screen. A George-like shape, distorted by my tears, is watching me closely, but he remains mute.

The tightness in my chest constricts my airflow, and I have to stop multiple times to put my head between my legs.

I'm doing the right thing. Please forgive me.

Signing Rhys's message with his nickname for me feels like the end. I refuse to believe that it's the end for us. It can't be. But the mere thought of him not forgiving me... My fingers are shaking so badly I drop the phone. George is at my side in two strides and clasps my hands between his.

"Please, look at me."

I can't.

"Miss Lilly. Look at me!" My body automatically obeys at his order.

He levels me with a look that is equally stern as it is...empathetic? My eyebrows draw together, and I study him. Emotions I have never seen flicker across his face. It's like he's lost in his own memory for a second.

"I'm not going to lie to you. I don't agree with your decision." I open my mouth, but he cuts me off. "However, I understand it." *He does?* "I had to make a similar decision once...leave someone behind that I cared about. The difference between you and me is, though, I believe you and Rhys will have a happy ending. He will be angry with you, but he loves you. You will find a way to work it out."

I'm not sure what to say. He left someone? Is that why he is so distant? Instead of responding, I wrap my arms around him and hold on tight. After a moment, he places his hands on either side of my head and pulls back gently. He forces me to make eye contact, and then...he smiles at me—a genuine, heartwarming smile.

"It will be okay."

And I believe him. Next are Den's and Wes's messages, saving the one for Heather and Tristen for last. Those ones are easier. Maybe because I'm all cried out. Maybe because I do trust George's words.

I decide to give my friends a watered-down version of Rhys's, that with Turner showing up at Natty's school and her being targeted by Katherine's sister, I can't risk anyone coming after them as well. When I get to Heather and Tristen's, I stare at the screen for a long time. I have no clue how much to reveal to them, so I settle on the half-truth. Turner is not who he pretends to be, and I'm scared for their safety if I stay. I start typing that I am with family but then erase the words and end the message with *Please know that I'm safe and that I will call as soon as I can. Love, Lilly.*

After reading over everything one more time, I send each message to Nate. My brother responds within minutes that he will make sure my family and friends will receive my notes. Glancing at the little clock in the corner, I'm surprised to see that it's not even six. We've only been here for about an hour and a half—over two more to go. I lie down on my side, clutching the burner in both hands. "Unstoppable" by Red starts playing, and I want to laugh at the irony. I don't turn it off, though. Instead, I scroll through the pictures that somehow made it onto the device. It's the same folder that I found on my phone at the vineyard, and I suspect Nate transferred them on somehow before George gave it to Rhys.

"Miss Lilly." Someone gently touches my arm. My eyes spring open, and I jackknife up.

Shit, my back does not take the abrupt motion lightly.

"Oww," I moan and try to focus my eyes. "Did I fall asleep?"

George stands above me, and the answer is kind of obvious, but he indulges me. "You did. The jet just landed and will be here in a few minutes. It's time to go."

My pulse picks up. It's time to go. Last chance to back out. But even as the thought crosses my mind, I know returning to Westbridge is not an option until Turner is out of the picture.

At that moment, the noise level rises to the point of having to cover my ears, the metal structure amplifying the sound of the jet's engines as it rolls in.

I step beside George right outside the office, and we wait for the aircraft to come to a halt. Men who I hadn't noticed before and, I assume, belong to the small airstrip jog over and start working on the plane. They put the chocks in, and one heads to a fuel truck parked right outside the hangar doors.

My heart is beating in my throat as I watch the door lower. A flight attendant—no, one of the pilots appears in the opening and descends the steps. He gives George a curt nod and makes his way to the airport employee.

"That is Joel. He is Nate's personal..." He trails off, and I follow his gaze to see what has him distracted.

My hands fly to my mouth, and my feet take off of their own volition until I am full-on sprinting. I reach him at the same time he steps onto the concrete floor and jump, wrapping my legs and arms around him like a monkey.

Sobs wrack through my body as his hands try to hold onto me without touching my injuries.

"Hey, sis. Shhh, it's all good," my brother coos, and it instantly calms the turmoil inside of me.

I pull back, and he lets me sink to my feet.

"What are you doing here?" My fingers keep clutching Nate's sleeves, afraid he'll vanish into thin air if I let go.

"I would like to know the same thing. What were you thinking?" George's voice comes from behind me.

"I was thinking that my sister needs me," Nate snaps in a tone I have never heard him use toward George.

I nervously glance around, expecting the workers and pilot to watch the exchange, but no one pays us any attention.

George steps closer to my brother. His next words are a low growl that would make most grown men pee their pants. "Get. On. That. Fucking. Jet. Nathan Edward Denton Hamlin. Or I will *put* you on it." He jabs his index finger at Nate's chest.

Oh crap, George using the F-bomb is not a good sign.

Wait... Edward Denton?

I peer at my brother out of the corner of my eye, not turning my back on George. I know he would never do anything to hurt me, but his current demeanor—despite no longer being scared of him—makes the blood in my veins run cold.

Nate rolls his eyes and grabs my hand, pulling me behind him onto the plane. "George will get your stuff. Won't you?" he remarks with a smirk.

I don't dare make eye contact with the man behind me.

The door is located at the rear, and my eyes bulge as I follow Nate on board. The inside is everything you imagine a private jet to be—and more. A door to the right is ajar and leads into a bathroom—an actual bathroom, not just one of those airplane lavatories you have to be anorexic to fit in and still can't turn around. The color scheme is light yet sophisticated. Each of the cream-colored leather seats could easily fit two people. There are eight in total, two opposite each other with a small table between them. Toward the front of the plane is a couch on one side with a bar across from it. A small kitchen area, a seat for a flight attendant, and the door to the cockpit could be closed off by a curtain, which is currently held back by a hook that looks like it's made of gold. *It probably is.* An almost-white carpet covers the floor, and a matching runner lays in the middle row.

Keeping everything this pristine must be challenging.

THE JET TAKES off an hour later.

As we gain speed on the runway, my heart is hammering out

of my chest, not because I'm scared of flying, but because of the unknown. I feel like I'm in the dark again—this time because of the future, not the past.

I curl up in one of the buttery-soft leather seats in the back. George stretched out on the couch, one arm over his eyes, after he had placed my bag on an empty spot across the aisle as soon as he boarded the plane. The next few hours are probably the only rest he'll get.

Nate sits across from me, his laptop in front of him on the table. He's been typing away since he made himself comfortable there—right after he showed me around the aircraft.

"I forwarded your messages as soon as you sent them."

My eyes snap to his. I hadn't even considered that he could send them while he was on his way here. He must've sensed my confusion, because he elaborates, "The jet has Wi-Fi. I wouldn't be able to work otherwise. I've spent a lot of time in the air over the years." The corner of his mouth quirks up.

Oh.

"Do we know if they got them?" My whispered question is barely audible over the pounding in my ears.

He clenches his mouth before speaking. "No. They were delivered and received by the devices, but I didn't have time to write a routine to check if they read them. I would assume they did, based on the time." He tilts his wrist, and I notice the fancy-looking watch on his arm for the first time. He follows my gaze and mumbles, "A gift. I was still wearing it when I left the house."

I smile at him. He always appears so...embarrassed?...uncomfortable?...when he has to showcase his money.

"You still haven't told me what happened," my brother prods carefully.

I draw in a shaky breath and expel it at the same rate. "Turner was at Natty's school."

Nate's eyes widen, and George sits up instantly.

I guess he wasn't sleeping after all.

I tell them about Natty being targeted by the kids at school, specifically Katherine's little sister, and conclude how she recalled Turner showing up during her lunch break.

"We need to figure out what he wants. His endgame." George has switched to security mode.

"I'll start digging more into his past. There has to be something, and I haven't gone back far enough." Nate immediately starts typing on his laptop.

"Can you do that from here?" I don't even attempt my surprise.

He glances up between his fingers flying over the keyboard. "Don't be silly, sis. I would never do that on such a minimally secured network. I'm letting Hank know that I am taking tomorrow off as well."

Nate just snubbed me. What the—?

THE REMAINDER of the flight is uneventful. Unable to do anything until we land, George resumes his pose on the couch, and eventually, he does fall asleep—soft snoring being the dead giveaway. Nate works on his laptop, and I listen to my playlist on repeat, letting the tears fall as they come. He looks up every so often but then leaves me to deal with it. If I want to talk about it, I will, and he knows that.

As we descend, the pilot's voice comes over the intercom. "We are approaching LA and will be landing shortly. Nate, I confirmed that your car is waiting for you in the hangar and that George's truck was also brought in."

Nate presses a button. "Thank you, Joel."

"Won't he wonder who I am? To you?" I assume everyone has seen my name plastered in the media by now.

"He won't."

That's all my brother gives me, and his expression tells me not to ask any further questions.

After touchdown, the jet taxis directly into a similar structure as we departed from. However, this one screams private airport, not dingy drug-smuggling airfield. As I peer out the window, I see a massive sign on the wall reading *Altman*, and my eyes widen.

Nate gets up and digs through a bag, pulling out a plain hoodie and a baseball cap. "Put this on."

I look down at myself. "I'm already wearing a hoodie."

Before he can respond, George steps up to us. "Yes, but yours has your school's logo on it. If anyone would take a picture right now, they could easily trace it back." After a pause, he adds, "Leave your hair inside the hood, pull the hat down low, and put these on." He grabs something from Nate's hand and presses a pair of black Wayfarers into mine.

I argue that I'll stick out like a sore thumb like this, but Nate assures me that Californians dress like Eskimos in seventy-degree weather, and no one will look twice.

Well, okay then.

HE WAS RIGHT. I don't get a second glance as I follow Nate to a fancy-looking car, which he identifies as an Aston Martin One-77. The first image in my head is how Rhys and Wes would drool over this *vehicle*. I shut down that train of thought as fast as it came—I can't go there. I can't break down in public.

George will follow us in his truck, a matte-gray monstrosity with blacked-out windows that would make Tristen proud. As we pass him leaving the airport, I'm able to recognize it as a RAM 3500.

We drive for almost two hours. LA traffic is something one has to experience to understand. Holy crap, what a cluster. Where are all these people coming from—or going to—in the middle of the day?

When we enter a neighborhood like ones I have only ever seen on TV, I crane my neck to take it all in. One wrought-iron gate after the next. Behind some, you can see mansions that make the vineyard look like a mobile home. Others have an endless driveway with no house in sight.

"Nate?" The awe in my voice is apparent.

"Hmm?" His shoulders are tense, and he doesn't look away from the road.

"Where are you taking me?" I don't think he would bring me to his house.

"My parents'," he replies absently.

It takes me a moment to grasp the meaning. He's letting me stay at his childhood home. The home he has barely set foot in in over ten years. My father's house.

"Nate," I choke out his name. "You don't have to. I can stay at a hotel or..."

"This is your house as much as it is mine," he cuts me off. "And this way...maybe I can associate that place with something good again."

Tears prick at my eyes. "Thank you," I whisper.

This time he turns to me. "For what?"

"For being here."

CHAPTER SEVENTEEN

LILLY

I DIDN'T THINK I WOULD BE ABLE TO FALL ASLEEP LAST NIGHT, but I was out as soon as my head hit the pillow. That's what staying up for almost two days will do—and still recovering from getting attacked by delusional high school girls with no backbones.

After we arrived, everything was a blur. Nate showed me around the mansion—there was no way to call this place a house. The bottom floor alone could fit Heather and Tristen's entire square footage twice, if not more. And did I mention that it had three stories with a full finished basement? Talk about ostentatious. This was *worse* than the vineyard.

The kitchen was fully stocked, and when I raised my eyebrows to my brother, he explained he had the house readied for me. No one had lived here since Brooks, so it had to be cleaned top to bottom and the pantry filled.

Still staring at the packets of instant oats and pasta in front of me, reality crashed in. This was where my father took his life, where Nate found the letters—the reason his mother and sister were dead. I shouldn't have been here. A simple motel would do just fine. As I expressed my concern, Nate pretended like I hadn't spoken at all and continued the tour. Acting oblivious was his way of coping, but it didn't stop the voices in my head.

The first floor consisted of several living spaces. Why would one need two dining and four living rooms? There wasn't even a TV—apparently, that was what the theater room was for. The second floor had several guest rooms, Brooks's home office, a library, an art studio—Payton loved to paint, as Nate informed me with a sad smile on his face—and Audrey's playroom. Nothing had been touched since the last resident of the home...*left*. The more I saw, the more I felt like an intruder.

We stood in the library, overlooking the back of the property, when thoughts of Rhys crept into my mind. I'd refused to go there since we spoke about the messages and Turner on the plane. Allowing my brain to even think his name brought me too close to my breaking point. I instinctively wrapped my arms around myself as if the gesture would make the ache disappear.

My brother glanced down at me. "Do you want to call him?" His tone was careful.

A pit opened up in my stomach. I wanted to talk to him more than anything, but at the same time, I was terrified of him not wanting to speak to me.

My inner conflict must've been apparent because he answered his own question for me. "I'll let him know that you are safe and that you'll call him tomorrow. I'll bring a computer over from my place in the morning and teach you how to initiate encrypted video chats. The burner is still just set up to call George's and my numbers." After a pause, he added, "If that is okay with you?"

All I could do was nod, my voice not working as I tried to keep the sob steadily building in my throat locked in.

"'Kay." He gave my shoulder a squeeze. "Let's find you a place to sleep."

Nate turned and led the way toward the staircase leading to the third floor where the family's bedrooms were. As we ascended, he informed me that there were two more guest rooms upstairs, besides his parents', Audrey's, and his old bedroom. He'd be staying in the other one, whichever one I didn't pick, and George would be on the second floor. I could choose between any of the spare rooms, but he'd prefer me to be on the top floor. I dipped my head in confirmation and then picked the first room he showed me. Funny enough, it was very similar to my room at the vineyard *and* in Westbridge. The nightstand and dresser were white with black hardware, the king-size bed had a gray, upholstered wingback headboard, though way fancier than the one I had gotten from our local furniture store in Virginia, and a matching bench sat at the foot of it. The bedding was a white pin-tuck duvet; however, the accents were cream and gold instead of lavender. If that also would've been the same, I would've walked right back out.

George was busy for the rest of the day, setting up a security perimeter since nothing besides an alarm system had ever been installed. Nate admitted that—in the past—he didn't *give two shits* if someone broke in, so he never bothered putting in one of his designs. By the end of the day, wireless cameras were set up outside on the property and at the entrances to the house. That would have to do for now.

Around 6:30, the three of us ate in silence, but I excused myself immediately after. Before we sat down, Nate had disappeared for about an hour and later assured me Rhys knew I was safe. He wouldn't elaborate on how he had communicated with him, and I was too scared to ask. What if he had spoken to him personally? What if Rhys had told him he wouldn't forgive me for leaving? I forced the dinner down simply because I hadn't eaten all day, but I didn't remember what we had.

I EMERGE from my room sometime after eight in the morning. I had slept for almost thirteen hours, and despite the multitude of conflicting emotions that have been wreaking havoc in my body and mind, I am semi-rested—at least physically.

George sits in the breakfast nook—nook being used loosely, as it could easily fit an entire football team—and is reading one of his weathered books. Nate is nowhere in sight. Pulling out the chair closest to him, I lower myself down, careful not to let my healing skin make contact with anything.

"Where's Nate?"

Without taking his eyes off his reading material, he replies, "He went to his house to pick up some items."

I stare at him for a long moment. "George?"

"Yes, Miss Lilly?" He won't look at me, and my chest constricts.

"Are you still mad at me?" My question is a barely audible whisper. "For leaving," I add.

This makes him pause, and his fingers tighten around the paperback. He slowly closes his book and places it down before turning toward me. "I am not angry with you, Miss Lilly. Never was. I am..." George lets his gaze wander to the opposite wall, where it lingers for several moments before returning to me. "Concerned."

My eyebrows pull together.

Concerned?

He draws in a deep breath. "For you. I have only been concerned for one person for over a decade, and that was your brother." There is a beat of silence before the corners of his mouth pull up, and the sudden boyish smirk shocks me almost as much as when he had reprimanded Nate yesterday. "Your brother was never in physical danger. He could take care of himself—for the most part. I'm not used to being worried like this about someone anymore. Not since—" He cuts himself off, and I want to ask who he's talking about. "If something happened to you—something else"—he is referring to the attack —"it would destroy Nate. He wouldn't come back from that.

And he would not be the only one. You have the ability to wrap people around your finger."

My face heats, and I'm speechless. Emotion clogs my throat, but before I can go all mushy on the Altman Head of Security, he gets up and makes his way over to the stove, turning on the kettle.

"Earl Grey, Miss Lilly?"

I smile. It looks like our *moment* is over.

"Yes, please."

I SIT AT THE ISLAND, my hands wrapped around the now empty mug, and let my gaze wander through the three sets of French doors. The property behind the mansion is as grand as the house itself. The bluestone patio is visible as far as the eye can see through the glass. There is an inground lap pool with adjoining hot tub and lush green grass that has been well cared for even if no one lived here.

Around ten, Nate walks in from the hallway leading to the garage. He balances a large white box in one hand while two black duffel bags are strapped over each shoulder.

"Too lazy to walk twice?" George remarks in a dry tone as he faces my brother.

Nate places the box next to me on the island. "Nope, just left the heavy stuff for you."

Their comfortable banter is new, and I don't know if Nate is this relaxed because I am finally where he has wanted me for the past week or if it's something else. My gaze ping-pongs between the two men, waiting for what happens next. I expect everything from George pulling his Glock—which is strapped to his side at all times—to walking over and smacking my brother over the head. Instead, his stoic face is on full display, and all he does is glower at Nate for several breaths before he walks out, muttering to himself.

I focus back on my brother. "What's all this?" I dip my head toward the items he deposited in front of me.

He unzips the first bag and reveals enough electronic equipment to put one of those Best Buy stores Dad dragged us to as kids out of business.

"What the—?" My eyebrows shoot upward.

"Everything you'll need, little sis." He shoves his hand into his jeans pocket, and something flies toward me. "Oh, and here."

I barely catch the object.

"Happy Birthday." He looks like the Cheshire cat.

This grin is never good.

Slowly, I glance down and frown at the item in my palm. Is that—? My eyes shoot back up. "You're giving me a car?"

Nate shrugs nonchalantly. "Well, it's kind of my fault you totaled your Jeep. So, it's appropriate I replace it."

I turn the key fob over and suck in a breath. "A Mercedes?" My voice is shrill, and I'm not sure if it's from shock or excitement. My rapid pulse could be from either.

Misinterpreting my outburst, his face falls. "If you don't like it, you can buy something else."

"Don't like it? ARE YOU NUTS?" I jump off the barstool and tackle my brother. "Thank you, thank you, thank you!"

He chuckles. "You don't even know what model it is."

I squeeze tighter. "I don't care." Peering up at him, I add, "I know you. You would never give me anything less than the best. You don't do *average*."

The corner of his mouth tilts up. "Guess you *do* know me."

Suddenly, I feel like someone has punched me in the stomach, and I jerk back. Nate scowls, about to say something, when my hands fly to my mouth, and I blink against the stinging sensation in my eyes.

It's my birthday. My eighteenth birthday.

"What's wrong?" He gently grabs me by the upper arms.

I haven't been away from Rhys on my birthday for as long as I can remember. Even when we didn't speak, he was always there that day—in the background, but he was there. Tears stream down my face, and I press my lips together, not to start sobbing uncontrollably.

"Good Lord, Nate. What did you do now?" George's exasperated tone brings me back to the present.

I wipe under my nose. "I'm sorry. It's just..."

"Rhys?" Nate concludes in a flat tone.

I nod. The waterfall is back in full force. I'm such a mess. I left to keep them safe then break down if someone just mentions his name.

"Let me set up the system, and we can call him?" Nate phrases it more like a question.

I want to hear his voice more than anything, but— I cut my thoughts off.

"What am I supposed to say? He probably hates me." The words barely make it out of my mouth.

"He doesn't hate you."

My head jerks in George's direction, who is depositing several medium-size moving boxes near the door to the foyer. His statement is spoken matter-of-factly.

"You talked to him." I hiccup yet manage to sound accusatory.

"I have."

"How?" My rasped question is followed by a growl from my brother. "Why is this the first time I'm hearing of this?"

I brought the burner with me.

"He messaged me last night. He has my number memorized, as you know." The unspoken *duh* is like a slap to the face. George continues without waiting for one of us to answer. "He wanted to know where you are and if I'm with you. I confirmed that I am but didn't tell him the location. He told Heather and Tristen that you are with family—"

"WHAT THE FUCK?" Nate's outburst makes me jump, and he drops his hands from my arms.

He what?

I press my hand against my chest, feeling my heartbeat under my palm.

"Rhys had to give Heather and Tristen something. What did you two expect?" George's irritation is apparent. All that's missing is the eye roll.

My chin starts wobbling again, and his eyes soften. "He is not angry with you, Miss Lilly. He is...confused."

"Confused?" Nate scoffs.

George flexes his jaw. "Get everything set up so Miss Lilly can talk to her boyfriend. She doesn't have to give him a location, but she does owe him an explanation face to face."

As much as his words sting, he is right.

"Whatever." My brother grabs one of the bags and marches toward the back staircase. "Bring the rest to the office," he barks at no one in particular, and I scramble for the second bag, even though I'm pretty sure he didn't mean me.

BY THE TIME I reach the top of the landing, Nate is nowhere in sight. He said office, so I assume he meant Brooks's home office. During yesterday's tour, he pointed out the room but only stared at the door. The look on his face as we stood in the hallway for several minutes made it clear that he still has a lot of unresolved issues with our father.

My father's office was the only one I didn't get to see, so my steps are hesitant. Slowly reaching out for the handle, George's voice comes from behind. "He's not in there."

I whip around, scowling at him.

I'm going to attach a bell to this man.

"This room hasn't been opened in a decade," George explains in a gentler tone than he used downstairs. "Besides the cleaning personnel, that is."

"Oh."

"He's in here." Turning around, he makes his way three doors down.

Following him at a slower pace, I step over the threshold and come to an abrupt halt. I try to take everything in, but my brain has a hard time catching up. This was one of the guest rooms yesterday, complete with a four-poster bed, dresser, armchair, and stand-up mirror. The low-sitting, cognac armchair is still there, and so is the tall, rustic-looking mirror, but the bed...is gone.

"What happened in here?" I mumble as I make my way farther into the...new office?

Nate straightens from the desk he is leaning over while attaching cables to various monitors. "You needed a place to work." His casualness makes my brows pinch together.

"Where is the bed? And the dresser?" I spin in a circle.

"In the basement," George inserts with a slight grudge. "Your brother decided to change his career to interior designer while you were sleeping."

"Oh, shut up, old man. You were just as excited to pick out the office chair as I was." Nate is now under the table, messing with more cables.

I smirk as their banter distracts me from what we're about to do. *Who* I'm about to talk to.

"What can I help with?" I carry over the bag.

"I'll show you how to set up a secure network so you know for the future. It won't be anything like mine but enough to get you started and call h—uh...Rhys."

It sounded like he was about to say *home*, but I let that go. Instead, I squat down and let my brother give me networking lessons.

CHAPTER EIGHTEEN

RHYS

LILLY IS SAFE. SHE ARRIVED AT HER DESTINATION AND **will contact you tomorrow.**

As everyone in the house is most likely fast asleep, I sit at the edge of my bed and stare at the message I received from UNKNOWN earlier this evening. I'm sure Dad's spyware alerted him of the incoming text, but so far, he has not started his interrogation. Why? Who the fuck knows these days?

Tomorrow. This one word makes me want to launch the phone across the room. She can't even let me know herself that she's okay. Wherever she is. What the fuck happened to us? Everything was fine—as fine as it could have been.

If someone would've told me, twenty-four hours ago, that Lilly would run away in a cloak-and-dagger operation while I was sleeping in her bed, I would've laughed in the fucker's face.

I focus on breathing through my nose until the red haze in my vision turns to a faint pink. My pulse has calmed enough for rational thoughts to make their way back into my brain. I refuse to accept that I have to wait another day.

Opening up a new message, I enter the number I memorized weeks ago: **I want to know where she is.**

The little bubble with the three dots pops up within seconds. **I cannot tell you that.**

WTF, G? She left me in HER bed and snuck out. U picked her up. I thought u were against her leaving.

It takes several minutes until the reply appears. At that point, I already assumed he wouldn't respond at all.

Rhys, as you know, your phone's activity is being tracked. I can assure you that she is safe, and she will contact you as soon as everything is set up. We are working on it. She didn't make the decision lightly. She is worried for her family and friends. For you.

Understanding hits that he *can't* tell me shit since my father would instantly know.

"FUCK!" I jump up and reach my desk within two strides, swiping everything on it to the floor in one motion. "AAAR-RRG." A roar leaves my throat, but I'm past caring who hears me. When no one, aka my father, bursts through the door, gun swinging, I look back at the screen. George needs to give me something. I don't give a flying fuck anymore who finds out.

Can u give me an idea when she'll call?

Great, now I sound like a whiney toddler again.

This time the answer is instant: **No.**

Motherfucker! My arm lifts to chuck the phone, but I catch myself at the last second.

AT 5:47 A.M., my bedroom door flies open. I still haven't gone to bed, and I switch my focus from the video game on my TV screen to the red-faced man taking over my doorframe.

I'm tired, and I'm pissed at pretty much everyone in my life for one reason or another, so I do what every mature male would do. I concentrate back on the game, casually acknowledging his presence. "Dad."

My father stalks into the room until he's in front of my bed, blocking my view of the zombie I was just about to blow up. "Who the fuck did you text last night?" He enunciates every word in a low growl that makes it clear he's a tad salty.

Well, tough shit.

"I don't know what you mean." I cock an eyebrow.

After George's last message, I let the confusion of why Lilly would leave without talking to me and the frustration of not being able to do jack shit about any of it turn into rage against my father. I convinced myself that if his fucking tracker weren't on my phone, Lilly's bodyguard would've given me something.

I expect Dad to explode at my defiant reply. Instead, he shocks the hell out of me. My father sinks down on the mattress and puts his head in his hands. All I can do is stare. What the hell?

We sit in silence for what feels like hours but a glance at my alarm clock reveals to be only four minutes.

Dad turns his face toward me, letting his arms drop to his thighs. "I've messed up with you, haven't I?"

"Uh..."

He continues, "All I tried to do was keep you...my family safe."

"Safe from who?" It can't be *just* Nate. He had no clue where Lilly was until we showed up in Cali.

"Did Lilly tell you why she can't remember?"

Of course he doesn't answer my question. "No." The memory of storming into my father's office when I had heard the raised voices and seeing Lilly's distraught face burned itself into my brain. Of-fucking-course I remember.

"I had consulted with a former associate on how we could help her cope. Lilly went through a lot at such an early age, and I didn't think she would make it out of it without long-term consequences, psychologically speaking." A lot? What the hell is he talking about? Dad's eyes are unfocused, and I clamp my mouth shut, afraid if I say anything, he'll stop talking. "She's a special girl, you know that?" The corner of his mouth tilts up, and he briefly catches my gaze before training it back to something on the wall. "She has a kind heart, always has. She spent a lot of time with our family as a little girl, and your mom and I *needed* to help her. I explained to your mother what my associate could do. Initially, she was furious with me for even suggesting such an option."

My stomach churns at his vague descriptions. What could he have suggested that would have made Mom that angry? I swallow hard. "What did you do to her?"

Dad zeros in on my face. He's torn between walking out and coming clean—a conflict I've never seen on my father's face. He's always confident in everything he does.

"Her memory was manipulated through a form of hypnosis and persuasion."

Excuse me, what?

I stare at the man in front of me, refusing to believe what I just heard. I know he's been ruthless when it came to his job, no remorse and shit, but his child—adopted or not. How could he?

"Get. The. Fuck. Out." My body is shaking, and I keep my voice low to not wake up my little sister at the end of the hall. It takes every ounce of willpower not to take a swing at him, my balled fists already twitching with the need to pound something. Someone. Him!

He must realize that it won't do any good to argue, so he draws in a deep breath, stands up, and leaves. As soon as the door clicks shut, I grab the closest pillow, bite down, and let out a guttural scream, followed by taking said pillow and ripping the case into shreds.

I DON'T LEAVE my room until my stomach growls so loud Lancaster—still camped out in the front yard—can probably hear it. I intend to go straight to the kitchen, grab every granola bar in the pantry, and head back upstairs—water from my bathroom sink would suffice for the foreseeable future. What I don't anticipate are the raised voices from Dad's office.

Heart beating against my ribs, I sneak down the hallway. The door is ajar.

"Honey, I'm sorry. I didn't want to give you another reason to worry. You barely agreed to stay after she was found. I took every precaution I could without packing up and moving us again."

"Three years, Tristen. Three. Years." Mom is crying—and not the pretty kind. The anger in her voice is apparent. "Has anyone had access to this footage? This is a complete invasion of privacy. Did you watch it?"

"I only checked the main living areas. The cameras in the bedrooms were just a precaution."

Slap.

Holy shit, did she just smack him?

My mother's voice turns hysterically shrill. "You made it sound like Hannah's death was an accident—a burglary gone wrong. Then I find out the person came back? Now this. Did *she* kill Hannah?"

Again with this Hannah person. Who is this chick? And who the fuck is *she*?

There is a beat of silence before Dad speaks. "I think so."

"Oh, my God!"

Fuck this shit.

I push the door open, finding Mom covering her mouth with her hands, tears streaming down her face and my father's arms wrapped around her.

"Rhys!" Dad's head snaps toward me.

"Who is Hannah?" No point in beating around the bush.

My father briefly closes his eyes in resignation, and Mom uses that opportunity to move away from him. She steps next to me. "Your father has informed me about the extent of the surveillance cameras in the house."

So, she really didn't know.

"Who is Hannah?" I repeat myself, enunciating every word. I'm running out of patience.

"Was."

"Huh?"

"Was. Hannah is dead," Dad clarifies in his normal, detached tone. I'm looking at Colonel McGuire, not my father.

"Hannah was our housekeeper. She started working for us when we moved back to Westbridge until she..." Mom won't make eye contact with Dad. "Until she was killed in our house."

"What the fuck?" My gaze jerks back and forth between my parents. So many questions assault my brain at once. How is this possible? "When was this? Why have I never heard of this person, let alone that someone killed her in our house?"

Mom has herself back under control and swipes at her smudged eye makeup. "We didn't want to worry you when it happened. Hannah would always come during the day when you were in school. It was easier for her to get her job done in an empty house. We never thought twice about the arrangement. Dad had her checked out, and we trusted her. We didn't have any reason to be concerned. She knew the alarm code and would arm it once she left." She draws in a shuddering breath and stares at the opposite wall. "One day, three years ago, the security company called us that the alarm was triggered. I was in the city. Dad went home to check on it and..." She trails off, fresh tears running down her face.

"I found her in the hallway," my father continues with a more subdued tone—so he was affected by it, after all. "She must've been able to hit the alarm button on the panel before she died. It happened on a Thursday, and I told Mom to take you straight to Grandma's house for a few days while I took care of every-thing. We excused the three of you from school, and since you always had clothes at Grandma's, it was easy to manage."

Holy shit, I remember that day. Mom came to pick us up from school and said it was a surprise trip.

"At the time, we were worried that it would trigger something in Lilly's memory, or you would let something slip about her past." He looks at me apologetically.

I narrow my eyes at him. "Oh-kay." Something in his story doesn't add up. Why would that trigger Lilly's memory? Traumatize, maybe, but what was she supposed to remember? "Sooo...someone broke into the house while Hannah was cleaning and off'd her. Why did that make you put in cameras in every single room in the house?"

Mom crosses her arms over her chest, avoiding Dad's gaze.

"The...person came back," my father finally declares.

The Person. The Killer. My eyes nearly bug out of their sockets, and I feel like trying to breathe underwater. This is fucking insane.

At his words, my mother's posture stiffens. Did she not know about that? Is that what they were fighting about? Besides the cameras?

"The police had already released the crime scene, and I had a cleaning crew go over the entire house. Mom was supposed to bring the three of you back the next day."

"What happened?" I choke the words out.

Dad exhales slowly. "I got another call from the security company. Someone had entered the house with the old code and triggered the alarm again. I had them disarm it and told them one of the kids must've triggered it by accident since we just changed it. I was at a meeting nearby, but when I got to the house, it was empty. We had cameras in the entryway and on all doors leading outside—something I've installed in all our houses since Lilly came to live with us. I pulled up the footage and saw the intruder exiting the house. She had several personal items with her, including Bobo."

She. Bobo. My thoughts are a jumbled mess my brain is scrambling to put in order.

"Lilly's bear? Why on earth—"

My father holds up a hand. "That's when I put the system in place. The person came back and stole personal items. I promise, it was a mere precaution, to be able to trace every step of a possible intruder if that would've happened again."

I study his face for several breaths, trying to wrap my head around why someone would kill our housekeeper and steal an old-as-fuck, ugly bear. Or would come back a third time, for that matter. Then something else clicks. "Why didn't you hand the footage over to the police?"

"It wouldn't have been of any use. They wouldn't have found anything."

"But you knew who it was." I'm not asking.

"The video feed never showed the person's full face." My mother, who has remained quiet the entire time, doesn't deny my statement.

"Let me guess, you are not going to tell me who you *think* it was." Sarcasm drips from my voice. Even now, we're keeping up the damn secrets.

When neither of them speaks, it's clear that that is Dad's way of shutting down the conversation.

I turn and leave the office without a backward glance.

Guess I'm keeping my secrets as well.

I've just scarfed down the third protein bar when my phone buzzes twice next to me on the mattress—text message. Tapping the screen, I scan the two words. The fuck?

OPEN ME.

The grudge-holding toddler in me wants to flip the small device the bird and ignore it. I pick up the game controller but then place it back down. Aww...shit, I can't do it. Taking the phone, I swipe the text open and tilt my head. It's empty. Seriously?

I still stare at the screen when an incoming video call pops up: LILLY.

My heart begins to pound in my chest. I briefly close my eyes before accepting the call.

Lilly's face fills the screen, and she smiles hesitantly. "Hi."

That voice. *Her. Voice.* I want to say something, but my mouth won't obey. I take in her surroundings. She sits at some type of desk. Behind her is a cream-colored wall with fancy artwork and crown molding visible at the top of the screen. Her face falls, and I instantly feel like an asshole.

She left you, a voice pipes up inside my head.

She didn't leave you, *asshole. She left to keep you safe,* reason yells back.

It's like having whiplash. I want to be pissed at her. For leaving. For not talking to me about how she felt. I understand "the why," but it has driven a wedge between us. Yet, I love her more than anything.

"Hey." I force the corners of my mouth upward, but the expression won't take hold. The last thirty-six hours have been too much to keep up any pretense.

"How angry are you with me?" Lilly's voice is below a whisper, and I contemplate how to answer her question without sounding like a resentful prick.

"I..." *Fuck.* "I'm not angry—much." I dig through my muddled brain to find the right words. "I'm disappointed. I guess I would've expected for you to come to me first." Truth.

Her chin dips slightly, and moisture builds in her eyes. I want to be there for her, but at the same time, she ran. I just can't. When she looks back up, there's a beat of silence. "That's fair."

My eyebrows raise. I expected her to defend herself.

Recognizing my confusion, she says, "I had a long conversation with George and Nate. I understand now that I should've filled you in on my plan. I was just..." She blows out a breath. "I was scared you'd talk me out of it. You're the only person who could have."

Somehow, her confession releases most of the tightness in my chest. "I guess that's fair as well."

We have to work through our double truckload of baggage eventually, no question there. We'll probably have a full-on freight train by the time this is over, but we've also already spent years ignoring each other. Well, I stayed away from her. That guilt will haunt me for a long time.

"I also had an interesting conversation today." My rational side wins out, and I shift gears.

"Oh?"

"Where are you?" I'm not ready to rehash my parents' newest revelation yet.

She inhales deeply followed by expelling all the air at the same rate. "Los Angeles."

I knew it! It's what I would've done. *Great, now I'm relating to a criminal billionaire.*

"How is brother-dearest's mansion?" What I can see in the background already looks like the shit.

"I'm..." She pauses, and I tilt my head. "I'm at Brooks's house."

Well, shit. I didn't expect that. I would've assumed he'd lock her into some fancy hotel penthouse if he didn't bring her to his house. "How do you feel about that?"

"Fine?" Lilly shrugs one shoulder. "I don't think I've really made the connection yet."

Instead of responding, I watch her closely, waiting for what comes next. Emotion after emotion flitters across Lilly's face before she speaks.

"How is everyone at home?" She looks everywhere but the camera.

Her question sends my insides into another tailspin. Is that how she's been since finding out the truth about her past? About Nate. This constant back and forth between *resentment/red haze/I want to pound someone's (anyone's) face* and *I understand/I miss her/I'm a fucking pussy for not staying angry* is turning me fucking bipolar.

"Depends. Den and Wes were pissed. I told them about Turner. And even though they want to help, they get it. I guess we all just want to move on."

More accurate words haven't formed in my brain all day.

"Me, too." Her eyes are on her hands, and by the slight twitch in her arm, I'm guessing she is flicking her thumb against the rest of her fingers.

"Dad was a little more pissed than the rest. But that was mainly after his little spy app informed him about my texts with George."

Her eyes jerk to mine.

"In the end, we got sidetracked." I picture my father sitting on the bed, revealing what he let someone do to Lilly. My grip instantly tightens, and the case around my phone crackles.

"What do you mean?"

I attempt to calm my temper by breathing through my nose, and Lilly waits patiently. She can read me better than anyone and knows when I'm about to *flip my lid*, as she calls it. Twenty-three inhales and exhales later, I'm sure I can recall both conversations in a manner that will not end in me destroying any more pillows or electronic devices. I say, "Dad told me what happened to your memory and why there are cameras in the entire house."

Lilly's hands fly to her mouth.

"You might want Nate and George there," I continue.

She stares at me for a long moment, probably trying to figure out why I'd voluntarily suggest speaking to her brother.

"Okay. Uh, give me a minute." She doesn't immediately get up but then shakes her head and disappears from the screen. I take in the framed paintings on the wall behind the desk and finally recognize the object on them as an abstract version of the same black horse, one galloping and one standing. The weird shit rich people hang on their walls.

It takes several minutes before Lilly is back. She lowers herself into the chair, and I hear rummaging in the background. A moment later, two tall figures are carrying more chairs into the picture. When all three are facing the camera, I'm not sure where to begin.

"Rhys," George greets me in his usual, unemotional fashion.

"G." I nod at him, mimicking his detached tone. Oddly

enough, I can remain pissed at him for picking Lilly up instead of putting his foot down—not that that really would've been an option.

My gaze swivels to Nate, who sits with his arms crossed slightly behind his sister. "Psycho."

Yup, still resentful for him allowing Lilly to leave.

Where Lilly glowers at me disapprovingly, George's lips twitch at the corner.

Nate simply rolls his eyes. "Why were we summoned, Rhys?"

Well, here we go. "My father explained to me how Lilly lost her memory and—"

"We already know how. George has a meeting with Lakatos set up for next week," he interrupts me.

Who—

"You didn't tell me that!" Lilly's head turns to her brother.

"I finalized the details yesterday. I didn't have time to fill you in yet," the other man inserts himself.

"Who. The. Fuck. Is. Lakatos?" the question is more a feral growl than an articulated string of words.

"He's the memory doctor." Lilly glances back at me.

I suck in a lungful of air. *Holy—* "Can he...uh, reverse what he did?" Is there a possibility for Lilly to remember?

"We don't know. I had to follow his extensive contact protocol before I could even set up a secure call with him."

"He's a paranoid motherfucker." Nate blows out a non-comical laugh.

George ignores his employer. "As I was saying, we spoke on the phone, and it took multiple days to agree on the terms to meet in person. The only reason he even considered it was my...reputation. He has heard of me, as I knew of him."

Well, if that isn't wonderful. "Maybe you can form a club." I can't swallow the snide remark that formed on my tongue.

This time, I'm at the receiving end of George's displeasure.

Thankfully, he doesn't evoke a sudden bladder release anymore, so I just shrug. "What?"

"Okay, now that we are all up to speed on that topic." Lilly narrows her eyes at the two men in the room with her before making eye contact with me again. "What else did you find out?"

Oh yeah, the *our-housekeeper-got-murdered-by-a-teddy-thief* news.

"I overheard Mom and Dad arguing in the office. Turns out, Mom had no idea about the cameras. She was li-vid." I want to relay in vivid detail how she slapped Dad but then refrain from that. "Anyway, when they became cryptic, I confronted them directly." Three sets of eyes look at me expectantly, and I repeat what my parents told me in Dad's office.

"I read about this teddy in the letters." Lilly's eyes light up as some puzzle pieces from her past finally seem to fit back together. Then her brows furrow. "Why would this person take Bobo?" Her excitement turns to confusion.

"They didn't tell you who the intruder was?" George sits up in his chair.

"No, they just said it was a she. But they know. I'd bet the Defender on it."

"Why wouldn't they tell us? Why would Tristen keep it from Heather until now? This makes no sense." Lilly searches my eyes.

I wonder if our family would even function if there were no secrets between us. I'm about to tell her that her guess is as good as mine, but Nate beats me to it.

"You got this teddy from our father? What did it look like?"

Lilly's face falls. "I don't know. I don't remember him. I only read about him in the letters."

"I do," I speak up. "No one could forget this ugly thing. He was ancient. You carried him around everywhere. He was white —well, I assume that was his original color. He was more gray-ish by the time it went AWOL. Very simple, one eye was miss-ing, and he was patched up on the back with some red fabric."

Nate turns chalk-white at the description, but with him sitting slightly behind, the other two haven't noticed.

I lift a finger and point. "Uh, why does he look like he's about to puke?"

Both heads jerk around, and we wait for Nate to elaborate.

He rubs his hands over his face before looking at his sister. "That teddy used to be mine. It was a gift from my grandfather when I was born."

CHAPTER NINETEEN

LILLY

I OPEN AND CLOSE MY MOUTH SEVERAL TIMES BEFORE I CAN get the words out. "B-Bobo was yours?"

Nate attempts a smile but looks pained instead. "His name wasn't Bobo at the time, but yes, he used to be mine. I named him Sir Denton, after my grandfather."

Something clicks, and my eyes widen. "*You're* named after your grandfather."

"Both, actually." Nate smirks. "Denton was my mother's father: Denton John Altman II," he clarifies, then adds, "Last I remember, the bear was in some keepsake box. Mom would save all the things she was sentimentally attached to. She probably never noticed that it was gone."

He doesn't elaborate on his other middle name, and I decide to ignore it as well. It's not important for the current topic.

"Why would anyone want that stuffed bear?" Rhys's question comes through the speaker, and I turn back to the screen.

I wrack my brain. "There was nothing special about him. Was there?" I peer at Nate, who shrugs in confirmation.

"Not that I remember."

"This shit is getting too fucking weird." Rhys rubs a hand over his mouth.

"Language," George barks from the chair next to me, and I roll my eyes.

"So, we finally understand why Tristen wired the house like a high-security prison. He wanted to be able to trace this person's every move—if *she* ever came back," I summarize.

Whoever this *she* was.

"Yup." Rhys pops the P in a bored manner. He moved to his desk, the phone propped up, and his arms crossed over his chest, leaning back in his chair.

"And they said for sure it was a she? That would mean Turner is out." I tap my index finger against my chin.

"We have not confirmed that he works alone." George stomps on my theory like one would crush a nasty bug under a shoe. "Everything I learned about Francis Turner, and what Nate was able to find, points toward him not having the intellect to mastermind all this."

"Well, who then?" Rhys's frustration is audible.

"I'll start digging more into his past," Nate informs Rhys of what he already told me on the plane. "But at the same time, I'm still trying to trace the money our father paid to that shell account. I'll work as fast as possible, but I have to make an appearance in the office tomorrow and Saturday since I missed two days this week. Hank is up my ass already, and Margot set up a lunch date with Julian and Cece for Sunday."

"You need to keep up with your life, Nate. You've been cutting it too close already. You"—George levels us with a stern face—"are not ready."

Guilt constricts my chest. *Nate has to take responsibility for his actions.* Between Turner and the shower attack, I refuse to go there. My brother will go to prison. Pulling my lips between my teeth, I stare at the desk, unable to make eye contact with any of them.

"You should talk to Mom and Dad." My eyes fly back to the screen.

"What?" I squeak. The tightness in my chest is replaced by an out of control beating heart.

"They deserve to hear from you. Face to face. Not just a text message that says, *I'm fine*." Looking past the camera, Rhys sighs. "I'm not their biggest fan either, and I probably would shut them out. Hell, I did for years. But you're a better person. There are too many fucking secrets."

"I agree with Rhys. Though, you need to keep it brief. Don't give details that could compromise you."

I shift my attention to George. When he doesn't say anything else, I glance at Nate, who just lifts a shoulder.

What am I supposed to say to them? Everything could potentially compromise where I am or who Nate is. I struggle to get my rapid pulse under control; it's of no use. The overflow of saliva combined with nausea steadily building tells me what's about to happen.

"Well, okay then. I take that as my cue to go back to cooking dinner. George, I want you to be in the room in case Lilly needs anything. Just...stay out of the picture, or Heather might have a heart attack, seeing your scary mug and all." My brother stands up, and his words snap me out of the oncoming panic attack.

Latching onto his arm, my nails dig into his flesh. I must've somehow agreed to it. Did I nod my head? Shit, I have no idea. "You want me to talk to them now?" I'm on the verge of being hysterical.

Nate levels me with an unidentifiable look. "Get it over with, little sis. It'll help you as much as it'll help them. Trust me."

What?

What is he not saying? Am I supposed to read between the lines? Is there another meaning to his words that I don't understand? Every neuron in my brain fires at the same time. His words don't match his expression. I open my mouth, but before I can form the words, my brother pulls me up and wraps one arm around my shoulders in a careful hug. He places a kiss on the top of my head and leaves the room.

I stare at the empty doorframe. What the hell just happened?

In slow motion, as if this would delay the inevitable, I swivel back to the desk. George has moved the extra chairs out of the picture, and I lower myself back down, closing my eyes.

I count to twenty before making eye contact with Rhys through the camera. He probably expects me to have a panic attack any second—he's seen enough in the last few weeks. Heck, I almost did have one just a few minutes ago.

I fill my lungs with as much air as possible and hold it in, releasing it only once my lungs begin to scream for air. "I'm ready."

"You sure?" His brows furrow.

I bob my head up and down as confidently as I can because— let's be real—I am nowhere near ready to face my adoptive parents.

Rhys regards me warily before he disappears from the screen, and I wipe my damp palms on my leggings.

"It'll be okay, Miss Lilly." I peer around the monitors to see George give me one of his half-smiles.

I'm unable to respond because fast footfalls echo through the speaker, and Heather's face appears in front of me. She merely stares—hands covering her mouth—as she blinks rapidly against a waterfall of tears.

"Hi, Mom," I whisper hesitantly.

A sob escapes her, and Tristen appears in the frame, followed by Rhys, who remains in the background. Tristen sinks in Rhys's desk chair and pulls his wife to his lap. A gesture that was nothing unusual for them before all of this began. It gives me some comfort that, despite all the secrets, the relationship between the two of them seems to be fine—as much as it can be.

"Hello, sweetheart," Tristen speaks first.

"Hi." The other end of the call starts to swim in front of my vision.

Tristen's expression is not what I am used to. The Marine is nowhere in sight. He is just my father. "How is your back?"

My bottom lip trembles, and I bite down on it to make it stop. His concern is worse than if he were to yell at me for again making irresponsible decisions without talking to them first. Eventually, I manage, "It's good. The burns are healing well."

"Rhys told us you are with family. Are you safe?" His tone is sincere, but he's gathering information.

"I am. I...I wanted to tell you, but there is so much I still have to figure out." The words tumble out. Scanning their faces —seeing them in front of me—Heather and Tristen are my parents. The two people who have raised me for as long as I can remember. *The only* parents I remember. All the secrets and lies, everything that has come to light, and everything still in the dark is unimportant. I want them to know I'm safe, and I hope, with time, they will understand and forgive me—when they learn the truth about Nate.

"Where are y-you?" Heather's question ends with a hiccupped sob.

"I'm..." I hesitate, not wanting to make it obvious that I'm seeking George's approval. He must sense my distress and steps toward the desk, dipping his chin in confirmation.

I'm about to respond to Heather when he mouths, "Nothing more."

Not wanting to make it obvious that there is someone in the room with me, I focus on the monitor. "I'm in Los Angeles."

Heather and Tristen's eyes widen. The irony of being so close to where it all started is not lost on me.

"Can we speak to your brother?"

My heart skips a beat, and I pause before coming up with the semi truth. "He's not here right now." Technically, he's downstairs.

"But he is keeping you safe. You left because of Francis

Turner. How do you know he won't find you there?" The Colonel is back.

"I have twenty-four-seven security at the house. My brother is...wealthy." Understatement of the year.

They exchange a look I can't decipher.

Heather focuses on me with something like hope in her features. "Do you have more family there?"

Brooks's face flashes in front of my eyes, followed by Audrey's, and I swallow over the lump. "No." I glance down at my hands.

"I see," she replies. "We have a lot to talk about." The sadness in her tone is apparent. If it's for me not having more family or if she's disappointed in me running away, I don't know, and I'm too scared to ask.

After an elongated pause, I peer back up. "We do."

Tristen leans forward. "Thank you for letting us know that you're safe, sweetheart. With everything that has happened in the last few weeks, it means a lot to your mother and me."

The flutter in my chest caused by his words could mean anything from relief, to utter confusion, to guilt. I'm in desperate need of my emotional purging ritual to make sense of today's onslaught of news. Instead of the frown that wants to take over, I force a smile on my face. "Thank you for not being mad."

"Honey, let's give Rhys and Lilly some more time to talk," he addresses his wife, ignoring my statement of them not being angry with me. They probably are. Who am I kidding? They definitely are.

"Wait!" My shout makes three sets of eyes swivel to me. "Where is Natty?" Why is my little sister not there?

"She's downstairs, watching a movie."

Oh. Does she not want to talk to me?

"She doesn't know you're on the phone. We wanted to speak to you alone first. We told her it's a special day and to rent whatever she wants since your mother and I also had to discuss a lot," Tristen continues.

"Will you call again?" Heather rushes out. "We'll make sure Natty is here next time."

They're not keeping her from me. Relief washes over me like one of my purging showers. They just want her life to remain as unaffected as possible—less unaffected after what she went through herself this week.

"I will." This time the corners of my mouth pull up on their own. I'll get to speak to Natty soon.

I sure hope Nate is fine with that.

"Okay. Good." She's about to stand from Tristen's lap when she turns back, "Oh, and Lilly?"

"Yes?"

"Happy Birthday."

ONCE HEATHER and Tristen leave Rhys's room, George exits as well.

Rhys drops down in his chair, and we stare at each other for six minutes, according to the clock on my screen. For the first time in a long time, I can't read him.

"What are you thinking?" I bite down on my bottom lip until I taste blood. Not being able to decipher the mask that has settled over his face is freaking me out.

He doesn't answer right away. When he finally does, he speaks so quietly that I have to strain my ears. "It's your birthday."

Oh.

"I've never not been with you on your birthday." His voice remains low, subdued.

"I know." I understand what he's really saying. Even before I became a McGuire, we would be together on this day. Heather has photographs from my first birthday to my seventeenth. Rhys is in all of them. Not being with me hurts him as much as it hurts me.

Tears representing a mixture of sadness, guilt, and love are slowly running down my face.

"Don't cry, babe." His expression morphs into something worse than the blank mask. Sympathy and understanding.

"I'm so sorry." I blink to clear my vision.

How do I deserve this boy?

Rhys's genuine smile calms my nerves. "We're still together. Maybe not physically, but we get to see each other. Talk. That's more than the last few years where I was in the same room, but we wouldn't speak."

He's right. This is more than we did over the last few years on either of our birthdays.

"I love you." The words are out before I can think about my response.

"I love you, too." After a pause he adds softly, "Happy Birthday, Calla."

The corner of my mouth pulls up. "Thank you."

We watch each other in comfortable silence until he suddenly perks up, changing the topic. "Well, Mom and Dad sure as shit didn't react how I thought they would." He rubs his neck with one hand, grinning crookedly.

I smirk at his way of shifting the mood. "Definitely not." Where was the yelling, the gazillion questions, the demands to come back? In the end, all they asked was if I was safe.

Rhys laughs non-humorously. "I gave up on trying to figure out why Dad does anything. They're clearly keeping a shit-ton to themselves. And they know we are too."

"I guess." I replay the entire conversation. "Do you think they know who Nate is?"

"Uh, should we be using his name? I mean..." Rhys glances at the ceiling where his camera is hidden. One would never see it if you didn't know. They blend in even better than what Nate has at the vineyard.

"The cameras don't have mics; there is no sound recorded. I think we're good," I explain.

He tilts his head. "Sooo...if he can't listen, why did we hide in the freaking bathroom all the time?" Sarcasm drips from his question.

Unable to stop myself, I roll my eyes and match his tone. "Because a) he could've seen us hovering over a phone neither of them bought us, and b) they could've heard us talking from the hallway."

I swallow the duh.

Rhys cocks his head then slowly nods in an exaggerated motion. "*That* makes sense."

His expression makes me squint at him. "How long have you been awake?" He's acting...drunk. Loopy.

He turns his head to glance at the alarm clock then shrugs. "Long."

"Okay, why don't you get some sleep and call me tomorrow?" I didn't realize how tense I was until all of it suddenly leaves my body. I sink lower into my chair. I'm not oblivious that I will have a lot to explain and work through with my family and friends when all this is over, but the fact that Rhys hasn't broken up with me gives me the strength to keep going.

His scrunched forehead brings me back to the present. "And how am I supposed to do that? You took the burner."

I explain, "The message you opened before I called disabled Tristen's tracker. As long as you don't restart the phone, he can't follow your calls or texts."

Rhys's brows shoot to the hairline. "Was that you or your brother's handiwork?"

"Kinda both," I admit sheepishly. "He told me what routines to use but made me write the execution myself." It's still a miracle to me when the programs do what I want them to do.

"I'm gonna call you Whistler from now on," he announces proudly.

"Whis— Wha—?"

"I told you before, you need some cool hacker name, and you're obsessed with Abigail Whistler." Rhys grins.

I shake my head but can't suppress a laugh. "You're such a dork."

I like it, though. Whistler.

We talk for a few more minutes. He tells me to call Den and Wes. I instruct him to memorize the number I'm going to send him and then delete the text. Even if Tristen can't follow Rhys's phone activity anymore, I don't want to risk it.

For the first time since leaving the house in Westbridge, my heart feels a little lighter.

NATE HAD to leave after dinner. Margot had been blowing up his phone with calls and texts while we were eating, and he ran out of excuses. Mostly because she figured out that he's not in the office—she checked with Hank and called my brother out on it.

Before he left, Nate hooked the little NCC upstairs into its big brother network and gave me full access. When he told me, I couldn't stop myself from clapping my hands and jumping up and down, which resulted in both men scowling at me.

"What? Can a girl not be excited about her tech?" I frowned right back with my hands on my hips. I could hack into the feed and watch Rhys. That wouldn't be borderline creepy at all.

Nate shook his head and walked toward the garage entrance. "I'll talk to you later."

George settled in one of the living spaces downstairs with another book. I have no clue where he always pulls them from. It's like he has a secret bookstore in one of his many green duffel bags.

I am left wandering the mansion.

Not knowing what else to do, I make my way to the library on the second floor. Why rich people all have these massive accumulations of books is a mystery to me, but I won't complain. I'd rather read than watch TV anyway. Shelves dominate the two walls flanking the door from floor to ceiling with the center wall across being one large window overlooking the back of the property. This room is in complete contrast to the vineyard's decor with white shelves and a cognac-colored leather seating area—two big armchairs and a matching couch divided by a low white coffee table—on top of a white-and-beige oriental rug. I browse until I find a section with romance novels. Seeing Rhys earlier has made me miss him even more, and reading about someone else's tragic love story sounds better than wallowing in my head for the rest of the night, questioning if I made the right decision. The books were all published prior to the last decade, which I guess makes sense with the house sitting empty for so long. I pull them out one by one, scanning the back until I find a plot that piques my interest.

Buzz, buzz, buzz.

My groan at the constant vibration coming from my bedside table is muffled by the comforter over my head. Whyyy won't it stoppp?

The book ended up completely sucking me in, and I finished it at three in the morning. Last thing I remember is plopping face-first into the pillows. Pulling the blanket down, I glance to the side where the alarm clock sits next to my phone, alerting me to yet another message. It's past noon.

Oh, crap.

I bolt into a sitting position and reach over, unplugging my phone from its charger. The number of messages on the screen explains why my nightstand sounded like a beehive had taken up residence in the top drawer.

Nate: Good morning, sis. Heading to the office and will try to swing by after work.

Nate: ?

Nate: Lilly, where are you?

Rhys: Hey babe.

Nate: George said you're still in bed. Everything okay?

Rhys: Called G since ur not answering. U sick?

Nate: Call me!

Chewing on my bottom lip, I wonder if George came up to check on me. I should've kept the volume up. I reply to Nate and Rhys that everything is fine, and I slept in. Both text back immediately, and I apologize several times for making them worry. I can't fault them; I would be freaking out if they were the ones not responding.

After breakfast, I trail the second floor twice—both times stopping in front of the same door—before finally gathering the courage to step into Payton's studio.

An easel sits near the window with a stool in front, a small roll table next to it with jars of brushes and paint tubes. There is no canvas on the stand, but several large frames are stacked along two walls covered with white tarps. If it weren't for the layer of dust, you'd think Payton would be home any minute to continue her hobby. A sudden wave of sadness crashes down on me. No wonder Nate hasn't set foot into the house in years. The memories are everywhere.

With my emotions somewhat back under control, curiosity wins out, and I slowly pull one cloth off of a stack of three pictures.

Oh, wow.

I didn't know what to expect. I couldn't draw a stick figure if my life depended on it and automatically assume most people are as artistically challenged as me. Payton clearly wasn't. In front of me is a stunning mountain range with a vast lake. The detail is breathtaking.

I move from stack to stack and marvel at her talent. Most of them are landscapes, but the last pile of smaller canvases contains portraits. The first one is of Audrey; the original picture is taped to the top corner. Behind that, I find a young Nate with Audrey on his lap, looking back at me. The reference photo she used is attached as well. Based on the backdrop, it seems like a professional photograph. The last one is of a small Nate and makes me suck in a sharp breath. He is around five or six, and the similarity between his and my own features at that age is shocking. But that's not what makes me pause. It's the teddy he is holding in the picture.

"Bobo."

The word hasn't fully left my mouth when my head is assaulted by what feels like several icepicks at once.

Owwww.

I grab my temple, and tears pool in my eyes. Why does it hurt so much worse than it used to? A groan breaks free, and I let myself drop to my knees.

Make it stop.

I'm at a small, round table at an outdoor café. Emily sits to my right, Brooks to my left, and they are arguing. My mother's expression is furious, and Brooks looks at her with an equally angry expression. Like in the dream I had at the vineyard, I can't hear what they're saying. I'm clutching something to my chest. Bobo? Brooks places a hand on my shoulder, turning to me with an unreadable gaze. His mouth moves. I try to read his lips, but Emily grabs my arm and yanks me away from him. His eyes turn wide, and he's trying to hold onto me, but I'm no longer in his reach.

CHAPTER TWENTY

LILLY

"Miss Lilly." Someone is shaking me. "LILLY, ANSWER ME!"

I slowly blink, but as soon as the daylight registers, fireworks explode behind my eyes again, and I moan. Why does it still hurt? I squeeze my lids shut and fist the hair around my temple. Maybe if I pull hard enough, it will make the feeling of someone filleting my brain go away.

"Lilly, if you don't tell me this instant what's wrong, I will...." I recognize George's voice, but at the same time, I don't. I've never heard him anything but calm. Angry maybe, but definitely not...panicked.

More awareness starts seeping in. I'm on my side, curled into a fetal position. I slowly open one eye to a tiny slit, letting it adjust to the brightness. The bottom of the canvas comes into view, and the memory floods back.

Emily and Brooks. Together. They sure as hell didn't look like they were still having an affair. The hatred was coming off of my biological mother in waves.

I release the strands of my hair and place my palms flat on the floor to push myself up. When my elbows buckle, hands grab me under my arms and pull me upright like a ragdoll. As soon as I'm on my feet, one eye still slightly open, everything begins to spin, and my stomach churns.

I clamp a hand in front of my mouth. "Oh, God."

Before I know what's happening, I'm airborne, one arm under my legs and one behind my back, pressing against the healing skin. Another wave of agony hits me as the pain receptors in my back join the ones in my head.

Bile rises higher, and it's clear there is no way to stop it. "I...need..." I attempt to communicate the inevitable, but George is already dropping me in front of the toilet in the hall bathroom.

I immediately empty everything in my stomach into the white porcelain. When the retching finally stops, I let myself fall back on my butt.

With my knees bent, I rest my head on top. "Fuuuck," I groan. My clothes stick to my skin, and a shiver runs through my body. I'm freezing, yet I want to curl back into a fetal position and just lie on the cool, tiled floor.

A hand awkwardly pats my head. "Lilly, what happened?"

"Memory," I mumble.

"I'm going to kill Lakatos." Knowing George, he would follow through on his threat, and a smile finds its way onto my lips. His loyalty and protectiveness is like a soothing blanket in my current state.

I slowly turn my head, and his face comes into focus. "It has never been this...bad," I admit.

"Do you want me to call Nate? Or Rhys?"

If I look remotely how I feel, there's no way I can face them. Rhys would instantly be jumping into the Defender and driving to the airport—if not straight to LA. I shake my head, which causes another wave of nausea to hit me. Swallowing, I manage to keep it at bay this time, plus I don't think there's anything left in my stomach.

"I'll tell them myself. Just...give me a few." I close my eyes again.

"Whatever you need, Miss Lilly," my bodyguard, and now nurse, concedes.

IN THE END, George refused to let me stay on the floor and walked me to my room to take a shower, only leaving after I reassured him that I'd be fine.

My body is covered in the remnants of cold sweat, and not aiming properly as my breakfast made a reappearance has left me with chunks of toast and banana in my hair.

So gross.

Emerging an hour later and feeling almost back to normal, I have a foot on the top step of the staircase to the first floor when George's voice drifts up to me.

"I tried. He refuses to come earlier." Pause. "No, there is nothing I can do. If I press any harder, he'll cancel the meet altogether." Pause. "No, there is no point for you to come right now. She is taking a shower."

Listening to his words, my pulse speeds up.

That traitor. He called Nate after all.

I make my way downstairs, not hiding my approach. George is standing in the large kitchen, already facing the doorway as I enter.

I cross my arms over my chest, glaring at the man with the large scar. I'm no longer scared of him. Unfortunately, my accusatory glower doesn't do anything to the former Marine. George continues his conversation with my brother without a blink of emotion, making the pounding in my ears become even louder. A sound resembling a growl escapes me, but George is still unaffected.

"She just walked in." He listens to something Nate says. "Yes,

I agree. Okay, I'll make the arrangements. We should wait until I'm back, though, in case—of course." His lips form a disapproving line, and he holds the phone out to me. "Here."

Is that directed toward my brother or me?

I hold the device to my ear. "Hey."

"Don't you hey me, Lilly Ann," Nate's barked tone comes through the earpiece, and I automatically scrunch my shoulders up. "What the fuck happened?"

"Uh..." My own anger shrivels to the size of a dried raisin. Why is he so mad?

"George calls me out of a meeting with an investor, informing me that he heard a thud upstairs, and when he went to check it out, he found you unresponsive on the floor. I'm asking you again. What the fuck happened?"

I cover the speaker and hiss, "Why on earth did you have to call him out of a meeting?"

This time, George's expression does change—and not in a friendly way. "Because it took me five minutes to get you to move, let alone react. I was about to call an ambulance."

My heartbeat seems to slow. Five minutes?

"Oh."

"Yes, 'Oh!'" Nate scoffs on the other end. He gentles his tone. "Tell me what happened, please."

"I had another migraine," I mumble.

"But you never passed out before," my brother states, wanting confirmation.

"No."

"What did you remember?" George inserts himself, and I put the phone down on the kitchen island, pressing the speaker button. "It was about Emily and Brooks."

I recall everything, including what I saw in the café and how Emily dragged me by the arm.

"Could they just have been arguing?" my brother questions, still convinced their affair was ongoing until his mother's death.

I shake my head, not that Nate sees it. "I don't think so."

Brooks's face appears in front of my mind's eye. "Brooks looked..."—I struggle for the right word—"almost desperate. Like Emily shut him down on something. I don't know, Nate. I was scared."

"Scared of whom?" George pulls my attention to his face.

I scan every inch of the man's features. Between his menacing glare and the scar, he can terrify everyone without saying a word, yet I've never felt as afraid as when I sat there between my parents.

"I don't know," I admit. "Maybe of what they were fighting about? Why can't I hear anything in these memories?"

"I will make sure to ask Lakatos that."

"Speaking of..." Nate interrupts my stare-down with George. "I want you to see a neurologist."

My gaze shoots to the phone. "What? Why?"

"It's one thing to have headaches with these flashbacks, but passing out is a whole different story. We need to make sure there is nothing...uh, missed."

Missed? Like something is not right with my brain? What else could be wrong with my head? I've already lost years of my memory. Black spots appear in my vision just as another possibility strikes me like one of the migraines itself. "You think I have a tumor?" My eyes widen in horror as my voice goes three octaves higher. They'd crack open my skull and literally rearrange everything inside, not just figuratively. What if it's terminal? I don't want to—

Nate interrupts my internal rant. "It needs to get checked out. We'll make the necessary arrangements for the day after George gets back. I want him to talk to Lakatos first. See if that is something he knows about and is...*normal*."

I cover my face with my hands.

Why is this happening to me?

"We should talk to Tristen."

My hands instantly drop, the panic of something growing in my brain forgotten, and I stare at the man in front of me.

"About what?" My brother vocalizes my own question.

"I never worked with Lakatos. Tristen has. He might be aware of that reaction and if it is to be expected," George clarifies.

I want to laugh at the absurdity of his suggestion. Heather would lose it. No matter what happened between all of us, I'm her little girl. She'd drag me back to Westbridge and lock me in my room in order to watch me 24/7. The fact that I'm eighteen and can support myself would be of no consequence when it came to my health. I'm so not going to tell them.

Their reaction isn't the only one that makes a pit form in my stomach. I refuse to even think about telling Rhys. I can't do that to him. I can't make him worry about anything else. I just can't.

"Let's see what we can get out of the memory doctor. Maybe he can reverse what he did." Nate sounds hopeful.

"Yeah, let's see." I don't expect anything to come from the meeting. I don't want to be negative, but I also can't bring myself to hope.

LATER THAT AFTERNOON, I work up the courage to call my best friend. I only type in her number three times before I finally hit the call button. Rhys talked to her, and Wes must've helped curb her best-friend-disappointment rage, because Denielle only chews me out for about fifteen minutes for packing up and *running*. She can take care of herself; let Turner try—her words, not mine. After that, she informs me that she has decided to book a flight and visit Charlie over spring break next week.

Spring break. I'm only excused from school for another nine days. What happens afterward, I have no idea. I haven't thought that far ahead, but I also didn't plan on returning to Westbridge until Nate and I have our answers and the people I care about are no longer in the crossfire of the press or stalked by a dead ex-Army Ranger. Not that Turner has physically threatened anyone, but we still suspect him to be at least involved in some of the articles. Plus, he faked his death. Who does that? And why?

I shake my head. Francis Turner is on the other end of the country. Hopefully, once he realizes I'm no longer in Westbridge, he'll leave my family alone.

You're delusional, the voice in my head shouts at me through a bullhorn, and I flinch inwardly.

I'm on my way to the third floor when I pass Brooks's home office and stop in my tracks. Curiosity to see the one room I haven't entered yet is making my body tilt toward the door.

Taking a deep breath, I turn to walk away but then halt again. Nate did not specifically tell me that I can't go in there. It's just that *he* doesn't enter his father's personal space.

I watch my hand reach out and clasp the handle. The metal feels cool against my skin, and I tighten my fingers, ready to push down.

"Miss Lilly!"

Shit.

I jerk my arm back and face George, who's jogging up the stairs.

"Yes?" My face is flushed. Did he see what I was about to do?

"Your brother wants you to call him on this number." He hands me a piece of paper.

I scowl. "Why a new number?"

"I believe he procured a second device to ensure there is no trace of you on his cell phone. It seems Miss Margot is beginning to question her fiancé's absence," he states.

I take the note and walk to the room Nate had turned into my mini NCC. Sitting behind the desk, I pull up the call function with the appropriate routine to mask the Caller ID and dial my brother's new number. A grin spreads across my face as I wait.

He answers after three rings. "George?"

"It's me," I say smugly.

"How—" Confusion clouds Nate's tone until understanding sets in. "You're getting good, sis. I'm impressed."

I chuckle. "Well, if you already have to get a second phone to erase me from existence, I might as well help with that."

"You updated the program yourself to match the parameters?"

"Yep."

A whistle comes through the earpiece. "Remind me never to let you near my computer again."

"Too late. You gave me access," I taunt.

"Ha. I did, which is why I wanted you to call me."

"Oh?" What has he planned now?

"We still need to figure out what to do with Psycho Barbie since you won't let me have George pay her a visit." He's joking about George, but the anger is apparent in his voice.

I roll my eyes even though he can't see me. George torturing her would give me some satisfaction, but it would also put me on the same level as her. "What do you have in mind?"

He gives me directions to a folder on one of the servers, and I suck in a breath at the title: Katherine Rosenfield.

"What's this?"

"This is what I pulled off her phone before I wiped it. You might find it interesting what she was up to when she was not with Rhys," Nate announces nonchalantly. "Call me when you see something you'd like to use."

What?

But he's already gone. I stare at the icon. I have no idea what to expect. When I finally click on it, I gawk at everything loading in front of my eyes. "Ho-ly shit!"

I scroll through what seems like over a hundred pictures with the occasional video in between. With every person I recognize in the photos and video stills, my pulse speeds up more. This is insane. Katherine has fooled everyone. At the very bottom is another folder labeled "E.S." Head slightly tilted, I let the curser hover for a moment before double-tapping on the track pad. My hands instantly fly to my mouth.

No way!

Fumbling with the keyboard, I redial my brother, who picks up after one ring. "You found it, huh?"

"Is this real?" I can't keep the shock out of my voice. This is a complete game-changer. It will destroy Katherine. She will no longer be the Queen Bitch—if she'd even stay at Westbridge High.

"Sure is. You recognize the other person?" Nate isn't asking for me to tell him; he already knows whose face is in the middle of my monitor. He just wants to confirm that I know who it is.

"I do," I croak.

"Soooo...any idea what we should do with it?" His voice has a sinister undertone, which is matched by the diabolical grin spreading across my face.

It's revenge time.

Tapping my index finger to my bottom lip, I ask, "How do I access someone's social media accounts?"

THE WAIT after Nate and I finalized the plan is excruciating. I am as giddy as I am nervous. They won't be able to trace it back to me, and let's face it, Katherine deserves every bit of what is coming to her, but a small part of me still revolts against being the mean girl. Katherine Rosenfield and her bitch squad have brought a whole new side of Lilly McGuire out. I still prefer to be kind to people, but some simply don't deserve mercy.

As Rhys and I talked last night, I was dying to tell him about what was going to happen in a few hours, but I bit my tongue. Him waking up to an entirely new scandal was too enticing.

So, when my phone rings at 5:22 Pacific Time, I am already sitting in front of my computer, a steaming tea next to me, and scrolling through the comments that started about an hour ago.

. . .

MEGHAN LG: Kat, what the hell?

   Kellan J: WHAT THE FUCK!

   Random football player: DAYUM, that's better than porn.

   Owen J: @Jager, you tapped that? High five, bro!

   Lisa Bennett: OMG, she needs help. This is disgusting.

   Random WH student: Why would anyone post that?

   Nora Ross: @Lisa, @Meghan:: Has E seen it yet?

   Meghan LG: I doubt it. She's going to lose it after what she did for that bitch.

   Kellan J: Someone take that shit down before McGuire sees it!!!!!!!!

   Nora Ross: @Jager:: Ohhhh, scared you'll piss your pants again?

   Kellan J: Fuck off!

I ANSWER the incoming video chat on the second monitor on my desk. "Hey, you're up early." I lace my greeting with innocence, even though I have the urge to bounce in my seat.

"That was you, wasn't it?" Rhys stares at me with a crooked grin. His voice is still raspy from sleep, hair sticking up in all directions, and he's shirtless.

Licking my lips, I trail down his chest to his muscled stomach that's peeking out from the comforter. A whole new sensation stirs inside of me, and I press my thighs together. What I wouldn't give to be able to—

"Calla!"

My eyes snap up. "Yes?"

"Up here." He circles his face but doesn't hide his satisfaction at me ogling him. "Admit it. You're responsible for this shitstorm."

I shrug casually. "If you mean Katherine Rosenfield's *coming out* announcement... Yep, that would have been me." I finally let the glee show and clap my hands like a lunatic.

Rhys shakes his head, laughing. "How the fuck did you get those pictures? And that video?" The awe in his tone makes me draw my shoulders back. Not that I had anything to do with the actual recording—that's all on the Wicked Bitch herself.

"Remember when Nate mentioned he pulled all her pictures off before wiping it last week?"

"Yeah?" He cocks an eyebrow.

"That's what he found on it."

"Oh, she is so fuuuuucked!" he sing-songs.

At that moment, someone storms into Rhys's bedroom. "Bro, wake up! Did you see—? Oh, you're already awake." Wes's voice carries through the speaker.

Rhys lazily glances past the screen at his best friend. "Good morning to you, too."

Suddenly, the camera shakes, and Wes appears at the corner of the frame. He has thrown himself down next to Rhys and is now also leaning against the head of the bed.

"Holy hell, Lil! How the fuck did you do that?" Rhys turns the phone to the side so I can see the other boy better.

Pride surges through me, and the little bit of regret is forgotten. Revenge is a bitch, and Katherine Rosenfield just fell off her throne as the reigning queen. Okay, I might have shoved her off. I brush some pretend lint off my shoulder and smirk. "It's called skill, my friend."

"It's called The. Shit! Jager blew up my phone to confess. He probably thinks telling me gives him a pass from getting his ass beat," Wes cackles.

"Nah, I don't give a fuck about that," Rhys answers, bored.

"Do we know who that is in the video?" Wes looks genuinely curious.

"Elisabeth Shaw." I throw the name out and watch the wheels in both guys' heads turn. When it clicks, their eyes nearly bulge out of their sockets.

"NO WAY!" Wes shouts.

"FUCKING HELL!" Rhys rubs his hands over his face.

I shift back to my other monitor and pull up the post I

published under Kat Rosenfield's name on her various social media accounts. The announcement is accompanied by a new album I copied to each platform.

I had to make sure *everyone* gets to see it.

The one thing I made sure of was that everyone outed was of legal age, including Katherine, when the video was taken. That's the one reprieve I gave her.

KAT ROSENFIELD:

I've been living a lie for the last three years, and it's time to admit to what I've known deep down for so long. I'm a nymphomaniac. I used Rhys McGuire to uphold an image I no longer can portray with a good conscience. To fill my life with everything I desire on a daily basis, I need to shed myself from the secrets of my past. In this post, I publicly admit to seducing every single one of the pictured individuals. However, none of these male objects have fulfilled my needs as satisfying as my dear friend and spiritual guide.

UNDERNEATH THE POST is an album containing twenty-seven photos and one video. Each picture displays Katherine with a different guy in various make out poses: tongue down each other's throat, the dude's hand on her boob, her hand rubbing along a guy's hard-on, some even completely naked. But the video is what tops it all. I had to watch it twice before I could believe what was playing out in front of me. I expected a lot from Rhys's ex, but that was not it.

The four-minute film starts with Katherine in a very compromising position between a pair of female legs. Based on the moaning, Rhys's ex found a taste for what she was doing with her mouth, and the other person holding the phone seemed to agree. "Ohhh, yes, Kitty Cat. Just like that, baby. Mhmmmm." After about a minute, Katherine lifts her head, wipes at her chin, and wiggles her fingers toward the camera. The phone switches hands, and after some shuffling, the second star of the home-made porn appears on the screen between Katherine's thighs.

That's when I made the video stop and zoomed in on the face. Elisabeth Shaw. My former friend, Emma Shaw's, mother.

CHAPTER TWENTY-ONE

LILLY

EVEN THE ARTICLE ANNOUNCING THAT *LILLY MCGUIRE WENT into hiding out of shame for seducing her adopted brother* couldn't undermine my satisfaction as I watched the comments multiply exponentially on *Katherine's* posts.

Every so often—whenever I came across an especially cruel remark—a pang of guilt crept in. Should I have felt this proud of causing Katherine's downfall? But then, all I had to do was lean against the back of my chair, and the still-present pain of my healing burns was enough of a reminder. Katherine Rosenfield deserved everything coming to her.

Sadly, by Saturday afternoon, someone—most likely the Wicked Bitch herself—disabled all her accounts. Another round of pride hit me, though, because it took her that long to get back in after I had changed her password and put extra authentication on it.

I wish I had recorded Denielle's reaction when she found out what I'd done. She called me immediately, and her three-minute happy dance included twerking, some very explicit cheers that would make half the football team blush, the running man, and a grand finale of *the worm*. In the end, we were both out of breath —Denielle from her spontaneously choreographed routine and me from laughing.

For the next few hours, random giggles bubble up in my throat whenever I visualize my best friend moving in front of the camera. I wish Rhys and Wes had seen it.

I miss my friends.

After I no longer have new comments to read through, I randomly snoop through folders on my brother's server. Maybe I can help with finding some answers. I'm three layers deep when my phone rings with an incoming video call: Rhys.

Weird, we didn't plan on talking until later.

I grab it from the wireless charger on the desk and swipe right. "Hey, what's—"

"Mom and Dad need to talk to you."

A pit the size of Nate's lap pool opens up in my stomach. "Why?" My voice instantly goes hoarse.

He draws in a long breath. "One of the families contacted Camden, demanding for you to be interrogated again. She wasn't aware that you're no longer in Westbridge and wasn't happy when she found out."

"What? Which family?" The hand not holding the phone begins to tremble, and I curl and uncurl my fingers in an attempt to make it stop. It's no use.

"No fucking clue. Dad just barged in here, demanding to talk to you. NOW!" Rhys exaggeratingly imitates Tristen's order.

Shit.

"Okay, uh...you want me to call back once they're there?" I shove my twitching fist between my thigh and the chair.

"No, I'll take the phone down. Hold on." The motion on the screen—Rhys taking two steps at a time down to the first floor —would make me seasick if I wasn't already nauseated from his news.

"Lilly is on the phone," he announces, and the device changes hands. A stern-looking Tristen sitting at his desk appears on the screen.

This is so not good.

"Sweetheart." He greets me with his usual endearment, but there is nothing pleasant attached to the word.

Tristen is shaking. What the hell? Wait. I tilt my head. He wasn't moving when he took the phone from Rhys. That's when I realize it's my nerves causing the device to literally vibrate. I clench my fingers around it tighter in an effort to stop the trembling.

"W-what's going on?" I address him just as Heather steps behind her husband and leans down to be in the frame.

"Hi, sweetie."

Unable to respond, I force myself to smile at my adopted mother.

"Agent Camden informed us that Ava Conway's father is demanding for you to be questioned further. There has been no progress on the case, and he is accusing you of protecting The Babysitter," Tristen explains.

I'm gonna throw up.

Oblivious to my inner panic, Heather adds, "We let Vivienne know that you are staying with family due to the incident at school, and you would be available via video conference if needed. Mr. Conway has no basis for his accusation. Ava is not a minor and has shown no interest in pursuing any actions regarding her case. From what we were able to find out, she is not even in the same state as her father."

Ava Conway was older than me when Nate...I force myself to complete the sentence...*took her.* But she's been off the radar for years. From what I found in my research, her parents have been divorced since she was a little girl. This makes no sense.

I inhale and hold the air in, forcing my rapid breathing to slow. Slightly calmer, I concentrate on the present again.

"What did Agent Camden say?" I suck on the inside of my cheek as I wait for their answer.

"Mr. Conway was contacted by a member of the press. He was told about evidence that you are faking your memory loss, and you are protecting the kidnapper." Tristen stares at me intently, and my heart sinks.

He knows.

At that moment, something crashes in Tristen's office, and a roar of "FUCKING TURNER!" bursts through the speaker on my end. All three of us jump at Rhys's outburst.

"Turner?" Heather narrows her eyes to somewhere behind the phone.

"Who do you think is behind that? A member of the press," Rhys mocks the wording. "Well, fuck that shit. Turner is trying to flush Calla out because he knows she's no longer here."

"Why would this man do that?" Tristen inquires suspiciously, and I tense.

Do not take his bait, Rhys. Please, please, please. I'm begging in my head.

There is a moment of silence until he answers, "Probably for the same reason some chick kills your cleaning lady and steals a teddy bear." He's playing the *you-have-your-secrets-we-have-ours* card.

I don't know how long we can keep this up. My phone starts shaking again, and I lean it against one of the monitors, sitting down on both of my hands this time. Thank goodness I answered on the small phone screen. The built-in camera on the desktop would have shown my whole body, revealing my physical state of panic. There would have been no hiding anything.

Heather's mouth turns to a slit before she focuses back on me. "I spoke to Vivienne, and she asked for you to come in once you are back in town. She wants to ask you some questions about both of your kidnappings."

"Okay," I choke the word out. The last thing I want is to answer any question regarding Nate.

Suddenly, the camera on their end moves violently, and I am face to face with Rhys, who doesn't look at the screen. "Now that that's all cleared up, there is nothing else to discuss." He flips around and marches out of the room and up the stairs.

As soon as he clears the threshold, Rhys kicks the door shut with one foot.

"MOTHERFUCKING COCKSUCKER!"

He knocks something off his desk, and I cringe. It doesn't sound like it was anything overly breakable, and for a moment, all I see are strands of his brown hair as he grabs fistfuls with the phone still in one hand. I wish I were there to wrap my arms around him and hold him. It becomes more and more apparent that my decision to run has made everything worse instead of better.

Eventually, his green eyes lock on mine sadly. He's back in the same position on his bed as this morning when he first called.

"Babe, this is getting out of hand."

"I know." I can't get my voice above a whisper.

I FIND George in the motor pool—calling it a garage would be like saying the Vanderbilt estate is a cute little cottage. His upper body is in the backseat of his RAM, one foot on the nerf bar, the other balancing in the air. He is maneuvering something large around in an attempt to get it under the bench.

"What are you doing?" I step behind him to get a better look.

He jerks, and the object slams into the opposite door with a clang. "Good Lord, Miss Lilly."

Unable to suppress the chuckle for actually startling the scariest man alive, I apologize behind a cupped hand. "Um, sorry."

He adjusts the large black box I can finally identify as a rifle lockbox. "More firepower? I thought you have at least two guns on you at all times." I purse my lips mockingly, remembering when Rhys told me about George's arsenal in Morristown.

"It's a custom design. I ordered it before Nate sent me to

Virginia. It fits under the backseat with the opening in the front. It's connected to a button in the dashboard, which will automatically unlatch the lid, and a mechanism inside moves the rifle out. That way, I can reach for it without having to bend back."

I lean in. "That's pretty impressive. Tristen would love that setup. He has to open his *manually*," I say, exaggerating the last word with a teasing eye roll.

"Did you need something?" George steps down from the truck.

Oh yeah, the reason I came to find him. Part of me wants to ignore all of it and be a normal girl, even if it's just for a few hours. But I don't get the luxury. Turner, Camden, the upcoming meeting with Lakatos, the possibility of *something else* being wrong with my brain...none of that will go away, no matter how much I want it to.

"Actually, yes." I swallow down the burning sensation in my throat. How do I phrase this? "It seems Turner contacted Ava Conway's father, who now demands for me to be questioned. I wasn't sure if I should call Nate or not." I steady my voice, suppressing the quiver that wants to break through at the thought of being interrogated.

George snaps to attention and reaches for his phone that's laying in the front seat. He doesn't have to wait long for my brother to answer. "We have a situation." Pause. "She is fine, but I would suggest for you to come by on the way home from the office." Pause. "That is unfortunate. Okay. Call me when you can."

After shoving the device a little too forcefully into the side pocket of his trademark gray cargo pants, George finally makes eye contact. "Nate is unable to come by. His little lap dog is glued to his side after not showing up in the office this week."

I narrow my eyes at the man in front of me, and he amends, "Hank Todd."

Oh.

. . .

NOT KNOWING what else to do and unable to look into Turner myself—my brother hasn't covered that aspect in his lesson plan —I aimlessly trail the mansion. The walls are starting to close in, and I've only been here for four days. George and Nate are adamant that I am not allowed to leave the property. The sudden onslaught of emotions knocks me back on my heels. What if Turner now goes directly after my family and friends? Did I make a mistake by coming here? I was so focused on my revenge against Katherine and the relief of Rhys not breaking up with me that I neglected all the other potential consequences. Why is Turner after me? What is my connection to a man that faked his death when I was just a kid?

I find myself back in front of Brooks's office. George is downstairs and won't come looking for me anytime soon. I shouldn't, but even as I'm still thinking the words, my hand reaches out.

If it's locked, I'll go to my room.

My fingers close around the cool metal of the handle, and it eases down without the slightest resistance. Letting the door swing inward, the hairs on the back of my neck stand like someone is watching me. There are no cameras in the house; Nate doesn't know that I'm here. Brooks was my father, too. I don't need to feel guilty.

My pep talk isn't working, and the guilt of my trespassing is taking over every cell of my body. I scan the inside from where I'm rooted to the floor. Brooks's home office does not look like the rest of the decor. Most of the mansion is bright, soft colors on the walls, light wood tones for the furniture. My biological father's personal space is... I try to find an appropriate description, and all I can come up with is 1950s Ad Agency. The walls are dark gray. The spaces around the big picture window hold identical shelves. Both pieces appear to be custom made; they're not attached but fit perfectly. Acorn boards are connected and held up by thin polished black metal bars with cabinet doors where the two lower shelf boards would have been. Centered in front of them is a massive, mid-century style desk made of the same wood. A high-back office chair behind and two low-sitting armchairs in front—all three of the softest black leather—complete the design.

I close my eyes and count to five. Nate never specifically said I wasn't allowed in here. I'm not doing anything wrong. Why do I feel like such an intruder?

Because you are, my inner voice sneers.

Three more breaths and my feet finally cooperate. I take one step after another until I'm in the middle of the room. The crew hired to prepare the house for my arrival must've cleaned this room as well since there is not one speck of dust anywhere. I spin in a circle and discover more identical shelves around the door. Books and different memorabilia decorate all four, while the two walls to the left and right contain large paintings that look suspiciously like the ones I found in the art studio down the hall. I wonder if Payton had a hand in decorating or if they hired someone.

I scan the books—some biographies, some business-related, no fiction anywhere. I stop at a small bronze Viking statue on a warship. The detail is captivating, and I have to force myself to move on. The more objects I discover, the more I come to the conclusion that they must be souvenirs from their travels. There is a glass with black sand, a mask, seashells, and a stand with several pipes.

When I reach the desk, I move the chair backward and slowly lower myself down. Placing both hands flat on the desk, I scan the room once more.

This is where Brooks used to work when he was not in the office. Did he read Emily's letters here? Nate's words come back to me: *I found a stack of letters and pictures in his desk at the house.*

My gaze falls to the drawers on either side of me. Swiping my palms on my pant legs, I glance back and forth between them. Screw it. I carefully slide the top right one open, unsure of what to expect. I don't anticipate finding all the answers in the first drawer I look into, yet there is a nervous flutter in my stomach.

All I discover are blank legal pads.

"What are you doing?" My brother's voice makes me jolt in the seat, and my head snaps toward the door.

"Nate." I'm like a deer in the headlights.

"What are you doing in here?" he repeats, not taking his eyes off my face. It's as if he refuses to acknowledge the room I'm in.

He wasn't supposed to come over. Shit.

"I...uh..." I stammer as I push away from the desk. When I step in front of him, all I manage is a strangled, "I'm sorry."

His eyes are still fixed on me, but his tense features soften. "I haven't seen this room in a long time."

"I shouldn't have come in. I—"

"You were curious about your father. I understand." Nate's tone is calm, yet his rigid posture screams *on edge*. This is where it all began for us, where he found out about me.

I gently place my hand on his chest and push against it. He lets me move him farther into the hallway, and I close the door on my way out. As soon as his view of the office is blocked by the wooden barrier, his stance relaxes, and he unfastens his stare from my face.

"I'm sorry," I say again, a little more confident this time.

"Don't be. I...it's..." He sighs, grasping for words. "You can enter any room in this house. I would never stop you. It's just...I..." He trails off again.

"*You* can't go in," I finish the sentence for him, and he nods.

I hope that one day, when we have our answers, things will change—that Nate can heal.

I FOLLOW my brother to the first floor where George is waiting for us in the kitchen. Sitting at the breakfast nook, I give both of them a detailed rundown on Heather and Tristen's news.

As I recall everything my adopted parents told me, Nate

grips the tabletop, his knuckles turning white. Anxiety is radiating off of him, and I'm not sure if this is because of Turner or because it's the first time we're actually talking about one of the other girls.

"You believe Turner is behind it?" George looks at me for confirmation.

My gut feeling is as strong as ever. "Who else would have reason to contact one particular family—not even the family, just Mr. Conway, and cause him to raise questions?"

"Mr. Conway could simply want to seek closure, and with no real progress in the case—"

"Conway is a drunk. There is no way he came up with that on his own. He hasn't spoken to his daughter in years," Nate interrupts.

A flush of adrenaline shoots through me, and I stare at him. "How do you know that?"

My brother holds my eyes. "After you *resurfaced,* I looked into everyone. I hadn't checked on them since uh...you know. After I brought you back to Santa Rosa and you started talking to me, I made sure they were all *okay.* I wanted to know where to find them when I turn myself in."

We have never spoken about it this openly, and somehow, I didn't think Nate was already making plans for... My mind refuses to finish the sentence. I reach over and place my hand over his, needing the contact. He glances from my hand to my face and back, turning his over and interlacing our fingers.

"You know that I will make it right. You trust me?" He searches my eyes.

My throat thickens, and I swallow hard. "I do."

Nate focuses on the third person at the table but doesn't let go of me. "Conway is a useless drunk; there is no way he is doing this out of worry for his daughter. His wife ran off with another guy when Ava was three. Ava bounced between both homes until she filed for emancipation. I haven't been able to find anything on her in the last few years. She has no bank accounts, no social media, and she definitely has not spoken to either of her parents."

I'm stunned about the details he found out about Ava.

George nods. "What are we doing about it?"

"Camden agreed to delay the questions until you'd be back in Westbridge?" Nate asks in confirmation, and I bob my head up and down, tightening my fingers around his. At this moment, he's my anchor. My big brother. Who will go to prison.

"As long as she doesn't change her mind, it doesn't matter then. By the time you go back, everything else will be over as well," my brother declares.

When I'm ready to go back, he'll have already turned himself in.

CHAPTER TWENTY-TWO

HER

IT TOOK GRAY TWO DAYS TO FIND A PILOT WILLING TO TAKE MY *substantial donation and take us to California without putting any of the passengers on the flight manifest.*

At this point, I have spoken to the informant seven times to get updates on Lilly's whereabouts—not that he has been able to give me anything but assumptions. Nate's socialite fiancée was of more use. Her social media post—a pouty-lipped Margot in a pool chaise, tagging Hamlin with the caption: "Fiancé on another business trip until Friday"—made it clear that he hasn't been around.

Brainless bimbo. Not even her non-profit work can make up for the air in her head that's only good to keep those ridiculous curls in place.

Gray limps after me into the beach rental my little helper procured for us. He grunts under the weight of our luggage, his leg bothering him with every step.

"Oh, shut up. The knife went straight through the muscle. I didn't even nick a blood vessel. You've had worse," I snap after he moans again, making his way with my bags to the bedroom I chose.

I dial Elise to check on my pawn. I had to leave him behind in Virginia since Doc refused to knock him out for the flight. Apparently, it could overwhelm his system with the increased dosage of paralytic drugs and anesthetics he's received in the last few weeks. Not that I care about his body, but on the minimal chance I require him to convince Lilly to do what I want, I have to keep him alive a little longer. Such a nuisance.

Elise assures me he is compliant and everything is good. I confirm her statement by pulling up the cameras Gray installed for me without her knowledge before we left.

"Elise?"

"Yes, ma'am?"

"Why is he reading a book?" Meaning, why the fuck are his arms not in the restraints?

The sharp inhale on the other end of the line tells me that she did not expect me to know that.

I speak very slowly. "If you value your position,"—sub-context: your life—"I highly suggest that you rectify your lapse in judgment immediately."

"Yes, ma'am."

I hang up before she can say anything else and watch her hurry into the room and rip the book out of his hands. His brows furrow, and her gaze flits around the room as she mumbles under her breath. His mouth sets into a grim line, and he holds out his hand for her to tie it back down. Always the gentleman.

Once I am satisfied that my order was followed, I find Gray in the kitchen, popping more painkillers.

"Do you think that's wise with your history?" I arch an eyebrow.

"I wouldn't have to if you would keep your temper under control," he mumbles between gulps of water.

Ignoring his insolent remark, I take the car keys off the counter and toss them at him. "Make yourself useful and do recon on the Hamlin estate. I want to know everything."

CHAPTER TWENTY-THREE

LILLY

I AM WIDE AWAKE. NATE'S WORDS ABOUT AVA KEEP PLAYING on repeat in my head. Hearing about her childhood—besides what my brother had done—made needles prick in the back of my throat. What happened to her?

Nate headed home around nine, after Hank started spamming his phone. My brother had given him contracts to go over so he could get away. Unfortunately, Hank figured out that said contracts had already been reviewed and started angry-texting. When Nate didn't respond immediately, he called. Twelve times.

As we watched Nate pull out of the garage, George excused himself to go to bed. Somehow, I never considered that the man requires sleep. Most of the time, he is so inhuman that it wouldn't have been a surprise to find a secret battery compartment under all his cargo gear.

By midnight, I give up. I swing my legs out of the bed, put on Rhys's old hoodie, and pat down to the second floor to my little computer room. Sitting down behind the desk, I reach for one of the laptops and press the space bar. Besides the missing wall monitors, it's an almost identical setup as at the vineyard. I love it.

I have no particular goal in mind when I open up the console, but my fingers guide me to the folder my brother mentioned earlier—the one he added after I came to Santa Rosa. It wasn't hard to find once I knew it existed. I laugh at myself as I briefly glance at the mouse sitting next to my keyboard and then ignore it. Like brother, like sister. Who needs a mouse?

A few commands later, I'm scanning the multitude of documents Nate compiled. He has detailed information on the other four girls, and I find myself reading file after file. He didn't exaggerate. He pulled up everything down to school records to check how they're doing. Meredith and Chloe seem to have overcome *everything* without long-lasting issues—my mind refuses to use the k-word. Both have good grades, play extracurricular sports, and their home life looks...normal. Rose is the youngest and most recent. She sees a therapist regularly, but other than that, she appears to be fine as well. None of the records indicate that her experience traumatized her.

I dip my head and close my eyes, letting the relief wash over me. They're okay. I seem to be the only one who didn't make it out of this unscathed, aka lost my memory and was transplanted into a fake family. Maybe by changing his approach?...Tactic?...Routine?... Shit, I can't even think about it. What kind of person am I for wanting to be completely oblivious to what my brother has done? Audrey's face flashes in front of my eyes, and my throat thickens at the thought of what her loss did to Nate.

When I get to Ava's file, there is not much to see. She dropped off the face of the earth after becoming a legal adult. From the few records there are, her upbringing doesn't seem to have been a happy one. Her father has several DUIs and one domestic violence charge. Her mother worked one minimum-wage job after another, sometimes several at once. They lived in a rundown one-bedroom apartment in a bad part of town. The guy her mother left her father for was arrested for breaking-and-entering when Ava was eight. No mention of another relationship since.

Where are you, Ava?

I sit at the desk, palms flat on either side of my keyboard, and stare at the wall opposite me. Getting more insight into the girls' lives has forced me to acknowledge what Nate did. I'm not able to deny or ignore it any longer, nor what the inevitable consequences of his actions would be: Nate will take responsibility and go away.

The selfish side in me doesn't want him to leave me. The bond we've formed over the last few weeks runs as deep as if we had known each other for years. The connection was instant, which is probably why I was never afraid for my life. He's my big brother.

Pride for him making it right makes my lungs expand. He had started setting everything in motion before I even mentioned him taking responsibility. I tell myself that I'm not going to lose him forever. Having all these thoughts running through my head also brings to the forefront how little I know about my biological father.

Before I can change my mind, I push the chair back and stand up. Nate's reaction to me being in Brooks's office still has me rattled. He appears so...*normal* all the time that I forget how deep his wounds lie. But he said I can go into any room in the house. Decision made.

THIS TIME, I don't hesitate to push the handle down. Flipping the light switch next to me, the room illuminates with several small lamps strategically placed around the space, giving it a warm feel. I hadn't noticed that there's no overhead light when I was in here before.

Suddenly unsure, I turn in a circle. I eye the desk then let my gaze wander to the file cabinet under the shelf closest to me. I doubt the desk holds anything of consequence, and I let my feet carry me the few steps toward the shelf. This is the first place one can see that the house stood empty for years. The cleaning crew did a great job on the surface but neglected cleaning inside the cabinets. The little gap between the doors has let dust in over the years, and the binders are covered in a thin layer. I grab a handful and lay them out in front of me—déjà vu.

Similar to the vineyard, most of the folders are case files. Some contain more financial statements, but they are either— what I deduce—the family account or Payton's personal spending—mortgage and car payments, random expenses. Then I flip a page and pause, my fingers turning into a vise around the paper. Holy—it's the same amount. The same large sum that was deposited into Brooks's account every so often.

He took the money from their family account?

My heart is pounding against my rib cage. This is huge. I fish my phone from the center pocket of my hoodie but remember I can't call my brother. He messaged earlier that Margot is staying at his house tonight.

SHIT!

I could wake up George, but what is he going to do? I slam the paper on the floor. Damn it!

Frustrated, I stand up and move to one of the shelves by his desk, leaving the files where they are. I need to keep myself busy until I can at least call Rhys.

I open the doors to that cabinet and come to a halt once more. Photo albums. Three black leather albums. I pull the top one out, expecting it to contain some Hamlin family pictures, but instead, I stare at myself.

What the hell?

With shaking hands, I skip through the pages faster and faster. It's me. It's *all* me. Holy hell, Brooks has more photos of my childhood—pre-six years old—than Heather and Tristen. Cold sweat starts forming on my forehead. How is this possible? There's even a picture of Rhys and me as toddlers. We're sitting together on a blanket in the park, a ball and some snack cups between us, a set of legs on either side of us. I let my index finger glide over the photograph, stopping on Rhys's face. A flutter in my chest replaces my rapid heartbeat. I start inspecting the photo closer when it hits me: this was taken from afar, through a lens. Based on the angle and focus, I'm sure of it. Did Brooks take it, or did he have someone follow me as a kid? And if so, why? He was still seeing Emily—or that's what we've been thinking.

Crap, I need to talk to someone about this.

I tap the screen on my cell phone that I dropped on the floor next to me and mentally add three hours to it. It's 3:47 a.m. in Virginia. My thumb hovers over the call icon until the little clock shows 3:49, and I click the side button, locking the device again. Ugh! If I wake Rhys up now, I'll just worry him more than he already is.

A yawn slowly builds up, and I press the back of my hand against my mouth, trying to suppress it. My eyes feel heavy, and when the second yawn escapes, I push myself up. There is nothing I can do for at least another couple of hours. Resigned, I leave everything where it is and head to the third floor to give my body what it obviously demands.

Buzz, buzz, buzz.

Buzz, buzz, buzz.

"What the hell?" I dig the heel of my hand into my eyes.

Buzz, buzz, buzz.

Buzz, buzz, buzz.

It's not a text message. Peeling one lid open, I squint at my phone slowly moving across the nightstand.

Buzz, buzz, buzz.

Buzz, buzz, buzz.

What is that? Groaning, I lean up on one elbow and reach for the device before it can tumble off the edge it's getting dangerously close to. I unplug it from its charger and flop back onto the pillow. Blinking my second eye open, I stare at the screen.

ALERT: Lilly subroutine activated. Message sent.

Huh? Oh.

"Oh!" A rush of adrenaline hits me like a cross punch to the jaw. It worked. Holy crap, it really worked!

Sitting up, I throw back the covers and take three steps at a time down the stairs, almost running into George, who's on his way to the first-floor staircase.

"Miss Lilly? Is something wro—" His confused question drifts after me as I speed-walk with my phone still in hand past him.

I drop into my chair and pull the keyboard close. With the computers hooked into Nate's private network, I don't have to go through the same motions as when I hacked into the security feed to his LA. house. I simply open the app for the system at the vineyard and select the camera to my bedroom.

There he is. My brother sits on the foot of my bed, staring at his phone.

A broad grin spreads across my face. I did it. I jump up and down in my seat, doing a little happy dance. Yessss!

"Miss Lilly?" George's voice startles me, and my head jerks toward the door, a blush heating my face.

"Sorry," I mumble, sitting down on my hands.

George chuckles. "No need. I enjoy seeing you happy."

At that moment, an incoming call pops up with my brother's name. I peer over at the security feed, and he is now standing in front of the bed, phone pressed to his ear and staring at the camera in the ceiling. He mouths, "Pick up!" and I bark out a laugh, accepting the call.

"How did you know I'd be watching?"

Nate smirks. "You're not the only one with alerts, little sister. I got a notification as soon as you activated the camera."

"Hey, no fair," I explain in mock outrage.

"That was quite a surprise." He ignores my pretend anger.

"Well, you told me to write a routine that gets activated by a voice command," I justify myself.

"I did," my brother confirms. He looks back up and smiles. "Thank you."

Warmth floods my body, and my mouth turns upward as well. "You're welcome."

When Nate kept me busy at the vineyard, one of his exercises was a subroutine for the camera and mic in my room. I chose to write a voice-triggered notification alert for the mic. He probably assumed I'd program something and test it myself to see if it worked. But instead, I set the trigger for "little sister," hoping Nate would eventually cause the alert to go off. Obviously, I had no idea when or if it would ever happen. When the words were spoken inside my room, it would send a text message to him: **How dare you enter my room without my permission! JK, big brother. (; Just wanted to tell you that I am glad we are finally a family again. XO, your little sister. L.**

Words I felt at the time but wasn't able to admit out loud yet.

My brow furrows. "Wait, what are you doing at the vineyard?"

Nate sighs. "Margot wanted our lunch with J and Cece to be up here on the terrace, so we took the jet for the day."

"Must be nice to be rich, huh?" I say cheekily.

"You are just as rich; don't forget that," he counters with humor.

Shit, I did forget.

"I'll be back later tonight," he assures me, and a calmness settles inside my chest.

The corner of my mouth pulls up until the memory of last night's findings surges to the surface like an erupting geyser. The statements and photo albums with my childhood pictures are still scattered over Brooks's office floor. I gasp, and Nate's eyes narrow at the camera in the ceiling as if he can see me.

"Lilly, what's wrong?"

OF LIGHT AND DARK • 223

"I need to show you something, but I don't know if we should do this over—"

"Darling?" a female voice comes through the speaker, and Margot appears in the frame on the camera. "What are you doing in here?" She glances around, confused. Understandable since, technically, the room Nate is in is just a random guest room.

"I had to take a quick call." Nate disconnects the phone, and I watch him usher her out of my bedroom, glancing up one last time.

Crap. I wanted to confess at least where I was last night, even if we didn't have time to discuss the rest until later. It feels like every time one of us makes progress, something happens— in this case, brunch at the other end of the state—and delays things. I push back from the desk a little more forcefully.

I should've woken him up last night.

George is leaning against the doorframe, watching me with an indecipherable expression.

"What?" I raise my eyebrows, waiting. Does he want me to elaborate on what I found?

The corner of his mouth tilts up. "It's good to see you and Nate together."

Standing up, I make my way over to him, point my finger, and circle it toward his head. "George, you're doing it again."

It's his turn to scowl. I clarify with a grin, "You're smiling."

My bodyguard just shakes his head, turns, and leaves, but not before I see his mouth quirk up at the corner. As he walks away, I hear him calling out, "You are quite the brat, Miss Lilly."

Rolling my eyes, I follow. I can make it until Nate is back later.

CHAPTER TWENTY-FOUR

RHYS

"He has pictures of me!"

It's Sunday morning, and after three days and several not-so-subtle comments from Natty, I finally took a shower. So, when the vibration of my phone on the nightstand drifts into the bathroom, I drop the towel and dive across my bed to answer the call.

Thank fuck my room is on the second floor, or Lancaster would have a front-row seat to my pussy-whipped nakedness right now. My best friend would simply barge in, and Denielle is off to Georgia, getting some ass herself, which leaves only one person to call me.

"Who?" I'm confused.

"My father!" Lilly snaps like I was supposed to simply *know*.

"Which one?" I huff out with a laugh.

"RHYS!"

Oh-kay, we're not in a joking mood.

"Sorry, babe. I'm assuming you're talking about Brooks?" I force myself to be serious, even though I think my pun was pretty good.

"Yes, Brooks. He has hundreds of pictures of me. *You* are in some as well!" she barks.

"Me?" That gets my attention.

"I found photo albums in his office. He has more pictures of me than Heather and Tristen. I just went back and am flipping through the ones I didn't get to last night. There are so many!" Her tone pitches toward the end. She's not quite hysterical, but it won't take much more.

"Anyone else? I mean, besides me?" I don't like this. How could he have gotten these photos—Emily, a P.I., himself?

Pages turn hastily in the background, and I tap the fingers of my free hand against my naked thigh.

I should probably get dressed.

I picture her, sitting on the floor, surrounded by photo albums—similar to the day I found her in her bedroom. "Emily and Henry are in some. I found one with all of us at what looks like a carnival," Lilly says absently. More rustling. "Oh, my God!"

"WHAT?" Come on, woman, speak!

"Brooks!"

"What about him?" I grind my teeth. I really don't care for cryptic responses when she's across the country and I can't do shit about anything.

Yup, I'm still bitter about it.

"There is a picture of Brooks and me. It's when he gave me —" She cuts off, something clatters, and I have to pull the phone away from my ear at the sudden noise.

"Ahhhhh!" a scream rips through the speaker, followed by another thud and then...whimpers. "Make it stop. Please m-make it s-stop."

The fuck—?

My heart starts racing. "Calla?!" She's not answering. "BABE, ANSWER ME!" I'm standing butt-naked in the middle of my room, shouting into the phone.

Fuck, fuck, fuck.

"LILLY!" I press the device harder to my ear and tug on my

hair with my free hand. "LILLY, ANSWER! Please." I'm begging more to myself than her since she's unresponsive. Motherfucker. When her moaning cuts off, so does my breathing. I can't draw any air in.

The worst possible scenario plays out in my head. Fuck. The pounding against my ribcage causes physical pain, and my gaze flies around the room as if I'd find the answers to what happened taped on my wall. What the fuck am I doing? I need to get help. I hang up and dial George, putting the call on speaker so I can cover my naked ass with the sweats I dropped on the floor earlier.

"Rhys?" he answers on the second ring.

"Something is wrong! She stopped talking and started screaming." I barely get the words out as I suck oxygen into my lungs.

"FUCK! Not again."

My stomach churns. George doesn't curse, let alone use the F-bomb.

Wait. Again?

"Where was she when she called?" I hear footfalls in the background.

"Brooks's office." Finally covered, I pick the phone back up and disable the speaker. I hope Mom and Dad didn't hear anything, or I'll have to answer a lot more questions.

I watch the blinking dots on my alarm clock disappear and light back up seventeen times before George speaks again.

"Miss Lilly!" Pause. "LILLY! Don't do this to me again." Another Pause. "Lilly, your brother will not be happy. Come on, wake up. Please." The last word is spoken with such desperation that my entire body begins to shake. I tighten my hold on the phone to not drop it as I sink to my mattress.

"George, what the fuck is going on there?" I try not to yell, but the rest of the house probably heard me anyway. My pulse is thrashing in my ears, and all I can do is clench and unclench my free hand, waiting.

"George?" Lilly's faint voice comes through the speaker.

Oh, thank fuck!

Air finally enters my lungs again, and I can feel them scream in relief.

"Yes, I'm here. You gave us quite the fright again, Miss Lilly." George's tone is gentle, a side I have not yet seen of the man.

"Us?" she mumbles, confused.

"JESUS CHRIST, GEORGE! PUT ME ON FUCKING SPEAKER!" I'm losing my shit. They must've heard me because there is rummaging, and then their voices are clearer.

"You were on the phone with Rhys. He called me when you passed out." His soothing tone does the opposite for me.

"What the fuck do you mean she passed out? Calla, are you okay?" I press my free hand against my chest. I'm not going to make it to my nineteenth birthday at this rate. My heart will give out before.

"I'm fine." Her groggy voice manages to calm my nerves a little, but not enough to stop the trembling in my extremities.

"Miss Lilly," he warns her.

"I haven't told him," she whispers to her bodyguard.

"Told me what?" Motherfucker. More secrets? I stand and start pacing the length of my room. She's not talking to me again. The silence on the other end tells me that they are either in a standoff or somehow quietly communicating.

"Told. Me. WHAT?" I bark into the device. I'm losing my patience—with both of them.

"I passed out after my last migraine," Lilly finally admits meekly.

"YOU WHAT?" Awesome, now I seem to have developed belated puberphonia.

"I am meeting with Lakatos on Thursday. I will discuss this new...development with him. In the meantime, Nate also set up an appointment with his neurologist for the following week."

My knees buckle mid-step, and I sink to a crouch, white-knuckling the device while my other hand is back at pulling

228 • DANAH LOGAN

strands of my hair out. "What does that mean?" My question is not more than a barely audible croak.

"We don't know. But we want to talk to Lakatos before drawing any conclusions."

Before drawing conclusions? The reason behind my rapid pulse shifts, and I see red. "Are you fucking kidding me?" I seethe into the phone. "She passed out. TWICE! Draw some conclusions. You don't pass out from a freaking memory if nothing is wrong with you!"

"Rhys," Lilly pleads with me. She sounds better than a minute ago, but I can hear her exhaustion in my name. "I promise you that I will have it checked out. There is nothing we can do right this second. I can't check myself into the emergency room here."

I let myself fall ungracefully on my ass and drop my forehead to my knees. She's right. The press would be all over it. *Lilly McGuire Suddenly Checks Herself into an LA Hospital*. Not to mention that George's presence would cause a whole other round of questions.

Fuuuck!

"I get it, babe. I do. But..." I inhale for four, hold, exhale for four. "Shit. I can't sit here and do nothing."

There is silence on the other end, and I fight the urge to hang up and drive to the airport.

"What was the memory about?" I grit out the question in an attempt to distract myself from the other *topic*.

"I saw Payton."

Huh?

"What do you mean?" George appears just as confused.

There is rustling on the other end before Lilly speaks. "Here. I found this picture of Brooks and me in his albums. It's the day he gave me Bobo."

"Can someone please switch this damn call to video?" I don't mean to growl into the device, but I can't help it. Frustration is making my jaw clench.

"Oh! Yes, hold on." An incoming video call from Lilly's phone pops up, and I accept, disconnecting George's number. Her face fills the screen, and I take in her disheveled appearance.

She's fine, my ass.

I bite my tongue. I'm sick of fighting, but there will be some conversations when we're in the same time zone again.

"Show me the damn photo, Calla," I order. My ability to communicate calmly left sometime between Lilly screaming and passing out and the understanding settling in that there might be something seriously wrong with her.

The screen tilts, and a photo of a young Lilly and a blond man comes into focus. It's the first time I'm seeing Lilly's biological father. The similarities between him and his children are instantly visible. Nate and Lilly have the same light hair and similar complexion, though Lilly is on the fairer side. Since the picture was taken with a frontal view of Brooks, Lilly partially from the side and back, his hazel eyes catch my attention immediately. He is holding the teddy bear I remember Lilly dragging everywhere for years.

Lilly comes back into view. "It's Bobo, isn't it?"

"Yes."

"How does Payton fit into this?" George inserts in a tone I can't interpret.

Lilly takes in a deep breath. "I'm not sure if it was the same day. I think it was, though, because I was holding the bear, and Brooks was by my side. The more I think of it...it has to have been." She holds the picture up again. "He is wearing the same clothes. I turned toward Emily, showing her the bear, when I noticed a woman in the distance. She was partially hidden behind a tree, watching us. I've seen enough pictures of her. It was Payton."

Lilly's gaze flicks between her bodyguard and me. "That has to mean that she knew about me, right?"

"Do you remember anything else?" George probes.

She hangs her head, defeated. "No."

"Where is Nate?" I ask, suddenly wondering why no one informed him of his sister's findings or losing consciousness.

"He's at the vineyard with Margot and Julian," Lilly elaborates. "He'll be back later tonight."

Rustling indicates George has gotten up off the ground. "I will give him a call. He needs to know what happened."

"Can that wait until he's back?" Her eyes are begging the man I can't see.

"No," is his last word before fading steps come through the speaker.

We sit in silence, and I watch her stare somewhere past the camera. When her gaze settles back on me, she whispers, "I wish you were here."

My heart breaks. "Give me the address, and I'm there by tomorrow." I would be.

She sighs. "I can't. We can't risk tipping Turner off."

"Do you really think that dude won't find you? Or do something to flush you out? It's clear that he has an agenda. *You running away* will not stop him!" All restrain breaks, and I can't stop myself. "And since we're already on the topic. What's going on with finding your answers? It seems like you only have more questions. Should I assume you'll hide in La La Land indefinitely?"

Lilly's eyes grow wider the more words leave my stupid trap. By the time I'm done, I'm breathing heavily again, and tears run down her cheeks.

Fuck.

"I, um...I think I'm gonna check if George got a hold of Nate," she stammers.

"Cal—" But before I can apologize, she disconnects, and I'm staring at my background picture—a selfie Lilly and I took one night, lying in her bed.

My leg kicks out and connects with my chair, slamming it into the desk. My room will be an assembly of broken furniture soon.

. . .

I TURN the knob without knocking, and my father's head snaps up at the unannounced intrusion of his office. It has always been an unspoken rule for anyone to announce themselves—even Mom. However, I don't give a shit right now.

"I want you to call Lakatos!"

Dad's jaw drops, and his eyes widen. He composes himself quickly, followed by taking me in from head to toe. I haven't bothered putting on a shirt, my three-day-old sweats are stained, and my hair is a semi-dried mess from almost ripping my scalp off from finding out Lilly has kept more secrets from me. Not to mention listening to her scream in agony. My fists at my side twitch, and the motion doesn't go unnoticed.

"Who is Lakatos?" My father's tone is even and gives nothing away. He's good, I'll give him that.

"Don't fuck with me," I snarl.

He cocks his head, doing another scan. "What happened, Rhys?"

He doesn't ask how I know the name?

Screw it. If Lilly decides to freeze me out, I have no reason to protect her damn secrets. "Your little brain-fuck with Lilly's head is making her pass out whenever she remembers something." I'm borderline yelling.

"What is she remembering?" The question is more careful this time.

"Does it matter? I fucking listened to her scream in pain before passing out. Call that motherfucker and HAVE. HER. FIXED!" The adrenaline raging through my veins is causing the all-too-familiar body trembles to start again, and my knees threaten to buckle.

Dad slowly pushes back from the desk and walks around to where I'm standing. His hands settle on my shoulders as he looks at me with a somber expression. My chest is heaving, and it's written all over his face that I'm not going to like his next words.

"Rhys, what was done to Lilly's mind is irreversible."

My legs give out. Bending forward, I clasp my hands behind my neck and start rocking back and forth.

No, no, no.

Behind my eyes, I see Lilly's unconscious body, lying on a floor, one day not waking up anymore. I'm starting to feel sick and begin to dry heave in the middle of my father's office.

"Rhys. Son!" I hear him calling out for me but don't have it in me to respond. Eventually, she'll pass out, and no one will be there to help her. She'll hit her head, or fall down the stairs, or— one scenario worse than the next plays out in my head. Another round of retching makes my stomach cramp.

Suddenly, hands grab under my arms and pull me up like a ragdoll. Dad pulls me over to the sofa, where he drops me with less care before sitting down next to me. My elbows rest on my thighs, and I bury my face in my palms. "I'm going to lose her for good." My muffled mumbling is accompanied by my eyes beginning to water.

Fuck, now I'm also crying like a freakin' baby.

My father's hand comes to the nape up my neck, where he squeezes ever so slightly, almost like a massage. "You will not lose her, son."

"How do you know?" My voice is hoarse.

"Because the two of you were meant to be together from the moment Emily dropped her off at our house and your mother placed her in your crib. Lilly was crying nonstop; we tried everything for hours to calm her down. You were never like that, so we were completely out of our element. In a final attempt, Mom put her down in your crib; you had just woken up from your nap. As soon this little tiny baby girl was lying next to you, you smiled at her, and she stopped. She fell asleep, and you watched her the entire time she slept."

I turn my head to see if he's shitting me, but he's sincere. At eighteen years old, I feel like I'm finally forming the bond with my father I should've had years ago.

"Why did you make me leave?" The moisture in my eyes spills over, and I swipe it roughly, embarrassment heating my face.

His expression shifts, and he's about to shut down.

"DON'T!" I order. "Don't you dare freeze me out, too."

He understands and dips his head in a fast motion. "There is a lot you don't know—"

"Whose fault is that?" Anger overtakes my senses again, and I'm grateful for the change. I don't like losing it in front of people, least of all my father.

He sighs. "I don't know how you found out about Hector, and I won't ask—*yet*. I have kept a lot from you—not just you, but also your mother—to keep this family safe. In my line of work, I've made enemies, and I was prepared for that. When my family was at risk, I handled it the way I knew how, which in hindsight was not the best solution. I..." My father swallows hard. "I pushed you away to not make you a target as well. Your feelings for Lilly made you reckless. The fact that everyone believed she was your sister was never a concern for me; that would've been an easy fix, telling people she was adopted. But I couldn't risk my son's life being threatened. It was only a matter of time before Lilly would be in the crossfire again."

"What crossfire?" He gives me answers, but at the same time, he speaks in riddles that raise more questions.

"I don't have all the facts either, Rhys. I have some, but a lot are suspicions. Some of them are probably accurate, but without confirmation or proof, I won't cause my family unnecessary panic."

"So, essentially, you're not giving me anything. AGAIN!" I bark the last word at him.

"I can give you one answer." His gaze jumps back and forth between my eyes. "I've never not cared for you. You are my son, and I would do anything to keep you safe. My methods may not have been the best, but I always knew where you were and made sure you were safe."

The steadily building rage deflates, and for the first time since being a little boy, I hug my father. He wraps his arms around my shoulders, and I feel him shudder.

I haven't gotten any answers for Lilly, but I have my father back.

CHAPTER TWENTY-FIVE

LILLY

NATE DIDN'T TAKE THE NEWS WELL—THE MIGRAINE-MEMORY *or* me passing out. Again. He made up some emergency in the office and got everyone on the jet within the hour. From the moment George told me he's on his way back, I haven't been able to sit still. He is bringing too much attention to himself. What if Margot checks with Hank again? She's been annoyed for days. She could follow him here. She'd find me, and Nate would have to turn himself in sooner. My thumb won't stop flicking against the rest of my fingers. Back and forth, back and forth.

In an attempt to distract myself, I go to the theater room and turn on a movie. It doesn't work; I couldn't tell you what the movie is about if I tried. My mind constantly goes back to Rhys. Is he right? Has my running put everyone more at risk? Should I let him come to LA? We could spend spring break together, and he could get to know Nate. A flutter in my chest makes me smile. Then, a new picture flashes in front of my eyes: Turner waiting for Natty during school. But that's not where the images end: Turner running Wes off the road with his car. Turner following Rhys to the airport and coming to LA, exposing where

I am. *Or* Turner hurting Rhys when he refuses to tell him where I am. Each scenario is worse than the next until I'm covered in sweat and am sitting bent forward, clutching my stomach with both arms. Inhale, exhale. Inhale, exhale.

That's all I do until my brother finds me. The door flies open, and Nate scans the room. When his eyes settle on me, he's at my side in three strides. Crouching down, he gently forces my chin up with his hand, and we lock eyes.

"Talk to me, sis." His careful tone is my breaking point.

The tears I've been holding in spill over, and I press my mouth together.

"Lilly." My name is just a whisper of a sound.

I let my lips part, and that's it. All my worries spill out. I word-vomit everything. The memory, the phone call with Rhys, my fears about Turner, and all the fucked-up scenarios I've cooked up in my head in which he kills off everyone I care about.

I've gone off the deep end.

Nate listens to all of it, not interrupting me once. When I'm running out of steam, he gets up from his crouch and sits down next to me.

"I'm so sorry you are going through all of this because of me." His arms wrap around my shoulder, squeezing me to his side.

My eyes flutter closed, and I lean against him. I'm emotionally drained. "I'm going to lose him, Nate," I mumble, sinking further against my brother.

"You won't," he soothes me, the words just a murmur.

I blink against a flickering light.

Where the hell am I?

I try to move, but an arm holds me in place. What the—? Slowly adjusting to the brightness, I'm able to open one then both eyes and glance around. I'm still in the media room. On the screen plays a muted action movie, bright explosions being the reason for my temporary inability to see. My head is fuzzy, and my eyes burn from my crying spell. Turning my head to the side, I take in Nate's slumped form—he's out like a light. I carefully disentangle myself from his large frame and move into the hall-way, closing the door behind me quietly.

I tap the screen of my phone. It's 4:21 a.m.—past seven in Westbridge. I stare at the clock for a whole minute before I make my decision. Screw it. Before I can stop myself, I pull up the recent call log and click on Rhys's name. It rings five times, and with every beep, my heart rate increases. He's not going to answer.

"Calla?" Rhys's groggy voice comes through the speaker.

"I'm so sorry," I begin to sob.

"Wha—?" He's instantly more alert. "What happened?"

"I'm sorry I ran. I was so scared Turner would come after you. Natty can't defend herself. I kept picturing him hurting you t-to g-get to m-me—" My words break off, and I lean against the wall opposite the theater, sinking to the floor.

The silence, on the other end makes my fear become a real-ity. I've lost him. I've kept too much from him.

"I...I'm not sure what to say, babe. I understand why you did it. I do. But—" He exhales slowly.

"B-but?" I hiccup, pressing the back of my hand to my mouth.

"I'm...pissed. I'm not gonna lie to you. You know that's the one thing I'll never do again. It's supposed to be you and me. *Together!* But you don't talk to me; you keep hiding things from me. I love you more than anything, but I... I can't handle any more surprises. I don't want to go to bed wondering if you're still going to be there in the morning. Or be close to a heart attack every time my phone rings, thinking this time you're gone for good. When you stopped screaming yesterday, I couldn't breathe. It was discovering your crashed Jeep all over again. I thought you had died with me on the phone, and I couldn't do shit about it."

Rhys's tone is getting angrier the more he speaks, and the fear of him leaving me overtakes every cell in my body. *You left him first*, the voice in my head sneers at me. *He has every right to break up with you.*

My hands shake violently, and I can barely hold the phone up.

What have I done?

The door across from me opens, and Nate looks down, hair disheveled and with worried eyes. Footsteps from the other end of the hall alert me to George's arrival. I've woken them both up.

I pull my legs close and let my forehead drop to my knees, ignoring the two men in the hallway with me. "Please don't leave me," I whisper into the speaker.

"I...fuck." Rhys exhales a sharp breath. When he doesn't say anything else, I lose all self-control.

My not-so-silent crying turns into uncontrollable panic. I rock back and forth while pressing the phone harder against my ear. "I'm sorry. I'm so sorry..." I can't get anything else out other than my hysterical apologies.

"Fuck!" he curses. "Calla. Babe? Put Nate or George on the phone. Please." His tone is softer than before but detached at the same time.

He doesn't even want to talk to me.

I hold out the device without looking who takes it. As soon as it's out of my hand, my arms bend, and with my elbows pressing against my knees, my hands find my head, and my nails dig into my scalp.

"Yes?"

Nate has the phone.

Silence. "Did she sound okay to you?" Sarcasm drips from my brother's question. "Yes." Deep breath. "George did everything he could without spooking the guy. He won't meet sooner." Pause. "I get it, man. She is my sister." Longer pause. "We're taking care of her." *Since when does Nate talk this civilly with Rhys?* "This won't make it go away. You get that, right?" More listening. "Mhmm. You get four days." This is more of a warning. "Friday. We'll be in touch as soon as George is back." Sigh. "I will."

I take in the conversation on this end without moving out of my balled-up position. Four days? What's happening on Friday? Suddenly, two arms pick me up behind the legs and shoulder blades, and I'm airborne. My eyes fly open, settling on Nate's face, and a squeak escapes my throat. My body is expecting the familiar pain to set in, but after a few steps, it registers. My back doesn't hurt—not like before. With all the emotional chaos, I didn't pay attention to my healing injuries. The physical tension leaves my body, and I cover my face with my hands. This is all too much.

MY BROTHER DEPOSITS me on a barstool at the kitchen island and places my phone in front of me. I'm numb. The panic, the fear, the guilt...it's all gone. Did my mind finally break completely?

Out of the corner of my eyes, George gets busy with the kettle, and a few minutes later, a steaming cup of Earl Grey is placed in front of me. My bodyguard remains leaning against the kitchen counter by the stove while Nate sits down next to me at the island, rubbing his hands up and down my spine.

"Rhys is asking for a break, baby sis."

My bottom lip begins to quiver, yet the emotion behind it is not there. It's like the connection between the limbic system and the rest of me is severed. When I remain mute, he continues, "You and I have put him through a lot the last few weeks. I'm as much to blame. We've been selfish assholes." A non-comical snort escapes him.

The rational part of my brain still works. He's right. I've only thought of myself—what I needed.

"The guy can only take so much, and as much as I tried not

to like him, I do. And I get it. He loves you. *He has loved you forever*. I would lose my shit, too, hearing what he did yesterday. Hell, I packed everyone on the plane without a real excuse and left them standing at the airport. And you're *only* my sister, *not* my soulmate." Nate pauses, waiting for me to say something.

I can't. Rhys wants a break. It doesn't mean we're broken up. He loves me. It's just for a few days.

My brother continues, "I told him we would call him Friday after George gets back. That gives him time to collect his thoughts, and it gives us four days to find as many answers as we can, including who Francis-Fucking-Turner is. Then, you and Rhys will work it out. One way or another."

"You think he'll still be there?" My voice sounds like a recording.

"He's angry and worried, but he made me promise to tell you one thing."

I turn my head toward Nate, eyebrows raised.

"He loves you, and you're stuck with him."

Those few words bridge the gap between my body and my brain. It's like a wave of emotions crashes down on me, and I'm suddenly drowning. Sadness, guilt, anger, fear, worry... I can't filter through them fast enough.

I cover my mouth with my hands in an attempt to muffle my cries. Nate reaches out and pulls me close by the back of my head until my face is against his shoulder.

"Give him time," he murmurs next to my ear.

I nod against the fabric of his shirt.

He holds me until I regain some control and pull back. George is still in the same spot, watching me with a wrinkled brow.

"Okay. Let's get to work, then." Nate lets go of me and gets up.

. . .

AFTER FORCING down breakfast which consists of tea for me and half a gallon of coffee for Nate, he follows me to Brooks's office. He remains standing in the doorframe for several minutes before slowly setting one foot in front of the other.

Seeing him struggle to be in here, I hold my breath. I pick up a stack of paper from the floor. "Do you want me to bring everything downstairs? Or—"

"I'm fine." His words are clipped, and it's clear that he isn't.

"Nate, I really—"

"I said I'm fine!" he barks, and I jerk my head up and down. I'm not going to argue with him.

He comes over to where I piled the statements for Payton's and the family accounts, and I hand him one containing the transaction amount.

My brother scans the papers, reaching for another and another before looking up. "He transferred the money for whomever he was paying off out of the joint account he and my mother kept for the property expenses." His expression ranges from confused to pissed off.

I nod and whisper, "Does that mean Payton knew about it?"

Nate's mouth turns down. "I always assumed the family accountant took care of most of the stuff. Both my parents had their own money, and they shared a joint account for all the big expenses—properties, cars, etc. My college tuition came out of the trust my grandfather set up when I was born. Audrey had her own. After my grandmother passed away, my grandfather called a family meeting where he went over everything the Altman's own. During that, my parents also laid out to me how our family's finances were set up. But they never specifically told me who managed them. After my father..." His hands tighten on the stack he's holding. "After he died, our accountant handled everything and just handed me the papers. I never read any of them. I was too—"

"It's okay," I interrupt him. He doesn't have to spell it out. "Do the accounts still exist?"

Nate looks up. "No. Everything got consolidated into mine or your trust, which is why I didn't recognize the account number the money came from. But—" Then his eyebrows scrunch together.

"What?" I ask, unable to follow his thoughts.

"Frank knew."

"Who?"

"Frank. Our accountant. He handed me all the papers, which means he at least saw the will if not even had something to do with setting your trust up. That motherfucker. He kept that to himself all these years."

"Are you sure about that? Why would he keep that from you?"

Nate jumps up and starts moving between the door and the desk. "I will find out." He pulls his phone out of his pocket and dials someone. The other person picks up after several rings.

"Hank! I—" Hank cuts him off, and my brother gazes at the ceiling. The voice on the other end is raised, but I can't make out what he says. Nate barks, "Yes, I can read the clock, asshole." He pulls the phone from his ear and glances at the screen before holding it back up. "It's 6:23 on a Monday; you should be up by now. Stop whining. Now, what I was going to say is I need you to find me the number for Frank Hollancomp." Nate listens. "I know he retired three years ago, but since we still send checks his way, his number and address are—" The knuckles on his fists turn white. "Because I'm busy. Just do it."

Nate hangs up without saying goodbye.

"Do you always talk to Hank that way?" I ask carefully with a raised eyebrow. I've seen so many sides of my brother by now, but this one is new, and I'm not sure how to react to it.

"Huh?" He focuses back on me. "Oh. Hank's been exceptionally bitchy lately. No clue what crawled up his ass."

"You sure that has nothing to do with you?" I keep my voice low and prepare myself for another outburst. I don't want to directly accuse him of being at fault for how Hank acts; I haven't seen much of it firsthand. But Nate has been absent a lot, and I assume Hank has had to pick up a lot for him.

He shakes his head, starting to flip through the statements again. "No, it started a few months ago."

"Hmm...okay then." I'll leave it at that.

My brother gives me a hug and informs me that he'll work on tracing the money. He hasn't done anything on that end since he ran into a dead end with the last shell corporation. He tells me he'll be at his house for a bit, and I should call if I need anything. He'll be back in a few hours.

CHAPTER TWENTY-SIX

LILLY

THE DAYS WERE BLENDING TOGETHER. NATE WENT BACK TO his *keep-Lilly-busy* strategy. By the end of Tuesday, I felt like some type of accountant—forensic, maybe? Who knows. Thank goodness I like numbers. He made me go over Brooks and Payton's financial statements. All of them.

After I had left California, Nate uploaded every shred of paper from the vineyard to his servers, and I probably went through more than half a decade of Altman-Hamlin personal expenses. It gave me insight into my biological father's habits, but that was pretty much the extent of it. Besides the outgoing large—six-figure—amount coming from the family account and the smaller—five-figure—ones going out from Brooks's, everything was normal. I began to suspect that Nate was simply trying to keep me occupied, which worked during the daytime. At night, not so much.

My sleep was shit, and when I did manage to doze off, I would wake up before the sun was up, my mind instantly spiraling. I'd been replaying the previous months in my head over and over. Not just since I started remembering, but before. Rhys has always put me first. After years of protecting his parents' secrets, I forced him to keep mine. He had to isolate himself from his best friend because of me. The more my mind ran with it, the deeper the pit in my stomach became.

I couldn't fault Rhys if he wanted to continue the break indefinitely.

Grabbing my phone almost hourly, I started typing several text messages to him but deleted them all. I promised my brother I'd *adhere to the radio silence*, as he phrased it, and give Rhys the space he asked for. What was Rhys doing right now? Instead, I spent the nights tearing the place apart for more clues while Nate was busy following the money trail. Hank and Margot kept him equally busy, and he could only work on our leads when they slept. Whenever I saw him, the circles under his eyes became more pronounced. I didn't like it.

Tuesday evening, George informed me over dinner that he'd be gone most of the next morning to prepare for his trip north to meet Lakatos. He'd be leaving around five in the morning *to meet someone* (who the hell meets that early—I probably don't want to know) and then run errands. He'd be back after lunch to finish packing.

This would be the first time I was alone in the mansion. At the thought, my pulse immediately sped up. I was safe here, but the emptiness of the ginormous house—even though George was still in front of me—made my stomach churn.

What was my gut trying to tell me?

ON WEDNESDAY, I wake up at the crack of dawn. Surprise, surprise. Not.

I glance at the clock; it's not even six yet. George is already gone. My hands clench around the comforter. I'm alone. I slept about three hours after spending the night unsuccessfully digging through more storage bins in the basement. My eyes are burning, and even the eyedrops George handed me are not helping.

I've been here for a week, and with no specific task for today, the walls are closing in. I press my palm to my chest, but my lungs constrict even more. I need to get out of here. NOW!

That's how I end up parked, before eight—in my new, white G-Wagon—in front of Flakes, a small café the search engine spit out when I looked for a place to get tea. Not that the twenty-three flavors of assorted black teas my brother stocked the kitchen with weren't enough. I simply needed a destination—a *lame* excuse to leave the property. Driving here, I marveled at how the streets were crowded like downtown Westbridge during Black Friday. Los Angeles is so different from everything I am used to; it's hard to wrap my head around it.

Sitting in the car, I can't bring myself to get out. "Nothing to Lose But You" by Three Days Grace plays through the speakers, and the outside becomes blurry. I haven't cried since Monday morning, but the lyrics hit deep, and a sob escapes me. I sink low in my seat, wrapping my arms around myself, and let the tears fall.

After the song finishes, it takes me over fifteen minutes before I can force myself to open the driver's side door. My face is dry, and I check in the rearview mirror that I don't look too much of a mess. My brother's order to remain inside the house at all times replays in my head. He's so going to kill me when he finds out. And he will find out; he's Nate Hamlin. Maybe I should go back. I pull on the handle to close the gap again, but before the lock latches, I pause. I need this, or I will go crazy. *Crazier*. Or I'll cave and end up calling Rhys. I push the door back open.

The street is not two miles from the ostentatious neighborhood of mansions where I've been hiding. The sidewalk is busy, people on their way to wherever, passing the fancy boutiques, restaurants, and cafés lining both sides. Even if Turner were to suddenly show up, he couldn't do anything without attracting attention. And I would make sure to bring attention to myself. A woman in a business suit passes and holds my gaze. A new thought slams into me: what if someone recognizes me? My one hand that's on the steering wheel tightens, and I scan the faces passing in front of my car. Are they looking at me longer than usual?

Shit. What am I doing?

I release the door handle and steering wheel to cover my face and take one deep breath. No one is looking for me here. I'll be okay. Pulling down the baseball hat I found in one of the many bins, I climb out of the Mercedes. I parked close to the entrance of Flakes and am inside within less than twenty feet. My shoulders relax instantly.

Scanning the inside, I miss Magnolia's. This place is nothing like it. Where Magnolia's is cozy and inviting, Flakes looks like a spaceship stuffed with junkyard scraps. A blindingly polished gray concrete floor, shiny silver high-top metal tables, white metal bar stools, white napkin holders on each table—also metal. The artwork on the walls consists of abstract photographs. The random shapes—whatever the objects in front of the lens were— are either too close, too blurry, or too over-exposed. Between the tables are life-sized—surprise, surprise—metal sculptures made out of random...well, junkyard crap. I almost turn around and walk back out but then stop myself. I'm here for a change of scenery and tea. Who cares what the ambience is like? Stepping up to the counter, I scan the menu hanging on the wall behind it. The pastries in the display look mouthwatering, and I order my usual tea and add a chocolate chip scone to it, because why not?

Keeping my face hidden behind a curtain of my hair and the low-hanging hat, I move to the side. I wait for the barista to pour water over the teabag and place my treat on a plate. She pushes both toward me with a smile, and I reach for them. I stifle the sigh of relief when I have my order in front of me and no one has called out my name or pointed a finger at me. In my current state of paranoia, I expected to either have someone jump up, yelling, "It's Lilly McGuire," or worse, Turner himself serving me my beverage.

Guess I'm losing it no matter what or where I am.

I've just lifted the plate and mug when a tall, hard body slams into me from the side. My arms jerk upward, sending my food and drink flying, and I hear the impact of the plate and mug several feet away as I go down myself. I manage to brace the fall somewhat, but the same hard body lands on top of me, and all the air gets expelled from my lungs.

Ouch.

My initial panic when I hit the ground is replaced by confusion and...annoyance. The dude—now sprawled out on me with his head somewhere in my armpit region—begins to laugh like a hyena on crack.

What the hell?

He is heavy, and all I see is his shaggy blond hair. It looks like it was styled at one point, but now the gelled strands stick out at all angles. When he doesn't move and just keeps cackling, I push on his shoulders. "Hey, asshole, get off of me!"

Heat surges through me, and the annoyance quickly morphs into anger. People are staring. So much for keeping a low profile.

Footsteps come from behind us, and a female voice shouts, "Jesus-fucking-Christ! Hudson, what the fuck! I left you for two minutes to pee!"

Hudson's dead weight gets dragged off of me, and my lungs sigh in relief. From my position—still on the floor—I notice he can barely stand. Swaying, he leans against the bar and closes his eyes, a green tint to his skin. A hand appears in my vision, and I glance up at the girl attached to it. She is gorgeous in an innocent kind of way. Her long, chestnut hair hangs wavy over her shoulders. Her face is bare of makeup, and she is dressed in a black jogger and soft-pink V-neck tee.

"Shit. I'm so sorry. I will replace whatever my dumbass brother just ruined for you." She throws a glare to the side that would make Denielle proud. Hudson, aka her brother, is slouching with his elbow on the counter, staring at nothing, and I get my first full visual of him. He's gorgeous. He's tall, probably around Rhys's 6' 1, bronze skin, the bluest eyes I've ever seen, and high, sculpted cheekbones. His washed-out designer jeans hang low on his hips, and his black dress shirt could use a wash and an iron. But despite him being a complete mess, almost every female in this place ogles him.

I focus back on the girl and grasp her hand. As she pulls me up, I mutter, "It's okay." I don't want more attention. Peeking at Hudson again, I add, "Is he okay?"

The girl snorts. "Depends." Just as she says the word, her brother begins to tilt forward, and she latches onto his arm, whisper shouting, "Jesus, H. Get your shit together." She drags him over to one of the high tops and deposits him on the barstool where he instantly drops his head on his forearms on the table. I cross my arms in front of my chest and watch the scene.

Turning back to me, a genuine smile spreads across her face, and she holds out a hand again. "Hi. I'm Elle. I figured I have to properly introduce myself and apologize for dumb-dumb over there one more time." She tilts her head toward a now snoring Hudson.

My brows shoot up at the sound coming from him, and Elle briefly closes her eyes, mumbling, "I'm so going to rip him a new one when we get home."

That makes me snort, their relationship reminding me of my own with Nate. Not that I've ever seen my brother trashed like this.

"So..." she chirps, "what do I get you?"

My pulse speeds up. "Oh, no, I...uh—I should leave."

"Nonsense. Tell me, or I order you one of everything."

Wha—? Who is this girl?

"Well, um...Earl Grey and a scone?" My response sounds more like a question.

"You got it." She nods. "Do you mind making sure baby bro doesn't faceplant off his chair while I get your stuff? And some black coffee for him."

How did I end up babysitting a drunk dude who cannot be much older than me?

"Uh, sure?" Again, more a question.

I warily eye Hudson as I perch on the barstool next to him. This is so not how I expected this morning to go. Elle is back a few minutes later, my tea and scone in hand, and the barista in tow with two coffees.

"I didn't catch your name earlier." She seems genuine, but every muscle in my body tenses. Shit.

"Uh...Lilly." I omit the last name. If she's seen the news lately or has access to the Internet, she knows who I am.

Her eyes widen for a fraction of a second before she composes herself.

Yup, she knows.

I sigh inwardly and take that as my cue. "I should probably..." I start pushing off the table.

"No! I'm sorry. Please stay!" Glancing at her brother, she adds, "I'm stuck here for a while. There is no way I can drag his ass to the car. Keep me company. Please?"

"I don't know." I let my eyes wander, but everyone else has gone back to whatever they were doing.

Suddenly, a hand covers mine, and I jolt. Elle pulls back. "Listen...Lilly. Most people probably would recognize you if they knew you were here. Your name...and face are all over the Internet. You just...surprised me. I mean, aren't you supposed to be on the East Coast or wherever?"

I stare at her, my mouth dry. What am I supposed to say to that?

Then she rushes out. "Never mind. It's not important. Just...

Let's chat." She shrugs, and her eyes turn sad as she looks at the boy sleeping with his head on the table.

"What's going on with him?" I whisper, feeling like I'm intruding on something private.

Elle sighs. "I wish I knew. He's spiraling, and it's mostly my fault. So, when he calls me in the middle of the night to drive to LA to pick him up at a frat party he has zero business of being at, I do it."

"He's in college?" He doesn't look like it, but I don't want to sound like a bitch.

She huffs out a laugh. "Hell no, we're both seniors. Though, H here is eleven months younger than me."

My eyes widen, and she quickly adds, "He's my half-brother. Different moms."

I nod. Who am I to judge anyone on their family history?

We chat about everything and nothing while Hudson snores peacefully beside us. I drink my tea while Elle sips on her coffee, sneaking glances at her little brother. It feels good to talk to someone who is not involved in my drama, and despite her initial recognition, she doesn't ask me anything about *the case* or Rhys. I almost feel normal—like making a new friend.

When my phone begins to buzz in my pocket, my heart stutters at the sensation. My initial thought is *Rhys*, but as I pull it out, Nate's number scrolls across the screen. My gaze skips to the top, and the clock on the screen tells me I've been sitting here for over two hours.

Shit, shit, shit!

I look at the girl across from me apologetically and answer the call. "I'm so sorry. I lost track of time. I'll be home in a few."

"What the fuck were you thinking?" my brother hisses into my ear. "George is not back until this afternoon, and I was on my way to the airport when I got the movement alert. Damn it, sis. We have no fucking idea where Turner is. Why would you put yourself at risk like this?"

Airport?

I sit up straighter, but instead of admitting that he is right, I lash out. "I've been stuck there for a week. I needed a break."

The elongated silence makes my guilt level rise even more. Finally, Nate exhales audibly. "Please get back to the house. I'm not getting on this damn jet until I know you're safe."

My eyes start to burn, and I blink several times. When the rest of his words sink in, my forehead wrinkles. "Where are you going?"

"There is a problem with one of the new hotels in Europe. Several of the local investors are freaking out, and I need to make an appearance and calm their rich asses." He sighs, exasperated.

"Why didn't you call sooner?" I keep my voice low, but it's clear by Elle's expression that she can hear my side of the conversation.

"Because you seem to be having a good time, and that Elle girl checked out clean."

No way.

"How do you...never mind," I trail off as I spot the camera in the corner above our table. Of course my brother hacked into the café's security feed. He probably got her name from tapping into the line verifying the credit card transactions or following her on traffic cameras back until he caught the license plate. Nothing would surprise me.

I sigh. "I'm leaving, okay?"

"Thank you, Lilly," Nate says gently before hanging up.

"Family trouble?" Elle inquires with a raised eyebrow.

I snort. "You could say that."

She smiles at me in understanding. "Hey, I really enjoyed talking to you. Why don't I give you my number, and well, uh...we can touch base when you have your stuff sorted out."

She waits for my answer, and after a moment of deliberation, I pull out my phone. Why the hell not? She rattles it off, and I put it in my contacts. I could use another friend. Worst case: I don't call her. Other than saying she has seen me in L.A., she can't do anything.

My life has taken on a status of utter insanity.

After we exchange numbers, I say goodbye, and as I walk out, I hear a slap on the table behind me, followed by, "Wake up, fucker. It's time to get on the road. I want to get back to San Diego before Hazel blows up my phone!"

San Diego?

CHAPTER TWENTY-SEVEN

LILLY

I PULL INTO THE GARAGE AND SHOOT MY BROTHER A TEXT. I confirm that the roll gate is down before getting out of the SUV and making my way through the mudroom to the kitchen. I've just put down the keys on the island when my phone starts vibrating in my pocket again.

Chill out, Nate. I would've called—

But when I see the name on the screen, my eyebrows scrunch together. Denielle. I didn't expect to hear from her until Friday when she'd be back in Westbridge.

"Hey, D. What's—"

"HE CHEATED!" My best friend's screech makes me pull the phone away from my ear.

"Who?" I'm genuinely confused.

"CHARLIE. WHO DO YOU THINK I'M TALKING ABOUT? THAT POOR EXCUSE OF A WALKING DICK STUCK HIS MINI-SAUSAGE INTO A SORORITY SLUT!"

Oh. Ohhhh! Well, shit.

"Um, I am seriously speechless, D. I—"

She interrupts me with more obscenities, followed by, "THAT SON OF A—"

The phone could be at the other end of the thousand-square-foot kitchen, and I'd still hear her loud and clear.

I gentle my tone. "Den, you need to turn it down a bit. My eardrum is about to burst." If she'd been in front of me, I would've lifted my hands in an *I-surrender* gesture. Anything for her not to bite my head off. I've rarely seen, *or heard*, her this livid.

A sigh comes from the other end of the line. "I'm sorry, babe. I'm just...I don't believe what just happened."

"What *did* happen?" I glance at the clock on the stove. It's midday on a Wednesday—not the most common time to discover your long-term boyfriend is cheating.

"He went to a frat party last night, and I didn't feel like going. He's been dragging me to one party after another since I got here." My eyebrows pull together. That doesn't sound like the Charlie I know, but I don't interrupt her. "When he didn't come home, I called his friend, who told me where the party was. I just knew something was off based on how his dickwad frat brother acted on the phone." She draws in a deep breath. "So, I get to the house. It was like a mass orgy, babe! Passed out naked people everywhere."

What the fuck?

"I step over the, uh...bodies—some seriously going at it right there in the middle of the day. Gross. And then I start opening random doors. The third one reveals Charlie dipping his dick into some blonde bimbo with fake tits."

Um, wow.

My jaw drops. Literally. And I force myself to close my mouth.

"What did you do?" I'm a little scared to ask.

"Nothing there." Her reply is just a quiet mumble.

"There?" My hand tightens around the phone. This cannot be good.

"I was too stunned to confront him in front of a house full of naked asses. I walked back to his place and..."

Uh-oh. "And?"

"I went a little crazy on his apartment," Den confesses.

"Explain, please." My tone is careful not to set her off again. My ear just stopped ringing.

"Weeell, his entire wardrobe is in the Goodwill dumpster down the road, and so is every electronic device I could carry there. The rest..."

"Jesus Christ, Den. What did you do with the rest?" I pinch the bridge of my nose, at the same time trying to stifle a laugh. You do not want Denielle Keller as your enemy.

"I may have just thrown it out the window. At least some poor soul will benefit from this."

Good Lord. "Are you still at his place?" What if he calls the cops?

"No, I grabbed my shit and took an Uber to the airport. I'm coming to you."

My heartbeat slows before it picks up double time.

"WHAT?" This time I'm screeching into the speaker.

"I'm landing at LAX tomorrow at one. I can't get out of this shithole until tonight and then have to sleep in Chicago. Thankfully, I can get into the lounge." She sighs, exasperated.

"Den, I don't know if that's such a good idea. What if—?" My mind goes haywire with Turner following her here. And I haven't even considered what George or Nate will do when they discover my best friend in the house.

"Babe, relax. I'm almost six hundred miles from Westbridge. No one followed me here, let alone stuck around for days to watch my cheating boyfriend make an idiot out of me." There is the bitterness I expected, but I appreciate her trying to downplay my anxiety.

"Fine," I concede. The couple of hours with Elle this morning made me miss everyone like crazy. I want to see my best friend.

I give her the address, making her memorize it. I tell her to call me when she lands, and we'll go from there. It'll also give me time to confess to Nate.

AFTER WE HANG UP, I stare at my screen. Charlie cheated on her. This is...holy shit. I mean, the boys had voiced their suspicions before, but still. He adored Den from day one.

Instinctively, I pull up my most recent calls. Rhys is number three on the list, and before I can talk myself out of it, I tap his name. I know I promised not to contact him, but this morning's events, including Nate leaving not just the state but the country, stirred up a multitude of emotions. The phone rings several times before it goes to voicemail.

"You know the drill. If I wanna talk to you, I'll call back."

Rhys has had this greeting forever, but under the current circumstances, it's like it's intended for me. Only me. He told Nate he loved me, but he's not answering. Standing in the middle of the kitchen, I spin in a circle, taking in the empty room. What the hell am I doing here? I've lost him. What am I — I can't inhale, my lungs have closed up, and I press a fist to my chest. A wheezing sound hits my ears, and I realize it's coming from me. I need air.

My legs give out, and I drop to my knees. Wrapping my arms around my midsection, I lean my forehead to the cool kitchen floor, close my eyes, and start counting—a last attempt to prevent a panic attack. Every nerve ending in my body is charged, and a film of sweat starts building on my neck. As I reach sixty-three, the beeping of the alarm system alerts me to someone entering the back hallway from the garage. "Miss Lilly?" George's voice calls out. Footsteps come closer and then speed up.

"Lilly! What happened?" Panic laces his question.

He's back early.

Hands clasp my arm and pull me upright until we're face to

face. I can barely make out the silhouette of him through my hazy vision. His grip tightens, and he shakes me ever so slightly. "Did you have another migraine? Are you in pain? Talk to me!"

"H-he is n-not answering," I stammer.

Reaching up, I swipe my eyes, and George's frown comes into view. "Who is not answering, Miss Lilly?"

Fresh tears spill over. "Rhys."

His mouth forms an O, but no sound comes out. He gives a curt nod and pulls out his phone. About to dial, I latch onto his wrist. "No!"

When the man in front of me cocks his head in confusion, I take a deep breath. My pulse is slowing, and my rational side takes over. "I got overwhelmed. I shouldn't have called. I'm not supposed to. But Nate was mad at me for leaving the house, and then he left. Den found Charlie cheating. I haven't talked to Rhys in three days because I've been a selfish bitch for months and he's finally had enough of me. And then I was alone in the house and—"

"Stop!" George emphasizes his command by squeezing my shoulders.

My eyes widen at the word-vomit that just came out of my mouth, and my chin dips down. Covering my face with my palms, I mumble, "I'm a mess, aren't I?"

A chuckle makes me peer through my fingers at my bodyguard.

"I wouldn't call you a mess, Miss Lilly. You've been through a lot in a very short period of time."

I attempt a smile at his words of comfort.

When his mouth pulls up in a smirk, I wrap my arms around his midsection and squeeze. George stiffens for a fraction of a second before he returns the embrace.

"You don't get hugged too often, do you?" I say before it registers that it's more an insult than a compliment.

He doesn't take it that way, though, and I hear a rumbled laugh in his chest. "No, not in a very long time." He holds me tighter for another second before releasing me with a genuine smile. "Thank you, Lilly."

I quirk an eyebrow. "Where is the Miss?"

He grins sheepishly and shrugs. "I think we're officially past it."

I can't stop myself from laughing out loud. What just happened? I was close to losing it, and this man that usually lacks any emotion—not that it's his fault, it's simply a trait his line of work brings with itself—completely snapped me out of it.

My mood sobers, and I confess in a whisper, "I don't know what would've happened if you hadn't come home when you did."

He seems to understand. After all, he has seen me through several episodes by now. "I'm glad I was here when you needed me." He looks around before his gaze settles back on me. "How about some tea, and we can go over the plan for the next two days."

WITH NATE HAVING to take the jet to Europe, George is going to take the RAM to meet Hector Lakatos. He'll be leaving in the early evening and driving through the night to make it to the agreed-upon location mid-morning. He wants time to scope out the area. After the meet, he'll check in with Nate and me, let us know what he found out, and get a few hours of rest before driving back. I ask why he wouldn't just fly—less physically draining and all—to which he gives me a stare like I've said something ludicrous. When I don't catch on, he just fans his jacket open and reveals his Glock.

Oh.

"Oh."

"The TSA people don't take too kindly to my security measures," he deadpans.

"You mean they don't let you bring an arsenal for a small town on a commercial plane?" I smirk.

He just winks at me.

George also is not too happy with me about taking the car for a drive. I have to swear up and down that I will not leave the *premises* while he and Nate are gone. I almost blurt out that Denielle will be arriving tomorrow but bite my tongue. I'll tell Nate later when he calls. Maybe. They'll find out eventually. A light flutter stirs in my belly. I can't wait to have my best friend here.

AFTER GEORGE and I eat dinner, I walk with him to the garage. He loaded his truck earlier, and I watch him pull out. He gives me another nod before pressing the garage opener on the visor. As soon as the gate is fully closed, an empty feeling settles in my stomach. I step back into the hallway and close the door, arming the system. A synchronous beep echoes through the house, and I clutch my cell phone in my hand.

The urge to call Rhys overcomes me again, but instead, I send Denielle a text: **Can't wait to see u tmrw.**

The response is instant. **Just landed in Chi-town. Thank fuck I'm not leaving the airport. Can u believe it's snowing here. IT'S APRIL!**

Just a few more hours and u'll be in the golden state. ;) It was 72 today.

The bubble pops up again. **TSNF. I'm freezing my ass off.**

I bark out a laugh, picturing my best friend at O'Hare, complaining at the poor lounge employees to bring her a blanket.

Get some rest. Call me when you land at LAX.
Will do. LY.
LY2.

Still standing in the hallway, I contemplate what to do. It's too early to sleep—not that I can anyway. I can't sit still long enough to enjoy a movie *or book*, and I don't feel like exploring new parts of the mansion—not while I'm the only person here.

My feet take me back to Brooks's office. The room has become oddly comforting to me, the warm colors and soft light of the lamps making the room cozy. When Nate started looking into the finances, I cleaned up what I had left on the floor, including the photo albums. Padding across the room, I open the double doors and pull the three leatherbound books out. I place all three next to each other on the desk and lower myself into the chair, pulling my legs underneath me. Sitting where my father used to spend hours on end makes me feel like I have a connection to him. I flip the first one open and start turning the pages. Not that I want to have another migraine, but there is a little spark of hope that has remained inside of me and is waiting for me to remember...everything. After an hour of scanning picture after picture, I still feel like I'm spying on a stranger's life. My jaw clenches.

Screw this.

I stack all three albums on top of each other and spin in the chair to put them back in their spot. As I turn, the pocket of Rhys's hoodie—which I've been wearing for three days in a row —gets caught on the desk chair's armrest. I try to disentangle myself while balancing the heavy leather books on one arm. With the weight wearing me down, I attempt a final pull. I'm free, but my force propels the chair in the opposite direction— straight into the other shelf. Books fall over, a framed picture of Brooks and Payton crashes to the floor and shatters into a thousand pieces, and as if in slow motion, I watch another row of books tilting like dominos. I watch in horror as the tipping books push the stand containing Denton John Altman II's pipe collection toward the edge. Dropping the photo albums, I reach out and watch the pipes sail past my outstretched hand.

No, no, no.

When Nate finally was past his anxiety, he told me about all the items displayed. As suspected, a lot were souvenirs from their travels, and it sounded like the Hamlin's did a lot of that.

That's my luck, ruining one of Nate's grandfather's favorite possessions. Shit!

I kneel, careful not to cut myself on the broken frame, and start picking up the antique-looking pipes. I carefully place one after another back into the stand—which, by a miracle, is still in one piece—but then suddenly halt. I turn the pipe over in my hand and inspect it carefully. This one doesn't match the rest. It's new and... I turn it again. It's plastic made to look like wood.

Taking it between both hands, I squint. Something looks weird. I twist the mouthpiece, and my eyes widen as I repeat the motion. With shaking hands, I turn and pull at the same time. My heart is hammering against my ribcage. What is this? The object slowly comes apart and—what the hell?

CHAPTER TWENTY-EIGHT

LILLY

I LEAVE EVERYTHING WHERE IT FELL AND RACE TO MY computer. It's just down the hall, yet I'm out of breath like I've just sprinted a mile. The adrenaline coursing through me puts every nerve ending on high alert. What is on this thing? Why was it hidden among the pipes? *In* a fake pipe.

I drop into my desk chair and hit the space bar repeatedly. Come on, come on, come on. It only takes a second for the monitor to come to life, but it feels like an hour.

"Finally." My voice sounds like a bullhorn in the quiet house.

With my hand wrapped around the small device, I hesitate for a moment. Uncurling my fingers, I stare at it. I should wait for Nate. No, this is important. Brooks wouldn't have hidden it otherwise.

Plugging the USB drive—*slash back part of the pipe*—into the adapter connected to my laptop, it instantly pops up in my Finder window: Nate and Lilly.

I suck in a sharp breath.

My hand is trembling as I navigate the cursor into position. I clench and unclench my hand before clicking on the device name. A single video file with the same title gets displayed on the right.

Shifting in my seat, all I can do is stare. My heart is hammering so hard I swear I can hear it. Slowly, I move the little arrow over the file.

Why did Nate have to leave town today? I have no clue if I can reach him. What time is it in Europe? Crap, crap, crap. I can't wait until he's back, though. Swallowing hard, I double click.

Oh, my God.

Brooks fills the screen, and when his voice comes through the speaker, tears begin to run down my face.

This is my father. My dad.

NATE. Son. I hope when you see this, Lilly will be with you and you've already found each other.

BROOKS'S FACE BECOMES BLURRY, and I hit the spacebar to pause the video. Seeing him—not just in a picture or one of my muted memories—actually *hearing* him, I can't contain the sob building in my throat. His voice is deep and calm. Kind. I rub my eyes with my fingers and apply pressure. Breathe. When I have myself semi under control, I continue.

I DON'T KNOW where to begin.

MY FATHER CHUCKLES and looks down for a second. Following his line of sight, I notice that he's holding a couple of photos. One hand lets go of the pictures, and he scrubs it over his mouth before focusing on the camera again.

.   .   .

IF YOU HAVEN'T FOUND Lilly yet, this will be one more revelation I wish I would've had the guts to tell you, son. There is no way to sugar-coat it. You have a half-sister. Her name is Lilly Ann.

She looks so much like you. I truly hope you have found each other by now.

HIS BREATH BECOMES SHAKY, and his eyes gloss over. The emotion on his face breaks my heart, and I cover my mouth with my hands in an attempt to mute my own crying.

IT ALL STARTED about seven years ago. I met a woman...Emily. Your mother and I went through a rough patch. After Audrey's birth, your mom was struggling with post-partum depression. We hired a nanny to take care of you and your sister because she couldn't.

HE PAUSES, and his face softens.

IT WASN'T HER FAULT—WE knew that—but Payton would blame herself for not being stronger. Just when she had recovered, your grandfather passed away. Payton was distraught. You know how much your mom adored your grandfather.

I had to take over the hotels' legal department, which was part of your grandfather's will, and I had no idea what I was doing. I was gone sixteen hours a day—sometimes even slept in the office.

Your mother was grieving, I was stressed, and we blamed each other for our failing marriage. We did our best to keep all this from you, and I hope we succeeded on that front.

HE GLANCES BACK DOWN at the photos that are now flat on the surface in front of him, but I can't make out who is on them. Are those of me? Are those the same pictures Nate found? My mind starts firing questions at me, and I draw in slow breaths. I need to focus on Brooks. He recorded this for a reason.

EMILY WAS MYSTERIOUS, energetic, spontaneous. I met her at a conference where she was visiting a friend; I forget her name. Her friend was pregnant, so Emily hung out in the hotel bar after her friend went to bed. We hit it off.

I'm sure you have no interest in the details...let's just say one thing led to another. After I got back to LA, we stayed in contact. We met a few more times. She lived in San Diego, and it was easy to make the drive and meet halfway.

We kept in touch through handwritten letters. She said they were more personal.

HIS EXPRESSION SHIFTS, and his face becomes hard.

A FEW MONTHS INTO...THE affair —I have to call it for what it was— Emily wrote that she was pregnant. I had planned to break it off the next time I saw her because your mother and I were finally doing better. We were working on our marriage, saw a counselor once a week, and I wanted to be there for you and Audrey—be the father you deserved.

Shortly before, I had also found out she was married, so of course, I questioned her if the baby was mine. We met, and she showed me proof that her husband was unable to father a child. She agreed to have a paternity test once the baby was born, and I told her that if the baby were, in fact, my child, I would be there for it. I would support her and the baby in any way I could, but the affair had to stop.

Emily seemed to understand and be agreeable. Lilly was born, and I got the confirmation that the little girl was my daughter.

· · ·

Buzzzzzzz, buzzzzzzz.

My eyes jerk to my phone sitting next to me. I quickly pause the video, not to miss anything.

Buzzzzzzz, buzzzzzzz.

I want to ignore whomever it is. I need to know what else Brooks has to say. But when I glance over, the one name that could make me drop everything flashes across the screen.

Buzzzzzzz, buzzzzzzz.

My heart skips a beat, and my hand flies to the phone. I answer the video call immediately.

When the connection is established, the screen is entirely black. *Uh.*

"Rhys?" I say hesitantly.

"Shit. Hold on." The rustling of the comforter comes through the speaker before his bedside lamp clicks on. "Sorry."

I don't respond; I just drink him in. He's as gorgeous as ever, and my belly flip-flops at the sight. His hair sticks up in all directions as if he just woke up. God, I miss him so much.

Rhys cocks his head, studying me. "Are you okay? You look out of it. Did you cry?" His concern gives me hope.

He still cares.

"Yes. No. I..." Instead of mentioning the video, I say, "You didn't answer your phone earlier." I try not to sound accusing but fail miserably. I am so high-strung from my discovery that my emotions are a ginormous cluster fuck.

Rhys sighs. "I know." He's glancing past the screen, and I picture him looking at the TV on the other side of the room. When his eyes find mine again, he says, "I wanted to. Wes was here. He's been on babysitting duty since D is gone. He saw that you were calling and took my phone."

A pang hits my chest. "Why?"

Why did he take the phone? Does he hate me, too?

"I made him promise not to let me talk to you. I needed time to clear my head, and when I hear or see you..." He lets the sentence trail off.

Needles prick in the back of my throat, and I press my lips together. It takes me almost a whole minute before finding my words again. "I'm so sorry. I should've never forced you to keep my secrets. I was selfish and didn't think twice about the position I put you in."

I want to apologize more, but how many times can one say it before it loses its meaning?

The corner of Rhys's mouth tilts up. "I get it, Cal. And I can't really fault you for it. Think about everything you've been through."

"You're doing it again," I tell him through the tears.

"Doing what?" He's genuinely confused.

A laugh bubbles up between my sobs. "Being understanding."

"Ah, what can I say?" He full-on smirks.

"Are we—?" I start in a whisper.

His eyebrows draw together. "Are we what?"

"Are we, uh...still together?" I sound pathetic, but I can't help it. I can't lose him. I need to find a way to tell him how much I regret my actions.

Rhys narrows his eyes at me, looking incredulous. "Did you think we broke up?"

My breath hitches. "Yes. No. Maybe?" I shrug. "I hurt you. You didn't want to talk to me."

"Babe," he sighs, "I know we haven't had the traditional dating start. Instead of fighting about where we want to go out for dinner, we argue about your secret brother, brainwashing, and a crazy stalker—two, if you count Kat. But that doesn't change the fact that we are together and will be for a very. Long. Time. If it's up to me. But we can still be mad at each other. Keeping the migraines from me and how they affected you was like a knife to the gut. The same goes for your cloak-and-dagger escape. But none of that changes my feelings for you. I just needed time to digest. We have to be better at communicating."

I hiccup a laugh between the waterfall running down my cheeks. I have no clue if these are happy or sad tears. Both, I think, based on my internal turmoil. "I promise I will never shut you out again."

"That's all I ever wanted from you, babe—to let me in. Well, maybe I also want your sexy body... No, I definitely want that as well." He winks.

"You are in. *I'm all in.*" He holds my gaze, and I add, "I love you."

"I love you, too, Calla." The A is drawn out by a yawn.

"Were you sleeping?" Is that why his hair is such a mess?

"I fell asleep during a movie. Wes just left, which is why I finally could call you back."

"I see." Hearing him say that he wanted to talk to me this entire time is like a soothing blanket. He's not breaking up with me. We're okay. He loves me.

He's not breaking up with me.

I keep repeating it over and over in my head.

I'm about to tell him about the video when he yawns again and rubs a hand over his face. "Shit, I'm so out of it. I haven't slept much the last few daaays." Another yawn.

As if on cue, I can feel one building up inside of me as well, and I try to suppress it—unsuccessfully.

"Why don't you go back to bed and call me in the morning?"

That way I can finish the video and tell him everything in the morning. I want to have all the information. My gut tells me there is a lot more on Brooks's video.

You're keeping the video from Rhys immediately after telling him you would never keep anything from him again, my inner voice accuses.

I'm not. I want to have all the details. I justify myself against myself. I'm losing it.

We say our goodnights, and another yawn escapes me just as we hang up. I need caffeine. With the video still paused on the screen and my phone in hand, I head to the kitchen to make some tea.

. . .

WHILE I WAIT for the water to heat, Brooks's words replay in my head, causing my adrenaline level to skyrocket again. What else is on that recording?

When the kettle signals that the water is boiling, I grab it with a trembling hand and pour the water carefully over the tea-filter.

I need to tell Nate about the video, but I have no idea where he is, if he's alone, or what. Hoping his phone is silenced, I type out a message: **Call me asap.**

Realizing how that sounded, I add, **I'm fine but found something. Need to talk to u!!!**

I place the phone down, not expecting an answer right away. I'm on my way to the trash can to throw the filter of soggy leaves away when the beeping of the alarm system chimes. I peer over to the panel installed in all the main rooms. The message on the screen makes the blood in my veins run cold. "Garage Second Entrance disabled."

I stare at the blinking notification. What the—?

"Hello, Lilly."

I spin around at the voice, sending the tea dripping from the filter spraying across the kitchen.

No!

CHAPTER TWENTY-NINE

RHYS

"Duuuude, what the fuck is wrong with you? Your aim is complete shit. I thought I left early last night so you could get some sleep and I don't have to kick your moping ass all day."

Wes is about to launch the controller at me for getting killed the eighth time in the last hour. Fucking zombies keep biting me in various body parts before I can react, which makes him lose as well.

The video call with Lilly left me wide awake until after four, and my best friend showing up here at nine sharp, like the last several days, didn't help either.

Mom stuck her head in, informing me that she was taking Natty and her friend Olivia out for a girls' day, including dinner at their favorite restaurant. That'll be good for Nat. She seems to be handling the current situation better than the rest of us, but that doesn't mean it doesn't affect her. On their way out, I pulled my little sister aside and told her that we're going to have a brother-sister date this weekend. Her face lit up like I had given her the best present ever, and my stomach sank. I have to be around more for her, get my head out of my selfish ass.

I knew that Dad was downstairs in his office, doing his secret spy work or whatever he does, but other than that, I hadn't seen him today.

I'm about to restart the game when my phone starts ringing. I peer over and see Denielle's name scroll across the screen. Why is she calling *me*? She's not supposed to be back until tomorrow. Wes told me earlier this week that she'd been bitch-texting him several times about how Charlie had turned into a serial party-drunk, but she's been radio silent since Tuesday evening. I assumed they had made up and were getting at it like the horny rabbits they are.

"Who is it?" Wes mumbles as he picks out his weapons for this round.

"It's D?" My tone makes it sound like I'm asking him.

"Huh? Why—"

The call cuts off, my voicemail probably picking up. Within two seconds, it rings again. That's odd. Maybe she came back earlier and needs a ride from the airport?

I pick up the phone and swipe to answer. "Hey, D. What's—"

"Have you talked to Lilly?" she bursts out so loud Wes glances over.

Huh?

"Uh...last night, yeah. Why?" I lock eyes with my best friend, who scowls at me. *Busted.*

"SHE'S NOT HOME!" Den yells into the phone.

"What do you mean? Where the hell are you?" My confusion turns into annoyance. Why can no one ever talk in complete, coherent sentences?

"I'm in LA. At her place. She's not here. Or at least no one is opening. She wasn't supposed to leave the house, so she has to be here. But she's not opening the door." She speaks so fast it takes my brain a moment to catch up.

LA?

My hand tightens around the phone. "What are you doing in LA?"

How the hell did she get there?

"Dear Lord, McGuire!" Her exasperated tone makes my blood boil. "I found my longtime boyfriend doggy-styling a sorority slut yesterday, so I jumped on the next flight to Los Angeles to see my best friend."

"And she let you?" I ask, half incredulously, half pissed. Pissed because Den is there and I'm not, but also at the way she talks to me—like I'm an idiot.

"I didn't give her a choice," she confesses. "I called her from the airport after I bought the ticket. She told me to let her know when I landed, but she didn't answer. I assumed she just didn't have her phone with her, so I took a cab. I had the address, and she must've put me on the list because this Harvey doppelganger at the gate let me through once I gave him my ID. Now I'm knocking and ringing the doorbell, and no one is answering. I can't reach G either." She draws in a shaky breath. "Rhys, I'm freaking out."

My pulse increases the longer she speaks. She's freaking out? What am I supposed to do? I'm across the fucking country. "What do you want me to do? You're there—" The phone is ripped out of my hand, and I glower at Wes, who is standing in front of me, *my* phone in one hand and the other lifted defensively so I don't clock him. I could still get a good punch in, though. His guard is way too low.

"You need to take a breath, bro. You're about to blow a gasket."

I'm gonna show you a gasket, fuckface!

I'm ready to launch myself at my best friend to fight him for my only connection to the West Coast when he lifts it to his ear. "D! I heard most of it. Walk around the house. See if you can find anything. Another door or something. Rhys is going to call Nate and George."

I narrow my eyes at him. Since when did he turn all drill sergeant?

"Okay," Denielle's voice comes through the speaker; he must've enabled it when he stole my damn phone.

We can hear the crunching of gravel, which I assume is Den making her way across the property.

"Rhys!" Wes snaps a finger in front of my face. "Get my phone and call George." He points across the room.

The fuck?

I want to break his damn fingers, but instead, I make my way across the room as ordered.

He's so going to get a beating for this.

While we're waiting for Denielle to tell us something, I dial the number I can recite three different ways to Sunday. It rings and rings and eventually goes to a non-descript voicemail.

"Motherfucker!" I hit end and dial again. And again. Pick. Up. The damn phone!

"Isn't he at that secret meet with the memory doctor?" D's voice interrupts my internal curse crusade against my BFF.

Fuck, she's right.

"He probably doesn't have his phone with him," Wes chimes in.

"Thank you, Sherlock," I snap.

"Just saying." He sounds a little less smug now, but I can't muster any remorse for my behavior. Lilly is fucking missing. A-fucking-gain!

"Oh no!" Denielle breathes into the phone.

"WHAT?" I bark, my heart instantly beating in my throat.

"The side door next to the garage is wide open," she whispers.

"Could she just be out for a walk or somewhere else on the property?" Wes tries to reason.

"I don't think so." Lilly's best friend's voice is trembling, and the saliva pooling in my mouth tells me I'm close to making a dash to the bathroom. I swallow several times before asking, "Why?" My voice sounds robotic.

"There is blood." Her response is barely audible.

I'm out the door and down the stairs before anyone can say another word. Wes is on my heels with Denielle on the phone as I push my father's office door open. It slams into the wall and bounces back, which results in me kicking it and leaving a size-twelve dent in the wood.

Dad's head jerks up. He's ready to ream me out—mouth already open—but I speak first.

"Get me on the next flight to LA!" I don't give him room for negotiation. I would get a ticket myself, but he can get me there faster with his connections.

His forehead wrinkles and he's about to say something when Wes's phone begins to vibrate in my hand. Glancing down, I recognize George's number. I answer the call before anyone else can utter another word. "SHE'S MISSING!"

Holding my father's gaze, his entire posture goes rigid when comprehension sets in.

"What are you talking about?" George snaps to attention on his end.

"Denielle is at the house. Lilly is not there. The side door is open, and there is blood," I summarize the last several minutes while clenching my hand around the device and fighting the urge to purge my revolting stomach.

He doesn't ask me why Den is in Los Angeles. Instead, he hangs up.

What the fuck?

"George is video calling me. Hold on," D's voice comes through the speaker. Her line goes dead.

My father glowers at me with an equally worried and murderous expression. I know I'm in deep shit, but I couldn't care less at this point.

My phone starts to vibrate in Wes's hand, and he holds it out to me. I latch onto the device and accept the incoming video chat at the same time.

Lilly's best friend, as well as George's face, fill the screen in two little squares. George is in his truck, and based on how he stares out the front, he's driving. The phone is in a car mount or somehow propped up to the side of him. Denielle looks directly into the camera, and our eyes lock. At the edge of the screen, I see her twirl a strand of hair over and over—something she does when she's upset. I've learned her tells over the last few months.

"Denielle, I want you to go slowly inside. Flip the camera around so I can see. If at any point you think someone besides Lilly is in the house, leave! Someone from my team will be there soon; I messaged him from my other device. I'm on my way but won't get there until late tonight unless I can charter a plane along the way."

"Rhys." I turn at my name. Still behind his desk but now standing with his arms crossed over his chest, my father speaks up for the first time. "What is going on?" His tone is eerily calm, yet the question holds a warning.

"Colonel McGuire, sir. My name is George Weiler. I am Lilly's bodyguard and her brother's head of security."

Dad stiffens while Wes's jaw drops. Den looks equally slack-jawed in her little square. George just told my father who he is.

"George Weiler?" Dad repeats slowly as his arms go slack on either side of him. "The George Weiler?"

The?

My heart skips a beat as my father addresses George. I'm taken back to the day I found out who Nate was—when I saw him holding Lilly as she had her panic attack. The shock back then mirrors what is currently going on inside of me. It's like my brain is trying to catch up with what's happening, but I'm two steps behind at all times.

"Yes, sir," George confirms, never taking his gaze off the road in front of him.

Dad moves around the desk and to my side, peering down at George. "You have been off the radar for almost twenty years."

"That is correct, Colonel."

My father stares between Wes, the phone, and me, an almost dumbfounded look on his face.

"Denielle?" George redirects everyone's attention.

"Yes."

"My associate will be there within thirty minutes. When you go inside, make as little sound as possible. I don't believe anyone is there anymore, but I want you to be careful."

Den turns the camera around, and we can see the half-open back door and a short, dark hallway behind. My free hand fists into the material of my pants. I'm holding my breath, and so is Wes from the looks of it.

Den exhales audibly and takes one step inside. When she doesn't keep moving, George starts directing her. His tone is calm, almost soothing.

"The hallway leads to the motor pool on the left and the kitchen straight ahead."

"There is blood on the floor," she whispers, her voice cracking.

My father swipes his hand over his mouth.

"Jesus," Wes mumbles.

"How much? Turn on the hallway light to the left of you," George orders.

My lungs are burning, and I force myself to let oxygen into my lungs. My free hand is now permanently balled into a fist and pressed to my chest.

"I don't know. Not much. Some drops and smears?" She tries to stay calm, but the quiver in her tone is audible. The light on her end flicks on, and we can see what she's talking about. It is not much, just like someone cut themselves and didn't have a Band-Aid. But it's blood. It doesn't matter how much or how little. Someone was hurt.

"Good, keep going."

The kitchen entry slowly comes into view. I want to yell at her to move the fuck along. I feel like someone is slowly gutting me with every snail-paced step she takes. Dad's hand lands on my shoulder, and he squeezes. I have no clue, though, if he's looking at me. I can't avert my eyes from the screen.

Den finally reaches the kitchen and waves the camera around before she aims it at a spot behind the massive kitchen island. "There is something on the floor. It looks like dried...tea? And a cup. Someone threw it."

Lilly!

She continues, "A broken fruit bowl." Den's breathing fast, and I can only imagine what her heartbeat is like. With mine beating in my throat, Den must be close to passing out.

She changes the angle, and we can see a large white bowl shattered on the ground—apples, bananas, and grapes on the floor.

"Is there any more blood?"

I'm gonna be sick.

"Oh no."

She still has the camera aimed on the fucking bananas.

"Denielle!" This time Dad directs his bark at her.

"Yes?" she squeaks.

"Don't. Do. That!"

"Please show us what you see." George is the only one able to keep his cool. He is doing his job. Dad's usual military mode went out the window as soon as the words Lilly, missing, and blood were spoken.

The camera shifts, and Denielle walks closer to an object on the floor—a small chef's knife. The blade is covered in blood.

I thrust the phone at my father, who barely catches it, and drop to all fours. Retching in the middle of my father's office, I expel the remnants of my stomach.

I DON'T REMEMBER MUCH after I saw the knife. Dad and Wes maneuvered me upstairs to my room, where I curled into a fetal position on the bed and watched Wes pace like someone waiting for his next fix and texting furiously. Dad said something about making phone calls and disappeared back downstairs.

It's 9:30, and I'm on a private plane—this time heading to

Los Angeles. I have no clue how my father pulled this off. One of these days, I want to know what the man really does for a living.

Wes sits opposite me with Dad across the aisle. Mom and Natty came home around seven, and Dad ushered her upstairs immediately. I have no idea how much or what he told her. I couldn't bring myself to ask, either. Her face was blotchy, and her mascara was streaked when she watched us pull out of the garage. According to Dad, Natty was in her room, and they told her that we would be visiting Lilly to bring her home.

Nice way of wording it. He's telling her the truth, but she has no idea what it really means.

Dad props open his laptop and starts typing.

Staring out the window into the dark, I ask, "Are there any updates?" My voice sounds like a stranger to my own ears. It's the first time I've spoken since my breakdown, and their focus is instantly on me. Out of the corner of my eye, I see Dad angling his body in my direction, and I turn my head to face him.

"I've been in contact with Weiler. He called earlier to inform me that his men are at the house with Denielle." He pauses, and I scan his face. His expression is blank.

Before he can continue, I interrupt. "You knew George." I don't ask, because from his reaction, it was clear that my father had heard of the Altman head of security.

Dad chuckles. "George Weiler is a legend. He's a...ghost. He went off the grid as soon as his feet hit U.S. soil after his last mission. No one knows what happened."

Well, well. I know something my father doesn't.

"I do." I try to keep my face neutral but can't stop the shit-eating grin that spreads across my face. For a brief moment, I forget the reason we're on this plane.

My father raises an eyebrow, but I shrug. "Maybe he'll tell you, too."

His nostrils flare. He doesn't like that I'm rubbing my secrets in his face, but I don't care.

Wes interrupts our standoff. "So, uh...D has been saying one of the two dudes who showed up a while ago and are 'processing the scene' is almost as scary as G." He makes air quotes around the words. "The other one—"

"How is Denielle holding up?" My father seems genuinely concerned.

Wes shrugs. "From her texts, she's anywhere between hysterical meltdown and B.K."

Bulldog Keller.

"We should get to the address Lilly's *bodyguard* gave me around midnight local time." When I don't react, he addresses me directly. "Son?" He waits until he has my attention. "When we have Lilly back, the two of you will tell me everything. The only reason I'm not putting you into an interrogation cell is that finding my daughter has priority. The cell is still on the table, though."

He's not joking, but I just turn back around and stare out the window into the blackness.

CHAPTER THIRTY

HER

GRAY HAS BEEN WATCHING THE HOUSE FOR THE LAST FEW DAYS. Nate was going back and forth between his office, his home, and the mansion. Weiler, however, did not leave at all—until a little change in plans forced the two men to go out of town.

The unexpected complications at the new Altman hotel in Paris forced Nate to take the jet out of the country, which resulted in an extended absence of Lilly's watchdog.

We had two days to get everything ready for Lilly, including her accommodations. I briefly contemplated making them a little more inviting than how the pawn has been stored for the last decade, but then, why? She has a mattress and a toilet at her disposal. That's more than he's gotten for years. I have not yet made up my mind on the restraints. Let's see how the girl behaves.

GOT HER. **The little bitch stabbed me.**

Gray's text lights up my phone at 11:53, and the corner of my mouth tugs upward. The kid has spunk, I'll give her that. The years of training that Tristen put Lilly through paid off. Too bad for her, though, that I brought some of the paralytic drugs with me.

I have to wait another hour before the garage door rolls up. I made sure not to wear white today; I'm still furious with Gray for ruining my new linen pants with his blood.

Standing in the door, I watch him get out of the SUV and walk around to the back.

"Did she give you any more trouble?"

He peers around the back of the car. "Not once I got the syringe in. Dropped faster than you can down a glass of your fancy wine."

"WATCH IT, Francis!"

He scowls at me. I haven't called him by his given name in over twenty-five years—unless he's pissed me off.

"Get her in the house and to her room." I turn and head straight for the kitchen. I've already gone through most of my pills, which means I have to resort to other means to calm myself. And stabbing his muscle more would be counterproductive; I need him to keep Lilly in check until I get what we came for.

"MAYBE WE SHOULD'VE REDUCED the dose? Or not mix it with the sedative. She hasn't moved in hours." Gray cocks his head as he watches Lilly on the monitor. It's been half a day, and I want to go back home and finally be done with this decade-long farce, but I learned a long time ago, things rarely go how you want them to.

"She wakes up when she wakes up. Enjoy the downtime," I say absently as I pour another glass.

"Christ, woman, it's not even noon." He purses his lips at me.

"That's rich coming from someone who gets high every chance he gets." His eyes widen. Yes, I know that he has not been as clean as he pretends to be.

"She's moving!" Gray suddenly exclaims.

I step up behind him to watch the feed, and a slow smile spreads across my face. "Good morning, Lilly," I whisper to the screen.

CHAPTER THIRTY-ONE

LILLY

Francis Turner is in my kitchen. We stare at each other, neither of us moving. I blink. He's still here.

How the hell did he get past the guard and alarm system?

The tea dripping from the wet filter onto the floor is the only sound in the room. Holding my breath, I'm waiting for the panic to kick in, but there is...nothing. Why is there nothing? Maybe it's the shock of seeing him in front of me, in my father's house in Los Angeles. It's got to be. I'm alone with no one to contact to help me. Definitely shock.

I glance to the side, mentally measuring the distance to the knife block by the stove. Too far.

Following my gaze, he cocks an eyebrow, and the corner of his mouth pulls up in a smirk. "I wouldn't do that, little girl."

My phone is where I left it on the counter—also on the other side of the kitchen. Why did I have to go to the trash can right this second? I scan everything in my vicinity. The white porcelain fruit bowl—which probably costs more than my old Jeep—is the closest item in my reach, and I lunge for it.

Unfortunately, he anticipates the projectile and ducks to the side. The crashing sound of the bowl is equivalent to the demolition of a high-rise in the quiet house. It also is what my brain and body need to catch up with the severity of the situation. Turner pulls something out of his pocket, and my adrenaline level goes through the roof.

Please don't let it be a gun.

My heart beats in my throat, and I take a defensive stance. I'm trained to defend myself against almost every weapon, but no one can match a bullet. I follow his movement like a hawk, ready to dive behind the island. When he pulls out a small object, I narrow my eyes. What the hell is—a syringe? This can't be real.

Every nerve ending in my body is buzzing with energy. This asshole is not going to get me. Through his evasion maneuver, Turner is now farther from the knives than me, and I don't hesitate. I sprint around the island, swiping my phone as I pass it and clasp my hand on the first handle I can reach. What I don't anticipate is for this tall and bulky guy to be so quick. An arm sneaks around my stomach just as I pull my weapon out of the block.

"Ahhhhh!" The sudden connection sends my system into overdrive. Goosebumps erupt where he touches me, and I fight the urge to scream and thrash uncontrollably. I'm trained for this. I need to be smart—in control.

My feet leave the ground, and his other arm comes around my upper body, immobilizing me. Expelling all my air, I throw my head back, but he's too tall, and I hit his chest.

Shit!

"Nice try, princess," he sneers close to my ear, and his breath of stale alcohol and cigarettes penetrates my nose.

I swallow hard not to start gagging.

He fumbles with the syringe, attempting the right grip to administer whatever he has in there. Using the opportunity, I flip the handle around in my hand—blade pointing backward—but almost lose hold of it, my palms being coated with sweat.

Before it slips from my grasp, I push it into the closest body part.

"Fuuuck! You little bi—" He stumbles and drops me.

I keep my fingers curled around my ticket out of here. The knife dislodges from wherever it entered his body, and I spin, holding my weapon in front of me with my other hand raised in defense. I follow his gaze down to his thigh, where his dark pant leg begins to look wet. *Blood.*

"What is it with you women and stabbing me in the legs?" he growls.

Huh?

Turner trains his ice-blue eyes on me, and his glare sends chills down my spine. It's at that moment that I realize I dropped my phone in the struggle. Crap, crap, crap. I flick my gaze across the floor, making sure not to take my focus off of my opponent for more than half a second.

Unable to spot the device anywhere, I take a step back to bring more distance between us. His pained expression turns into a shit-eating grin, and he leans down without breaking eye contact.

"Looking for this?" He wiggles my phone between his thumb and forefinger. My heart is pounding like a jackhammer. He lets go, and I hear it smash into the tiled floor. *No!* He glances down, back up at me, and shrugs once before he brings his heel down on the screen. I don't have to look to know that my phone has been rendered useless—the loud crack made it clear.

I'm breathing heavily, running through possible ways out of this situation in my head. Then something hits me: the alarm system. It has a button to notify the security company and most likely send an alert to Nate. The closest panel is about thirty feet away, next to the French doors to the back patio. Turner is on the other end of the kitchen, and I have a straight path to the keypad. Before I can think more about it, I push off and sprint toward help, using the coursing adrenaline to my advantage.

I'm almost on the other side, reaching out my hand, when

something hits me in the back, and I go down. I try to brace my fall, but with the knife in one hand, I'm only able to block the fall with the other one which, by the force of my impact, doesn't do much good. My forehead hits the floor, and everything goes black for a moment.

Do not pass out.

As the darkness clears, the room is spinning from the impact, but I force myself on my hands and knees.

I need to get up.

My thoughts are sluggish, and I shake my head in an attempt to clear the fog. Footfalls behind me announce Turner coming closer. Suddenly, my head gets yanked back by the hair. A sharp prick punctures my neck, and I fall to the side, dropping the knife.

Oww!

Faintly I register that I'm lying in something wet when the smell of Earl Grey hits my nose. He threw my freaking Yeti at me. I peer up at Turner, who becomes fuzzier by the second. His head is tilted to the side as he glares down at me.

"Nighty night, Lilly."

CONSCIOUSNESS SLOWLY STARTS CREEPING into the dark void. I'm awake but unable to move. Maybe I'm dreaming. Please let this be a dream. Or a memory. I'd even take a memory at this point. Why won't my eyes open?

The syringe.

The visual of Turner standing over me and everything slowly turning fuzzy slams into me like a freight train. He drugged me. My heart rate increases, and so does my breathing, but drawing in the air my body demands is like running a marathon through water. Whatever he gave me prevents me from moving. No, no, no. What if, this time, there is permanent damage? What if it doesn't go away? What if I can't ever move again? I'm trapped. I try to open my mouth to scream, do something, but my body won't obey. The sound reverberates inside my head, but on the outside...I'm mute. I start counting my breaths in an attempt to calm my heart rate.

Inhale, four, three, two, one.

Exhale, four, three, two, one.

It takes several rounds, but my pulse eventually slows enough that my lungs no longer feel like they're closing up from the lack of oxygen.

I have zero sense of time. It could be days, hours, or ten minutes—definitely feels like days, though—when there is a twitch in my index finger. Instantly, my adrenaline level spikes again, and I consciously attempt to bend my finger. It's just the slightest of movements, but it's there. The drugs are wearing off. I'm so relieved I could cry.

I'm gonna be okay. I'm gonna be okay. I'm gonna be okay.

In an attempt to measure how long it takes for me to become fully mobile, I start counting. My brain needs to do something, or I'm going to lose it. I have no clue how accurate my seconds are, but by the time I get to 783 I can sense both my arms and most of my legs. I want to laugh and cry at the same time. By 1,341 I can consciously make my chest expand—breathing has never felt so good. I've just reached 2,127 when my eyelids snap open. At first, I think it hasn't worked, but then the faint glow from my right draws my attention. I only move my eyes, afraid to alert someone close by. There is a small gap under a door that allows light in.

When nothing happens for several minutes, I slowly turn myself to the side, taking stock. I'm on a mattress, and I'm having a hangover from hell—worse than what Nate and George pumped through my system—but I don't sense any new injuries. My clothes are in place, which is a relief I never thought I'd have to experience. Not knowing what Turner wants from me, my mind has come up with the most horrific scenarios. My back is sore, but that is most likely a result of lying on it for so long, which I am still avoiding whenever I can.

With my hands pressed into the scratchy surface of my makeshift bed, I push fully upright. My eyes have adjusted to the darkness, and I scan the inside of the room. Besides the mattress on the floor, there is one other door, but I'm not brave enough to go exploring.

A click makes my head snap toward the sound. I instinctively scoot backward until I'm against the wall and hold my breath. It slowly opens inward, and the light from the outside blinds me. Holding a hand over my eyes, I can only make out a shadow standing in the now open door, but his voice identifies him instantly.

"Took you long enough, princess."

I wait for my eyes to adjust before responding, "Well, maybe you shouldn't have used a fucking horse tranq." My words sound brave, but my insides lack the courage I'm trying to portray.

He snorts before turning his tone to ice. "I would be a little more careful about how you talk to me. I'm not your *last kidnapper*. I didn't bring you here to play family."

The hair on my neck stands, and I whisper, "What do you know about that?"

"We know everything, Lilly," a female voice comes from behind the tall man.

What?

He moves out of the way, and a woman enters the room. My attention is at her naked feet. Slowly, I let my gaze travel upward past the black leggings and over her dark tank top. She is slender and toned but not overly muscular. Her arms are folded over her chest, and when my eyes meet hers, I inhale sharply.

No!

I stare at the face I have seen in so many pictures over the last several months, and yet, my brain refuses to comprehend who I'm seeing.

"I don't understand." My words are slow, detached.

"I came to take back what you took from me," the woman explains in an equally robotic tone.

My forehead scrunches. How is this possible? Why is she with this supposedly dead former Army Ranger?

"Gray, give Lilly some water and bring her something to eat. We will continue our chat later." She turns and leaves me alone with...*Gray?*

"Who is Gray?" I ask the man I thought was Francis Turner.

He smirks. "That would be me. Francis Garrison Turner—or as she's called me since we were kids, Gray."

"Kids?" My hands are trembling, and I cross my arms in front of my chest, just to realize that that's the exact posture she just had. I quickly untangle myself again and sit down on my hands.

What is happening?

I follow Turner...Gray—whomever this man is—with my eyes. He walks over to the other door and opens it, revealing a bathroom. He grabs a plastic cup that, apparently, was already in there and fills it with water, only to place it on the floor, out of my reach.

"I'm not coming anywhere near you, princess. I already have two stab wounds, and I know what you've been trained to do."

My brows shoot up. How does this guy know everything about me?

He senses my unspoken question. "I've been watching you for her for over a decade, princess. I probably know you better than you know yourself."

I don't reply, and he snorts, shaking his head. "Drink water; it's the best way to get over your hangover."

"How—?"

But before I can finish the sentence, he is gone, and the door clicks shut, a lock snapping in place outside.

My entire body starts trembling, and a sheen of cold sweat coats my skin. I pull my knees close and wrap my arms around my legs, rocking back and forth. My eyes sting, and I let the tears go.

This can't be real. I'm still unconscious. She cannot be here.

I'm chanting the same three sentences over and over—my

lips moving but no sound coming out. With every repetition, my pulse quickens, and nausea makes my stomach churn. I swallow the saliva, but it's no use. I uncurl from my position and try to stand. My knees buckle at the first step, and I end up crawling to the bathroom on all fours. Thankfully, my captor left the light in the small room on, and I don't have to search for the toilet in the dark as the bile makes its way up. I retch several times, but since my last meal was...I don't know when, there is nothing to throw up. Eventually, the sensation subsides, and I sit back, wiping the sweat off my forehead.

Too exhausted to pull myself up and wash my face, I crawl back to the mattress and curl into a tight ball.

"WAKEY, WAKEY, PRINCESS." A not-at-all-cheery Gray pushes his foot into my back.

Facing away from the door, I arch away from the contact—not from pain but revulsion that this man is somehow associated with her. My eyes instantly gloss over, and I reach up, swiping at the moisture with the heel of my hand.

"Get up. She wants to talk to you. And you need to eat something. You've been out for almost thirty-six hours. Given the fact that you'll probably puke everything right back up, let's get the show on the road. I have more stops to make while I'm in this fucking country." He pushes me again with his damn boot.

Heat surges through my body the more he rants, and I whirl around, hook my elbow around his ankle, and use the little energy I can muster to kick both legs up. My feet connect with his groin region, pulling his leg out as soon as he is off-balance from pain.

Fuck you, asshole.

Gray topples over and lands ungracefully on his side. "You dirty little cunt," he yowls.

I push myself up into a sitting position and wait until his eyes meet mine before speaking. "Don't ever touch me again."

A snort comes from the open door. When my eyes meet hers, the empty pit in my stomach opens back up.

"Why am I here?"

She ignores me and addresses the curled-up man on the floor. "Get up! I told you to give her food, not get emasculated by a teenager." She kicks the brown bag I hadn't noticed before by the door toward me. When Gray doesn't move, she barges into the room and grabs him by his black hair. "I said get the FUCK UP!" She screeches the last word into his ear, and he winces.

She is psychotic.

She's about to turn and leave when I push myself off the mattress. My legs are still weak, but I force my spine straight and my tone calm. "Why am I here?"

She lets go of his curls, and her eyes snap to mine. "Not now, Lilly."

Her dismissive tone stirs a familiar sensation in me, but instead of cowering, I do the opposite. "Yes, now, Emily!"

CHAPTER THIRTY-TWO

RHYS

A RENTAL CAR IS WAITING FOR US AT THE PRIVATE HANGER AS soon as we arrive. With Wes in the backseat, we make our way to the address George gave my father. There are several moments where I am ready to jump out and walk—I probably could beat them there. This traffic is fucking ridiculous; it's the middle of the night.

Thanks to the WiFi on the jet, Dad has been in constant contact with George and the security staff positioned at the Hamlin Estate. Denielle has been texting Wes, who attempts to give me updates, but when I ignore him, he also leaves me alone. I have no clue what he—or my father—told Wes's parents to explain his sudden departure across the country. Don't care either. Since our one-sided chat, Dad seems to understand that I don't give a shit about what he has to say unless it involves Lilly's location and getting her back.

Thank fuck for that. I am over talking.

We pass a security guard, who meticulously dissects everyone's IDs before letting us enter the gated community. As we drive past the different properties, all separated from the road by various styles of walls, fences, and gates, I hear Wes mutter to himself, "Who the fuck lives here? The president?"

After what feels like years since Denielle's name lit up my phone today, we approach the wrought iron gate the nav chick directed us to. Dad opens his window and types something into the keypad like he's been here a million times.

What the hell?

I focus out the windshield, taking in the massive structure coming into view. In front of the house are two blacked-out SUVs and an even more decked-out RAM. Several men stand in front of the main entrance with a slightly shorter, dark-haired girl next to them: Denielle.

Arms wrapped around herself, her head snaps up as our car approaches. The men turn as well, and I recognize George instantly. How the hell did he get here before us?

Dad stops behind the farthest SUV, and Denielle takes off down the drive. Wes pushes his door open before we're fully stopped. Den jumps him koala-style and latches on. By the way her body is shaking, she is sobbing into my best friend's neck.

I exit the car a little slower, aiming straight for Lilly's bodyguard. I have tunnel vision.

George faces me as I reach the group. He's about to say something when I pull my arm back and let my fist fly. I clock him straight in the jaw, and his head snaps back. This is the only punch I get in, and the only reason I was able to make contact was the element of surprise.

I shake my hand out, even though I feel nothing. I move forward again. "YOU WERE SUPPOSED TO PROTECT HER!"

"Holy shit!" Wes exclaims somewhere behind me.

"I TRUSTED YOU! WHAT GOOD ARE YOU IF THIS PSYCHOPATH WALKS STRAIGHT IN?" My voice cracks, and tears are streaming down my face. My chest heaves, yet I feel like I am suffocating.

Two of the guys grab me by the arms and secure them behind my back, assuming I'll attack again.

"Let him go," George commands, and they instantly remove their hands. George steps closer and looks at me with such sorrow that it's clear he blames himself more than anything. Dipping his chin ever so slightly, it's like a signal. I throw myself at the man like a little kid.

George's arms wrap around me, and he says, "I will bring her back. I promise you."

Unable to speak, I nod into his shoulder. I'm losing it in front of everyone.

George shifts but doesn't let go. "Colonel McGuire. It's an honor to meet you."

I draw in a shuddering breath and step to the side, wiping my face with both hands.

My father holds his hand out. "George Weiler, how is my daughter connected to *The Ghost* no one has seen in two decades?"

Lilly's bodyguard doesn't answer his question. Instead, he says, "Let's get everyone inside and settled. Then we'll talk."

WE CONGREGATE in the living room—or one of them, as we passed two more on the way in. I scan my surroundings as I trudge after George. The money in this house is visible but not *in your face*. Everything is decorated subtly and tastefully—Mom would approve.

Mom. A pang of guilt hits my chest. We just left her there. I wonder what she's doing right now. If she and Natty will come to California.

I drop in the first seat available, which puts the kitchen in my direct line of sight. Two men and one woman are moving around. It looks like they're cataloging everything, taking pictures, and, as it seems, also looking for fingerprints. It's like we walked into a scene from one of those hyped-up crime TV shows, and I have to turn away. Someone broke in here and kidnapped Lilly, right there.

I avert my gaze. Den and Wes are on either side of me, with Dad standing by the door. George lowers himself into the closest armchair, and the remaining men distribute themselves in and outside the house.

"Where is Nate?" I break the silence in the room.

George's expression shifts to something unreadable, and it's like an invisible hand is choking me.

"What?" The word is just a rasped whisper.

George glances around the room before his gaze settles back on me. "Nate has been missing for over twenty-four hours."

My eyes widen. How is this possible? I open my mouth to ask exactly that but am interrupted.

"Could he be involved in Lilly's disappearance?" my father inquires in the same tone I've heard him speak in so many times on his business calls.

"No way!" I snap at my father, whose eyes widen at my outburst. I press my hand against my chest, feeling my heart beating against my palm.

"No," George replies, a lot calmer. "Nate would do anything for Lilly. He's been searching for her for over ten years."

"Ten?" Dad's eyebrows shoot up.

Ah, he's catching on.

No one elaborates, though, and George continues, "Nate landed in Paris around midnight local time. He texted me that he would get some sleep and be in touch in the morning before his meeting. That was the last time I communicated with him. I tried his phone and Hank's several times, but they went straight to voicemail."

"Hank is with him?" I narrow my eyes.

"Hank goes everywhere Nate goes." There is disdain in George's tone that I've never heard before.

"What about Joel?" Lilly told me about Nate's pilot.

George nods approvingly. "I contacted Joel. He went to

Nate's suite at the hotel. No one was there. He alerted our local security staff and was working with them last we spoke. I've been focused on this scene since. Nate is capable; Lilly is my first priority."

My father has been typing on his phone the entire time when his eyes suddenly snap up. Something must've clicked, and he walks out of the room like his ass is on fire.

"What's up with your dad?" Wes mumbles to me, but I only shrug.

"Who the fuck knows." *Or cares.*

Denielle yawns, and I glance at the antique clock in the corner. It's almost two in the morning, and I can't stop my own yawn.

"Now that everyone is here, I am calling Joel again. Why don't you three get some rest? I'll get you if we receive any news." George sweeps our faces one by one.

He's out of his mind if he thinks I'd be able to sleep.

But knowing George, there's also no use in arguing. We're dismissed—for now. We follow him upstairs, where he shows Wes to a spare room. Denielle walks past all of us and disappears inside. I cock an eyebrow at my best friend, who shakes his head at me—*don't ask*—and then follows her, closing the door.

I turn to face George, who is already making his way to another set of stairs. Too exhausted to question him why I'm not staying on this floor, I follow. I get my answer when he opens a door on the third floor.

Lilly's bedroom.

My eyes wander over the cream-colored décor. The bed is unmade, and clothes are hanging over the chair in the corner. I swallow over the lump in my throat as I step farther into the room.

"I'll be on the first floor if you need me." I nod, acknowledging him but not turning around. The click as the door closes indicates that I am alone.

· · ·

I DON'T EMERGE AGAIN until 10:30.

After taking a shower and changing into sweats and a t-shirt, I had sat down on Lilly's bed. Falling backward, I pulled one of her pillows over my face. The remnants of the same shampoo she uses at home registered in my nose, and my eyes started to burn.

I was so fucking sick of bawling like a baby.

Clutching the pillow tighter, it muffled my sobs. I imagined her moving around the room, standing by the window, looking out. I want her back. This...situation makes everything else seem so unimportant.

I didn't think I would sleep, but I must've passed out eventually. The next thing I know, I'm blinking against the sunlight. My mouth is dry, and the back of my throat feels like I gargled acid —damn crying.

Not bothering to change, I pad downstairs barefoot, where I find George and my father in the breakfast nook of the kitchen. The only reason I am willing to be around anyone is that I need to know if they have news. Two laptops and three phones—one of them more remnants of one—sit between them. My stomach instantly drops, recognizing the device for what it is...was— Lilly's.

I scan the room. The kitchen appears like nothing ever happened, which, on the one hand, is a relief—I don't think I could've handled seeing the result of the struggle—but on the other hand, it ignites a rage I haven't felt since I discovered what my psycho ex did to my girlfriend. The rational side of my brain is fully aware of how *irrational* I am. Still, with the room being this impeccable and the two former Marines lounging there like they're long-lost buddies, chatting casually over some joe, I want to take another swing at George. Or Dad. Or both. Definitely both.

Dropping into a chair on the other side of the table, I look at the two men. Like, really look at them. Some of my rage deflates at the realization that neither of them has slept a wink. Dad has dark circles under his eyes, his hair is disheveled like he ran his hands through it one too many times, and both are in the same clothes as last night.

A steaming cup of coffee is suddenly thrust in my line of vision, the dark liquid almost spilling over. As I follow the arm attached to it, an equally tired Denielle looks down at me. One corner of her mouth twitches, and I assume it's her attempt at a reassuring smile—which epically fails.

Out of the corner of my eye, Wes pulls out one of the barstools and leans against it. I take the mug from Den, not even attempting a positive facial expression, and she immediately steps back to Wes's side.

The bond the two of them have developed over the last months cause me to turn away. I want Lilly, my best friend and my girlfriend, back by my side. Seeing them so close causes a surge of jealousy that I am embarrassed to even admit to myself.

"Anything new?" Wes is the one to break the suffocating silence.

"We—" George starts when a door somewhere flies open— the front door maybe? And the noise of numerous footfalls echoes through the first floor. Every head turns as Nate stumbles into the kitchen, followed by a man in a pilot uniform and several of George's guards.

Lilly's brother is half bent forward, clutching his side, and George is out of his seat in a second. Good thing he was sitting in the corner seat, or he either would've climbed over the table or pushed my father out in the process.

"Nate, you're not supposed to be on your feet."

"What happened?"

"Where is my sister?!"

The man I assume is Joel, George, and Nate speak at the same time. Just as the words leave his mouth, Nate's legs buckle, and his pilot and head of security reach for him. George catches the brunt of his employer's large body and has to brace himself by stepping one foot back.

Nate grunts, and Joel supports him by wrapping his other arm around his shoulder. "He shouldn't be standing. Can we put him down somewhere?"

"I'm fiiineee," Nate responds in a slur.

I narrow my eyes at him.

"Dude, you don't look so fine," Wes remarks dryly, and Denielle elbows him in the ribs. "Ow." He scowls down at her.

"WHAT THE HELL HAPPENED?" George bellows, and everyone—except my father—flinches at his outburst. George doesn't raise his voice.

"He was stabbed," Joel explains with fear in his eyes as if George would hold him responsible. Maybe he does. What do I know about the inner workings of them.

Stabbed?

Everyone's gazes falls to Nate's side, where he's holding himself.

"How the hell did you get stabbed?" George addresses his boss, the momentary anger gone.

"Hank," Nate grunts.

"Hank? What—" Eyebrows scrunched, George turns to me as if I know what happened.

How would I know? I take a step forward, shouldering the poor pilot—who looks like he's about to piss himself any second —out of the way.

"Let me have him. I'll take care of Psycho-brother-in-law," I say, unable to stop myself from using my nickname for him. I grasp at anything that makes me not feel like floating in a dark void, and taking a verbal stab at Nate briefly does it for me. He's my connection to Lilly.

"You're funny, little brother-in-law." Nate chuckles then winces. "Fuuuuck."

"Come on, I gotcha."

Nate shifts his entire weight on me, and I brace his body as we make our way to the closest living room.

George breathes down my neck, followed by Denielle and

Wes both staring like they're watching *Alien vs. Predator* about to battle it out. I guess I can't fault them for that. This is the first time I've been face to face—in person—with the guy who kidnapped Lilly. *Twice.* But as we hobble toward the couch, several things register in my brain. My anger and resentment toward this man are gone. I don't know if it's temporary or if both of us losing the one person we care most about has shifted things. We'll have to wait and see.

Panting—the dude is fucking heavy dead weight—I deposit him on the couch. Half sitting, half lying on the sectional, I take a seat close to Nate, but not too close to be in his personal space. George sits down on the small coffee table right in front of us and leans forward, reaching for the hem of Nate's shirt.

My father is standing behind George, watching the scene with a frown.

Denielle walks in with a glass of water and a pill bottle. I didn't even notice she'd left. "Joel says he has to take these." She thrusts both items at George, who inspects it closely before uncapping the lid. He hands Nate two white pills and the water.

"Can you guys stop hovering already?" Nate mumbles as he takes his, what I assume are, painkillers.

"*We* are not the ones who got stabbed," I deadpan, crossing my arms over my chest.

"Nate." George waits for him to make eye contact. "What happened?" He's running out of patience.

Nate shifts so he is more upright. "The fucker stabbed me."

"Hank?" I ask just to confirm once more.

The confusion on everyone's face is as visible as the fact that the dude is dead meat if he did what Nate claims—which I don't doubt.

Winkey-Hank won't be winking much longer.

Nate nods his head in my direction. "We were eating break-fast in my suite, as usual, preparing for the meeting. I was sitting on the couch while the little cunt, *aka Hank*, was telling me what to expect. Then my phone vibrated." Nate pauses and shifts, grabbing onto his side. "I'm going to kill this fucker," he mumbles.

"Nate." George holds a warning in his tone, trying to get Nate to focus. The crease between his eyebrows tells me he doesn't like seeing Lilly's brother in pain. George is way more than just an employee to Nate.

"Sorry." Nate groans then mercifully continues, "I picked it up, and I saw that it was a notification from the house alarm system. It was disarmed." Nate's eyes settle on George. They both stare at each other, and it seems like a silent communication is taking place between them. George's expression turns murderous, and Nate jerks his head up and down.

"Where is he?" George growls.

"No clue, man. I woke up in the fucking hospital with no ID or any way of communicating. You know my French is shit."

My pulse increases, and I'm starting to lose patience with the two. My fingers have curled inward and have left crescent-shaped indentations in my palms. "It's great and all that the two of you can, apparently, read each other's minds, but I want to know where my girlfriend is. So, *please*, tell the rest of us unknowing mortals what the fuck happened?" I glare at both men.

All eyes are on me, but I don't care. They need to start fucking talking.

Nate adjusts his position so he can address me. "The house alarm system is set to send me notifications whenever it is armed or disarmed. It's part of the system I have at all my properties. I added the protocol here when Lilly moved in. Additionally, everyone with access to my properties has their own code. No one uses the same. The message I received showed an alert for Hank's code disarming the security system in this house." He pauses and waits for the rest of us to catch on.

Holy fucking shit!

"You are telling me that your bitch assistant has something to do with Lilly being kidnapped?" I grind out between clenched teeth. My entire body is vibrating from rage.

Nate presses his lips together. I turn and fling the first object within my reach across the room—a small, golden elephant statue from the coffee table. It makes a decent size dent in the drywall before crashing into the glass table underneath. I can't muster any remorse for the property damage.

"What next?" My father's voice brings everyone back to the present. He has remained silent since Lilly's brother stumbled into the house. Observing the scene.

"I told him I was gonna go take a leak. I started dialing George—fuck the meet with Lakatos. Lilly was in danger. That much was clear. The little shit must've realized that I was onto him, and next thing I know, I have a sharp pain in my side, and something hits me in the head." He inhales slowly. "I woke up in a Parisian hospital, and it took them two fucking hours to find someone fluent enough in English to get me a phone and call the hotel to find Joel. Their damn landlines wouldn't connect to a non-French number. It's like the stone age."

"I had already searched the suite when you called me." Joel stands in the corner of the room and addresses George. "Besides Nate's clothes, nothing was there. I packed everything up, and I went to the hospital. It took several more hours for them to agree to discharge him."

"We drove straight to the airport and came back," Nate finishes.

"Why didn't you call me?" George admonishes him.

"Because I had no clue if anyone else was involved, if someone had gotten into my system, or what the hell was going on. My laptop was gone, and I couldn't check the feeds." Nate is one of the best, and for him to consider someone breached his *homemade* security system—not to mention hijacking his business partner and turning him against Nate?

Fuck.

George suddenly stands up and turns to one of his men. "I want an APB out for Hank Todd. He is your number one priority." The guy jumps at the order, bobs his head up and down, and storms out.

"Um, shouldn't they look for Lilly?" Denielle asks, wringing her hands together.

"No, they can concentrate on the traitor. I'll find my sister. That son of a bitch is not smart enough to *not* leave a trail," Nate sneers and turns to George. "Have one of your guys go to his place and bring me everything he left. Laptop, phones, a fucking carrier pigeon if that's how he communicated with Turner. I want it all here within two hours."

His head of security nods and pulls his phone out, putting it to his ear as he follows the other guy.

Then, Nate turns to my father and pushes himself up until he's slightly swaying on his legs. "Mr. McGuire." He reaches out his hand. "I'm Lilly's brother, Nate Hamlin."

Dad looks between Nate's face and his hand. I can see the wheels in his head turning before he takes it. "Nate. Call me Tristen."

I expel a breath I didn't realize I was holding. I have no clue what I was expecting.

They both shake, followed by Nate turning to me. "Can you help me upstairs? I need to get to work."

Surprised that he wants my help, I'm momentarily stunned, but then I wrap his arm around my shoulder and slowly lead him to the stairs.

Behind me, I hear Dad tell Den and Wes that he's going to go check in with Mom. I don't know what they're going to do, but the selfish prick in me doesn't give a fuck.

Nate is here, and he is our best chance of finding Lilly.

CHAPTER THIRTY-THREE

LILLY

GRAY PUSHES HIMSELF UP, BUT WHEN HE PUTS A HAND ON HIS thigh for more leverage, his leg buckles, and he groans. I narrow my eyes at him—that is not the leg *I* stabbed.

He stumbles out of my room and slams the door. The familiar click follows right after, and I sink to the floor. The adrenaline is quickly leaving my body, and my hands begin to shake. Pulling my knees close, I wrap my arms around them and let my forehead drop forward.

What the hell is going on here?

I sit like this until the trembling in my body subsides enough to drag myself on all fours over to the paper bag without my arms or legs giving out. I'm starving, yet the thought of eating causes my stomach to churn as if someone has dared me to eat some type of insect—alive. I have to, though. If it's true that I've been here for over a day and a half, I need food. And water. The fighter in me knows I have to keep my strength up until Nate and George—oh, no, Denielle. In all of this, I completely forgot about her coming to LA.

Shit, shit, shit!

I gave her the address and put her name on the visitor list. She should be able to—another thought *backhands* me. How did Gray get on the property, let alone in?

My brain pulls me in so many different directions that my tired mind can't keep up. I eye the bag that supposedly contains nourishment again. Please let it be something edible.

Pulling the top apart, I could weep in relief: two plain bagels. I reach for the water that still sits in the middle of the room from...last night? Whenever Gray put it there. Gulping it down, it's like a drop of water over a hot stone. It doesn't satisfy my body's need one bit. Dropping the now empty cup, I take two large bites out of the bagel. Not a good idea. My stomach instantly begins to cramp. I clamp my mouth shut and crawl as fast as I can into the adjacent bathroom, reaching the porcelain bowl just in time for everything to make a reappearance.

Cold sweat covers every inch of my skin, and the full-on body tremors are back. I groan as another wave of nausea crashes down on me, but all that's left is bile.

"Make it stooooop," I mumble into the empty space and lean my cheek against the seat. My inner germaphobe is too exhausted to be grossed out. Gray apparently knew what he was talking about.

When my legs can support my weight, I pull myself up on the rim of the sink and rinse my mouth—what I wouldn't give for a toothbrush right now.

On the second try, I know better. I take small sips of water, pick the dry bread apart, and nibble on it slowly. It takes forever to finish both, but it remains down. Win-win.

Sitting back on the mattress, I prepare myself for a long wait time but am surprised when I hear footsteps outside the door and the lock unlatches.

I'm not completely blind anymore when the outside glare

hits me since I've left the little light in the bathroom on. Gray enters the room, followed by Emily. My mother.

I'm still considering that I'm hallucinating.

Both scan the empty bag on the ground, and Gray smirks. Emily is the first to speak. "I see you ate. Good."

Her tone is dismissive. Detached. She acknowledges it but couldn't care less.

Remaining where I am with my back to the wall, I stare at both of them. They are such an odd pair. Where Gray is all creep, she is put together and impeccably styled. She is still wearing black leggings, but her top is light-blue today. Her blonde hair is curled in precise waves, her subtle but professionally applied makeup making her look younger than her forty-eight years.

I steady my voice. "What do you want with me? I don't assume you want a happy family reunion."

With some of my strength returning, my attitude also resurfaces. Though, it's different than when I had faced Nate for the first time. With Nate, I somehow felt he wouldn't harm me, but I'm not so sure with these two. Gray probably would enjoy getting revenge for the stab wound and kick to the balls. I draw my shoulders back, forcing my inhales and exhales to remain steady.

I refuse to show them fear.

Gray leans at the wall beside the door as Emily walks closer. She squats down with her elbows on her knees and slants her head, scanning me up and down. She is far enough away that I'd have to leave my spot to reach her—a strategic move on her part.

"You grew up nicely." Her voice is cold, and the hairs on the back of my neck stand.

What kind of statement is that?

"Is that a compliment?" I cock my head in an identical way and mimic her expression.

She huffs out a non-comical laugh. "I see you haven't lost

your attitude." I open my mouth to make a sarcastic remark, but she continues, "Heather and Tristen did a good job. Unfortunately, not good enough. I didn't plan for you to meet your brother."

What?

My pulse increases, but I remain mute, letting her do the talking.

"All you had to do was turn eighteen. You would've never known any of this. I had it all arranged."

Eighteen?

The pieces are falling into place. "This is all about the money my father left me?" I stare at her incredulously. She dumped me and went off the grid to wait her time for...money?

"What else would it be about?"

Unable to stop myself, the little girl in me speaks. "Me?"

My mother chuckles as if I've said the most ridiculous thing. "Oh, my dear Lilly, I never wanted children. Yet, fate had different plans for me." Her tone is sugary sweet, and goosebumps appear on my arms. "That's why I chose Henry; he told me on our second date that he was infertile. He was perfect. I would never have to go through that again. He was my ticket out of the life I grew up in."

Again? But she doesn't give me an opportunity to speak.

"We got married and moved to San Diego to be closer to my childhood friend. Life was normal for the first time. Then, I went to visit Heather at a conference and met Brooks. I didn't see him coming." Her eyes become vacant for a second before they harden again. "He made me feel."

Behind Emily, Gray shifts, and his expression becomes unreadable. I narrow my eyes at the man. She said something that made him react.

Oblivious to the change in her...partner? Accomplice? Whatever he is to her, she continues, "When I found out I was pregnant, I even considered keeping it. But then he told me he went back to his wife. He wanted to make it work with her for his children's sake." She sneers the last words, and I fight the urge to press closer against the barrier behind me.

Her face contorts. "I WAS CARRYING HIS DAMN CHILD!"

I jump at the outburst and fight the urge to wrap my arms around my midsection. *Holy hell.*

Emily stands up in a jerked motion and starts pacing. I trail her every move while keeping Gray in my peripheral vision. I cannot let my guard down with them.

"But nooo, that wasn't good enough. I wasn't a rich, stuck-up bitch. He would've lost everything if he had left Payton." She suddenly spins and gets in my face. "I had to bide my time. And if he wouldn't come to me willingly, I would at least get what I deserved another way. So...I kept you."

I press the back of my head against the concrete wall. "What you deserved?" I whisper with raised eyebrows.

But she ignores my question. "He wanted you. Did you know that? He wanted to raise you. The red-headed bitch would've taken you in as her own." The smugness in her tone makes the hair on my nape stand. "We couldn't have that now, could we?"

Good Lord, this woman is crazy.

"It was all fine, as long as he was paying his child support, but—"

My snort interrupts her, and her eyes snap to mine. *Shit.* I didn't mean to do that but can't take it back now. Thankfully, the anger that has slowly been building the more she rants gives my voice the backbone I need. "Child support? Are you kidding me? Twenty-five K a month is not child support. You blackmailed him!" Another puzzle piece is in its place.

Her sudden stiff posture tells me that she didn't expect me to know that fact.

My *mother* composes herself and moves on without acknowledging my statement. "He should've just kept sending the money, and everything would've been fine."

My muscles tense. I don't like where she is going.

"When Gray and Mara were in town one weekend, and Gray noticed someone following me, it was time to show your dear father what it meant to ignore my instructions. I didn't crawl my way out of the life I was born into to be made a joke out of."

I stop listening after Gray and Mara.

Who the hell is Mara?

"So Gray and I came up with a plan." She stops talking, which brings my attention back to Emily. She's standing in the middle of the room, hands on her hips, and looking at me expectantly. She's waiting.

Replaying what she has said so far and—oh, no. Please no! I cover my mouth with my hands, whispering, "You killed Payton?"

Her face lights up, and she puts her palm against her chest like she is proud of my deductive skills. "Well, not me, personally. I just gave Brooks the nudge to set things in motion."

Set things in motion. *What—?* I can feel the crease between my eyebrows grow deeper.

"We made Gray disappear. A dead man could not be prosecuted." She sounds almost chipper.

My eyes flick between the two people in front of me, swallowing several times. I let my gaze rest on Gray, who still hasn't moved. One foot propped against the wall, his arms are crossed over his broad chest. He'd appear bored if it weren't for him clenching his jaw.

I can't look at her, so I address him instead. My voice is a mere rasp. "Who was in the car?"

The car that went over the cliff on Pacific Coast Highway.

"My brother," Gray answers without emotion, and I choke on my saliva, coughing violently to the point of my eyes watering.

"You killed your brother for *her*?" The pitch in my tone is rising. "You both are fucking insane!"

With blinding speed, Emily is across the room and in front of me. Her hand shoots to my throat, and she pins my legs with hers. "You know nothing about me," she hisses in my face, and I can smell the wine on her breath. I'm going to be sick.

"No, I d-don't. Y-you left m-me," I croak, trying to dislodge her clawed hand from my neck.

She lets go and moves back, smoothing her hands over her top and pants. "Let's continue our chat later."

As she struts out, I gulp in all the air I can get. Watching her retreating form, I place my hand at the side of my neck where her nails dug in. Gray follows close behind, and I'm alone again. Wetness under my fingertips makes me pull the hand away again. Blood. She scratched me to the point of breaking skin.

I'm starting to feel glad that I don't remember this woman. Was she like this when I was a child? How could Henry stay married to her?

Henry! I jump from the mattress and race to the door, banging my fists against it. "EMILY!" I hit the barrier until my arm hurts, but there is no response. Exhausted, I turn, leaning with my back against the door, and slide to the ground. Tears fill my eyes, and I let them fall, uncaring if they hear me.

"What did you do with Henry?"

It's hours before I see either of them again.

I'm on the mattress, my back pressed against the wall. *Never let yourself be vulnerable in a hostage situation*, Spence's words from one of our sessions come back to me. Back then, I laughed. What hostage situation did he think I'd get in? Did he know more than he let on? After Gray's boot against my back, my trainer's advice has become like a mantra in my mind. These people are crazy. I'm in a hostage situation.

The door opens to a small gap and another paper bag projectiles in.

"EAT!" Gray's barked command echoes through the bare room, and the door flings shut again.

So much for getting more answers anytime soon.

Resigned, I comply. My stomach has been growling for a while, and I'm not one of those idiots that goes on a hunger strike to defy their kidnappers. Fuck that! Emily's insanity, what she said, her attack... I touch the marks on my neck. I should be more hurt that she obviously never wanted *me*. I was at first, then I remind myself that I do have a family. Two, actually. I don't remember this woman, and from what I've experienced so far, I hope I never will remember. She is a stranger. She won't break me. I'll go down fighting if I have to.

Eventually, I must have dozed off and tipped over because I'm now horizontal and staring at Emily's bare feet.

Does this woman ever wear shoes?

I struggle to push myself into a sitting position. *Shit.* Gray is in his usual spot next to the doorframe. His eyes are drooping, and even from here, I can see that his pupils are the size of a pinprick. Is he high?

"Darling, please excuse that it took me so long to get everything in order." Emily sounds like a doting mother.

In order?

"Where is Henry?" My fingers curl in. I refuse to let her distract me from the one question I want an answer to.

She places a stack of papers with a pen on top in front of the mattress. "If you sign here, everything will be rectified."

Is she high?

"Where is Henry?" I repeat myself slowly, purposefully talking as if she has trouble comprehending simple English. There is a buzz running through my body, a combination of rage and fear, and my fists press into my thigh.

Her nostrils flare. "I guess I was right to keep him around, after all."

My pulse speeds up. "What do you mean?"

"My *husband* is currently indisposed, but I might be inclined to let you speak to him if you sign the papers," she states sweetly.

The reason why George abandoned his position during my

attack comes to the forefront of my mind, and my eyes widen as I stare at Emily. "The drugs," I whisper.

She scowls, and I elaborate louder, "The ones he bought in Virginia." I flick my gaze to Gray. "They weren't for me—at least, not all of them." I rub the spot he drove the needle in.

Emily slowly swivels on her heels and focuses on her helper. "You were followed?" Her voice turns void of emotion. Her mood swings are starting to freak me out; there's no indicator of what sets her off.

The tall man shrugs. "You have her now. What difference does it make?" His words are slow like he has to concentrate hard to form them.

"What. Difference? WHAT. DIFFERENCE?" she shrieks and is across the room in a flash, grabbing onto Gray's thigh and squeezing.

He winces but won't buckle as her nails dig into what I assume is the other stab wound.

"What else have you been hiding from me, Fran-cis?" The shrill tone has turned to an icy whisper, and I have to strain my ears to follow the conversation.

"Nothing, Em."

"What if Weiler would've followed you to the house, huh?"

"No one knows where you stashed the cripple."

Cripple?

My heart starts pounding, and I jump up. "What did you do with Henry?"

She doesn't turn when she responds, eyes locked with the man she's torturing with her talons. "I simply kept him in line. But one phone call from me and he will no longer be of your concern. Or mine."

White-hot rage surges through me, and I lunge at the woman who gave birth to me. I tear her off of Gray, but she spins and backhands me with a force that makes my head snap to the side.

"You will not touch me. I'm your *mother*!" she seethes at me, getting right into my face.

I slowly turn back to her. "You are not my mother," I grind out. My cheek is burning, but I refuse to raise my hand to the sting. "Heather is my mother. Hell, Payton was probably more a mother to me than you—and I never even met the woman." A voice in my head screams to shut up. Emily is obviously mentally unstable, but the words were out of my mouth before I could stop myself.

Instead of responding to my verbal attack, she flips around and takes two long strides to Gray, whose eyes widen at her sudden intrusion of his personal space. She pushes her hand between the man and the wall and pulls out...a knife?

Shit. I scurry backward as she approaches me like a predator advancing on its prey. "Do you want to repeat that, my daughter?"

I flatten myself against the wall and move sideways away from her, but she keeps following with the knife held low toward me. I can deflect a blade. That was one of the first lessons Spence taught me, but the shock of *my mother* coming after me with a weapon has temporarily wiped my brain of all defense moves. Before I can collect myself, Gray's arms wrap around Emily, and he stops her.

"Em, you need to calm down. If you hurt her now, she most certainly won't sign the money over."

When did he become the voice of reason?

She lowers the knife and stops struggling. Gray seems to know that the immediate threat is over and loosens his grip.

"Sign the damn papers, and you can have Henry. That's the only reason he's still breathing anyway," she barks out before shouldering out of Gray's hold. She spins on her heel and marches out.

Gray remains in his spot for a moment longer, eyeing me. "Piece of advice, princess. I've known your mother all my life. You need to watch your mouth if you want to come out of here..."—he pauses and quirks an eyebrow—"with a pulse."

CHAPTER THIRTY-FOUR

RHYS

NATE DROPS INTO THE DESK CHAIR WITH A THUD, AND I PULL another one around from the front. I keep it near the edge, not wanting to be in his way but so I can still see what he does.

His hands hover over the keyboard before he turns back to me. "I didn't think I'd like you much."

What the—?

"Excuse me?" I cock an eyebrow at Lilly's brother. "I just carried your heavy, injured ass upstairs and—"

"That came out wrong," he interrupts me, chuckling, and wipes a hand over his mouth. "The big brother in me was suspicious about your intentions with Lilly."

I open my mouth to tell him where he can shove his big-brother attitude, but Nate holds up a hand. "Chill, I know I'm the last person who can claim the brother-of-the-year award." He blows out a breath. "What I'm trying to say... I can see why my sister would argue about the existence of a soulmate with me. Everything Lilly told me about you two—your past. Plus, when you and I talked before and now meeting you in person... You're not so bad."

Soulmate? He must be high from the pain meds.

I do a goldfish imitation, no clue how to respond to that.

He focuses back on the monitors and presses the space bar. One of the monitors comes to life, and he's about to hit the other keyboard when he pauses. "What the fuck?"

Nate's face pales, and his eyes nearly bulge out of their sockets. I lean over to see what has him so unhinged and almost fall out of my chair. Brooks's face is paused on the screen.

"What is that?" I ask hesitantly, pulling myself back into the chair and scooting it closer.

Nate ignores me and hovers the curser over the play button. He closes his eyes for several inhales and exhales before they snap open, and he clicks—almost as if he didn't want to give himself a chance to change his mind.

SHE THREATENED *to tell Payton about the affair. About Lilly. She wanted me to come back to her. Said she'd leave her husband. It was like she had built this fantasy in her head about us. A relationship that never existed. When I didn't change my mind, she started threatening our daughter's life.*

HEARING BROOKS THROUGH THE SPEAKER, the fingers of Nate's hand in his lap dig into his leg. The other, still on the trackpad, begins to tremble. Then the words sink in. *She started threatening our daughter's life.* She. Lilly's mother. Emily. Emily was threatening Lilly? My stomach rolls, and I wrap one arm around myself.

I *SAW ONLY ONE OPTION. I told Payton everything. As you can imagine, your mother didn't take the news well. I had an illegitimate daughter. She left me for a few weeks. You thought your mom took Audrey to stay at your aunt's house during that time.*

When Payton came back, we sat down and talked. We talked for days, and by some miracle, your mother forgave me. We agreed that our family would come first, and we would find a way to have Lilly be part of your and Audrey's lives. That's who your mother was. She loved and cared for everyone. None of this was Lilly's fault.

TEARS STREAM down Brooks's face, and his voice cracks with every other word. A lump forms in my own throat. He recorded this video for his son. Peering at Nate, his eyes are glossed over, and his spine is rigid.

"This is why he mentioned the pipes in his will to be given to me..." Nate mumbles to himself.

"Huh?"

He pauses the video and turns to me. His tone is subdued. "I inherited everything my parents owned, which made the will pretty simple. When they read it to me, my grandfather's pipes were listed specifically, nothing else. I never thought about it. I didn't want shit to do with what's in this house—what my father cared about."

I narrow my eyes. "You think that was his hint for you to find this?" I gesture to the screen.

"Yes," he whispers.

"But why hide it?" This doesn't make sense.

Nate shrugs. "At this point, who cares? It could've been anything. Not wanting for anyone to find out before me, he could've been afraid Emily would come after him, or he was simply drugged out of his mind from the antidepressants."

Then why didn't he hide the letters and pictures Emily sent?

"But he didn't hide the photos and let—"

"I DON'T CARE, RHYS!" he barks, and I take that as my cue to shut up.

Without another word, Nate restarts the recording, and I focus back on the screen.

. . .

MOST OF THE TIME, Emily acted completely normal. We were two adults who made a mistake and conceived a child.

Then, a phone call would come, not one of her handwritten letters. She'd threaten me, Lilly, or on a few occasions, even you and Audrey. Said that if she couldn't be with me, she wanted money for raising my child. For keeping the secret from her husband.

The first time I questioned her about why she wouldn't come clean to him, she ended the call. Next, I received an email from an unknown sender with a picture of Lilly sleeping in her crib—nothing else, no context or message. I didn't know what it meant, but I couldn't reach Emily for days.

Eventually, I drove to San Diego and started following her. Everything seemed normal. Lilly was fine. She sent another handwritten letter with new pictures, and your mother and I chalked it up as a random occurrence.

Then, she called again. She demanded more money than we had already given her. The amount was outrageous, and when I told her so, she hung up.

I received another email with a picture of Lilly. This time, she was playing in the yard—again, no message. Something wasn't right, and Payton decided to contact a PI your grandfather sometimes used when their regular guy was already on a job.

REGULAR GUY? Is he talking about George? Nate's mouth is pressing in a thin line as if he has come to the same conclusion. Did George know about any of this? Nate makes no indication to stop the video and confront his employee, though.

WE HAD him look into Emily's past as well. The information he showed us...her childhood...it wasn't a good one. There were holes in her past. She'd disappear for months at a time until her husband came into the picture. But all the evidence led to her having...mental problems. I don't know if her husband knew about it or if she was such a good actor around people that she fooled everyone. She had fooled me for months.

BROOKS SIGHS and clutches a picture in his hand. My heart is hammering against my ribcage. I want Nate to stop this video. I've heard enough, but at the same time, I need to know the rest.

AFTER THAT, we looked into getting custody of Lilly. Our attorney even said we had a good chance if we could prove that Lilly was in physical danger. With Emily's husband not being her biological father or having legally adopted her, we could sue for sole custody. However, neither Payton nor I would've kept Lilly from him. Not if he was...safe.

THERE IS such a long pause that I begin wondering if Brooks is going to say anything else.

THE NEXT TIME EMILY CALLED, I informed her that I had looked into requesting shared custody. Your mother and I had agreed that we didn't want to spook her right off the bat with taking Lilly away; we would've accepted joint custody. Emily didn't take that...well.

WELL? Please don't say what I think you're going to say. I'm so high-strung that my entire body feels like it's vibrating.

THE NEXT DAY, I received an email with another picture. Lilly had a bruised eye and a split lip. S-she was b-barely a year o-old.

. . .

I'M GOING to be sick. Tears are streaming down Brooks's cheeks as he recalls everything. Nate's hands cover his mouth, not making any attempt to conceal his crying. Someone was hurting Lilly. Nate's mother knew about all of it. My mind starts to take off on its own.

THIS TIME, the email had a message. Either I would pay the mother of my child the agreed-upon amount every month on the same day—meaning the five figures Emily previously demanded—or there would be no daughter.

We didn't know what to do. Payton wanted to take Lilly from Emily against her will. But when we received another email with more...photos, I agreed to pay. Emily, or whoever did this to my little girl—I don't believe her husband had anything to do with it...they were serious.

I...I couldn't risk my daughter's life.

MY HANDS ARE SHAKING SO BADLY I tuck them under my armpits and clamp my elbows to the side of my body. Brooks doesn't go into any details about what kind of pictures the second email contained, but I can guess. This is some fucked-up shit, and it all revolves around Lilly. How is it possible that my parents, who supposedly cared so much for her, didn't know any of this? Or did they? I want to confront my father, but I can't get out of the chair. My legs won't obey.

Nate's complexion has turned a chalkish gray with a hint of green. His leg is bouncing so fast my messed-up brain associates the tapping sound of his foot with that Irish dance-tap show Mom was obsessed with when we were kids—River-something. What the fuck is wrong with my head?

I concentrate on breathing through my nose as the video continues to play mercilessly. How much more is there?

· · ·

Payton and I met with Emily. She had Lilly with her but refused to let me hold her. Nate, she looked so much like you and Audrey. The same blonde hair, the same eye color. She was such a happy baby, smiled the entire time.

During that meeting, we agreed to pay Emily the sum she had demanded under the condition of regular updates and me being able to see Lilly. I wanted to be part of her life. I had to.

Payton cried the entire drive home, but we knew we would risk Lilly's life if we came after her in any way at this time. We hoped that if we played along and bided our time, we'd have a better chance in the future.

I CAN BARELY SEE the screen. I have to untuck my arms and wipe my eyes. I have no words for what is being revealed in front of me. Has Lilly seen this? Her father loved her. He wanted her. Hell, even Nate's mother wanted Lilly. We had it all so fucking wrong.

A few years later, we received the demand to increase the amount, and we complied without hesitation. Emily had kept her end of the deal, I visited with Lilly regularly, and our PI also kept an eye on her. From what we were able to see, she was safe and happy.

We wanted to wait a few more years before starting the legal procedures of getting custody. We hoped that if Lilly was older, the likelihood of her getting physically hurt was less.

What we didn't consider was Emily finding out about the private investigator. To this day, I don't know how, but she saw it as a violation of our agreement.

ALL THE COLOR has left Brooks's face, and the blood in my veins runs cold. Nate has gone completely still. I don't think he's even breathing. Hell, I know whatever comes next will break me, and the man on the screen is not even my father.

I RECEIVED AN EMAIL—THE first one in years. But instead of a picture of Lilly, it contained two photographs. One of Payton and one of Audrey. From that morning.

FUCK.

I IMMEDIATELY CALLED your mother and told her to get Audrey and go to your grandfather's vineyard. We had never been there, and no one knew about it. He purchased it not long before he passed.

Two hours later, the police came to my office. Your mother and sister had been in a car accident. They told me she had run a stop sign.

You knew your mother. She was the most cautious driver out there. There was no way she missed the sign.

BROOKS'S SHOULDERS shake with sobs as he finishes.

AUDREY D-DIED O-ON IMPACT. The car was h-hit on her side. They said your mother had s-suffocated. H-how could s-she suffocate in a car a-accident?

I CAN'T BREATHE. My lungs have closed up, and I'm unable to draw in a breath. Nate slams his hand on the keyboard, which *finally* stops the recording of horrors. He starts retching and turns to the side, dropping out of his chair until he's on all fours. He reaches for a trash can I hadn't noticed before and pukes right into it.

Chin dipped to my chest, I wrap my arms around my midsection and rock back and forth. In addition to the smell coming from my side, a sour taste coats my tongue, and black spots appear in my vision. I close my eyes and start counting—one, two, three, don't throw up, four, five, six, don't throw up, seven, eight...

I'm waiting for someone to burst in here and demand to know what's going on. George, my father, or even Wes. But the door remains closed.

The gagging sounds from Nate have stopped, but neither of us speaks. I have no fucking clue what to do. It is clear what Brooks was saying, or rather *not saying*. Audrey and Payton's death wasn't an accident. Payton didn't die from the impact.

I turn my head in Nate's direction. One arm draped over the trash can, he lets it support his body. The other hand is holding his side, and he groans. "Rhys?"

"Yeah?"

There's a pause and another groan. "I can't get up."

Huh? Oh.

"'Kay, uh, hold on." Unfolding myself, I place my palms on the armrest and push myself into a standing position. When I'm sure my legs will support me and I won't faceplant next to Nate, I bridge the short distance between us. I grab him under his arms and hoist him back into his chair.

"Oof. Dude, you're not that much taller; how can you be so heavy?" I grunt.

Nate chuckles. "Itth called dead weith." His words are slurred again. He should probably rest, but I doubt this will happen anytime soon.

"Should we finish...this?" I peer at the monitor with a frozen Brooks on it. Nate remains quiet for so long that I'm not sure he heard me. Suddenly, he hits the space bar, and we watch Brooks trying to regain control.

. . .

Lilly, if you are with your brother, I am so sorry that I never got the chance to come for you. Please know that you were always on my mind. On Payton's mind. And that all we tried to do was keep you safe.

Holy shit, this video was for Nate and Lilly.

Nate, if Lilly is already part of your life, take care of your little sister. If not, please find her. You deserve to have your family in your life.

I'm sorry I wasn't a better father to either of you. I will never forgive myself for being the reason my wife and daughter died and that my son went to a mental hospital for something I caused. I'm so sorry. Please forgive me.

Nate, I never said it enough, but I'm proud of you.
I love you both with all my heart.

CHAPTER THIRTY-FIVE

RHYS

I HAVE NO FUCKING CLUE HOW LONG NATE AND I STARE AT the black screen once the video cuts off. So many thoughts assault my brain at the same time, and I dig the heels of my hands into my eyes. I press so hard until it hurts, but nothing stops the onslaught of emotions and new information needing to be processed.

The affair didn't go on for years.

We were wrong.

Nate's mother knew about Lilly.

Admiration for the woman's compassion and understanding makes warmth spread through my body.

Emily was blackmailing Brooks for money.

A bucket of ice douses the warmth.

Emily hurt her own daughter. Over fucking money.

Rage slowly begins to course through my veins. Lilly as a toddler flashes in front of my eyes. I've seen so many photos of her as a little girl, always laughing and smiling. But instead of remembering those good times, my brain alters them, inserting injuries into the mental pictures. One worse than the other. The sound of her crying reverberates in my ears, and I want to clamp my hands over them.

Nate's mother and sister were killed. Murdered.

My heart is beating so fast I feel dizzy.

Brooks wanted to take care of Lilly. He was a good person who made a shitty mistake during a weak moment.

"I blamed him for everything," Nate mumbles, interrupting my inner rampage. I remove my hands, glancing at him. His gaze is vacant, still on the monitor. "I told him at the funeral that I hated him. I refused to take his calls. He tried to visit after my arrest, but I made the staff send him away." He turns to me. "My father wanted Lilly to be part of our family. He didn't have an affair all those years." His gaze flips back and forth between my eyes.

"I..." Fuck, what do I say? "You couldn't have known. He didn't tell you any of that."

"I didn't let him. He probably tried," Nate bursts out, and I jump at the sudden shift. "He *killed* himself."

"None of this is your fault, Nate." George's voice makes both of us jerk around. Neither of us had noticed the door opening. He remains in the threshold.

"Did you know?" I grind out between clenched teeth.

"No." George steps inside and closes the door. "I came to check on you. I heard...sounds, then your father's voice." He tilts his head toward the computers. "I knew your family had someone else they worked with occasionally when I was busy, but never what cases they put him on. It wasn't my place to ask."

"Emily killed my mother. She didn't die in the accident. There *was* no accident." Nate looks like a little boy as he peers up at George, and my chest tightens.

George steps closer, pulling Nate up and wrapping his arms around him. Both men stand like this for several minutes, Nate's shoulders shaking silently. Averting my eyes, I stare at the floor.

When Nate regains some control, he moves back but

instantly sways on his feet. Both of us jump into motion and latch onto him before his legs give out.

"You need to rest." George's tone is commanding yet laced with worry.

"I need to find my sister," he pleads after he lets us guide him back into his chair.

"Dude, you are no good for anyone if you collapse," I snarl. *Shit.* I didn't mean to sound like an asshole. "I—" I'm about to explain when Nate waves me off. He gets it, and a sigh of relief escapes me. I can't handle much more.

With George, Nate starts the video over, and we conclude that Lilly must've watched the beginning but got interrupted— by whoever *took* her.

She would've told someone otherwise. She would've called me.

When we get to the part of Brooks recalling Lilly's abuse— there is no other way to say it—I fly out of my seat. "I, um...I'm gonna get some coffee for, uh, you. And me." There is no fucking way I'll listen to this one more time.

SEVERAL HOURS, and even more cups of coffee later, everyone in the house was up to speed. As per usual, my father remained mute. I wanted to punch the answers out of him. There is no way he didn't know about at least part of this. The man has eyes in the back of his head, for fuck's sake. How could he have missed Lilly being used as a punching bag by her psychotic mother? *My mother's* best friend.

I wanted to rip my hair out.

Denielle had burst into tears, and Wes dragged her to their room for her to calm down. Dad disappeared with his phone plastered to his ear before I could confront him. A need to be with Nate while he looks for Lilly kept me from searching for my father.

Sitting back in my chair, with my arms folded over my chest

and my ankle crossed over my knee, I watch Nate at work. The guy is good—and fast. His hands are flying over the four different keyboards on the desk. And Lilly is on the fast track to being at the same level—at least that's what Nate said to her. Lilly. Fuck, where are you, babe? Please be okay.

I squeeze my eyes shut. "You need to work faster."

"I work as fast as I can," Nate responds without pausing what he does, not taking my stab personally. He's better equipped and smarter than any authority we could've brought in, but at the same time, it's not fast enough.

There are still so many questions, but after Brooks's video, I'm convinced that everything is connected to the affair. It was the start of everything. Hell, Lilly has been saying it for weeks. I wonder if she has memories that were buried under the fake ones but were not fully erased—that, subconsciously, she knew.

Emily killed Payton and Audrey. She had an innocent woman and child murdered and then disappeared off the face of the earth. If she's involved now, what is the purpose? What does she want? My mind shifts. If she took Lilly and she had no problems harming an innocent child—two if you count Lilly *and* Audrey— I don't want to think about what she would do to someone who is an actual threat.

I need to get my ass out of this rabbit hole, or I am going to lose it. Again.

I focus on Lilly's brother instead. Nate switches between typing on the two wireless keyboards and the laptops simultaneously. On one, he pulls up information about Hank, aka the traitor, which looks like his personnel file based on the Altman logo. Two monitors show command line windows, and I quickly zone out of those. The last one is the security feed for the property.

I move closer to get a better look. Nate pulls up the video from Wednesday night, right before the alarm system got disabled, and we watch the outside view to all the entrances.

"I don't have any cameras inside this property," he murmurs as he fast forwards. George gave him more pain meds, and the three cups of coffee seemed to have done the trick. He no longer sounds drunk or looks like he's about to pass out. He's jittery, but I blame the caffeine for that.

We watch the feed until a dark SUV with tinted windows pulls into the drive. Nate switches the vantage point to another camera. "It's a rental."

Scrunching my eyebrows, I glance between him and the screen. "How do you know?"

He points at a sticker in the window.

Just then, we watch a tall man get out: Turner.

No. Fucking. Way!

"Motherfucker!" I feel like someone just kicked me in the junk. Fucking Turner works with (or for) Emily—if she's behind this. And so does Hank, the bitch assistant.

It's all connected. Every-fucking-thing. How?

"He disguised the license plate." Nate's voice is detached, and I eye him warily.

I follow his line of sight and scan the car. The plate is smeared with something reflective to the camera, and I curse under my breath.

We watch Turner leave the frame, and with no camera's inside, all we can do is wait. Nate skips ahead thirty seconds at a time until we hit the nine-minute mark. Turner reappears, carrying Lilly over his shoulder, and throws her in the backseat— literally throws her.

No!

I want to scream. Destroy something. He hurt Lilly. She's unconscious. What if she's seriously injured? My hands begin to tremble, and I clench and unclench my fingers.

Oblivious to the havoc raging inside of me, Nate keeps watching then zooms in. "Intelligence level of a damn amoeba."

That snaps me out of it. "Huh?"

"Hank got them the car. The moron used the company we hire for all the out-of-state board members' rentals. They have built-in GPS tracking."

I snort. "I didn't take him for that dumb." We can track her.

Nate pauses then starts typing again. "It's too easy. He'd know I'd find that trail in less than thirty minutes."

Fuck!

NATE IS CORRECT. One of George's men finds the SUV abandoned in a less desirable part of town—keys in the ignition. Turner switched his mode of transportation, and with where he did it, there is a zero chance of finding a reliable witness. It is a fucking miracle the car is intact. George sends it for processing, but even if we find fingerprints, we know Turner is involved, so I have no clue what the purpose is.

Later that afternoon, George comes in with a single laptop, declaring that it was the only electronic device left in Hank Todd's apartment.

"It's questionable if he had any intention of returning when you left for France or if he never had anything of value in the place," he tells Nate as he hands the computer over to me.

Something registers in Nate's brain. "I've never been to his place." He locks eyes with his head of security, then me.

George doesn't show any reaction, but I squint at him. "How long have you known him?"

"Long."

"You think he's been spying on you this entire time?"

"At this point, I wouldn't rule it out." He blows out a breath. "Let me see how far back I can search his bank account. His business cell phone was clean, but he could easily have a personal device I don't know about. And if he uses a burner, there is no way for me to find that without a receipt."

"So, we're back to square one." I grind my teeth. The urge to throw something makes my hands twitch.

"Not yet."

. . .

AFTER WATCHING Nate for another couple of hours and learning that his curse vocabulary is as extensive as my own—if not larger —my patience is wearing thin.

He has run into several roadblocks, and Hank's laptop was useless. All it had was company documents—which Hank was supposed to have—and porn. A lot of porn. To the point where even the guy in me who wants to jump his girlfriend every possible occasion had to cringe.

I yell at Lilly's brother to work the fuck faster and to suck it up since his stab wound didn't hit any major organs. To which George tells me to go cool off for a while.

Whatever.

My ass is asleep anyway, and I need to move.

Entering the kitchen, the clock on the stove shows it's past seven. Den and Wes are—I do a double-take. "Are you guys playing Monopoly?" I stop next to the kitchen island, rubbing my eyes.

My friends turn, and Wes shrugs. "We found it in one of the cabinets in living room number two. It seemed like a better option than watching a movie." He tilts his head toward Denielle. "This one wouldn't sit still, and it was driving me nuts."

"Fuck you, Sheats," D murmurs while rolling the dice.

I take in the board. Each of them has a whole battery of houses and hotels and an even bigger chunk of multicolored money in front of them.

"How long have you been playing?" I raise an eyebrow.

"Dunno, man." My best friend taps the screen of his phone. "About three hours."

I bark out a laugh then sober. "Listen, uh... I'm sorry I've been holed up with Nate. I—"

"Rhys." Denielle brings my full attention to her. "We get it. We do. I'd take my mother's entire stash of benzos right now if I had access to them."

I hold the air in my lungs until my chest begins to burn, and I let fresh oxygen into my body. My gaze swivels between my two friends before I pull Den off her stool and wrap my arms around her. She instantly returns the embrace and buries her nose in the crook of my neck.

Her shoulders shake, and she hiccups. "Just bring her home."

I cup the back of her head and hold on just as tight as my gaze locks with Wes. "She'll be home soon."

I have no clue if my words hold any truth, but I have to believe that between Nate, George, and my father, they will find Lilly.

We talk a little longer. My father informed both of their parents that Den and Wes are in LA, visiting Lilly with us. Denielle had to come clean to her parents about Charlie, who immediately agreed to let her stay with us. Her dad chewed her out for jumping on a plane without telling them, but the mass orgy her long-time boyfriend was involved in quickly overshadowed her father's anger for her purchasing a first-class ticket across the country. Mr. and Mrs. Sheats already knew where Wes was since Dad had cleared it with them before he got on the jet with us.

Dad.

"Where is my father?"

Wes is about to take half of D's cash after she landed on one of his streets with three hotels. "Haven't seen him in a while."

WHEN THERE IS no trace of my father on the first floor or the second, I try the third. He's nowhere to be found.

What the hell?

I make my way back down and walk past my friends who are bickering about how much *play* money one of them has to fork over to the other. At least this way they're distracted.

I find the basement door ajar and hadn't even considered looking down there—I was on my way to the garage to check if our rental was still there.

Opening the door all the way, I take two steps when I hear

my father's muffled voice. His tone is...tense. I slowly make my way down, conscious of minimizing any sound that could alert him to my eavesdropping. I'm at the bottom step when I can hear him clearly. I flatten myself against the wall and stay out of sight.

"I'm positive, yes." Pause. "I don't know, honey." He's talking to Mom? "I promised I wouldn't keep anything from you anymore, but you need to stay calm."

From the shrieking that I can even hear from my hiding spot, my mother is anything but calm. "Heather." More yelling. "Heather! Stop!" Dad uses his command voice, and it shuts Mom up. "We need him. He is our best chance of finding our daughter." *Who—?* "I don't like it either. The father in me wants to bash his head in, not even hand him over to the authorities." *Fuuuuck.* "But for one, we don't have any proof. Yet. And two, he seems to truly care about her. I'm not sure what to make of it. And we don't know how much the kids know." He listens again. "I will. I haven't been able to be around Nate much; Rhys has been with him the entire time. He seems to trust him." Pause. "I agree." Another pause. "Okay, I'll keep you posted. Please try to stay calm. We'll get her—" Mom doesn't seem to like his last statement. "As calm as you can, honey. For Natty's sake. How is she?" Dad is quiet, and I've heard enough. Tiptoeing back up the stairs, I halt outside the basement door.

Dad knows—or at least suspects that Nate is The Babysitter. FUCK, FUCK, FUUUUUCK!

I HIDE for the remainder of the evening, an easy feat since everyone already waits for me to lose my shit and doesn't question my behavior—like, at all. I could run through the mansion in the blowup unicorn costume the team forced on Owen during last year's Homecoming prank, and no one would bat an eyelash. Well, maybe George, but he still would remain his stoic, lovable self.

Lying on Lilly's bed, I've gotten well acquainted with the ceiling over the last several hours. There is a tiny cobweb I want to remove tomorrow once I find a broom or a ladder. And some type of water stain I need to mention to Nate. But besides coming up with a maintenance list for the bedroom, I have no fucking idea what to do. Telling Nate about Dad is out of the question. He needs to concentrate on finding Lilly. I'm a selfish prick for that, but there is no way I'll let him get distracted.

By one in the morning, the walls are closing in. Not that I mind being alone. Besides watching Nate work, I prefer it that way. The pity looks everyone tries *not* to give me—and fails epically—make it impossible not to go apeshit. Nate's the one with the ability to find her when the big bad Marines can't.

I keep picturing my father changing his mind and having Nate arrested or taking it into his own hands. I don't think he would do it here—with George and his men around—but my mind has played out more scenarios than Denielle has shoes. Eventually, I swing my legs off the bed.

I need to talk to someone.

I pat down to the second floor. The lighting in the house is muted, the hallway fixtures dimmed, and most doors closed. It's eerily quiet after the commotion all day. The only room lit is Lilly's office. When Nate first dropped that tidbit of information on me, I choked on my water. Because despite being aware of her newfound affinity for the digital world, imagining her sitting behind this desk with all the screens, command line windows, and her hair up in a messy bun with her glasses gave me an instant hard-on. So inappropriate for the current situation.

So. Inappropriate.

I peer into the room, and my eyes widen when I see Nate's head resting on his forearms, asleep. My jaw clenches, and I want to shake him, yelling what the fuck does he think he's doing? But the momentary surge of heat is quickly replaced by understanding. The guy got stabbed, flew across the world, and has been in this room for twelve-plus hours.

With a sigh, I ease back out and pull the door closed.

On the first floor, I come to an abrupt halt when I find George sitting in the kitchen, a laptop and a mug in front of him. He looks like shit—like, the pile someone stepped in and then tried to smear it across the sidewalk to get it off their shoes.

His eyes flick to mine, but he doesn't show a reaction otherwise.

"Have you slept at all since Wednesday?" I ask as I sink down opposite him. He sure doesn't look like it, and Lilly went missing almost thirty-six hours ago.

"Some." He leans back and folds his arms over his chest, waiting.

"Where is my father?"

"He took the spare room next to Weston and Denielle. He said to get him if we find anything new."

I nod, avoiding direct eye contact. I scan the kitchen, focusing on nothing in particular.

We sit in silence for several minutes. I keep glancing back at the man across from me several times, but he just raises an eyebrow, his scar pulling the corner of his eye up with the movement.

"My father knows about Nate," I blurt out when I can't take it anymore.

"What exactly would that be?"

I want to pound the calmness out of him.

"That he's The Babysitter." I drop the bomb, but George doesn't seem surprised.

"I'm aware." He places his hands flat on either side of the computer.

"You're aware?" My head rears back in disbelief.

George dips his chin once. "Your father has quite the reputation of his own, and despite my focus being on Nate, I've watched him closely from the moment they were both in the same room. He was suspecting something."

This is all kinds of fucked up. "But you didn't know what?"

"There is not much it could have been. Nate is well known, and your father can easily pull up his past. Nate's...breakdown was well documented by the press. The timeline between his discharge and Lilly's disappearance, in combination with his parents' tragedy...your father is a smart man. Especially after we informed him about the video." He says it all with such a lack of emotion, I grind my teeth.

"And you're not worried he'll call the authorities?"

"No. Tristen is fully aware that Nate is Lilly's best chance. Plus, he's not putting all his cards on the table."

My eyebrows pull together. "What do you mean?"

"There is something he's keeping from us."

My jaw is starting to cramp, listening to his monotone report.

"Is this, like, a thing you do?"

He just cocks his head.

"Both of you act like this is one of your secret spy missions." My voice rises. "This is Lilly's LIFE!" I shout the last word at him.

"That's exactly why we are doing what we're doing. Lilly is our number one priority. If your father had the facts that would help bring her back, he would share them."

AFTER MY LITTLE chat with my BFF, I go back upstairs. I want to pound on Dad's door, demanding answers, but him spilling his secrets is about as likely as getting *him* to wear the blowup unicorn costume. I watch the blinking dots on the alarm clock until my eyes start to droop around five in the morning.

Bang. Bang. Bang.

What the—?

"Dude! Get your ass downstairs!"

Wes's voice jolts me upright.

What time is it? One of the worst head rushes I've ever experienced makes me squeeze my eyes shut. Slowly blinking them open again, I glance to the bedside table—2:34 p.m.

Holy fuck, I passed out for over nine hours.

I jump up and pull the door open. My best friend is standing with his hands in his pockets in the hallway. His blond hair is a mess, and he hasn't shaved since we got here. He stares at me with a grim expression.

"What?" I know this guy better than myself half the time. "Spit it out."

His eyes harden. "Nate's got something."

I tear past him without waiting for more information.

Voices lead me to the office, and I find Nate, George, and my father behind the desk, with Den in front of it. She's chewing on her thumb, a gesture I have never seen on the always-confident Denielle Keller. Wes moves past me into the room and takes his spot next to Lilly's best friend.

All eyes are on me, and Nate breaks the silence. "I found her."

CHAPTER THIRTY-SIX

HER

MY DAUGHTER IS AS DEFIANT AS SHE WAS AT SIX YEARS OLD. *A trait that made me want to throttle her back then and, apparently, still does. If Gray hadn't interfered, she would also have a few holes in her legs.*

Never go for the vital body parts; that's what growing up where I did taught me. I rub a palm over the outside of my right thigh, remembering that particular incident. I was fourteen and had to make up excuses for weeks about why I couldn't join Heather at the pool and skipped P.E. One more reason he got what he deserved in the end.

I pour another glass as Gray walks in.

"If my husband is not enough incentive for Lilly to sign over what should've been mine long ago, we will take other measures." I don't turn as I speak.

"Yours?" His question makes me clench the bowl of the wine glass.

"Ours," I correct myself. I really can't deal with one of his tantrums right now.

He lets it go and switches gears. "Have you heard from your little bitch?"

Hank—the informant—Todd.

"No. He is still in Paris with Nate." I neglect to tell Gray that Hank should've given me an update yesterday, but my messages have been unanswered.

I need to speed things up.

Facing Gray, I tap my index finger to my lips. "How many paralytics do we have left?"

His eyes shoot up, and he opens and closes his mouth a few times. "You want to paralyze her?"

Why is he so shocked? We both have done worse over the years. Well, mostly him. That's why he's here.

I pull up one shoulder. "Just her legs. She might be more inclined to comply if she thinks she is in mortal danger."

"Is she?" He eyes me skeptically.

Heat surges through my body. "What do you care? It's not like you can claim the father-of-the-year award. When have you last spoken to either of them?"

Gray's nostrils flare. He doesn't like when I bring them up. After all, he left them behind for me.

"Get the drugs," I bark at him.

After a moment of hesitation, he turns and storms to his bedroom. Spineless idiot.

I face the sliding glass door and take in the ocean. It's not as blue as at home, but good enough for the few days I have to endure this place.

CHAPTER THIRTY-SEVEN

LILLY

IT DOESN'T TAKE LONG BEFORE THE DOOR OPENS AGAIN. Besides a five-second pee break, I haven't abandoned my spot on the mattress. My birth mother has proven by now that she is certifiable, so there is no way I'll turn my back on her.

Emily stalks toward me with Gray close on her heels. I crane my neck to see their faces as they stop in front of my makeshift bed. Taking in my mother's expression—or lack thereof—my pulse increases to an uncomfortable level.

Her eyes are dead, and she looks at me like one examines a bug right before squashing it. My gaze flicks to the man behind her, and he appears almost conflicted, which scares me even more. What's going to ha— I see her hand move out of my peripheral vision, but before I can react, I feel the sting in my thigh.

"Ahhhh!" I jerk my head around and stare in horror at the syringe sticking out of my leg.

"Now that this is done"—she pulls the needle out and holds it up for Gray to take—"we'll chat when you're back."

Back?

Still thinking the word, both of them turn fuzzy and then—

VOICES REGISTER IN MY BRAIN, but it's hard to concentrate on them. I feel like I'm lying on a merry-go-round with my eyes closed. What. The. Hell is going on? My forehead wrinkles as I'm straining to make out the words. Slowly they're starting to make sense.

"—been out for too long. How much did you put in?"

"The same amount the doc always gives."

Slap.

"Did your drugs finally reduce your IQ to the single digits? She is half the size of him. We wanted her unconscious for a few hours, not an entire day. The addict in you should know that you need to adjust the dose based on body weight."

Another slap.

"She'll be awake soon. Why are you in such a rush? Your fucking wine and beach chair aren't running away." Gray's tone seeps annoyance.

"What's the rush?" she barks followed by a grunt.

"Stop slapping me, Em," Gray growls.

He stops her from making contact a third time.

With the dizziness slowly subsiding, I peel my eyes open, and the white ceiling comes into view. I take inventory—how many freaking times have I had to do that in the last six months? I'm on the mattress. Okay, they didn't move me. Turning my head, I notice that the door to the room is open, and Emily and Gray stand out in the hallway. They don't pay me any attention. Their guard is down, which is...odd.

I wiggle my fingers then my toes. Where are my toes? I can't feel my toes. I bolt up—or more like attempt to, because from the belly button down, there is nothing.

Instant panic sets in. "Oh, God!" I exclaim before I can stop myself. I scramble up onto my elbows, one arm buckling once before I can steady myself and stare at my lower half. They're there, physically, but there's no sensation in either of my legs. Or my butt.

My stomach revolts. I feel sick. Quickly, I turn to the side and heave, but nothing comes up.

"You're back!" Emily's cheery tone makes the hair on my nape stand. She talks like I just came home from school. This woman is insane.

Lifting my gaze from the floor, I choke, "What the hell did you do to me?"

"Nothing permanent—yet," she chirps.

Yet?

Gray remains at the other end of the room, watching both of us closely.

Emily picks up the plastic cup I had put down next to the mattress and holds it to my lips. I want to refuse her offer. I don't want her anywhere near me, but my body demands the water. I greedily gulp it down, though it's not nearly enough.

I'm not going to ask for more.

"So, my darling daughter." I focus on Emily, who's still squatting in front of me.

"Why did you send me to Heather and Tristen?" I interrupt her before she can get to the point: *her* money. The question has been on my mind since the day I found out who I'm not.

"They wanted you," she answers simply without a pause, and I read between the lines: she didn't.

"You could've just left me with Nate." The words are a mere whisper, and I speak them as they pop into my head.

"Oh, I was planning on that, but your idiotic brother, despite his intellect, also doesn't know how to administer sedatives properly." She throws a glance over her shoulder. I follow her gaze and notice Gray scowl. Why does he let her talk to him like this?

"Anyway"—her conversational tone gives me the creeps —"when he brought you to the hospital, and you told them your name, I had to be the relieved mother, didn't I? Though, Nate's messages worked in my favor; everyone thought he was a threat." She rolls her eyes. "Henry was not at all for Tristen's idea. Why Tristen came up with that plan, I have no idea, but you don't look a gift horse in the mouth, right? They wanted you, so why fight them?" She smiles, but it doesn't reach her eyes. Her eyes are dead, and I have to avert my gaze. The longer she speaks, the harder it gets to breathe. Her confession gives me the answers I wanted, yet with every new word, my heart breaks a little bit further. No child wants to hear how her mother didn't want her. Emily continues her story without seeing or acknowledging what it does to me. "Did you know Henry even wanted to run with you? The silly man." She laughs. "I convinced him that it was in everyone's best interest for you to go with Heather and let her raise your bratty behind. That mouth on you as a child..."

"You really had Brooks fooled," I mumble more to myself.

Her eyebrows shoot up. "Brooks?"

I meet her incredulous gaze as needles prick at the back of my throat. I force myself to speak over the pain. "He left Nate and me a video. I found it the day he"—I dip my head toward Gray—"broke into my house."

"Your house?" Emily cackles. "Child, did they brainwash you again?" She shakes her head. "Oh well, none of that is important now. I was astonished to hear your father had the sense to change his will beyond the trust I knew he had set up for you. He was so out of his mind in the end. It was a pleasant surprise when I got the final number a few weeks ago."

My shoulders and neck start to cramp, but I force myself to remain propped up. The emotional tidal wave drowning me in everything from unimaginable sorrow to white-hot rage about who this woman is and what she has done is draining me fast.

"Let's talk about you putting your signature on the dotted line." She switches back to the topic that matters most to her. "If you do so now, this will be your only dose, but if you keep refusing, you may end up like my dear husband."

Henry.

My heart skips a beat at thinking his name, and I'm briefly distracted from her tirade.

"What did you do to him?" My voice is barely audible over the pounding in my ears.

"He's alive, if that's what you want to know."

Tears well up in my eyes. She hasn't killed him.

"But that can easily be rectified," she amends with a grin that I've only ever seen on a villain of a horror movie. She is pure evil. How can this woman be my mother?

"Where is he?"

Is he here? In this house?

Her expression turns smug. "He is in Westbridge."

What?

"I had to leave him behind after your little disappearing act, but I'll gladly hand him over—if you give me what belongs to me."

"Are you delusional?" I look between her and Gray. It sinks in, too late, that my words could have been interpreted as a refusal to give her the money, because that's exactly how she takes it.

Emily's hand shoots out, pushing me back into the semi-soft surface of the mattress. Her perfectly manicured nails dig into the flesh around my trachea again, constricting air from reaching my lungs. Choking seems to be one of her go-to torture methods. I latch onto her wrist, but I'm too weak to put any force behind it.

"I can't—" I rasp, barely audible.

"Em." Gray's warning tone penetrates the rushing in my ears, but she doesn't ease up.

Instead, the pressure remains, and she leans down, hissing in my ear. "*I* was meant to be at Brooks's side. He was supposed to leave the rich whore for *me*. ME! Which was the only reason I didn't run to the next clinic when I found out about you. But he wanted you. Only you. He cast me aside like trash."

Tears run down the side of my face, and black spots begin to form in my vision. In the back of my head, I know I won't stay conscious much longer. My eyes flutter closed, and my hand loosens around her arm, dropping to my side.

"Emily. You're choking her," Gray's voice gets louder.

He has come closer.

"If I couldn't have him, he couldn't have you," my mother hisses. "But he would pay. I was going to take everything from him and finally have the life I deser—"

The pressure around my neck disappears, and I suck in as much oxygen as I can. I'm faintly aware of shuffling, raised voices, and then a door slamming shut, but my entire focus is on breathing. I have no idea how long it takes before I open my eyes and come face to face with the man who has given me the creeps since the first time I saw him at Magnolia's.

"Princess, I told you to watch your mouth if you want to come out of here alive," he chastises me as his gaze moves down my legs then up to my face. "Or walking."

He doesn't mean it as a threat. It's a simple fact. He said he'd known my mother her entire life. She would paralyze her own child without a second thought.

"She can have the money," I croak, lifting a hand to wipe my stinging eyes.

I don't care about that. I only had it for, what, a week? I never planned on being rich. I was going to go to college on a partial scholarship and get a job. All I want is to go home to Rhys and my family. Fresh tears start to fall. *Rhys.*

Gray nods, no sympathy for my current state visible on his features. "Good. I'm gonna leave the contract here." He lifts it and glances down, stiffening. His eyes narrow, and he flips the pages. His nostrils flare, but he smoothes his features. Placing everything within my reach, he locks eyes with me once more. "You have quite the amount in your name." He pushes himself up, and with one last glance down at me, he leaves.

. . .

I REMAIN on my back for a long time after Gray leaves. Emily's words replay in my head over and over. It never crossed her mind that her words could hurt me—her daughter. It's like she has no feelings.

Eventually, I force myself to stop letting her verbal slap to the face break me further. I have a family. I have a mother, a father, and a sister. I have Rhys. And I have Nate. This woman means nothing to me. I repeat those words over and over in my head until Emily's slowly begin to lose their meaning.

Gathering the little strength I have left, I attempt to maneuver myself into a sitting position against the wall. With still no feeling in my legs or butt, this simple task is the equivalent of a two-hour sparring match with Spence. I'm drenched in sweat. I topple over twice due to the lack of sensation in my lower half, and frustration makes me slam my palm into the mattress until my hand hurts.

I. *Smack.* Refuse. *Smack.* To. *Smack.* Give. *Smack.* Up. *Smack.* *Smack.* *Smack.*

"Arrrrrrg!" With one last push, I am finally upright.

I eye the cup in front of the mattress. Out of my reach. *Shit.* I need water, but it's empty anyway. And there is no way for me to refill it myself. Fuck!

I glance at my legs and poke a thigh with my finger. Nothing. A pit opens in my stomach, and it feels like a hummingbird took residence in my chest—and not in a good way. What if Emily was wrong and it is permanent? She said Gray gave me too much. I poke the other leg. There has to be a way to make the numbness go away. I reach behind one knee and pull the leg up, but as soon as I let go, it flops to the mattress. I keep pushing into the muscles, no idea if it'll do anything, but I have to try something. Stay busy.

I'm on it for who knows how long when the door suddenly flies open, and I whip my head in the direction of the noise.

"What did you do?" Emily is standing in the door, legs apart, her arms hanging at her side. Her tone is so low and void of emotion that the alarm bells in my head immediately go off.

"W-what do you mean?" My heart starts pounding as my mother stalks toward me. I notice that she is holding something in her hand. Gray's knife. It's not hard to recognize, given the fact it's a KA-BAR. Tristen has several of those, and I've even seen some in George's arsenal.

"Where is Gray?" I press my hands into the mattress and my back further against the wall.

"*Gray* is sleeping off whatever he shot up his veins this time. Now, tell me, what did you do?" she snarls.

"I have no clue what you're talking about." Fear settles in my bones. Has she completely lost her mind?

"I can't reach Elise." Where I sound like a hysterical mouse, her tone is calm and monotone.

"Who the hell is Elise?" I press sideways as she takes a step closer, but it only makes me fall over again.

Fucking damn it!

"Elise was supposed to watch Henry while I took care of you."

I remain mute, focusing on pushing myself away from her as she continues her prowl.

"She didn't give me the usual update, and when I called, her phone went to voicemail. The doctor isn't supposed to be back until tomorrow, so I'm asking you again...what did you do?"

"I've been here the entire time, you crazy bitch. What do you think I did? Pulled out my magic phone and called the police in Westbridge, sending them to an unknown location where you're hiding my not-father?" Apparently, her drugs have also paralyzed my rational thinking because the words are out before I can stop them.

Of course, my outburst pushes her over the edge. Emily loses it and attacks.

"WHO DID YOU CALL A BITCH?!" I see the knife go in, but I don't feel a thing.

Eyes wide, I stare at the hilt sticking out of my thigh.

Oh. God. Oh, no. No, no, no. I'm going to be sick, and I manage to turn sideways before it comes up. She pulls out the blade, and my pant leg begins to turn dark red. Emily holds the handle in one hand and pokes her index finger with the bloody tip of the blade.

"Did you know that my father, your grandfather, stabbed me in the exact same spot once?" She peers down at my leg with an unreadable expression. "Gray and I were out with Ronnie, Ronnie wouldn't drive me home when he was supposed to, and Daddy lost his temper. He never liked when he didn't get his dinner on time." She goes on as if I'm not bleeding in front of her. "When I blamed Ronnie for what happened the next day, he slapped me then laughed and made Gray take me to the hospital to get stitched up." Her eyes are vacant, lost in her memory. "But that wasn't the only time I got acquainted with his knife. See."

My breathing is labored. If from the shock of what just happened, from the pain I cannot feel, or from the entire situation...I'm not sure. It doesn't matter anyway. All I can do is stare at the woman who gave birth to me as she keeps going on.

Emily holds out her free arm, turning it so I can see the inside between her biceps and triceps. A jagged scar, about three inches, is clearly visible. "Ronnie also didn't like when he didn't get what he wanted."

Who the hell is Ronnie?

"Maybe we should try your arm next—the one you don't need to write, that is." Emily is now on all fours on the mattress next to me.

"You can have the money," I croak the words out before she can inflict more damage.

She doesn't hear me; she is too far gone. She lifts the blade and pokes the tip against the skin of my upper arm. I fling out my other one to deflect her weapon, but it's no good. Between the drugs, the exertion from sitting up, and now the blood loss, I have the strength of a malnourished stray kitten. All I accomplish is cutting my palm on the blade.

"Ahhh!" I can't stop the scream, nor do I want to.

Suddenly, there is a loud bang somewhere outside the room followed by shouts and footfalls echoing through the house. Emily doesn't seem to notice any of it. She pokes the end of the knife just underneath my ribcage, twisting it until it breaks skin.

A whimper escapes me, and tears run down my face.

I don't want to die.

"STEP AWAY FROM HER, EMILY!" The command penetrates the room, and both of our heads snap to the door.

CHAPTER THIRTY-EIGHT

LILLY

THE BLOOD LOSS IS MAKING ME HALLUCINATE. BLINKING several times, I wait for the two blurry shapes to disappear, but all they do is slowly enter the room and spread out, circling us from both sides.

Emily shifts to straddle me, moving the knife at lightning speed to my neck. "Tristen, what a surprise," she chirps as if she ran into her long-lost friend in the grocery store. Then, her gaze swivels to the other man. "And George Weiler. I did not expect you two to ever join forces." She cocks her head.

"And why is that?" George mimics her expression, unfazed.

"Well, would you expect Lilly's father"—she chuckles, smiling sweetly at Tristen—"excuse me, adopted father, to work with the man who is his daughter's kidnapper's accomplice?"

No, no, no.

Unable to move in more ways than just being paralyzed, my gaze flicks back and forth between the men. Tristen and George are going in and out of focus, and I'm blaming my current physical state for that. What I do see, though, is that neither of them shows an emotional response to the bomb Emily dropped. Does Tristen know? My mother adjusts her position on top of me, pushing the knife deeper into my flesh.

"Ahhhh," a high-pitched gurgle comes out of my mouth.

The pain receptors in my upper half work perfectly because the intrusion of the metal in my skin sends a searing sensation through my body. My heart rate has exceeded any acceptable rhythm and has moved to an unhealthy, call-an-ambulance-immediately pace.

It fucking hurts.

This is the first time George and Tristen acknowledge me. They scan me from head to toe and settle on my leg. It's mostly covered by Emily sitting on it, but they see it. The blood must've seeped through my pants and into the mattress. Their eyes narrow, and both lift their arms simultaneously. Until now, I hadn't noticed their guns. George's Glock 19 and Tristen's Sig P365XL are both trained at my mother.

"Get off my daughter," Tristen commands in an eerily calm voice. He locks eyes with me, and just then, everything blurs again. Ugh. Squinting, I try to focus on the scene in front of me, but it's no use.

"Not until she signs the papers." Emily's response is just as calm. She reaches back with her free hand and squeezes my injured leg. I can feel her torture. My stomach flips; the sedatives are wearing off. Unfortunately, my relief is short-lived. That also means I can feel the agonizing assault of my wound. Make it stop.

A whimper escapes me, and I clench my jaw not to scream out loud and distract George and Tristen from their target: my mother.

George jerks a step forward at my pained sound, but Emily expected one of them to react, and she digs in deeper. Every cell in my body is suddenly on fire, and I can't stop myself. A gut-wrenching cry erupts in my throat.

"Ahhhhhhh!"

At that moment, all hell breaks loose.

"CALLAAA!" Three sets of eyes jerk toward the door as Rhys bursts into the room.

"Rhy—" I can't finish his name before my voice gives out.

He tries to get to me, but George moves lightning-fast, dropping his gun and wrapping his arms around him, pinning him in place.

Rhys struggles against the hold, George having a hard time keeping control over him. Rhys is losing it. "LET ME GO, YOU COCKSUCKER! I'M GOING TO KILL YOU, YOU CRAZY BITCH." He's screaming at George and Emily at the same time, his eyes blazing, never leaving mine.

I want to soothe his pain.

I don't like seeing him like this.

Please don't let him get hurt.

What is he doing here?

My thoughts are all over the place; I can't concentrate. This is all too much.

Tristen flicks his gaze to his son before focusing again on his target. "Emily, if you don't let go of my daughter immediately, you will not walk out of here."

But instead of complying, she starts laughing hysterically. "You are such a joke, Tristen. What are you going to do? If you so much as twitch that finger, I will slice her open so George's face decoration looks like a beauty mark. Tell *my daughter* to sign over the money, and you can have her. Hell, you can have all of them. I'll give you Gray on top of it. He's the one who killed Payton anyway. I had nothing to do with that."

"No, you cunt, you only physically abused your child, gave her up, and now kidnapped her. For what? Money that the man who didn't want *you* left to *her*?"

"RHYS!" Tristen barks at his son's outburst.

"FUCK THIS SHIT. SHOOT HER! You're faster than this

crazy bitch!" Rhys rears his head back to slam it into George's face. Rhys is trained, but George has years on him, and he turns his head at the last second. All I can do is watch, tears streaming down my face.

Please don't hurt him or let him get hurt.

"That's enough!" George roars in Rhys's ear and somehow gets through. Rhys stops his struggle—or that's what he makes everyone believe. As soon as George relaxes his arms, Rhys lets himself drop and goes for the abandoned Glock.

"Noooooo!" The scream bursts out of me, and I try to buck Emily off my body, but she is already gone.

Both men follow Rhys's abrupt movement, not realizing that Emily anticipated the action and dived for it a fraction of a second faster. My mother and Rhys both grasp for the gun at the same time.

I can't see who reaches it first. They're in a tangle of arms and legs when a gunshot makes everyone freeze. George and Tristen are staring with wide eyes at the two slumped forms on the ground, and I register something splash across my face.

Oh, please, no!

Time is frozen. I can't breathe. Someone do something! I want to crawl over, but as soon as I shift, the pain in my leg immobilizes me. I need to get to him. *No, no, no.* I wipe my eyes. But the tears are falling faster than my weak hands can remove them. Then, everything springs back into action, and both men dive toward Rhys, who is buried underneath Emily. Pulling my fingers back, I see the crimson color on them. My face is not only wet with tears.

"RHYS!" Tristen roars.

The world fades away, my eyes glued to my fingers. Red. Blood. I can't lose him. The thought repeats itself over and over in my head. I can't lose him. I don't pay attention to anything that's happening around me. I can't lose him.

A shadow appears above me, and my focus changes.

Gray.

My surroundings turn silent. Everything besides Francis Garrison (Gray) Turner is on pause. He peers down at me, his eyes briefly flicking to the side before returning to me. He squats down, and for the first time, I let my head turn toward the center of the room. I still can't make out what's going on. My eyes are burning. Tristen kneels on the floor, his back blocking most of my view. All I see are Rhys's legs and part of my mother sprawled on the ground. My face is grabbed by the chin, a rough hand forcing me to look back up at the man who broke into my house and kidnapped me. Something in his expression changes, but I don't understand what.

He leans down further until he is close to my ear. "No one betrays me. Our paths will cross again, but until they do...take care of her."

He shoves something into the pocket of my pants before he stands back up and disappears.

Her?

It's as if someone has pushed play again, and sounds filter into my brain. Rhys! I attempt to turn myself over once more, but the agony shooting through my leg is unbearable, and I whimper. The paralytics must be completely gone because the pain is worse than the blade to my neck, worse than the shoulder injury after my car accident, or the burns from the shower attack.

I manage another gurgled cry before everything goes black.

TOO TIGHT IS my first thought after I come to. Someone is holding onto me—no, not holding on. Focus. I'm nestled in someone's lap, arms wrapped around me. Whoever is cradling me is rocking back and forth. Saliva pools in my mouth, and I swallow down the nausea. My body doesn't like the motion. I want to tell whomever it is to stop when something wet hits my face from above.

More noise registers. Commotion to the side of me.

Someone barking orders. Feet shuffling. More commands. A hand comes to my face, and I lean into it—a touch as familiar as my own.

"Open your eyes for me, Calla," a voice begs between sobs. I know that voice. *I love that voice.*

With an excruciating amount of strength, I peel my eyelids back.

Green eyes dulled by tears find mine. "There's my girl," he breathes.

My stomach flips. "Rhys." I can't muster more than a whisper, and my lids want to close again, but I force them to remain open.

"Hey, babe." His thumb brushes the moisture under my own eyes away.

"You're here."

He chuckles. "Where else would I be?"

I attempt to turn toward the noise, but he cages me in. "Don't."

My forehead scrunches.

"Let me see," I whisper, my pulse increasing with anxiety. What is he hiding?

Rhys slashes his mouth, his gaze flicking to something beyond my peripheral vision.

"She can handle it," George says from somewhere close by.

Rhys's grip loosens, and he helps me shift to a half-sitting position leaning against his chest. I can see the entire room—my prison cell.

There, in the center, is a body in a pool of blood. Emily's body. My mother. I feel nothing. I don't remember her being my mother, and after everything I've learned the last few days, I don't want to remember. I no longer fault Tristen for what he did. I let my gaze linger a moment longer, scanning the room. Tristen is talking to a man by the door, and George is next to us, but his focus is also toward the other men.

I turn back to Rhys. "You shot her?"

Rhys shakes his head. "No. She got to the gun first."

My mouth parts.

"She was on top of me, the gun against my side, but she didn't get the safety off fast enough. Turner killed her."

Wha—?

CHAPTER THIRTY-NINE

RHYS

THREE MONTHS LATER

THE DAY HAS COME. The day everyone has been working toward since I carried Lilly out of that house. The sun is slowly coming up, and the outlines of the buildings around the original Altman Hotel in Los Angeles are morphing into actual structures—we never closed the blinds last night.

I yawn and peer down at Lilly's naked body sprawled over my chest. Her hair is fanned around her face and down her back. Scanning every inch visible above the massive down comforter, I swipe away a strand that fell over her eyes. I haven't been able to get any shuteye in days. The last two, I've been solely surviving on the constant stream of caffeine Wes has provided for me.

Every time I close my eyes, I relive that day. See the blood. Hear her screams. And today, nine months after the fateful homework assignment, everything comes to a close.

Wes and Denielle, together with my parents and Natty, came a few days ago. Lilly and I never left Los Angeles.

We finished the school year on the West Coast. Lilly refused to set foot into Westbridge High again, and I wouldn't leave her side.

There had been yelling, tears on Lilly's and Mom's sides, scowling from Dad, but in the end, we're eighteen. Mom and Dad *agreed* to let us stay under the condition we finish our coursework online—not that they could've forced us back east anyway. But I preferred the amicable resolution over another family shit show.

No fucking clue how Mom pulled everything off with the school, but she did. After what happened to Lilly in the locker room, they probably would've said yes if we had asked for our diplomas without finishing the year.

Lilly and I moved into the Hamlin mansion permanently, and George stayed at the house with us because Turner, aka Gray, being on the loose had everyone still on edge. Mom, Dad, and Natty flew in every two weeks for a *check-in*—the perks of suddenly having a private jet at our disposal.

EVERY TIME my mind wanders to those few days after Denielle's phone call, it's still a miracle to me how Nate found Lilly. Despite his injury, he worked himself into the ground. The only time he slept was that night in the office, and he had literally passed out from exhaustion.

Because of Nate, I can hold Lilly in my arms today, which is one of the reasons my preconceived psycho-kidnapper opinion changed. He's still a criminal, but that's just one of his many sides—most of them are actually pretty tolerable. He also handed me the keys to the R8 a few weeks ago. What idiot would say no to that?

While I was passed out in Lilly's bedroom that night—or day —Nate had dissected Hank's personal life down to the color of his dishtowels. When the bank accounts showed nothing out of the ordinary, Nate started digging. Deep.

Hank's credit history listed several joint and active cards linked to his mother. The same Mrs. Todd who had been in an assisted living home for over a decade and had not used a debit or credit card for just as long. Nate shifted his focus to her, and after finding several domestic accounts through various banks all over the country, he tracked down an offshore account with a *considerable*, multi-figure balance. Money Hank did not earn with his job for the Altman Hotels, nor his mother, who was the primary account holder.

Whoever helped set all this up knew their shit, and if it were anyone but Nate, we probably would've never found Lilly in time.

He followed the deposits to Mrs. Todd's offshore account back to one containing a sum that was suspiciously close to one Brooks had paid Emily over the years. Said account was with a bank in South America, not too far from where Nate ran into a roadblock when tracing his father's transfers. He had lost the trail when the entire amount was withdrawn on the receiving end, and the account was closed.

The amount was obviously not exactly the same anymore, but close enough. The living expenses in that region were not very high, and one could afford a decent lifestyle from the interest alone and accumulate more.

Don't ask me how he did all this. I probably don't want to—or shouldn't—know.

This also solidified our suspicion that Hank worked for Emily Sumner.

Nate then convinced one of the tellers at the financial institution to identify the account's owner who was supplying Hank with the funds. The helpful employee received a check that will support her family for years to come and immediately picked Lilly's biological mother out of the stack of pictures Nate emailed to her.

To not just provide her one option, he attached pictures of

my parents, the Kellers, and Mr. and Mrs. Sheats—none of whom the lady obviously recognized.

And with that, we had the proof. Turner kidnapped Lilly. Hank provided Turner with the vehicle for the abduction. Hank received money from Emily Sumner, Lilly's mother. Emily and Turner were linked.

Mrs. Todd's credit history also listed a brand-new lease for a bungalow on the Pacific Ocean. With Hank's passport still not back on U.S. soil—again, not asking so I don't have to plead the fifth if it ever comes down to it—George and Dad agreed that the house was most likely where Turner took Lilly.

All of this developed while I was sleeping on the third floor. Initially, I was pissed that no one woke me up, but it was probably better in the end. I wouldn't have been much help with my impatient nature. I can admit that now.

While the two were talking strategy, Nate pulled up the CCTV around the location. Between Turner breaking into the Hamlin estate and how long it would've taken him to get to the beach house, taking into account that he switched cars at least once, Nate narrowed down a time window. He recruited Denielle and Wes to watch the feeds with him, and Denielle was the one who spotted another dark SUV on the camera closest to the beach property.

The license plate to this one was not covered, and with some more *information seeking*, Nate soon had a close-up security camera picture of Francis Turner renting the car, though the name on the agreement was Ronald Turner, Francis's brother who had not been seen in—have a guess—almost twelve years.

MY RECOLLECTION GETS INTERRUPTED as Lilly begins to stir, and I look down. Her eyes are moving rapidly under her lids. The nightmares are another outcome of everything she went through. She admitted that it's always the same but won't elaborate on the details. I suspect it has something to do with Emily, but what? No clue. I pull her close and wrap both arms around her body. She stills instantly, which makes warmth spread through me.

I watch her steady breathing for several minutes, counting each inhale and exhale. Something I've come to do after preventing a nightmare from fully taking hold. It calms me enough to usually go back to sleep myself—not today, though. My thoughts carry me back to that day.

AFTER THEY FINALLY WOKE ME UP, George had been on the phone with his team while Dad and Nate went over more details of the property. The ins and outs, closest neighbor, and whatnot. Watching my father in action was new to me. He had talked about his job before, but seeing him focus on a mission was as impressive as it was intimidating.

"When are we leaving?" I asked as George got off the phone.

Both men looked at me expressionless yet as if I had asked to go skydiving without a parachute.

"You are going home. I've already contacted Joel. He will take the three of you back to Virginia."

I stared at my father incredulously. Was he fucking serious? He couldn't be. He was.

FUCK!

Anger started to build deep in my core and spread throughout my body. "I'm not getting on the damn plane!"

"Yes. You are," he stated as he checked the chamber of his P365XL.

"The fuck?" I ripped the gun out of his hand.

In hindsight, that was an irresponsible and completely dumbass thing to do. I mean, it was a loaded fucking gun. But the chance of keeping my temper in check was about as likely as jumping out of the previously mentioned airplane without the parachute and surviving. No chance at all.

If they seriously believed I would get on that damn jet while

Lilly was held hostage by her psycho bio-mom, they were more delusional than my ex thinking I'd come back to her.

Dad stared at me with a murderous glare, not just for ignoring every gun safety rule, but for interfering with his mission. And bringing Lilly home had become his mission.

"I'm not having you anywhere near the place when we go in. We have no idea what to expect. We don't know if it's just the two of them or if there are more. Henry is still missing, for Christ's sake," he barked at me.

Henry. I completely forgot about him.

"You think he is involved?" I narrowed my eyes at Dad.

"No." My father's response came so quick and convinced that I paused.

We stared at each other, and then it clicked. "She did something to Henry."

This time, he didn't answer, which was everything I needed to not hear. George had told Dad about Turner's visit to the warehouse district and what he most likely procured there.

Dad and George ended up letting me stay with Nate, but Denielle and Wes were put into a car to the airport with George's guys. They were going home—Den kicking and screaming. Even Wes couldn't calm her and, eventually, had to step back. George's men caged her in and deposited her in the SUV by her hands and feet. It was not a pretty sight, and I don't think she has forgiven George since.

Nate was to watch me which, let's face it, was fucking hilarious—I didn't point that out, though. What was the guy gonna do? He could barely keep his eyes open, let alone stand straight between his exhaustion and his stab wound. He'd been avoiding the pain killers after he fell asleep because he didn't want his brain to turn all fuzzballs again. But once Dad and George were ready to move out, he finally agreed to self-medicate.

It only took five minutes for Nate's eyes to droop, and I was off. The keys to Lilly's G-Wagon hung with the rest of the cars in the entrance to the massive garage. I put the address I had memorized from earlier into my phone and was no more than maybe ten minutes behind the rescue operation.

Looking back, following them was, by far, the most reckless shit I've ever pulled. I'm fully aware that I would've died that day if it weren't for Francis Turner.

Turner had been Emily's lapdog since they were kids. But we didn't know that until my mother arrived in Los Angeles.

The moment I walked into the house, all I had to do was follow the screaming—Lilly's screams. My pulse was pounding in my ears as I crept along the hallway toward the noise. A lot of what came next was a blur.

Should I remember it? Process what I saw? What happened with Emily and the gun? Maybe. Okay, probably. But I have no desire to hash that shit out with the therapist Dad has had me see once a week since. Lilly is alive. I'm alive. The bitch is dead. Moving on—or pretending to. All I want is to get through today, and I know we'll move past it eventually. Dr. *How-Do-You-Feel-About-This* is not going to be part of that progress.

I do think about everything that followed Lilly coming back to consciousness, though, and it sends me into a fucking tailspin every single time.

Maybe I should open up to Doctor McShrink?

George had stayed back at the house of horrors with his men, securing the scene and dealing with the authorities.

I bet that was an interesting conversation.

Dad tried to take Lilly from me so she could get medical attention, but as soon as he reached for her, every muscle in my body locked. I braced my legs, my arms tightened around her, and my hands curled into fists, clutching her clothes. Even if I had wanted to hand her over, I couldn't. The thought of losing contact with her in any way had my chest constricting, and I felt like someone was choking me.

We made it to the G-Wagon, but the events are distorted. Skipping. It's like my brain has blurred it all out of focus.

Self-preservation?

Lilly was in the hospital for three days. Dad took her to a clinic that catered to the privacy of its patients. They whisked us into a room upon arrival. It was not a traditional hospital room. It was a full-on hotel suite with a queen bed, sitting area, and a spa-like bathroom.

Lilly was examined, cleaned, and her leg got stitched up. They ran a gazillion blood tests, gave her multiple transfusions, and monitored her for side effects. By some miracle, the psycho bitch didn't hit any major blood vessels.

A lot happened on the outside during those three days, but I didn't give two shits. My focus was on Lilly and making sure she was okay. I ignored my phone—let it die—and the only people I spoke to were the ones that came to us: Nate, George, Dad, and the medical staff.

Lilly and I didn't talk much either. I mostly held her, needing the constant contact. No one blinked an eye when they discovered me under the covers with her. The first time she was able to go to the bathroom by herself—with the help of crutches—my hands started trembling, and my entire body was covered in a sheen of sweat. After that, I made it a habit to follow her and wait outside the door.

The attending physician's main concern was monitoring her bloodwork. The amount and combination of sedatives and paralytic drugs her body had to process caused her to lose sensation in her legs twice more in the first day and a half. When that happened, my pulse would pound in my ears, and my entire body shook like I was the one experiencing the possibility of not being able to feel my extremities again. I would yell at whomever was in the room, go completely ballistic, followed by George or Dad having to restrain my ass before I lost it on the poor nurse checking Lilly out.

Nate's neurologist also paid us a visit. Having money apparently makes the medical professionals come to you, not the other way around, but I didn't complain. He ordered a CT scan as well as an MRI followed by several hours of more exams. The helplessness as we waited for the results was as excruciating as watching the nurse check on Lilly's numb legs and not knowing if the sensation would come back this time. When the neurologist informed us that Lilly showed no signs of a tumor or brain injury, everyone in the room, including the two big bad Marines, had tears in their eyes.

No wonder my brain turned the events into a distorted movie. Who the fuck would want to remember all that in vivid detail?

One particular conversation, though, keeps replaying in Technicolor. And every single time, my chest feels heavy, as if someone has put a hundred-pound weight on it. I was sitting next to Lilly on her extra-wide bed, Nate in a chair to her left, Dad in one to her right. George had just returned and stood at the foot of the bed. It was day two, and Dad had let us know that Mom and Natty would be arriving in LA the next evening. Natty got excused from school for two weeks and would complete her work online—no issue there. She'd probably finish the entire school year in those two weeks if she had all the materials.

Arms folded across his chest, George eyed everyone in the room one at a time.

"G, what has your cargo panties in such a twist?" Nate smirked, hands interlaced behind his neck and legs propped on the bedframe.

Lilly's brother actually has a decent sense of humor once you talk to him about more than stalking reporters and rescuing his sister from her birth mother. Another trait that made me like him.

Lilly had a good day, no more losing the feeling in her legs, and we were all in a decent mood.

All eyes were on my BFF, and I was about to add an inappropriate comment when he blurted out, "Lakatos agreed to try and reverse Lilly's memory loss—as long as it's at a location of his choosing. I've been negotiating with him over the last few days."

Wha—? Dad said it was impossible.

Nate leaned forward in his chair, dropping his feet to the ground with a thud, and even Dad's entire posture stiffened. Did he know there was a possibility and lied to me back in his office, or did Lakatos tell his clients it was a one-way street? George's meeting with Hector Lakatos was a week ago, but no one had mentioned it since. We all had other things on our minds, which is why this felt like a punch to the gut. How could I have forgotten?

"That's okay." Lilly's soft voice came from the side, and every head turned to her.

I arched an eyebrow, and she whispered, "I don't want to remember."

"Are you certain? He said he has never done it, but he would try." George's question was filled with concern, which was mirrored in Nate's eyes when I let my gaze wander to him.

"I am."

I wanted to demand why, but her tone was stern, and it was clear that she wouldn't discuss it further. Not at the time.

My father pulled me aside later that day and assured me that Lakatos always said it was impossible—it was even part of his contract—and that he didn't lie to me. He knew my mind had gone there.

We've talked about it several more times over the last few months, especially after my parents' confessions a few days later, but Lilly has remained adamant. She says the only thing she regrets about her choice is that she may miss a memory of Brooks, but with everything in his video message, Emily herself, and what my parents revealed to her, Dad did the right thing.

Her forgiveness had my father bawl like a baby the day he and Mom told us the rest of the story—the day we learned more unnerving facts about Emily.

CHAPTER FORTY

RHYS

THE WEEKEND AFTER LILLY WAS DISCHARGED, WE WERE IN sitting room number three at the Hamlin estate. Number three was the one with direct access to the backyard. Wes and I had numbered all the duplicate rooms after missing each other twice when we were going stir-crazy waiting for Nate to find his sister, and *'I'll meet you in the living room'* was a one-in-four chance.

Natty, Lilly and I, together with Nate, had been playing board games all afternoon. It was something we used to do a lot before everything went down the shitter three years ago, and having Nate join us was one of the most bizarre experiences of my life—not counting the whole kidnapping and almost-dying thing, of course.

Nate had left a few minutes earlier. He was all vague and secretive about his whereabouts and whispered something in Lilly's ear that made her eyes bulge and hug him tight.

He placed a kiss on the top of her head. "I'll be fine."

Lilly didn't look convinced, though. "Call me after."

He nodded and walked toward the garage. She could read the guy as well as she read me.

"What was that about?" Mom, who sat in one of the armchairs, scrunched her eyebrows.

"He is going to end it with Margot." Lilly sounded...sad.

Oh.

"Why?" I couldn't stop myself from asking. Not that he had spent any time with his fiancée, nor had he answered her calls in days. Hell, he barely left the house. He even slept here instead of his own mansion the size of a medium-sized apartment complex.

"It's not my place to tell." She smiled softly at me. Her loyalty to her brother was admirable. But that was Lilly. When she loved someone, she loved fiercely and never betrayed the person's trust.

Mom asked Natty to help George make dinner—the man could actually cook like a Michelin Chef—and then turned to me. "Can you two meet Dad and me on the back patio?"

Uh. A hollow sensation settled in my stomach. Sending Natty to George and asking us to come outside...not good.

Lilly was right behind my parents, but I followed at a slower pace. Much slower. Maybe if I took my time, they would forget whatever they wanted to say. Unlikely, but worth a try. Subconsciously, I already knew that I wasn't going to like what I was about to hear.

"RHYS!" my father's bark assaulted my ears.

Fuck! "Coming."

I sat down in one of the cushioned wrought iron patio chairs surrounding the matching eight-person table—Lilly and me on one side, Mom and Dad across from us. The whole scene felt like we were in one of Mom's court proceedings.

When the prolonged silence turned beyond uncomfortable, I reached over to grab Lilly's hand. She squeezed it in return, just as my mother announced, "We know who Nate is."

Mom's words were like a bucket of ice in the face followed by several precisely executed uppercuts. I mean, we sorta knew, or at least suspected, but no one had said a word since I overheard Dad's phone call in the basement. Lilly's fingers turned to a vise around mine, and I, unsuccessfully, stifled a grunt as two of my fingers cracked under the pressure. "Argh."

"He's going to turn himself in," Lilly rushed out, not letting go of my hand.

She's going to break my damn fingers.

"We know," Dad inserted himself.

My eyes widened, the pain in my hand forgotten.

Holy fuck? How did that happen?

Mom took one deep breath before explaining. "Dad found out while you were still...missing." She looked at Lilly with a pained expression. None of us talked about those days unless we had to. I wasn't the only one in avoidance land.

"The moment Dad told me, I dialed Agent Camden on the house phone," she declared. "I was furious with your father. How could he not turn him over immediately?" She took a long breath and stared at her folded hands on the table. "But then he convinced me to hold off."

Convinced her?

Lilly's grip loosened—thank you, Jesus—and I peered over at her. She was completely unmoving, not averting her eyes from my mother.

"If it hadn't been for Natty, I would've been on the next flight out. Dad kept me up to date." Her voice cracked, the guilt from not being with Lilly when she was in the hospital written all over her face.

My heart was jackhammering as I waited for her to continue.

"I honestly had no idea what to expect. For one, we were talking about Nathan Altman. I looked into his case as soon as Dad gave me his name. He almost killed a man in college." Her voice got louder, and Dad placed a hand on her thigh.

"He paid for—" Lilly came to Nate's defense, but Mom lifted her hand to stop her. She kept shifting between lawyer- and mom-mode, and I was getting whiplash.

"He has, but that's not my point. He has a media focus that makes the one you previously faced look like an interview with the high school's newspaper. When your relation to him comes out, you'll be in the same spotlight as Nate. Not to mention what he'll be charged for."

The kidnappings.

I swallowed several times against the sudden overproduction of saliva. Another topic everyone had been avoiding—until now. Lilly's bottom lip began to tremble, and I scooted my chair closer to wrap my arm around her shoulder.

"He'll come forward and go to jail," Lilly whispered as the first tear ran down her cheek. We'd known for weeks that this was the inevitable outcome, yet seeing Lilly like this broke my heart.

"He told us."

My eyes flew to my father, who had Colonel McGuire on full display. I wondered if he needed this *side of his personality, his life,* to deal with the situation.

"Nate, Mom, and I sat down last night. Over the last week, I've gotten to know him in a way that I will never be able to repay him. Without him, Emily would've killed Lilly. I'm not under the delusion that she would've just sent her home after she got what she wanted." He looked at his adopted daughter. "Emily was...*ill.*"

"Ill?" My forehead scrunched. What the hell did that mean?

"I met Emily in kindergarten. Back then, her name was Emily Kaczmarek. Did you know that?" Mom's tone was low, and Lilly and I shook our heads at the question. Nate dug further into Emily's past, but with everything else, he hadn't had a chance to tell us what he found. It seemed my mother was going to fill in some of those blanks.

"We attended the same schools all our lives since Lake Robertson only had one for each grade level." Mom grew up in a relatively small town in the Midwest, but when she left for college, our grandparents moved as well, so we've never actually seen where she grew up.

She looked at a spot behind us as she continued. "We were

close. Emily had been my best friend from the day we were put at the same table in school, but there were things I never knew about her. I've asked myself many times over the last few weeks if I was too self-absorbed with my own life or if I didn't want to see it." Mom wiped under her nose. "She would come to school with bruises. One time, in middle school, she didn't show up for a week. When I asked her about it later, she gave vague answers that made no sense. She never let me come to her house. Maybe if I had...if I had just shown up, things would have been different. I could've helped her," Mom's voice turned desperate.

"Honey." Dad forced her to focus on him. "We've talked about that. There was nothing you could've done."

She nodded and then leveled us with a serious expression. "Emily was always around two brothers when she wasn't with me. Their names were R.J. and Gray."

R.J. Ronnie. Turner's brother. Holy shit.

Lilly sucked in a breath, and I could feel her beginning to tremble. I tightened my hold around her shoulder, wanting to reassure her that she was safe and ignore my own inner turmoil at the same time. It was easier to manage when I focused on Lilly rather than what my parents were revealing.

"I didn't put it together until Dad told me what Emily called Turner in front of you." She looked at Lilly. "R.J. was a few years older. He gave me the creeps. As the years passed, the rumors around him started. He was the local dealer, and his little brother functioned as his runner. I confronted Emily once, but she lost it on me. Yelled at me to mind my own business and that my rich ass had no idea what I was talking about." The corners of Mom's mouth turned down.

Rich? My grandparents were maybe upper-middle class—at most. Anger against Emily flared in my chest, even though all this happened years before I was even born.

"Her behavior became erratic. She would have mood swings, be her normal sweet self and then start yelling for no reason. At the end of our junior year in high school, Emily disappeared. She

would call every few weeks but refused to tell me where she was
—said she needed a change of scenery. I was too busy with
myself to question her further. We had grown apart when her
behavior changed, and I was already focused on getting into
college—the future. We would still talk occasionally, but I didn't
see her again until I was already at Georgetown. She came to
visit and wanted to repair our friendship. Thinking about it now,
maybe she had gone into a rehabilitation facility?"

Mom trailed off. I glanced at Dad, and he picked up from
there. "Mom and I met during sophomore year, as you know, and
Emily would come to visit a couple of times a year, but that was
it. It was usually short visits, a long weekend, but even during
those times, she would have moments where her behavior
was...unpredictable and, at times, inappropriate for the
situation."

What the fuck did that mean?

I scowled at my father but clamped my mouth shut, afraid
that if I interrupted, the hour of truth would be over.

"Shortly after I started my position at Pendleton, she moved
with her fiancé to San Diego. We met Henry once before, and he
was a good guy. She seemed better. Then she got pregnant.
You"—Dad made eye contact with me—"had just been born, and
your mother was so excited for our children to be so close in
age." He glanced over at Mom sympathetically. She picked at her
pantleg, avoiding the three of us, and dread filled me with what
would come next.

"But Mom was taking care of our newborn son and didn't see
the changes in her friend," he continued. "It wasn't your mom's
fault. Not by a long shot."

Huh? What wasn't—?

"Lilly was born, and Henry adored his little girl, but he had
to travel a lot during the early years for his job."

"What did he do?" Lilly interrupted, speaking for the first
time since the topic had switched to Emily. She still didn't know
much about Henry.

"He was the lead architect for a national construction company. He would be onsite for a couple of weeks and then commute back and forth. That left Emily alone with Lilly a lot. She would drop her off with us every other day, sometimes leave her overnight."

"I loved having you, so I never questioned her for it. I should've..." Mom interjected fast, and Dad moved his hand from her leg to cover her hand on the table.

"Honey." He addressed her, and her shoulders slumped. He turned back to Lilly. "Mom always saw the good in people, so she would've never suspected anything being wrong with your biological mother." He emphasized the bio part. "You were at our house more days than not when Henry was gone. You were about a year old when you started having bruises that didn't add up with the stories Emily gave Heather. One day, you were around five, and you had a split lip. She said you had slipped after your shower and fell on the tiles in the bathroom. That was when I consulted with an associate about it. I didn't tell Heather about it at first. I didn't want your mom to worry or, worse, act differently and tip Emily off. You can't just accuse someone of child abuse without valid proof. My associate, Hector Lakatos, specialized in mental illnesses and, as you know, other areas of the brain." Dad paused, letting us digest all the information. Lilly's chest was rising and falling as if she had just run a couple of miles at full speed, and I didn't feel much better. I had the urge to jump up and pace the entire length of the estate.

"Hector owed me a few favors. He had me keep a log of Emily's behavior. I made a point to invite her and Henry over. We would meet them or make day trips together—anything that would allow me to study her. I cataloged every little thing and handed it over to Hector. One day, he asked me if any mental illnesses ran in her family, and I started digging into her past. There was not much to find, though. Emily's mother was institutionalized for endangering herself and her family when Emily was a toddler. She died a few years later. Her father was mostly unemployed and eventually dropped off the face of the earth when Emily was a young teenager. Hector managed to get a look at her mother's medical files somehow and concluded that Emily may have a form of Schizoaffective disorder."

"What the fuck is that?" I burst out.

God, I needed to get out of this chair. My leg started bouncing of its own volition.

Mom pulled her hand out from under Dad's and clutched the arm of her chair as she explained, "It's a mental health disorder. The person displays a combination of schizophrenia symptoms, as well as mood disorders, such as depression or manic behavior."

Motherfucker.

"Do I have that?" Lilly squeaked, her gaze ping-ponging back and forth between my parents.

"No. Hector didn't find any indicators when he...treated you," Dad reassured her.

Treated. *Brainwashed.* I closed my eyes and counted backward. Five, four, three... When I opened them again, I found my father staring at me with furrowed brows. He was expecting me to lose it, flip the table or something similar, and he wasn't too far off. I was working hard on controlling my anger, though.

I let out a breath I didn't realize I was holding.

"When you disappeared and she wouldn't do anything about it, Henry was beside himself. Emily refused to go to the authorities. She acted like you were...visiting someone," Mom added with tears running down her face.

"That's when I filled your Mom in on what I had been doing," Dad admitted with a sigh.

"I was horrified that I had been so blind. All the signs were there when Dad laid them out, but I didn't see them." Mom was full-on sobbing at that point.

"You turned back up in Santa Rosa, and I saw it as the right time to suggest for you to stay with us for a while. I meant to fill Henry in on my suspicion and hoped we could get Emily to seek help while we took care of Lilly getting past her...experience. But I never got the chance to talk to Henry in private. Emily heard Mom and me discuss it in the hospital and instantly agreed. She said she would speak to Henry and, shortly after, came to us saying he also thought it was a good idea under the circumstances. We never saw Henry after that. According to Emily, he had to leave to go to another job site."

"We should've questioned her further. Henry wouldn't have just left you. But we were so focused on you, worried because of the messages Emily kept getting," Mom pleaded with Lilly. She blamed herself for what Henry went through. "I just wanted for you to get bet—" She broke off, covering her face with her hands.

"Honey, please." Dad wrapped his arms around her, and she sobbed into his shoulder.

I was shocked to realize how much guilt my parents were carrying around—misplaced guilt. They made mistakes, no question there, but what Lilly's psycho mother did should not have been part of that.

After my parents filled us in about their knowledge of Emily's past, and Mom had somewhat calmed down, we sat in silence. Lilly flicked her thumb against the fingers of her hand when she suddenly stopped.

"So, you had Lakatos wipe my memory because of Emily, not *just* Nate?"

Huh?

"Something happened while you were, uh...gone." Dad didn't use the word kidnapped, and Lilly and I both noticed it—her tick stopped abruptly.

"We never figured out what. We talked about it last night. Nate was 100% transparent with us on everything that happened while you were with him. Whenever Emily would come near you in the hospital, you would start crying, cringing away. Even scream. You would cling to whomever was near—Henry, me, your nurse," Mom whispered. "It was heartbreaking.

Nate couldn't tell us, either, what the trigger may have been. You were scared and wanted to go home, but there was nothing that would explain why you reacted toward your mother the way you did. You were terrified."

"I informed them what Hector would be able to do," Dad redirected the conversation before Lilly could get too worked up over what her mother may have done. "Emily agreed without a second thought." Dad scrubbed a hand over his face. "In hindsight, she probably wanted you to forget. I'm starting to suspect that your reaction in the hospital had something to do with what she did to you."

"She never wanted me." Lilly's words were barely audible, yet it was like she shouted them at us. My mother gasped and jumped out of her chair, rounding the table.

"Oh, sweetheart." She wrapped her arms around Lilly.

"You helped her by taking Lilly away," I told my father, who nodded solemnly.

He blinked slowly. "I never anticipated her being that—"

"Psycho?" I supplied with a raised eyebrow.

Neither of my parents contradicted my statement.

Lilly wrapped her arms around Mom, and they both lost their battle against the waterfall of tears. When Lilly calmed down enough, she disentangled herself from Mom and pushed off the chair. She rounded the table to where Dad was sitting and sank down in the empty chair next to him.

Placing her hand on his on the table, she said, "Thank you." Her face was still wet, and a fresh tear ran down her cheek again.

Dad's eyebrows drew together in confusion, and she smiled. "Because of you, I got a childhood I will *never* forget. You and Mom"—her gaze swiveled to my mother—"are the best parents I could've wished for. So...thank you. For everything." She peered over at me with glossy eyes, and her meaning was clear. They also brought us together again. Who knew what would've happened if Lilly had stayed with Emily? I was sure Henry would've done his best, but we'd never find out—which I was fucking glad about.

Emily visiting my mother during that conference had set a chain of events in motion no one could've ever anticipated.

By the time Lilly finished her sentence, Dad was bawling and hugging her to him. I stood up and opened my arms for my mother, who dived in and clung to me, her shoulders shaking.

It took a long time before anyone was calmed down enough for me to ask the question. I wasn't sure if Lilly forgot about it or didn't want to ask, but I had to.

"Are you going to turn Nate in?"

Lilly flipped in my direction in shock, but I kept my eyes on my father.

"No," my mother spoke up, and I jerked my gaze to her.

"You aren't?" Lilly was as surprised as I was.

"No," Dad confirmed. "Your mother and I spoke about it at length last night after Nate approached us."

He came to them?

"Nate will turn himself in. He laid out his plan to us but left it up to us whether we would give him the time he needs to get everything in order."

AND HERE WE ARE, three months later, in the penthouse suite of the Altman Hotel.

A HAND TOUCHES the side of my face, and I'm pulled out of the memory. I dip my chin. My girl is awake, and her hazel eyes look at me with concern.

"What are you thinking about?" Her thumb moves over my cheekbone.

I lean into the contact, loving the feeling of her skin on mine.

"Just remembering."

She understands the meaning behind my vague answer and nods, continuing her caress. I don't insult her by pretending it's all good. That's not who we are. We've been through too much to disrespect one another by putting on a façade.

"The alarm hasn't gone off yet," she states.

I loosen my hold and trail my hands down her arms, letting my gaze follow the motion. Goosebumps erupt where my fingers make contact with her skin, and seeing her reaction to me stirs a flutter in my chest. Reaching her elbow, I tug until she's on top of me. Her breathing increases.

"No, it hasn't," I confirm, locking eyes with her again and brushing my lips over hers.

The memory is forgotten. All I see is her. The now. The future.

She pulls back slightly, scanning my face. Her eyes darken, and I know what's going through her mind. My dick knows it, too, and stands at instant attention. No matter where in my fucked-up headspace I am, what situation we're in—or with whom—one look, one touch, and I lose all control over my body (part).

In those moments, we're like your typical couple in a new relationship—horny all the time. Lilly can feel my response as well. She rocks into me, and I groan, regretting that I had put on briefs after the last time she sat on top of me just a few hours ago.

You could already be inside, the voice in my head whines.

As if reading my mind, her mouth quirks at the corner. "I told you not to get dressed."

We haven't spent a night apart since we found her on that bloody mattress, and I don't intend on being away from her anytime soon. I no longer have panic attacks when she leaves the room, but the need to be close to her—and inside of her—is as overpowering as ever.

Lilly leans in and bites at my bottom lip, followed by her

tongue soothing away the sting. Heat shoots to my toes. "Fuck, Calla."

She knows exactly what this does to me but enjoys the torture. She starts trailing kisses down my neck, over my torso, until she reaches the unwanted barrier between us. My chest heaves as Lilly continues her exploration. She studies me through her lashes, a devilish grin spreading across her face.

"Babe?" I prop myself up on my elbows, tilting my head.

Her fingers curl into the waistband of my briefs, and she tugs on them until my cock springs free. She pushes the fabric down until it reaches my ankles, and I kick it off hastily. Trying to rid myself of the damn thing, I also kick the comforter off the bed in the process—*I swear I'll go commando from now on.*

Lilly crawls toward me on all fours until her face is level with my—fuuuuck.

She's on me before my brain fully comprehends what's about to happen. My eyes roll back inside my head at the sensation of her mouth on me, and my arms give out—I drop back into the pillow.

The mattress shifts, and a hand grips my painfully hard length in addition to her mouth. Holy fucking hell. She bobs her head. Whenever her lips near the crown, she swirls her tongue around my tip before sinking back down. She continues mercilessly. My chest is heaving as I lie on the bed, letting her do to me whatever she wants.

"Fuck, babe." Every nerve ending in my body is on fire, and I have to fight the urge to thrust into her, not wanting to choke her. The combination of her stroking my dick while her mouth works me...I bite the inside of my cheek not to blow any second.

"You...need...to..." Eyes still closed, my hands fumble for her until I find her hair. Her tongue is pressing against the back of my cock as she continues to suck on me. My body has a mind of its own, and my hips jerk. I hit the back of her throat, but Lilly doesn't let up. She moans, and the sound alone is enough to push me almost over the edge. With all my willpower, I tug on the strands of her hair, signaling for her to stop. I raise my head off the pillow and peer down at her.

What a view.

Lilly takes mercy and glances up, eyes twinkling with mischief. "Something wrong?" She licks her bottom lip, and I groan.

"If you don't sit down on my dick right this second, I will bend you over that chair over there and show you what's wrong." I smirk, dipping my head toward the armchair next to the bed.

A picture of me fucking her from behind on said chair while smacking her firm ass conjures in my head, and I want to follow through with my threat.

We can always have a repeat on the chair later.

Lilly tilts her head as if considering the idea as well. Please say yes! I raise an eyebrow in challenge.

Pressing her mouth together, she stifles a laugh before scooting up on the bed. She straddles my waist but remains up on her knees as I let my gaze trail from her beautiful face, over her gorgeous tits, to what's now perfectly aligned with my one body part that probably loves her more than the rest of me.

She leans forward, placing her hands on my shoulders, and our eyes lock, all playfulness gone. We don't need pretty words anymore. Even though we've only been together for just about six months, we know each other better than most couples after years.

Lilly sinks down, never breaking eye contact. She moans, biting her lip, and I can't wait any longer. Grabbing her hips, I pull her down until I'm all the way inside.

So fucking tight.

Mine, a growl echoes in my mind.

Sitting up, I let my tongue swipe over one of her nipples before sucking it into my mouth, my hand palming her other breast. Her fingers dive into my hair, nails scraping over my scalp, and I gently bite down, having learned over the last several months that this is something she likes—a lot. She arches her back, giving me better access, and I oblige, tugging on her skin.

"Yesss, just like—" Lilly rocks herself into me, creating more friction over her clit. My girl knows what she wants and doesn't hesitate to take it. Another reason she's perfect for me.

My hand, the one not already occupied, finds her ass, and I press her further against me, thrusting up in the process.

"Oh, God," she breathes next to my ear before starting to kiss right underneath it—my weak spot. A shudder of pleasure runs down my spine.

"Babe, I..." I'm so fucking close. It's embarrassing how she can make me come in less than ten minutes. Thankfully, it never takes long before I'm ready again, or my ego would be shot by now.

Lilly starts increasing her speed, and I meet her every move. The only sounds in the room are our ragged breathing and the sound of flesh on flesh. I release her nipple, and her mouth instantly finds mine, opening up. My tongue tangles with hers, and she purrs.

The sounds that come out of this girl.

Both my hands move to her back, pulling her to me until we're flush together. She moans as my fingers dig into her back, and I feel her walls tighten around me.

"Come for me, Cal." I watch her fall apart in my arms with my cock buried deep inside of her. The look of ecstasy on her face is enough to push me over the edge. I groan as my cum releases inside of her, biting down on her shoulder. Thank fuck we're past the condom stage.

Still need to send a letter to whomever invented oral contraceptives.

Once our breathing evens out, she places both hands on either side of my face and puts our foreheads together. She looks at me, and I tilt my head, our lips brushing together.

"I love you." Her tone is soft.

"I love you."

CHAPTER FORTY-ONE

LILLY

I STAND IN FRONT OF THE DOUBLE-SIZE MIRROR IN THE bathroom of our hotel penthouse. Of course, we don't just have a room; we have one of the two penthouse suites on the top floor —Nate staying in the other—with my friends and family one floor underneath in the *slightly* smaller suites.

My wet hair hangs down my back, and my stomach clenches as I'm debating the appropriate hairdo for today. Curls, straight, up, down, French twist...how should one look coming out to the public as the illegitimate heir to a billion-dollar empire? Not to mention the other news that will drop today. My pulse increases, and my fingers tighten around the edge of the vanity. I close my eyes, taking a deep breath.

"Calla?"

Rhys's voice startles me, and my eyes snap open. He's standing in the doorway—butt naked. I let my gaze trail his body. Rhys has bulked up over the last three months. He's been training with George every day, and it shows. Every muscle in his body is toned. Between his bulging biceps, defined pecs, and ripped abs, heat pools in my core, and I have to clench my thighs together.

Hell, he just gave me a mind-blowing orgasm not twenty minutes ago.

He chuckles. "Don't do that."

"Do what?" I ask innocently, meeting his eyes. I'm fully aware of him noticing my shift in stance. And I can certainly *see* how it affects him.

"We don't have time." His face turns serious. "G called. Henry landed."

Henry. My heart starts pounding. Henry is in Los Angeles.

HENRY HAD BEEN in a hospital in Virginia when Heather and Tristen filled Rhys and me in on everything they knew or had suspected about Emily. From there, he went straight to one of the best physical rehabilitation facilities in the country. Nate took care of the logistics, and I couldn't have been more grateful to him. At first, it was debatable if he would ever regain full functionality of his legs after years of paralytic drugs. The doctors labeled his one almost-escape a fluke. He shouldn't have been able to stand on his legs, but he did—one time.

Henry got the best therapy, and because of that and his hard work, he's regained 75% of his leg mobility over the last few months. He still relies on a wheelchair, but his right leg is stronger than his left, and on a good day, he can move around on crutches for a little while or stand in one place on his own.

It took me almost a month before I found the courage to call him. Whenever I put in his number, my hands started sweating, and I'd become nauseated. The guilt about Emily's actions was eating my insides. Everyone kept reassuring me that none of this was my fault, and deep down, I knew they were right. After all, I was a kid when it started, but still. He was trapped by her for years—because of me.

I confessed my feelings to Heather during one of her visits to

LA. We were in the kitchen, preparing dinner at the time, with Natty doing her online schoolwork at the breakfast nook. Heather wiped her hands on a dishtowel, placed it on the countertop, and walked over to the island where I was chopping onions. I don't remember if the tears running down my cheeks were from the vegetable or from the deep-rooted feeling of being the reason my father...stepfather—we still hadn't defined his role—was partially paralyzed for years. She hugged me before pulling back and placing both palms on either side of my face.

"My sweet Lilly, I'm going to repeat myself as many times as you need to hear it. None of this is your fault. None. Henry is not upset with you. Quite the opposite."

"But I still haven't talked to him," I interrupted her reassurance. My hands started to shake, and I had to let go of the knife's handle.

"He is processing himself, sweetheart. Tristen and I have been in touch with him. We feel just as guilty because we didn't see Emily's...problems either. Not how sick she really was. Henry is working with a therapist to move past his guilt of not noticing Emily's mental issues before it was too late, letting his daughter get physically abused and later not being able to protect her from his wife's plans."

"But he couldn't have done anything about it." Sudden anger makes my cheeks heat.

"Exactly. And neither could you. Both of you were victims in a game that used you as pawns." She placed a kiss on my forehead, and when she pulled back, I nodded at her. She was right, but there was no saying how long it would take for me to truly believe it.

"Did you know that Henry spoke up for Emily's employees?" I asked Heather. Nate had informed me the night before that Henry gave a testimony that the maid, Elise, and the medical staff, who were charged as accessories, had all been threatened or blackmailed by Emily and Gray.

"Yes, I heard about it. The court will have to decide how to proceed with that." She directs an apologetic smile at me. She wouldn't give me any more answers on that topic. Her professional side never gave any predictions on a legal matter. We would have to wait and see on that one.

Heather was just moving back to the stove when I swiveled on my heels.

"Mom?" Heather had become Mom again. She was my mother. My anger toward her for keeping me in the dark had long since been replaced by light. She had cared for me since I was a baby, even when I wasn't yet her daughter.

She turned back around while continuing to stir the sauce. "Yes?"

"Do you remember what you said to me at Hill Crest?" The hospital where George dropped me off in Nebraska.

Her eyebrows rose. "We said a lot while you were there." Her expression turned pained for a fraction of a second, but she smoothed it out just as quickly. "You have to be a little more specific."

I drew in a deep breath. It'd been nagging on me for weeks, months, but it'd never been the right opportunity to bring it back up. "After I told you that I knew about me not being your daughter...biological daughter," I correct myself, and she smiled softly at that. "You said to me, *'No matter what you know or think you know, you are my little girl.'* What did you mean?"

Heather—Mom scrunched her forehead and looked up at the ceiling. When she found my gaze, she opened and closed her mouth several times before speaking. "That was a very emotional day. Dad had just confessed to me about his suspicion that Henry was not your father. Yet, I didn't know how much more there was."

"Hannah and the cameras," I finished, and she nodded.

It was the other bombshell that Tristen confessed to Rhys and me when Heather first came to LA. He had kept the extent of the home surveillance to himself for years to not scare his wife and children. He didn't understand why Emily would come after our housekeeper—after no communication from her since I had moved in with the McGuires—and steal my teddy bear, of all things. Was it because Brooks had given me that bear? Was it her way of making a point? That she could get to me if she wanted to? Or was it simply part of her mental illness, and there was no real reason? Hannah was most likely a victim caught in the crossfire. We may never know. Not unless Francis Garrison (Gray) Turner shows back up. He'd been missing since the day he shot Emily, and we could only speculate about his motive. I repeated his words to my family. *No one betrays me.* But none of them could make sense of it either. *Did Emily betray him?*

Heather's eyes were shining with love as she explained, "You were confused about who you were, and I wanted you to know that you will always be my daughter, even if I didn't give birth to you."

This time, I walked over to her and hugged her.

ARMS CIRCLING my stomach bring me out of my memory. Two thumbs caress the spot underneath my belly button, and I let my vision come back to focus and face Rhys in the mirror.

"Where did you just go, babe?" He cocks his head and studies my face.

"Just thinking about Henry."

He nods and pulls me tighter to him, his erection pressing against my back. One hand moves upward and cups my breast, his mouth peppering my neck and shoulder with kisses.

I lean into him, tilting my neck, and close my eyes. "Mhmm...didn't you just say we don't have time?"

He blows out a resigned breath, and the cool air against my neck causes goosebumps on my arms. "I did, didn't I?" he murmurs, placing another kiss on my shoulder.

He loosens his hold and steps back, his gaze moving down to my butt. He sighs dramatically, and I bark out a laugh.

"Go take a cold shower, big boy."

He smirks, and I add, "Alone."

Rhys gives me a one-sided shoulder shrug before he turns on the spray. "Not my fault I have the hottest girlfriend."

The hornets in my stomach go haywire at his words, and I shake my head. Then, I meet my reflection in the mirror again, and the hornets turn to dust, a black hole opening up in my stomach.

IT'S TIME. With my hand safely secured in Rhys's, we make our way from our penthouse to the elevator down the hall. I knocked on Nate's door, but there was no answer. He must've already gone down.

When we arrived yesterday, Kevin, the hotel's bellhop of forty-two years, informed me that the top floor is reserved for the Altman family. No one else is allowed to stay there unless Mr. Nate—or now I—gave permission.

When I looked at him with confused eyes, the gray-haired man smiled. "You look like your father and brother."

My mouth dropped open, unable to form words.

"The second suite has been empty since Miss Payton and Miss Audrey left us. Mr. Nate always stays in his grandfather's suite," he said with a bowed head as the elevator ascended, and I fought against the lump in my throat.

Rhys, who had remained quiet, wrapped his arm around me and pulled me into his side. He saw that this friendly man's words had almost caused me to break down.

My biological mother was the reason why the penthouse had been empty for over a decade.

Now standing in the elevator, my heart rate is increasing. My palm is getting damp in Rhys's, and I focus on our reflection in the mirrored doors. Rhys is dressed in dark-gray slacks and a white button-down shirt. His short hair has the perfect amount of gel in it. I shift to myself. I decided on a navy-blue pencil skirt with a white cap-sleeve blouse and nude heels. After blow-drying my hair, I twisted it in a low bun, letting a few strands hang loose around my face. I want to look put-together but still like myself. When my gaze lands on my free hand, I snort, which draws Rhys's attention back to me. I was flicking my thumb against my fingers and didn't even notice.

I am more nervous than I want to admit to myself.

LATE LAST NIGHT, Nate and I met in the grand ballroom to go over everything one more time. Rhys patiently waited for two hours, sitting in one of the chairs on the stage. Today's announcement would only take thirty minutes. George and I, along with Agent Lanning, Agent Camden, and Doctor Stern, would be onstage together with Nate. We would need law enforcement, and after several heated discussions between myself, Nate, Heather, and Tristen, we all agreed Lanning and Camden were the best choices. Both were shocked, to say the least, when we flew them out to LA and introduced them to Nate. It took some convincing from Heather and Tristen to give us two more weeks to finalize the plan.

We also have several members of the hotel's security team, as well as George's own team, standing against both walls. George took charge of that. Everything is planned meticulously, down to the most superficial detail. Where Nate just wanted it all over, George and I refused to leave anything to chance.

That's how it happened that the first two rows are reserved for the families of *the girls*. I personally called each of the parents and asked them to be here today. They knew who I was—obviously. We took care of their travel and accommodations, but none of them knew the true reason why they were summoned. I only told them that it had to do with the case, and it'd be important for them to attend in person.

We were at the vineyard during that time, and before the first call, I had a complete panic attack. Rhys almost called 911—

if he would have known how to navigate Nate's NCC set up. He almost tore the door out of the hinges, yelling for Nate.

The third row is for the board members, and the fourth will be occupied by my family. Rhys was pissed that I wouldn't let him be onstage, but Heather sided with me on that. "She needs to do this alone. She'll be safe."

He hasn't left my side in months. Wherever I go, so does he. I see the looks Heather and Tristen give him, and he probably should work with his therapist on his fears, but I'm also selfish. I don't want to be without him as much as he doesn't want to be without me.

We have time to deal with the past when today is over. To heal.

WE ARRIVE on the second floor where the ballrooms are located. My heart is beating in my throat, but as the doors open, we're greeted by a familiar face, and my nerves calm a little. Marcus has become my shadow—as Rhys and Wes call him— whenever George isn't with me.

Between Gray and Hank both missing, I have a 24/7 security detail. Hank still has not returned to U.S. soil, and Nate lost his trail after he left the hotel and got into an unmarked car.

Marcus is one of George's men and is around Nate's age. He was personally trained by George for years, which was why he was chosen for the role.

He dips his chin, and without a word, he falls into step slightly behind me. We make our way to the side entrance, avoiding the press waiting in the back by the main doors. Rhys's hand never leaves mine, and I know he won't let go until the last minute. He's my anchor. He is worried, and if I'm honest, I am too. Not for my safety, but for how the audience will take what we have to say.

The press conference is to start in ten minutes, and the room is already buzzing. I stop abruptly when I step onstage and notice that the block of chairs has been moved back twenty feet. My eyes find Nate's, who's standing next to an uncomfortable Doctor Stern, and he slowly moves toward us. He is dressed in a custom navy suit, white shirt, no tie. We look like we color-coordinated.

"George and the hotel's head of security decided to put distance between us and, uh...the families."

Oh.

I bite my bottom lip and look between my brother and the first row. Before I can say anything, Rhys speaks up.

"Good." He nods at Nate. "We have no fucking clue how this will go down."

I bite harder. They are right, but I can't help the guilt that's settling in my stomach. We are about to turn these people's lives upside down as much as we will give them closure.

As much as we can after what my brother did.

I scan the room, and most of the seats are already taken. I'm met with nervous glances as well as glares from the first two rows. I should've expected that after everything that went down when I *reappeared*. I see almost everyone, except Ava Conway. Her mother is there with a woman that must be her sister. But neither Ava nor her father, who had demanded my interrogation, are present.

Ava's mother meets my gaze, and I avert my eyes, my mouth going dry. In the fourth row, I spot Heather and Tristen quietly talking to another man. *Henry.*

As if he senses my stare, he turns his head, and it's the first time—that I remember—I see him in person. He does a double-take, and I swallow against the needles in my throat. I squeeze Rhys's hand, making him follow my gaze.

Leaning closer, he whispers, "Go to him."

I jerk my head around. "I...I can't." The nervousness I felt entering this room is replaced by the imminent fear of facing the man who was held hostage for a decade because of me. My free hand finds my lower abdomen.

I feel sick.

"Well"—Rhys glances back toward the audience—"he's coming to you."

Every muscle in my body tenses, and I slowly swivel in the same direction. Henry is in his wheelchair and slowly approaching the podium. As if giving me an out, he doesn't avert his eyes from mine. One signal, and he'd turn around.

When he is right in front of the stage, my feet slowly move toward him. There was never a question of me stopping him. A multitude of emotions causes my stomach to somersault. I'm glad that I skipped breakfast today.

With Rhys on my heels, I descend the four steps and come to a halt in front of—

"Daddy?" my barely audible voice breaks. I feel my insides shatter like a crystal chandelier plummeting to the ground, breaking into a million shards and pieces. My hands fly to my mouth as I take in every inch of his face.

Henry's eyes spill over, and he pushes himself out of the wheelchair. Rhys steps to his side for support, but he shakes his head. Fully upright, his arms fall to his sides, and I launch myself at the man I only consciously know from my migraines. Subconsciously, a deep-routed sensation starts spreading through me. He was my father for my first six years. He is still my father. I never got to meet Brooks, but I have Henry and Tristen. He wraps his arms around me, and I squeeze his midsection.

"Hey, honey." His voice is deep and smooth. I can feel his chest rise and fall against my cheek while his hand cups the back of my head. I don't remember him, yet I do. It makes no sense, and at the same time, it makes perfect sense.

"I'm so sorry, Daddy." I'm sobbing, ruining his light-blue dress shirt and most definitely my makeup, but I don't care.

"Shhh," he soothes. "You have nothing to be sorry for." He pulls back and searches my face. "We have all the time in the world to talk. I'm not going anywhere."

I nod, wiping with one hand under my eyes. Glancing to the

side, Heather is mimicking my motion under her own eyes, and so is Denielle. A hand touches my shoulder, and I turn, facing George.

"It's time."

Already? I look back at Henry, suddenly unsure and feeling like a little girl.

He gives me an encouraging smile. "I'll be right over there." He tilts his head toward the edge of the fourth row.

I nod hesitantly, unable to form words. My knees feel weak, and I'm not sure I can make it back up the steps to the stage.

Rhys retakes my hand and squeezes it. "You sure you don't want me with you?"

Yes, please stay with me.

"I have to do this alone," I tell him with as much confidence as I can muster, given the pit that has rooted itself in my stomach and my voice cracking.

"Ok." He kisses me on the cheek, and I expect him to follow Henry, but instead, he levels George.

"If anyone harms her, I will hold you responsible. I don't care that you make everyone shit their pants just by looking at you. If anything happens, you jump in front of her, or I will come after you with your own gun. I know the combination to your safe; don't forget that." I am shocked at the menace that rolls off Rhys's tongue but equally touched by it. He loves George. The two have a bond that none of us understand, but he is one hundred percent serious.

George bows his head. "I will." He doesn't say anything else, but there is also no need for more words. We all know that this man would put anything on the line for Nate and me.

With one last squeeze of my hand, Rhys lets go and walks past the first three rows. He positions himself next to Henry's wheelchair, not moving into the row to sit down.

The sudden loss of his contact makes me almost double over. My anchor. Before I can change my mind and race after Rhys, begging him to come back, I turn and follow George.

I make my way to my assigned seat between Agent Lanning and Doctor Stern. The poor man looks like he's going to pass out any second. He probably never expected to be in this situation, but his testimony is prudent.

THIS IS where we wait until George taps the microphone on the podium in front of us. "If you would please all take your seats. The press conference is about to begin." I scan the room and take in several sets of wide eyes staring at the man who just addressed them. It's almost comical how intimidating he is despite being dressed all professional in a pressed suit.

CHAPTER FORTY-TWO

RHYS

I STAY NEXT TO HENRY IN THE AISLE AND CROSS MY ARMS IN front of my chest, focusing on the stage. Out of the corner of my eye, Mom gives me a disapproving glance. She wants me to sit down but knows why I've positioned myself here. I want a direct line of sight to Lilly and to be ready to move at any moment. Several of George's men, including Lilly's shadow, are closer than me, if it came down to it, but I don't care.

Lilly's eyes find mine from her seat between Lanning and Nate's doc. Holy fuck, the guy's face is all kinds of green. Guess he should've paid more attention to the shit he prescribed to his patient. If the situation weren't so serious, I'd laugh my ass off.

There is movement in my peripheral vision. Denielle shuffles past my parents and stands behind Henry, followed by Wes, who stops behind me. I glance back without losing sight of Lilly on the stage. She is nervous, flicking her thumb against the rest of her fingers.

"She'll be ok," Denielle whispers.

I'm not sure who she's trying to reassure or if she truly believes it. Hell, I have no clue what's going to happen in the next thirty minutes. This whole thing is fucking insane. I thought Lilly having her memory erased was the craziest thing that I would ever experience in my life. Never in a million years would I have expected to find myself here, in the fanciest hotel in freaking LA, after Lilly—*and I*, thanks to being the reckless idiot I am—almost got killed by her biological mother, now waiting for Lilly's brother/first kidnapper to admit to his past crimes.

I couldn't make that shit up even if I wanted to.

GEORGE APPROACHES THE PODIUM AGAIN, and I hear several intakes of breath behind me from the press rows. It's hilarious that this scary-ass guy with a massive scar across half his face is like a doting father to Lilly and Nate. I remember the night he stepped out of the shadows in Den's backyard; I almost pissed my pants.

"Ladies and gentlemen..." The room goes eerily quiet, and all eyes are to the front. Lilly, however, is looking directly at me, and I give her the slightest nod.

You got this, babe.

"Mr. Hamlin has called for this press conference for several reasons. One is to announce a change in ownership for the Altman Hotels. However, the main objective is for him to inform everyone in attendance of the truth in the disappearance of the five girls that went missing and reappeared *unharmed* over the past ten years."

Instantly I hear chairs scrape against the floor, flashes go off, and reporters behind me start shouting questions. "What does that mean?" "What do the Altman Hotels have to do with a string of kidnappings?" "Why are we here?" "Who is the man next to Miss McGuire?"

I recognize that voice.

I glance over my shoulder, and sure enough, Lancaster is

front and center. The dude will cry like a baby after losing his life's sole purpose today.

George ignores all of them and taps the mic again. When the press realizes that he will not answer their questions, they slowly sit back down one by one.

Shit, this guy is good.

"My name is George Weiler, and I am the head of Mr. Hamlin's personal security." I notice how he purposefully neglects the fact that he is also Lilly's security. They probably don't want to use her name until Nate and Lilly announce who she is.

"The press conference will proceed as follows. Mr. Hamlin will address you first, followed by several other speakers who will comment on what Mr. Hamlin is about to tell you." Again, he doesn't mention any names. "We are asking all of you to remain calm and seated the entire time. We will *not* allow questions during *or after*. The objective is for all of you to receive the same informa-tion at the same time. Any questions can be submitted in writing afterward and will be answered by the Altman legal representatives and the assigned authorities. Anyone who disrupts the press conference, does not remain seated, or attempts to approach the podium will *immediately* be removed by my security staff." George nods to both sides of the room, and it's almost as if everyone just now notices the men standing against the walls. Several gasps are audible throughout the large room, amplifying the sounds.

"Does anyone have an issue with the rules?"

Nothing. Not one sound. I'm pretty sure the entire room is holding its breath.

"Very well. Mr. Hamlin will address you first." With that, George steps to the side, and Nate slowly moves forward. He looks at Lilly before taking the last step, and she gives him a tight smile.

It's written over her entire face how much she loves *and supports* her brother. She has forgiven him for what he has done to her and what she went through because of his actions. Not many people would be capable of that. As scared as I am for her and for what is to unfold in the next few minutes, I am even more proud to call her mine.

"LADIES AND GENTLEMAN," Nate's voice rings through the ballroom. "My name is Nathan Altman Hamlin. My legal name is Nathan Hamlin; however, since taking over the Altman Hotels, I have used my mother and grandfather's name to conduct my business affairs. The two names have allowed me to live *two* separate lives, but this will come to a close today." Nate pauses and looks down at his notes. Where he sounds calm and collected, Lilly's posture is rigid, and even from a distance, I can see the white knuckles of her clasped hands.

My entire body is tense, and I fight the urge to march up there and throw myself in front of her. Denielle must've noticed the shift in me, because she gently places her hand on my lower back, keeping me in place. Behind me, hasty typing and the clicking of cameras is audible, and I assume the press is also holding up microphones. I don't turn around. My focus is on our current speaker and his sister behind him.

"As my head of security has already mentioned, we will not accept any questions. However, I am aware that some of the information I am about to share will be unsettling and upsetting to you, but I have to ask you to remain calm, or we will not be able to continue. Please let all the speakers finish."

Taking a deep breath, Nate turns one last time to Lilly, who locks eyes with him but doesn't show any expression. I haven't seen this blank mask in a long time. I don't like it, though I get that it is the face she has to put on.

"You were wondering who the people behind me are, and I will explain each of their roles to you in a moment. Most of you"—this is directed toward the press—"are aware of my past: my mother and sister's fatal accident, my father's suicide, and my altercation with another student, resulting in his hospitalization and my stay in a psychiatric facility. Doctor Stern"—he nods toward the small and, by now, extremely sweaty man in the farthest chair—"has been my therapist for the past *ten* years and will explain the medical aspect of this to you.

"On the other side, you have Agents Lanning and Camden of the Federal Bureau of Investigation. You may have heard their names over the last several months." He's alluding to the case without saying it directly. "Agents Lanning and Camden are here to ensure that the appropriate legal measures are taken once this is over."

A murmur runs through the crowd, and I almost expect someone to speak up, but George moves forward, and everyone quiets.

Fascinating.

"Before introducing the last person onstage, I would like to express my deepest apologies to the four families in the first two rows. I now understand what you have been put through, and there are no words that can ever erase the pain you experienced...through my hand." This is it. My adrenaline level shoots through the roof, not that my blood pressure wasn't already in the unhealthy range.

Flashes go off, people behind me jump up, and from my angle, I can see the shocked expressions of the parents in the front. Slowly the information sinks in. The women all sit with covered mouths, some crying, some in their husband's arms. One man jumps up and attempts to reach the stage when two security guards stop him.

"YOU MOTHERFUCKER! YOU TOOK MY BABY GIRL!" the man is shouting, and I feel Denielle behind me cringe at his words. The woman next to him starts crying harder and pulls on his arm, trying to tug him backward.

I force myself to remain rooted in place. Lilly is not in danger. I inhale and exhale through my nose, watching George slowly make his way off the stage and quietly address the man. I have no idea what he says to the outraged father, but all of a sudden, his shoulders slump, and he lets the security guard guide him back to his seat.

I did not expect that.

Focusing back on the stage, I realize that Lilly stepped up next to Nate and has her hand on his forearm. Glancing around, others have noticed the same gesture and are now looking at the two with a mix of curiosity and contempt. They know who Lilly is—at least part of it.

Nate covers the microphone while Lilly quietly talks to him. He shakes his head vigorously as she keeps addressing him. Her entire focus is on her brother; she has tuned everyone else out. Where Nate looks pained, she is serious, and knowing Lilly, there is no negotiation. George joins the two, and after Lilly seems to bring him up to speed, George places a hand on Nate's shoulder, nods at him in his typical no-bullshit fashion, and slowly guides him toward the chair Lilly vacated. I hold my breath as she takes the podium.

She is not in danger.

I curl my toes inside my shoes to keep myself in place. As soon as she stands behind the microphone, everything goes quiet.

"Ladies and gentleman of the press, Mrs. Conway, Mr. and Mrs. Scagliotta, Mr. and Mrs. Lynn, and Mr. and Mrs. Ashbaugh, thank you all for coming today. I would like to introduce myself first before continuing with the rest of the information Nate was about to share with you. My name is Lilly Ann Hamlin."

A collective gasp goes through the room, and I expect someone to speak up, but no one does.

From my angle, I can see Lilly clutch the notes Nate left behind. Lilly takes a deep breath before looking straight at the people in the first two rows. "I am Nate Hamlin's sister and his first"—she pauses for what I count seven breaths—"victim." Lilly's chest is heaving, and I know the signs. Unless she can calm herself, she is going into a panic attack. I take one step, and her eyes find me instantly. I halt, waiting for her cues. She looks at me, and I hold her gaze. I don't know how long we stare at each other when she finally dips her chin and faces the parents again. She's back in control. I expel a sigh of relief.

"My apologies. This is still hard for me, as well. As I said, I was my brother's first victim. My biological mother had an affair with Nate's father, Brooks Hamlin. Neither Nate nor his mother or sister knew about me, nor I of them. After Audrey and Payton Altman's death, Nate found out about his father's affair through a number of letters my mother had sent to him. At the time, my brother was in a very dark place. He had just been released from his stay at the hospital and was highly medicated. Medication that impacted his judgment and thinking to a point where—"

"ARE YOU MAKING EXCUSES FOR THIS FREAK'S CRIMES?" the man from earlier shouts in the first row.

Fuck. This is getting ugly.

I'm ready to storm to the stage; Marcus is already front and center.

Lilly faces the man with a sad smile. "No, Mr. Lynn. I am not. My brother needs to account for his crimes. I have told him that from the day I found out who I was and what he had done to your daughters and me. There is no excuse for that." Someone else is standing up, about to say something, but Lilly holds up her hand. She looks like she does this every day, and my chest swells. I'm even a little turned on.

This is so not appropriate right now.

"Please let me finish. I understand that this is hard for you, and I promise you will get the answers you need. I have had time to come to terms with what has happened to me and worked alongside my family and my brother to deal with the past."

"Why didn't you come clean when you reappeared last March?" Lancaster shouts.

So much for no questions.

"Mr. Lancaster, please let me proceed. As our head of security has informed you, we will not allow questions."

I can't help myself and glance back at the guy who had camped out on our front lawn for weeks. His face is a mixture of surprise and shock, and I grin to myself. I wonder how many times he's been told off by an eighteen-year-old.

Lilly continues. She tells the room everything. Every detail that led to today. With some topics, she's vague, like how she lost her memory. With others, there is uncensored explicitness, like Emily's blackmail and abuse. When Lilly mentions Henry, all eyes are on him, but he only focuses on his daughter. At Lilly's recollection of Turner breaking into the Hamlin Estate and what Emily did to her to get her inheritance, a collective gasp goes through the room. One of her hands leaves the podium and rubs over the scar hidden underneath her skirt. She does that whenever someone brings up those few days.

"The reason I am telling you all of this is for you to understand why it took so long for my brother and me to hold this conference. The Altman board of directors was notified last week of my existence and that I will take over for my brother, effective immediately. While I continue my education, I will rely on the board's experience and guidance to make sure my family's business is handled appropriately. Upon completion of my degree, I will take on the official role as the president of the Altman Hotels until my brother returns."

"Returns from where?"

Fucking Lancaster.

Lilly ignores him and focuses back on the parents of the four girls. "My brother has given his statement to Agents Camden and Lanning of the FBI. Upon finishing this press conference, he is voluntarily checking himself into a facility specialized for this type of disorder. At the same time, his attorney will collect the testimony of the pharmaceutical companies, Dr. Stern, who prescribed the medication that caused his impulsive and erratic behavior, and any witnesses before taking the case to trial. During his treatment, my brother will learn how to cope with his actions and—"

"THIS IS FUCKING RIDICULOUS. THE BASTARD NEEDS TO GO TO JAIL!"

Lynn is losing it, and this time, neither his wife nor George can calm him down. His yelling becomes louder, and when he takes a step toward the podium, George's men are on him, grasping his arms. Marcus has positioned himself directly in front of Lilly, making her peer around his large frame. The guys drag Chloe's father to a side entrance while his wife stands there staring after her kicking husband.

Suddenly, Lilly moves around her shadow and down the steps. Marcus says something, but she waves him off.

What the hell is she doing?

The only reason I'm staying where I am is that Marcus is right on her heels. She approaches the woman, who now stares at her with wide eyes. Lilly has her hands clasped in front of her body and quietly speaks to Chloe's mother. Mrs. Lynn keeps nodding, covering her mouth with her palm as she wipes her eyes with her other. Lilly gives her a genuine smile before she climbs the stage again, and Mrs. Lynn takes her seat.

"My apologies, ladies and gentlemen. Mr. Lynn will remain outside until the press conference concludes. However, I would like to say that his reaction is justified given the circumstances. I appreciate the rest of you following Mr. Weiler's instructions, and we will finish as quickly as possible."

Lilly takes a step back, and a shaking Dr. Stern approaches the podium. Instead of sitting back down, she remains at the side of the stage, flanked between George and Marcus. She studies Nate with furrowed brows, who has his gaze trained on the floor. His lips are pressed in a thin line, and—is he flicking his thumb against his fingers?

My attention gets redirected as Stern introduces himself, followed by giving a brief explanation of the medication Nate received over the years. He only states facts and doesn't go into the many side effects these drugs can cause. I guess that'll be part of the trial. Agent Camden is the last to speak and updates everyone on how this impacts the case. When she finishes, Nate stands from his seat, and Lilly and Camden turn. Agent Lanning reaches behind him and pulls out a set of handcuffs.

Why the hell did no one tell me that this would happen?

Lilly stands stock still, and George places a hand on her lower back as they watch Nate placing his hands together and Lanning putting the cuffs on. Tears are streaming down Lilly's face, but she doesn't make any move to remove them. Nate lifts his eyes to his sister, and before the two agents lead him back toward the other side entrance, he mouths, "I love you."

It's over.

EPILOGUE

LILLY

Six Years Later

IT'S BEEN fifteen months since I last saw my brother face to face, and my body is buzzing with nervous energy. We're approaching the small airport in Northern California, and I'm trying to get some notes to my assistant before shutting off the computer for the next week.

After finishing my degree, I took over the Altman security department. Thanks to Nate beginning my intensive training before he went *away,* and my education, I turned the Altman Hotels into one of a kind. People all over the world choose our hotels for their security measures and privacy.

"Babe, how long is that damn email going to be?" Denielle barks at me from her seat across the aisle.

I flick my gaze to her before returning it to my screen.

"Leave her alone, D. You know if my wife doesn't get her work done, we won't see her for the remainder of the trip."

I glare at Rhys over the top of my laptop, but he just smirks and winks. He'll never let me live it down for disappearing during our rehearsal dinner to fix a bug that one of my developers built into the custom system at an offshore location. I was still in college but had already started taking over parts of the business.

Instead of snapping a retort at him, I concentrate back on my screen. The sooner I get this done, the faster I can focus on what's important for the next seven days.

Typing, I listen to the conversations around me. Heather and Tristen are in the front, murmuring to each other. Natty is sitting in the other seat in the front row, reading a book. She's attending an online high school, which allows her to move between Westbridge and L.A. every few weeks, or in this case, fly to the vineyard with us.

"How was the beach?" Hudson asks Wes behind me. Hudson and Elle were able to make it; the others would fly in tomorrow.

Wes snorts. "Oh, you know. The girls played in the ocean until they passed out from exhaustion, and then I had to take care of myself—even cook my own dinner." *Smack.* "Ouch! Woman!" I glance over my shoulder and see Wes rubbing his arm, glowering to his right.

Grinning, I turn back around.

"You guys never learn," Elle laughs. "Don't antagonize the women who feed you."

Her voice gets closer, and she squats down next to my seat. "Hey, girl."

I smile at my friend. "Hi."

Who would've expected that the day she drove to LA to pick up Hudson and ran into me while I was escaping my gazillion-square-foot hideout would result in a friendship that will last a lifetime? We've visited each other a lot over the years, especially after Elle moved to Colorado for college and offered to give me free ski lessons. I dragged Rhys to the jet that same week, and after that, it became a tradition that brought our two groups of friends and family closer together with every visit.

"I just wanted to say that we're excited to be here for the big occasion. Too bad not everyone could make it today. Hazel was livid she couldn't be on the jet with us today and has to fly commercial. You know how she is." She laughs then chews on her lower lip, and I cock an eyebrow, waiting.

"Has he met her yet?" she asks carefully.

I avert my eyes as butterflies take hold in my stomach. "Not yet."

Rhys watches me closely.

"I'm not going to have a panic attack," I snap at him but immediately regret my unwarranted reaction. "Shit, babe, I didn't—" I cover my face with my hands. There is a high chance I will have a meltdown, and we both know it. I haven't had one in years, but I've been a mess since we found out about Nate's early release date and that it would fall close to this week. Nate was officially discharged three weeks ago, but besides a handful of phone calls, I've spoken to him less than the years he was in the facility.

Fingers clasp around my wrists and pull until I let my hands drop away from my face.

I lock eyes with Rhys, and he interlaces our fingers on top of the table that's separating our seats.

"Everything will be fine," he reassures me calmly.

Not letting go of him, I stand, and Elle moves out of the way to let me out. I step to Rhys's side, and he tilts his head. Without a word, I straddle his lap and wrap my arms around his neck.

"Ahem..." Elle clears her throat. "I'll take that as my cue." There is laughter in her voice, and I know she's not offended.

I brush my lips over Rhys's and whisper, "I love you."

He pulls me closer, his mouth less than an inch from my ear. I feel his breath on my skin as he replies in a murmur, "I love you more," and a shiver of need runs down my spine.

Closing my eyes, I move my hips, but Rhys stills me, chuckling. "Do you really want to do this on a jet full of people? In front of my parents—*your in-laws?*"

Heat surges into my cheeks. *Dear Lord, how could I have blocked them all out?* I hear a snicker from across the aisle— Denielle—and I bury my face in Rhys's shoulder.

He's shaking underneath me with silent laughter. After all these years, I still can't get enough of this guy.

"We'll make sure to get some alone time later," he says in a low tone, full of promise, and the heat spreads to other parts of my body as well.

Joel's voice comes over the intercom for everyone to take their seats, and I reluctantly move back to mine and buckle in. Across from me, Rhys is adjusting his pants and throws me an accusatory glare when he catches me watching. I shrug, and his eyes crinkle.

"Tonight," he mouths.

TWO LARGE SUVs wait for us in the hangar, and I spot George instantly. He leans against one of the vehicles but pushes off as soon as we step off the jet.

Initially, he was supposed to accompany us on the flight since it was Marcus's week off as well. Then, last Friday, he called, saying he'd be staying at the vineyard with my brother, and Marcus would be in charge during the travel. Something was off, and my mind immediately started coming up with all kinds of scenarios in which Nate was not okay. But when I asked, George kept assuring me that Nate was fine. That man was, and still is, a closed vault. If he doesn't want to talk about something, there is no way to get it out of him. *My shadow* was kept in the dark as well. He has never kept anything from me, no matter how bad the news was—and there have been many instances over the years. The media is ruthless.

Marcus has become like a second big brother and one of Rhys's closest friends. Even when he isn't on duty, he always hangs around. Marcus is also George's second in command when it comes to our security, which made me worry even more that he had no clue what was going on.

"Lilly." A huge smile turns George's mouth upward, and some of the tension leaves me. If it were something serious, I have to believe he'd tell me—warn me. *Nate is fine.* Everything will be okay.

I hug the man who's become an integral part of my family. "Hi, George."

"G-man." Rhys comes around me and gives him one of his usual clasp-hands-side-shoulder-man-hugs.

Oh, how things have changed.

"How was the flight?" George looks over my shoulder where Heather is carefully maneuvering down the stairs.

"Great, slept almost the entire time." Rhys puffs up his chest.

George's grin turns wider, and I snort.

"I don't need your help." Den's growl echoes through the hangar, and I sigh before turning around. My best friend and Marcus are standing on the top step, and she's tugging ferociously on the handle of her suitcase he is attempting to carry for her.

"Dude, just let go. It's not worth the tongue lashing she'll give you if you take Louis away from her," Wes shouts from the back door of the second SUV where he's waiting for his turn to climb in.

"Fuck off, Sheats!" Denielle barks at him, but Wes only grins wider and blows her a kiss.

"Fine. Whatever. I'm done," Marcus snaps before disappearing back inside the airplane.

Rhys bursts into laughter, and even George can't hold back a chuckle. I shake my head and stroll over to Heather. This week will be interesting.

. . .

WE PILE into the two cars. George is driving ours with Rhys in the passenger seat, Den and me in the middle, and Heather in the third row. Tristen and the rest went into the other SUV.

"Henry called right before we took off," Heather announces, and I turn in my seat.

"He did? Is everything okay?" I had spoken to him just this morning, and the jet is going to pick him up two days from now. He isn't able to make it earlier due to his current project.

After his recovery, Henry moved to Virginia, and Tristen helped him get an architect position with a well-known builder in the city. Whenever Rhys and I visited, I would make sure to spend a few days at Henry's as well, and over the years, we've been able to grow our relationship.

Besides the few migraine memories of Henry, I never remembered anything else prior to being six years old. But between him, Heather, and Tristen—their stories, as well as all the photos —I could picture it. That was how I wanted to remember my childhood, and not once have I regretted my decision to not meet with Hector Lakatos to let him try restoring it.

"Everything is fine. He was just asking if he should bring any of the travel toys you left at his house last month," Heather explains.

Oh.

I sigh in relief. The anxiety that instantly shot through me disappears, and I glance down at the middle seat where George expertly strapped in the baby carrier. My heart skips a beat. In just two days, this little one will be one year old. She rubs her eyes and slowly blinks them open.

"Good morning, sleepyhead. Did you have a good nap?" I coo at her, caressing her cheek with the tip of my index finger.

Her big green eyes slowly take in her surroundings, and Rhys twists in his seat.

"How is my princess?" Hearing his voice, she immediately gets antsy and tries to reach for him.

When she can't see or touch him, her fussing gets louder.

Whenever Daddy is near, no one else matters. "You need to wait a few more minutes. Then you can go to Daddy," I try to soothe her, and Den chuckles.

I glare at my best friend, and she makes a zip motion across her mouth. Denielle thinks this is hilarious.

George also laughs in the driver's seat, and my daughter's undivided attention switches to our head of security. Yup, I'm officially in third place; she prefers our bodyguard to me. I can't be mad, though. The men in her life adore her and spoil her rotten. Who wouldn't want that all the time? I smile down at her little round face, and the image of an old baby picture instantly appears behind my mental eye. I blink a few times. This is not the time to cry.

WE PULL straight into the garage, and I let George and Rhys get out while I unbuckle our daughter. I barely have her out of the car seat when she reaches for Rhys, who has just opened my door.

"Here you go. There is your da—" is all I get out before she dives into his arms.

He grins down at her proudly and hugs her to his chest, placing a kiss on her blonde curls. "I missed you, too, princess."

I climb out of the car and grab the diaper bag. My pulse increases as I scan the motor pool. His car is here, but why is he not coming to say hello?

"Where is he?" I address George, who's already halfway through the door leading to the east wing. Turning, he first looks at Rhys then at me. "He is in the kitchen."

Heather steps to my side. "You go on. I'll make sure everyone gets situated, and then we'll meet you in a little bit."

I hug her absently, my gaze not leaving the now empty door-frame to the house. "Thank you."

She is starting to direct everyone to their rooms.

With shaking legs, I step from the garage into the hallway.

The smell of garlic tomato sauce drifts into my nose, and I'm instantly taken back to one of my first meals here so many years ago.

So much has changed since then.

Nate has spent the last several years in a psychiatric facility, taking responsibility for his crimes. He was taken off medication for the last three and solely focused on therapy. I'm so proud of him for what he has accomplished.

Rhys and I finished college, got married, had a baby—not to mention what went on in our friends' lives. Life was never...ordinary.

Rhys places his free arm around my waist, smiling down. "Let's go. It's time he meets his niece."

My stomach is in knots the closer we get to the kitchen, and my feet are moving slower and slower until Rhys begins to herd me. I don't know why I'm so nervous. Maybe it's because I haven't seen him in so long, or because we've barely spoken the last few weeks, and I'm worried something is wrong.

Slowly, I push open the door and pause. Nate is standing at the stove, his back to us. His hair is longer than I remember, and he is wearing faded blue jeans and a white long-sleeve shirt.

"Nate?" I call out hesitantly.

He whirls around, and our eyes lock. My throat thickens. I've missed him so much this past year. I was on bed rest for the last few months of my pregnancy and then didn't want to leave my daughter overnight. Rhys and I also were extremely overprotective of her. We avoided everything that could bring her to the attention of the media. Hence, we didn't take her to see Nate.

I can't stop myself and run over, wrapping my arms around his waist and holding on as tight as I can. He returns the embrace and places his cheek on the top of my head.

"I missed you, too, little sister," his voice cracks.

His words make me squeeze him even tighter, and a sob bubbles up in my throat. We stand like this for several minutes until a tiny squeal alerts me from the door that there is someone else my brother needs to greet.

I disentangle myself from him and wipe at my eyes. Still keeping one arm wrapped around him, I guide Nate away from the stove while Rhys slowly walks into the room. When we are only a few feet apart, Rhys turns our daughter in his arm so she is sitting on one arm, and he secures her with the other against his chest.

Nate's gaze moves from my face to his niece, and he sucks in a breath. His free hand flies to his mouth. With tears in his eyes, he glances between my daughter's, Rhys's, and my face.

"She looks so much like..." a hoarse whisper comes from my brother. Our little girl's eyes fly to her uncle's, and she immediately starts grasping for him, opening and closing her tiny fists, squirming in Rhys's arms until he can barely contain her. He looks at me for help on what to do. Feeling the moisture in my own eyes spill over, I simply nod, and my husband hands our baby girl over to my brother.

Nate cradles her like she is the most precious treasure in the whole world. She peers up at him, and her small hand tries to pat his face.

With my arms now wrapped around Rhys's waist, I wait for my brother to meet my gaze before saying, "Nate, meet your niece, Audrey Hamlin McGuire."

Lilly & Rhys

THE END

Make sure to check out the acknowledgements
in this book for a few more secrets that will be revealed **soon**.

But first, keep reading for an exclusive preview of
Because of the Dark, Book Four in The Dark Series.

KEEP READING

**Because of the Dark
(Prologue)**

WES

MY HARLEY STREET BOB VIBRATES UNDER ME AS I WAIT FOR the light to turn. I'm still in disbelief about how Kai finished the entire bottle of Patrón and was still standing upright when I walked through the door of our shared townhouse. The guy has a capacity for liquor I've never seen before and is still fully functional. But of course, I'm stuck replacing it once we run out. Allowing him behind the wheel of his Rover—functioning or not —is not something I can do with a good conscience. Thankfully, this task has become easier since June, when I turned twenty-one, and I no longer have to rely on a fake ID or bribes.

The red finally switches to green, and I'm moving again. Two more blocks until The Moose's Head. After almost twenty-four long-ass (and most of them cold as fuck) months, I'm still dumbstruck by the names of bars, restaurants, or local shops. You'd think just because we're in the Treasure State, surrounded by mountains and wildlife, we'd still have something like Whole

Foods or Binney's. No, we have *The Farmer* and *The Moose's Head* —TMH for the locals.

Turning off the ignition in front of the liquor store, I take in the decked-out Jeep MOAB next to me. The car screams badass. Matte black, five-percent tint all around, black rims, light bar, chrome tube steps—that's what I call a sweet ride.

I take a step toward the double doors when a familiar ping sounds in my wireless headphones.

"Message from Rhys McGuire."

Fuck me. As if my day isn't already bad enough.

"Wes, bro, you can't avoid us forever. It's been two years. We know you got the invitation. Calla misses you. Call us," the robotic female voice reads me the text from my former best friend.

You bet your rich ass I can keep avoiding you.

They're the reason my life turned into this dumpster fire. I don't bother pulling out my phone. Seeing the words will only result in me sending it flying, and I can't afford a new one. Instead, I walk into The Moose's Head and veer toward the aisle with the hard stuff.

After this, I really need to replenish our stash. Thank fuck I brought the hiking backpack. That way, I can load up triple time.

Getting everything I need, I add a pack of Big League Chew to my liquid purchase—never heard of that shit until arriving in Podunk, Montana, but it's addicting, and now I buy it whenever I come here.

I head back to my bike, bottles clinking together on my back despite the layers of paper bags I ordered the flannel-clad clerk to wrap around them. My gaze sweeps over the Jeep. After the text, I forgot all about it.

I wonder who owns this baby.

I'm standing at the light right off of TMH's parking lot,

waiting for it to turn, when I see the Jeep pull out of its spot in my side mirror.

Weird. I didn't notice anyone leaving the store behind me.

"Radioactive" by Bullet For My Valentine blares through my headphones as I drive down 19th to our house on the south side, near the university. I approach another intersection just as it turns red, and I slow the bike down. Almost stopped, I glance in the mirror and spot the Jeep speeding toward me.

What the—?

I'm about to abandon my Harley to save my ass, when the driver hits the brakes and brings the car to a standstill about a foot from my rear tire, leaving skid marks on the asphalt.

Adrenaline is pulsating through my body, and my hands tighten around the handlebar. This dude is asking for it. Still riled up from the text, I wouldn't mind planting my fist in someone's face. I'm about to get off my bike to march toward the MOAB when the light switches, and the jerk beeps at me.

Lucky motherfucker.

I've never been a hothead. Rhys used to be the one who tended to lose his temper in our friendship. Not that I was a pussy; I simply didn't have the desire to pick a fight. I was the jokester—the person no one took seriously—until everything was ripped from under me. The day I punched my best friend across the face...that was when I changed.

The Jeep drives behind me with less than the mandated safety distance, and I clench my jaw.

Give me a reason, fuckface.

I switch lanes as I approach Bear Court, where I have to turn left—yup, even the streets have ridiculous names here. The dick navigating the Jeep follows suit and comes even closer. Fast.

At the last moment, the Jeep moves back into the right lane and halts next to me. The light turns green, but neither of us moves. I glower at the blacked-out driver's side through my visor —equally tinted—when the window suddenly lowers about halfway. My heart stutters when a girl with wavy, dark-blonde hair comes into view. Wayfarers cover half of her face that's visible, and despite not seeing her eyes, I can feel her gaze on me. Somehow, I know that she is stunningly beautiful. My body is instantly buzzing with...recognition?

Have I seen her before?

I hold my breath as something in her expression changes. She is smirking. The crinkle around her eyes is noticeable even though most of her face is hidden from me. Lifting a hand, MOAB Girl salutes and takes off with screeching tires.

Stunned, I remain at the intersection until I can no longer see her lights down the road.

I have no idea what just happened, but the thudding beat of my heart tells me that it was the most exciting thing since exiting the plane two years ago.

She was running from her past.
He was fighting for his future.
Together they face a love destined to fail
before it even began.

ACKNOWLEDGEMENTS

I can't believe this is the end of Rhys and Lilly's story. I can't tell you how many times I've cried toward the end of this book. I've lived with these two in my head for three and a half years. They've grown with me, and I've learned from them.

Never in a million years would I have expected this journey to be such a wild ride. Lilly, Rhys, Den, Wes, Nate, George, even Natty...they all have become a huge part of me.

Certain scenes, especially in this book, were extremely challenging and emotionally exhausting to write for various reasons, but in the end, I am glad I worked through them. Because of those moments, you get to experience Lilly and Rhys in their rawest and truest form. Every character in this series has their own strengths and weaknesses. They are selfish yet loyal to a fault for the people they love. And when they love, they love fiercely.

Even though this concludes Lilly and Rhys's story, this is not the end for them. **You've met several characters in these three books that will make a reappearance** in future books in The Dark Series, as well as get their own books or even series.

I'm aware that there are still some **unanswered questions**, but I can promise you, **they will be answered**.

- Where is Gray? Why did he really shoot Emily, and what was on the note he gave Lilly?
- Make sure to add *Because of the Dark*, Wes's book, to your TBR on Goodreads.

- What happened to Hank after he stabbed Nate?
  Good question. I have a vague idea on that part but
  have to have a few more conversations with Hank on
  that. ;-) What I do know: he will be back.

With that being said, Wes has been *yelling* in my head for
over a year and a half, and Denielle's story has slowly been forming, and even Nate and George have more to say. I hope you are
as excited for Wes as I am. If there are any other loose ends that
you would like to know when they will be tied up, message me.
I'd love to hear from you.

The list of people I need to thank has been growing over the last
few years.

First and foremost, I need to thank my husband. His endless
patience and support made this possible. He gave me an office,
he put up with me when I was in one of my characters' head-
spaces and my emotions would run wild (aka, my crazy side took
over), and he accepted that, for the past year, I've barely cooked
(besides for the kiddos) and he had to fend for himself.

D., I love you. This book is for you!

Abbi, who is the reason I started this journey. Thank you for
believing in me and pushing me to do something I never thought
I could.

Sammi (S.J. Sylvis) and Eleanor (Aldrick), my amazing and
wonderful author friends, who took time out of their busy
schedules to read my books and give me valuable feedback.

Maria, for your help on all the legal questions that came with
this book.

Laurin, for taking my random text messages day and night
and answering medical questions.

Mary, who started as my beta for *In the Dark* and has become
not only my alpha, beta, and proofreader, but also one of my
dearest friends. I can't wait to come up with more plots with
you. And I'm sorry, but you still can't take residence in my head,

munch on popcorn, and watch the stories unfold. There are already too many people in there. ;-)

Lyndsey, my side chick and beta, who shares my love for books and has endless conversations with me about the characters as if they're real. I mean, they are, right? Don't tell me they're not. :-P

A big thank you to my editor, Jenn Lockwood, who had to deal with my constant schedule changes and also re-edited books one and two multiple times until I finally stopped adjusting the plot. Pantser all the way! (Note to self: Not great when you write a continuous trilogy.)

And of course, THANK YOU, THANK YOU, THANK YOU to all the readers, bloggers, and reviewers! Without all of you, none of this would've been possible.

Wes, let's do this!

XOXO
Danah Logan

STAY CONNECTED

Add me on Facebook
www.facebook.com/authordanahlogan/

Follow me on Instagram
www.instagram.com/authordanahlogan/

Visit my Website for more content and other places to stalk me
www.authordanahlogan.com

ALSO BY DANAH LOGAN

The Dark Series:

In the Dark, Book 1
(Lilly and Rhys)
Out of the Dark, Book 2
(Lilly and Rhys)
Of Light and Dark, Book 3
(The Conclusion to Lilly and Rhys's Story)
Because of the Dark, Book 4
(Wes)
Followed by the Dark, Book 5
(Denielle)
I Am the Dark, Book 6
(HIM)

The Davis Order

REZONED
(Ethan)

Evan 2578,
0877922578,

Made in the USA
Middletown, DE
28 March 2023

27706005R00257